# Advance Praise for *T*

With a cast of relatable and
reader to participate as a juror in a very human case. Marriages begun and ended, institutional failure, the ability of one man to make a difference or not - all are present in a story which on the surface is about church polity and the church as an institution. More than once, I felt my open heart-strings tugged as I recognized my shared humanity with Ewing's characters. Whether a member of the UMC or not, readers can take away much insight on how to be human both in private and within the church. Well done indeed and highly recommended.

– *Josh Zotta*

*The Trials of Dan Davidson* is a gripping narrative that you will emotionally respond to as you read. It details factual experiences in the UMC struggles of orthodox theology and political wrangling within the denomination. I could not quit reading it and I was very curious to see what ending Terry Ewing offered the reader since the struggles are not yet fully resolved.

– *D.A. Bennett – UMC pastor, recently disaffiliated with the denomination*

Enter the jury box as you read, *The Trials of Bishop Dan Davidson*. Examine the evidence and take a good long look at the church, its members...and yourself. This book is well-written, challenging the reader to dig deep!

– *Linda Snowberger, Plumbline Ministries boardmember*

I'm hooked, you've drawn me in and it's hard to put down. The amount of detail and description truly brings the characters to life, all the while tying in historical theology and our faith is outstanding.

– *Tony Proctor, Plumbline Ministries board member*

I was struck by the pull-back-the-veil perspective of the book; the inner workings of church life in relationship to an ordinary life. This is such a good book I wanted to slow down and take my time but found it difficult to stop. I am glad to see the author articulate the theological critique of the UMC church in America. This book validated some of my personal church experiences. Finally, the heretical church leadership has been held accountable.

– *Roy Shiplet*

ISBN: 978-1-960810-16-8
*The Trials of Bishop Dan Davidson*

Yorkshire Publishing
1425 E 41st Pl
Tulsa, OK 74105
www.YorkshirePublishing.com
918.394.2665

Published in the USA

# THE TRIALS OF BISHOP DAN DAVIDSON

### TERRY EWING

Yorkshire Publishing
TULSA

# INTRODUCTION

This genre of novels has been referred to as historical fiction: completely fictional books with plots rooted in factually accurate historical events. Since many of the events depicted in this novel are current, it would be easy enough to determine who the book's characters are representative of. Therefore, it is imperative that I assure you, the reader, that I have taken many liberties in developing these characters far beyond what I know to be true about them.

On the other hand, I have exercised diligence in representing the United Methodist Church, as an institution, as accurately as I possibly can. As the story line and trial narrative progresses, I will give myself very little creative license. Of course, as the court-case and the personalities involved therein are fictional, but the antidotal stories, petitions, and evidence incorporated into the book will all be drawn from published documents and accounts which I have participated in firsthand and have been verified by others present at the events. Although identities will be protected (which also means that dates and places may have to be changed), you can assume that the events occurred as recorded and that the documents referred to are real and accurately reported.

Yet a problem remains. You see, I believe that the United Methodist Church (as well as any other denominational hierarchy) is much more than an institution. I believe that in many ways the United Methodist Church is representative of the strengths and weaknesses, gifts and gaffs, virtues and sin patterns of the people who comprise the membership and leadership thereof. As such, the United Methodist Church cannot be characterized fairly. Still, the denomination has an identity. I have done my best to represent the denomination with all the objectivity I can muster. To help me maintain my objectivity I have created a main character who I can truly love and admire. This character serves as the primary representative of the denomination: Bishop Dan Davidson.

Bishop Davidson's character is based on a real person whose identity is easily determined by those familiar with the denomination. During the trial, numerous events are cited which directly involve Bishop Davidson. All these events are the actual experiences of ONE person. I have not combined actual experiences of several people into one.

Even though I am familiar with the actual person, I have no intimate knowledge of his personal history, faith, or convictions. The conversations I had with him were always within the context of our mutual service to the denomination. In these conversations, I was attracted to his ability to seem unimposing even as he acted in utmost confidence and authority. I longed to know if I could trust what he said. I imagined what mixed emotions and conflicted hopes he must live with. I transferred to him my conclusions about a sincerely conflicted denomination struggling to integrate its most divergent parts

I would be remiss not to acknowledge that I have very personal reasons for wanting to write this book. Having grown up in the denomination and having served as a UMC pastor for fourteen years, I am deeply invested in its theological ambiguities and ambivalence. Many of my personal experiences as a UMC pastor are incorporated into the book through the Kyle Fedder character. Yet, his appearance, personality, and virtues are not mine.

All the experiences cited during the trial by Kyle Fedder

are my own. I have not added fictional experiences or the experiences of others in the representation of this character.

It is only right to also acknowledge that the fictional narrator of our story, attorney Sonny G. Richards, may so closely resemble the actual person this character is based upon that he also is easily identifiable. Therefore, I want to emphasize that I am not limiting myself to an accurate portrayal of my friend's character, faith, or courtroom principles.

Utilizing historical events in the United Methodist Church as the backdrop for a civil trial, issues as broad as the cultural impact of the practice of abortion and of hope for an individual's marriage are presented for judgment. The reader will be captured by the human complexity that blurs legalisms and yet requires him to reach conclusions. The courtroom drama builds on every level: legally, socially, theologically, spiritually, relationally, and personally, yet maintain sympathy and love for those taking opposing actions.

# PROLOGUE

I asked Ben for his favorite "Dan Davidson story."

"I think, maybe, a story that best incapsulates who I know Dan to be happened at our ten-year High School reunion," Ben answered. "We had hired a hypnotist for the entertainment on that Saturday night. The hypnotist was as good as any I have ever seen. From a crowd of over two hundred of us, he took ten volunteers, and promised them that under hypnosis they wouldn't do anything they would be ashamed of afterword – maybe a little embarrassed, but not ashamed. Dan was one of the ten. The hypnotist did a couple of 'give me your attention' exercises and narrowed the group to five.

"Those five were told to relax, listen to his voice, and that they were all going to enjoy themselves. When he told the group of five all their friends were wearing pink hot-shorts and big pink hats, the group started pointing and laughing. When he told them that their new language sounded like the sounds a pig makes, the five began talking with each other with oinks and squeals. When he told them they each weighed five hundred pounds, they all began moving around ponderously. And, finally, he told them two of their former classmates had been high school sweethearts but had gone to different colleges and had pined over each other ever since. He told them that this reunion was the first time they had been together since then. He described how their passions had gotten the better of them and they were stripping naked and commencing to make love in the back row of the auditorium at that very moment.

"While the others were looking away or maneuvering to see into the back row, Dan stood, walked to the front edge of the stage, and called out to the couple he perceived were in the process of disrobing. 'Please, my friends,' he called to them, 'please take a moment to consider what you are doing, because this seems like something you will each regret for tomorrow. Can you take a moment and consider what the God Who created you, Who loves you, and Who knows what is best for you is saying to you even in this moment?'

"I'm sure that Dan had more to say but the hypnotist redirected everyone's attention to himself and changed the scenario. I can't really tell you what happened the rest of the show. I just spent the rest of the night thinking of what I would have said or done in that same situation and hoping to God that I might be more like Dan."

Then Ben anesthetized me. He applied a local anesthetic, waited a minute, then gave me three shots into my gums.

Ben is my dentist, and I was in his office for a root canal.

Ben and Dan had grown up together, best friends.

Ben knew that I was a lawyer preparing a class action lawsuit against the United Methodist Church. Dan was now better known as Bishop Davidson, and he would be a key witness on behalf of the denomination. Dan was not only a witness for the defense but would also be the man I would need to prove was a charlatan, a conman, a fraudulent religious leader … a sham and an accurate illustration of the true nature of the majority of leaders within the denomination.

As Ben began to drill into my diseased root, I imagined how I would have been crying out in pain without the anesthesia. I wondered how such a profound and sensitive man, who would minister to the greatest good of his imagined infatuated and reckless classmates while under hypnosis, could become so numb to the immense pain and destruction of peoples' souls that he not only allowed, but then participated in, promulgating apostasy, promoting systemic racism, and abusing his authority during his term as a bishop in the United Methodist Church.

# CHAPTER 1
## THE ATTORNEY

*"It is not the critic who counts, not the man who points out how the strong man stumbles, or where the doer of deeds could have done them better. The credit belongs to the man in the arena, whose face is marred by dust and sweat and blood, who strives valiantly … who knows the great enthusiasms, the great devotions, who spends himself in a worthy cause, who at the best knows in the end the triumph of high achievement, and who at the worst, if he fails, at least fails while daring greatly, so that his place shall never be with those cold and timid souls who have never known \*neither victory or defeat."*\* — TEDDY ROOSEVELT

My name is Sonny G. Richards. I am an attorney. I've been acclaimed by some as the most successful civil trial attorney of my generation. I know it may sound self-aggrandizing, but I want to share with you some of the secrets of my success.

First, I have never thought of being an attorney as a career, but as a calling from God. Courtrooms and laws are just my workplace and tools. I see them as the settings in which I challenge judges, juries, witnesses, and even my clients to be honest and just people (at least in that specific time and place). I have taken on the risks of cases other attorneys were unwilling to accept. If the client is deserving, or if the case is important, I will take it on. If my client wants to press an advantage to gain money, power, or revenge, I will challenge his motivations, ask him to reconsider, and offer to withdraw as counsel in his case. If the judge has any personal motives attached to his judgments (which occurs much more often than you may imagine; see my book, *Black Robe Fever*),

I will not hesitate to challenge him. I have been charged with contempt of court many times, although the charge is generally dropped or negotiated down to a small fine.

Second, I am not afraid to be honest with anyone about anything (see my book, *Fear is not Your Friend*). If someone misuses or abuses the Truth, my task becomes focused on exposing him. This is my "style," my "strategy," my "approach" to life, both personal and professional. I have learned how to ask soul-piercing questions as gently as possible. I have learned how to humble myself while asking others to do the same. I have learned communication techniques for conflict resolution and for building intimacy. It has been a long learning process that has cost me relationships with many who simply could not join me in pursuing painfully honest transparency and openness to personal healing and growth. I invite intimate conversations with anyone I think is capable. I consider it a compliment to a person's emotional health to challenge his thinking and invite the same from him. As such, there are few things more offensive to me than people who misrepresent themselves, others, or me.

Because I am better at this than most, people often view me as narcissistic. I don't deny it. I must be able to hear truth if I claim to be all about speaking truth to others. And, since I am an "external processor," there are very few thoughts that I keep to myself.

As a Christian, I am deeply offended when a pastor, church, or denomination misrepresents themselves. So now, at the ripe old age of 72, I feel called of God to expose the truth about an entire denomination, the United Methodist Church. I began writing this book as an account of my reasons for filing a class-action lawsuit against the United Methodist

Church (remember, I am an external processor). I was going to write about my passion for justice, my dreams and visions (which I hope you would agree were given to me by God), and my plan to put all my legal experience and knowledge to this last great legal task. In other words, I planned to write about MYSELF.

Then I met Bishop Dan Davidson. While preparing for this trial I gained extensive and intimate knowledge of the man. I was the plaintiff attorney, and he was one of the primary witnesses for the defense. He, above all others, was the man I needed to display to a jury as a cold, calculating bureaucrat. I needed to convince a jury that he was protecting a corporation guilty of misrepresenting itself to millions of its constituents and intentionally entering fraudulent contracts with hundreds of its employees. Although I believed the United Methodist Church was indeed such a maliciously manipulative entity, I had some problems with my case that I might as well admit to you right now.

In technical terms, the United Methodist Church has protected itself from outside influences. The doctrine and polity (its *legal representation* of itself) grant powers of discipline, including legal rights to jobs and property to the hierarchy of the church. In other words, even though my clients were once in positions of responsibility and power within the denomination, they no longer were. My clients all withdrew from the denomination, stepping away from positions where they could press for the enforcement of the policies of the church.

My clients gave up on holding the denomination accountable. They surrendered their ordinations, resigned their position, and removed their membership. Legally, they gave up their rights within the denomination. The jury maybe very reluctant to interfere with any denomination in the exercise of their faith … "Separation of church and state," you know.

I had to convince the jurors that my clients had been intentionally misled into believing the denomination enforced its doctrine and policy within the church, rather than just utilizing them as guidelines. It was my job to win the sympathy of the jury for the no-win situations my clients were put in. I had to show the jury that a contract my clients entered in good faith was broken.

Of course, even if I did win a jury verdict, I knew the defense could make their legal appeals to the higher courts. So, maybe, my best hope was to prepare the best case possible while hoping the denomination saw the wisdom of settling the case out of court.

My second problem with this case was that the public and many members of the denomination had been led to believe that the primary issues creating division within the UMC were the social policies concerning abortion, whether pastors should participate in the weddings of homosexual couples, and if a self-avowed practicing homosexual should be considered for ordination. It was my job to demonstrate that those surface issues were direct results of those who have rejected the essentials of the Christian faith (Jesus as fully man and fully God, His virgin birth, His physical resurrection, etc.) and yet continued to seek ordination, serve as pastors, and occupy positions of power in the denomination. The traditional Christian terminology for those who use the Christian faith as an allegory, but reject the literal, historical reality of the statements of faith is "apostates."

For many parishioners it could seem unthinkable that

their beloved pastors were being very cautious when referring to the incarnation and resurrection of Jesus to not let them know they only believed in these events as symbols, parables, and analogies. It would feel like a thirty-two-year-old being told for the first time that they were adopted. Then, even though the secretive adoptive parent may say that it's all the same, the child surely must recognize the betrayal was more about the secrecy than the secret.

It is the same for the apostate clergy. They insist that their only concerns are the social policies concerning the ordination of self-avowed practicing homosexuals, while they redefine common theological statements to hide their rejection of orthodoxy. And, finally, when someone like me tells the truth of the situation, it may very well sound like I am a radical conspiracy theorist throwing mud at pastors whom they grew up trusting.

And it got worse! I also accused the hierarchy of the denomination of practicing a blatant and intentional systemic racism. Of course, this was an accusation that some might be prepared to consider if the accused are old conservative white men, but I must make the case that it is true of the old liberals who are pictured as being compassionate to the marginalized of our society.

However, I was confident that any open-minded juror would quickly see that I was not just slinging mud. The history of the systemic racism practiced by the old liberals in the hierarchy of the denomination was easy to see and obviously self-serving. The old liberals in power of the United Methodist Church have directed and manipulated the system so that the members of the African churches have less than half the representation at General Conference that their membership numbers would otherwise require. By limiting the African delegations to General Conference to only 240 of the 1000 representatives to General Conference, even though the six million two hundred thousand members of the African UMC is more than fifty-one percent of the total twelve million world-wide members of the denomination, the African delegation has been allowed only twenty-four percent of the representative positions at General Conference. The apostate hierarchy would have lost their positions and possibly their ordinations in the denomination if the conservative votes of the African churches were to ever be given their appropriate representation.

Nevertheless, I will have to show that the blatant and obvious systemic racism being practiced by the liberals had also constituted a breach of contract with their fellow believers in the U.S. whom I represent.

I also faced a difficulty of a different kind. I found it hard to address a heart-felt righteous indignation toward Bishop Davidson. You see, I failed to maintain my objectivity toward Dan. Over the course of the two years of trial preparations, I learned just about everything there was to know about the man. I learned details of his youth through mutual relationships I didn't even know we had. My secretary of twenty years went to Junior High and High School with the man. My pastor once served the church where his parents were members. My dentist, Ben, had been Dan's best friend since elementary school. They even roomed in college together. Ben agreed to share all of his "Dan-stories," unconcerned that Dan would want any of them kept confidential. One of my best friends was also one of Dan's seminary professors. Coincidence? I don't think so.

Dan shared things in depositions so deep and personal that his attorneys advised him to seek therapy (as if he were using the depositions as a form of personal catharsis). And, to my great amazement, I had come to think of him as my very good friend.

Dan and I have told each other our life stories. We began by having dinner together after a day of depositions. Then, Dan invited me to stay at his home on a weekend I had to stay over between days of depositions.

We shared at the level of mutual therapists. I know of his hurts and fears. He shared dreams he had that seemed to relate very directly to dreams I had. I challenged myself to view his life and his decisions in the most positive terms possible.

His ex-wife was deposed as a witness for the plaintiffs as were a host of pastors that have served with him. Most have also exceeded the expected bounds of personal disclosures. Even the pastors whom I represent as plaintiffs in this case have shared details of their personal interactions with Dan.

So, maybe my biggest problem in presenting this case, with Dan as the principal witness for the Defense, was that I had come to admire, appreciate, and truly love the man. I saw a beauty about him that made me wish to be around him more. I wanted to be like him in ways I can even now hardly begin to identify. I now want to give each person my full attention like he does. I want to live with a sense that we are all bigger than and more important than whatever our present circumstances are like he does. I want to be able to evaluate historical events with clear, sharp insights of faith – like he does. Or maybe I should say, like he used to.

My final problem with this case was, for the first time in my life, I was believing a lot of things and making a lot of choices based upon subjective data. Before, I had prided myself on being able to set aside my personal thoughts and feelings and to observe people and situations logically and objectively. I knew some might dispute this claim because much of what I believe is based upon Biblical principles. Yet so much of what I think and do lately is based upon convictions, the call of God, passionate ideas, and even dreams I had been having. I will share these experiences with you, the reader, but I cannot present them to the jury.

My solution to these problems all came down to one strategy. I didn't intend to screen the potential juror. I don't really have any guidelines for how to filter out any juror based on his religious perspectives. Everyone has their own personal experiences and interpretation of the meaning of his religious experiences or lack thereof. The jurors came with their own presuppositions. I would not be able to present mine. If I got a juror who didn't value the Christian faith, he may have decided that the differences in the faith of the plaintiffs and the defendants were not significant enough to award damages. If I got a juror who highly valued the ministries of the denomination, he could be unwilling to cripple the ministries by awarding damages to my clients. If I got a juror who valued the Christian faith and was part of the large percentage of Christians who have little denominational loyalty, he may have had no sympathy for my clients who didn't "move on" to the next church much sooner than he did. So, in short, my strategy was to simply treat the jurors with respect and hope to earn a small measure of respect in return. I'm convinced that is all I will need to make my case.

# CHAPTER 2
## THE CLIENTS

*"They may be misplaced, forgotten, or misdirected, but in the heart of every man is a desperate desire for a battle to fight, and adventure to live, and a beauty to rescue."*

— JOHN ELDREDGE

My friend, Kyle Fedder, became a preacher in the United Methodist Church when he was nineteen. He was surprised to be offered the "appointment" to a very small church in a very small town where he would serve four years as a student pastor. He didn't learn until several years later the cabinet (the bishop and the district superintendents) didn't expect him to have a successful ministry there. They expected the church to decline just enough to meet the requirements of being partnered with another nearby Methodist church to become a dual charge, sharing one pastor with another, nearby, congregation. Instead, maybe due to the community's compassion toward Kyle's youth, the church steadily grew during his tenure there.

Kyle is likable. If I asked you to pick out the most likable guy from a crowd of fifty people his age, most of you would end up with Kyle. He is physically unimposing: 5'9"and hefty, with brown hair and intelligent eyes. He smiles as often as appropriately possible, and genuinely happy to meet anyone.

Kyle is intellectually capable, but not conceited. He is interested in all kinds of subjects. Although he doesn't keep the details in his head, he understands the concepts of his subjects and can draw them together. This makes him an interesting conversationalist whether the subject is sports, theology, music, cars, economics, cooking, or any combination of so many subjects.

Kyle's most endearing quality is that he really, truly, honestly enjoys people. He is interested in them and about them. Whether you are the homeless drug addict or the CEO of a major corporation, he wants to know you. And, if you are okay with it, he wants to encourage you in whatever stresses, needs, hurts, or doubts you may have. He doesn't need you to, but it will be hard for you not to like Kyle.

Maybe the most telling thing about Kyle is that he was somehow able to marry above his station. Even though I won't be writing more about her, Kyle's wife makes him look good maybe she's been a big part of the reason he is good. A minister's daughter, she has understood and embraced her role as a pastor's wife better than Kyle understood what it meant for him to be a pastor (at least in the early years). She is more physically attractive than Kyle, which, obviously, makes people wonder what she sees in him. Given the opportunity, she can happily tell you what she sees in him.

Kyle's wife doesn't seem to need nice things or many comforts. She seems to have always known what she wanted in life: a good man to make a family with and to serve God beside. She found what she wanted in Kyle.

Through Kyle, I became aware of the fraudulent practices of the United Methodist Church.

When I met Kyle, he had already withdrawn from the denomination. He returned his ordination papers and walked away from the local churches he loved after fourteen years of pastoral ministry. During his first four-year student appointment, he completed his undergraduate degree. He served his second student appointment for three years while he completed his Master of Divinity Degree. It was during these years that Kyle began to realize what he and his fellow students were being taught about United Methodist doctrine and polity was not what he was experiencing in his encounters with the church leaders.

Kyle was one of the very few seminary students who was serving as an appointed pastor in the denomination. And, of those who were appointed, he was the youngest, yet had been serving the longest (no others having served as a pastor during their undergraduate studies). Therefore, he lived with conflicting emotions when he witnessed the failures of the United Methodist Church to live up to *The Book of Discipline* it promoted. His first exposure to the failure of "the Church authorities" came during his second year of service.

Kyle was at a District Ministers' Meeting when a woman named Darla introduced herself to Kyle, stating that she had heard him preach on the college campus (which he had done several times on the invitation of a para-church college ministry). She explained that she was serving as a graduate assistant while completing a Master's degree prior to entering seminary and seeking ordination as a UMC minister. Kyle and Darla enjoyed each other's company and began seeking each other out at the District Ordained Ministry meetings they were both required to attend.

At the Leadership Seminar, in which each candidate for ordination was tested for and educated on the strengths and weaknesses of their natural leadership styles, Kyle and Darla sat together. After completing and self-scoring their leadership style surveys, they shared their results. Kyle's predominant leadership style was "explanatory," with scoring gaps separating the other three options. Darla's results grouped three of the styles within a point of each other, with only three points separating the fourth from the other three options. In other words, her styles were evenly scored.

The instructor explained the nature of each leadership style and their possible blends in the event that two of the styles shared a high score. Kyle and Darla puzzled over what it meant for her to have all four of the styles so evenly scored. What they soon learned led to the end of Kyle and Darla's friendship and the beginning of Kyle's concerns about the integrity of those in leadership of his district's Committee on Ordained Ministry (COM).

The instructor concluded the seminar by encouraging those who were unable to distinguish their leadership style to seek help through counseling. He warned that this result (like Darla's) was indicative of some identity confusion, a lack of core-awareness and acceptance.

As the seminar concluded, Darla sat alone with Kyle and confided in him her uncertainty concerning her beliefs, her values, and even her sexual orientation. She cried as she admitted her confusion. Kyle offered to go with her to discuss her situation with the counselor who was hired to work with the candidates.

That was the last time that Kyle and Darla talked together.

The next time the two were together for a meeting, Darla avoided Kyle. Kyle assumed that Darla was embarrassed by their last encounter and determined to give her some time. But when Kyle approached Darla at their next encounter, she muttered, "Leave me alone, Kyle," and turned away from him.

Kyle determined to express his concern for Darla to their district superintendent. Almost as soon as Kyle began to explain his desire to make sure that Darla was getting the help she needed, the superintendent cut him off.

"This process is not one that justifies the spreading of gossip … Darla is one of our most promising candidates for ordination.… Yes, Darla has spoken to our counselor, and we have been advised to help her maintain her distance from those with harmful prejudices against her."

Kyle left the conversation with his head spinning. The more he thought of the conversation, the more stunned he became. Before he could even focus to drive himself home, he had to sit in a nearby park for an hour and sort through what he had just experienced.

He assumed that there were factors involved that he didn't know, and trusted that the necessary means of caring for Darla had been carried out by those in positions to do so. But, as Kyle interacted more and more with those in positions of authority, his confidence was continually eroded.

Kyle served as a UMC pastor for fourteen years in local churches that he dearly loved, before his trust in the denomination's accountability to *The Book of Discipline* was destroyed and he reluctantly submitted his resignation and surrendered his ordination papers.

By the time I met Kyle, several years had passed since his resignation from the United Methodist Church. Kyle was managing a new restaurant in our downtown area while pastoring a fast-growing, newly begun church. He asked to meet with me due to the encouragement of our mutual friend, Fred Whitaker. Fred, a lay-person who had grown up in the UMC, had withdrawn from the church after similar disillusionments.

What began as a lunch appointment, with each of us tentatively exploring whether we really needed to be talking together at all, ultimately developed into an abiding friendship and a calling that would dominate my life for years to come.

I could not believe some of the stories Kyle shared with me concerning the UMC documenting his encounters with church authorities throughout his fourteen years of service would fill a book as long as this one. As the details of his experiences illuminated for me how the structure actually worked, the more offended I became on his behalf, and the more incredulous I became toward the denomination.

The text of the trial to come will detail a select group of events that you may have difficulty believing any organization could get away with, and you may understand the dream I began having (and will share with you later) that increased my passion for trying this case.

The first task after committing myself to developing a class-action civil lawsuit against the United Methodist Church was a very critical one. Could I find enough former clergy and lay-members of the denomination to justify the suit? I found all the encouragement I needed to commit my time and resources to this case when this first task literally fell in my lap as a *fiat accompli*.

One of the most difficult prerequisites for filing a class-action lawsuit is identifying and screening those who will join as plaintiffs in suing the defendant. How would I find those who have been injured by the defendant? How would I define "injured" in a significant enough way to justify suing for damages? How would I screen out those who misrepresent themselves in hopes of free money, emotional motivations, and/or attention (all of which are very possible in this case)?

You may remember me saying I met Kyle through my friend Fred Whitaker. Well, Fred had no intention of being involved in a lawsuit against the UMC, even though he strongly felt that the pastors who had left the church should themselves consider suing. I'll tell you now that Fred did finally consent to joining the lawsuit, becoming my primary lay witness during the trial. But, before all that, Fred was excited about the possibility I would represent Kyle and other ex-pastors. When Fred realized that Kyle and I were very serious about pressing the case, both of us encouraged by dreams, he contacted a reporter he knew who had contributed a number of articles for the monthly *Conserve our Faith Coalition Newsletter.*

Before this part of our story will make sense, I need to explain that the Conserve our Faith Coalition was the latest organization representing conservative members of the denomination in exposing the efforts of the more liberal organizations to change the doctrine and polity of the United Methodist Church. The monthly newsletter documented examples of how *The Book of Discipline* was being ignored or subverted by the more liberal bishops, district superintendents, pastors, conference boards and committees, and local churches. The newsletter detailed the efforts of the apostates to change the wording of certain doctrine and polity statements in *The Book of Discipline* every four years at the General Conference. Invariably, every four years at General Conference, amendments are proposed to conservative (pro-life) statements about abortion, the prohibitions to ordaining self-avowed practicing homosexuals, and the prohibitions to clergy conducting marriage ceremonies for same-sex couples.

Within a couple of months of speaking with the reporter, the newsletter ran a short article stating my intention to press suit against the United Methodist Church. The article only gave some basic information, with no editorial commentary. For such a small article, the reaction was nothing short of incredible.

Our case was made known by word of mouth, and was even reported in local newspapers. My law office received over five hundred calls within the first week after the newsletter went out. It was taking two full-time secretaries to handle the calls that were coming from reporters and applicants. In less than a week, I published guidelines for interviewing prospective clients in this case:

*A lay person must submit (dated, signed, and notarized) to us a record of giving to the U.M.C. that exceeds $2000 a year for at least ten years, and a personal statement describing what event(s) within the U.M.C. led to his or her withdrawal of membership.*

*A clergy person must a) have served in full-time ministry within the UMC for no less than five years, b) provide us tax statements for the last five years of their time in ministry as well as the following five years, and c) a personal statement (dated, signed, and notarized) describing what event(s) within the U.M.C. led to his withdrawal of membership.*

These simple guidelines disqualified over 50% of those making inquiry, yet the number of applicants continued to amaze me. With Kyle's and Fred's help, I trained a group of paralegals to eliminate any applicants whose written statements did not detail events that signified a breach of contract according to the *Book of Discipline*. Within two months, we had identified and contracted with two thousand ex-laymen and one hundred and forty ex-pastors. Though we could have generated even more interest through marketing our case, we determined my law firm was already being stretched to its limits, so we closed off applications. As it was, we would never have been able to fully depose even a small percentage of our clients, and I began formulating a court strategy that would allow for a select few of our clients to represent them all.

I informed the defendants they could depose any of our clients they chose to, so long as they paid for their time and travel. Though they were disgruntled by this, they made no motion to challenging it.

So, our first major task, one many cases never move beyond, was handed to us on a silver platter. We literally got to choose our clients.

# CHAPTER 3
## COURT STRATEGY

*"Christianity, as it currently exists, has done some terrible things to men. When all is said and done, I think most men in the church believe that God put them on the earth to be a good boy. The problem with men, we are told, is that they don't know how to keep their promises, be spiritual leaders, talk to their wives, or raise their children. But, if they will try real hard they can reach the lofty summit of becoming … a nice guy. That's what we hold up as models of Christian maturity; Really Nice Guys. We don't smoke, drink, or swear; that's what makes us men. Now let me ask my male readers: In all your boyhood dreams growing up, did you ever dream of becoming a Nice Guy?"* — JOHN ELDREDGE

The case was working out for me. I won't bore you with all the details about the procedures, motions, and other motions that went into preparing a trial strategy for the court. The court needed to know how many witnesses we would call, how much time we anticipated using, and what key issues would need to be addressed before the first juror was chosen. The court would need these details to create its own "strategy" (scheduling the judge and the courtroom, and anticipating the needs of the jurors, the legal teams, and the media). And, based upon what the court would accept, the defense's strategy would directly influence my strategy. My strategy was vital, not just because I wanted to win, but because this case was unique in many respects.

It was only the second class-action lawsuit ever filed against a religious denomination, the first being the lawsuit against the Catholic Church regarding their systematic cover-up of pedophilia cases. The differences in this case, though, were that we didn't have the same limiting factors screening the number of plaintiffs against the UMC, and there were no criminal accusations against individuals.

I was filing this case as a breach-of-contract complaint against the United Methodist Church. I was filing it on behalf of individuals who invested in the church under the false pretense that the church was accountable, in its polity and doctrine, to *The Book of Discipline.* As such, their interpretations of this contract and their perceived damages were both diverse and numerous, with over one hundred and forty former pastors, and more than two thousand former lay members of the church represented. As a result, the court was challenged with creating a strategy that allowed a jury to understand the accusations brought against the denomination.

Bob Chaney was the counsel for the defense, and he and I agreed to be limited to the smallest number of witnesses, while being granted the maximum amount of flexibility in the use of these witnesses. Our recommendations focused on three dynamics:

1. We agreed to bring in an expert witness concerning the history of the denomination for whom we would each submit six questions.
2. We were limited to listing two witnesses each, one clergy and one lay person.
3. We were allowed to "redirect" our witnesses after each issue of their cross-examination.

Although this would make for a very back-and-forth examination of our witnesses, it would help keep the focus on one issue at a time. This unique strategy would make it possible for the jury to understand the complicated issues of the case.

Bob Chaney, for the defense, asked for and received one additional witness, a representative from the Conserve our Faith Coalition. He argued that the jury should be given a chance to hear from a pastor with "exemplary conservative credentials" who had chosen to remain within the denomination. I offered no objection to this because, as you will come to see, I believed this witness would serve my case better than the defense.

Perhaps the greatest task I gave myself is to identify the "cards in play." Let me explain. I see a trial like a card game. In order to win this card game, I really need to know where the important cards are and, of course, I hope to have all the aces in my hand. In the actual trial, the "aces" are those elements that will most powerfully influence the jury. Attorneys often disagree as to what an "ace" is. Some think the aces are the evidence they bring. But, if the evidence of the case can only be interpreted to support one side, the case will almost always be settled out of court; both sides can recognize irrefutable evidence. When a case goes to trial, however, it is because at least one side believes the evidence can be repudiated. Therefore, in this case, the aces will be in the development of the case. An ace may be a juror, an especially inspiring witness, a helpful ruling by the judge, etc. To win, my four aces must be ones that Chaney never sees coming.

By getting a representative of the Conserve our Faith Organization added to the witness list, Bob thought he had gained a queen or a king. I knew he was very wrong. Instead, I was giving me my first jack, something I could turn to my advantage.

There was one more wrinkle I planned to take advantage of, and that was how the jury viewed the witnesses. If, for example, they viewed each witness as being equally important, then they will focus less on the institution, and more on which attorney they trust most. It becomes a form of popularity contest, and so, I needed to make sure the jury loved me. I would be stern but caring in how I treated the witnesses and the court, and I would respect everyone.

I am a big man, 6'4", yet, my voice is gentle, my movements are graceful and my demeanor is attractive. I always appear to be in search of the truth, the whole truth, and nothing but the truth (because I truly am). I have all my hair: light grey (the color of wisdom) in a background of black (the color of determination and strength). I'm too old to be a power seeker, a fame seeker, or a social reformer. Yet, I'm too sharp minded and physically fit to be put on a shelf. In short, juries love me based on nothing more than first appearances.

In the arena of winning the jury's love, Bob Chaney is, unfortunately, outclassed. Bob is brilliant, professional, articulate, and immaculate, but the jury wouldn't love him. He is twenty years younger than me, but I could take him in a foot race. Slightly shorter than me, he is just as grey, but has a large bald spot noticeable only from behind, as if he were trying to hide it. He has a round face with heavy jowls, which may be due to genetics, but which jurists tend to associate with overindulgence and, dare I say, laziness. He hides his flabby core in expensively tailored suits which, again, leads juries to distrust him. He talks longer than he needs to, and louder than the situation calls for. Perhaps most damaging is that he talks down to the plaintiffs. Condescension in an attorney is never attractive. There is one thing that Chaney can use to turn the jurors against me. I will be seeking damages for my clients more than eighty million dollars ($60,000 per pastor and $20,000 per member who were forced by their commitment to their faith to leave the denomination, with the balance being paid to my law firm).

Yes, my firm stood to make approximately fourteen and a half million dollars on the case. It could be much more if the jury decides to expand the 'punitive damages' I will ask for, which is often the case when a jury is sympathetic to the plaintiffs. It should be noted that I would not be allowed to inform the jury that the plaintiffs committed all their potential award to establishing a trust designed to meet the needs of the UMC churches in Africa. I also feel the need to mention that our law firm made the same commitment (minus our expenses, of course).

The jury knows that a civil trial is all about the money, and they know the lawyers get their shares. What they didn't know was I invested over two years of my professional life on this case (before the trial even began), and that we used lawyers, legal assistants, secretaries, and investigators who put a combined nine years of labor into this.

# CHAPTER 4
## JUDGE BROWNE

*"My friend would like to think of himself as a peacemaker, but in truth, he serves in the role of a peacekeeper, a false prophet saying, 'Peace, peace,' when there is no peace."*

— TERRY EWING

Bob Chaney and I both met Judge Browne for the first time the day we mutually declined arbitration and submitted our requests for court dates. Until then, I had hoped that the UMC would offer out-of-court settlements to my clients. It seemed as if that might be the case until we realized that our beginning points for negotiations were so terribly far apart.

Bob, on behalf of the denomination, offered one to two thousand dollars (depending on the length of time each had spent as members of the church) for the former lay members, and five to ten thousand for the former clergy. If all my clients had met the maximum payout guidelines, the United Methodist Church's offer would stand at five million, four hundred thousand dollars. I later learned their total offer was not to exceed seven million dollars, and that was less than a tenth of what we were seeking.

You may be surprised to know it took us over a month to acknowledge we would not be able to reach an agreement.

Next, we were asked to allow an arbitrator to evaluate the case and their resources in order to make a binding decision. I don't like the idea of binding arbitration. Arbitrators are pragmatists concerning everyone except themselves. They pride themselves on not being influenced by the emotions, passions, or convictions of the respected "sides." My issue with this process is that arbiters are rarely, if ever, interested in the strengths and merits of our cases. They begin with the idea that each side has merit, then delude themselves into thinking they can contrive to create a "win-win" option. It completely ignores who is right and who is wrong and doesn't even begin to address issues of justice for, or reform of, the offender(s).

Nevertheless, I did not want to be the one to decline arbitration; it tends to put us in a bad light with the judge. Furthermore, though I detest arbitration, I think I could have lived with their conclusions. Even a "mid-range" settlement would look bad for the denomination, would raise questions from the media, and would cause significant harm to the normal operations of the denomination. Of the over 2,100 plaintiffs I was representing, I would be surprised if 5% were motivated by the money. They had a larger agenda, far more interested in informing the laity in the church who were too loyal or too naive to question what is really happening in the UMC leadership. They were also hoping to cause a significant enough financial crisis for the UMC that it would be forced to divide assets and separate itself or die.

So I didn't want to accept arbitration, but neither did I want to be the one to refuse it. Therefore, it came as quite a relief when Bob contacted me and asked if I would join them in declining arbitration. Not only would mutual declination serve my purposes, but it would also put Bob in debt to me. I quickly cashed in this debt while we were drafting proposals for structuring the court's strategy.

That brings us to our meeting with Judge Browne, who would be responsible for facilitating the trial.

It is not unusual for a seasoned civil trial attorney to not know the judge, especially when the trial is in a federal court, being held in a neutral jurisdiction, in this case Colorado, since the UMC does not have a national headquarters. Each Conference has its own headquarters, and with conferences in almost every state, any Federal Court site can be considered neutral. I pushed for Denver because of the religious influence of several national conservative Christian ministries head-quartered in nearby Colorado Springs. I hoped this would be beneficial to my special desires for the jury pool.

When we made our first trip to Denver it seemed to me that God was smiling on me. Where better to be throughout the summer dates of the trial than in one of my favorite cities, surrounded by green places and mountains?

I felt even more blessed when Bob and I went to the courtroom to meet Judge Bowne.

I must confess I assumed she had asked to meet us in the courtroom in order to impress upon us the authority of her role. She quickly dispelled my cynicism. Judge Browne met us at the courtroom doors and introduced herself with a smile.

She was a trim, clear-eyed, young woman in her late 40s. Her black hair was streaked with almost white strands, her smaller stature hidden behind her strong presence. She was attractive, but not distractingly so, and was "aware" in a special way: aware of those around her, aware of the purpose for each moment, aware of the adversarial system and its demand that she remains neutral. She seemed to blend into the court-room environment, and commanded a quiet type of respect, but also respected Bob and I. It was her courtroom, but we each had a role to play

She sat down at the plaintiffs table, motioned to chairs spaced around it, and asked us to tell her about our propos-als. Soon we were all three talking together like old friends.

The minor adjustments she made to our proposals were only to accommodate the procedures of this particular building. Otherwise, she showed no interest in disturbing Bob's and my agreements. The dates were set, less than a month away, and our work was quickly completed. I fought the urge to give the judge a fatherly hug and tell her what a good job she was doing. I decided it wouldn't be proper to do now, but that I would probably have to do so as soon as the trial was completed.

# CHAPTER 5
## EARLY YEARS

*"He [Satan] is perfectly content to see you becoming chaste and brave and self-controlled provided, all the time, he is setting up in you the Dictatorship of Pride."* — C.S. LEWIS

Before I give you my account of the trial, I think it is important you meet my friend, Bishop Dan Davidson. I want you to feel like you really know him. You will get to know him as the person and the professional he is today as I detail the events of the trial. But to really know a person, you need to know his or her history.

Dan told me that he had always thought of himself as the product of the very epitome of a Christian home. He had absorbed his mother's affectionate nurturing and respected his father's strict discipline. Since his parents seemed to have no trouble reconciling their divergent roles, neither had young Dan. He grew up feeling the same about his father's verbal corrections as he did about his mom's warm hugs. He associated them both with love. When his dad insisted on a strict schedule of meals, homework, and bedtimes, his mother smiled and nodded. He had developed a sensitive nature that found freedom within the parameters dictated by a sharp and ordered intelligence. The combination of these gifts produced a calmness that was almost contagious to those around him.

His faith also reflected his parents' relationship. In the way so common to us, Dan's image of God the Father was shaped by his relationship with his dad. God the Father is the one with the plan and the rules that go with the plan. He wants the best for us and doesn't want us to mess it up.

For Dan, his mother revealed the Holy Spirit, a nurturer and encourager. Therefore, Jesus came to be the imaginary older brother he never had, a sibling who did things first then told his brother how to do it, too.

As a second and third grader, his Sunday School teachers were impressed with him. Not only was he good at sitting quietly and following instructions, but he also seemed to care about the lessons they taught. It was in his third grade Sunday School class his remarkable insight and caring nature were first noted and began being talked about.

One such memorable Sunday, Mr. Sloan was teaching about the love of God (his most common theme). He had just read about Jesus healing the man by the pool of Bethsaida when Dan's classmate, Kendal, spoke out. "Mr. Sloan, God loves my mother too, right?"

"Of course, He does," the teacher answered. "Then He is going to heal my mom's cancer?"

Mr. Sloan moved to Kendal's side. "I don't know, Kendal." "But Mr. Sloan, my mom deserves it. She deserves for God to heal her."

"I'm sure she does," the teacher hesitated, "but. …"

"No, she doesn't." The words were said kindly, but firmly. Mr. Sloan looked around to see who had spoken. Then Dan continued, "None of us deserve God's miracles."

"Mr. Sloan," Kendal redirected, hoping for a different answer, "my mom deserves for God to heal her."

The class grew silent as Mr. Sloan considered what to say next.

Again, Dan, in the same tone of voice, insisted, "None of us deserve God's love, but He promises to never leave us anyway."

Following another short silence, Kendal looked to Dan. Dan insisted, "That is still a pretty good promise, isn't it?"

"It certainly is," Mr. Sloan agreed. "What do you think class?"

One by one different students spoke up. "It is good to never be alone." "I think your mom would like that promise." "I'm glad we don't have to deserve God's love."

It was the most wonderful experience Mr. Sloan had ever had in Sunday School. He told the story often.

From childhood, through adolescence, and into adulthood, Dan's ability to give and receive love matured side-by-side with his freedom to stand alone. His enjoyment of reflective thinking went as deep as his capacity for self-expression. Throughout his Junior and Senior High School years, he had never been among the most attractive, athletic, or popular of the kids. However, as his peers would look back on those years, they would inevitably agree that Dan was liked by almost everyone. He had been the guy who seemed comfortable in every setting: he was a good enough ball player, an excellent student, could ask the new girl on a date, and could tell the bully to calm down. If his peers had been mature enough to truly appreciate the beneficial effects his presence had on them, he would have been their hero. Even Dan had no idea of how his unassuming stance for what was right had influenced the atmosphere of his school and his church.

In Dan's ninth grade class, Jeremy Watts had clearly distinguished himself as a potential world-class athlete. Jeremy didn't play on the ninth-grade football team or the ninthgrade basketball team: he played on the High School Varsity Teams. He was as good as any player on the field and would only get better over the next three years. Needless to say, he was very popular, which, unfortunately, led to him becoming very arrogant. When it was learned that Jeremy would not be allowed to run track with the varsity team, due to a rule concerning age requirements established by the Conference Track and Field Policy and Procedures Committee, Jeremy was incensed. He seemed to truly believe that the rule had been established as a personal attack on him. His hostility was directed toward Vernon Bates, the coach of the ninth-grade track team.

Jeremy took a special license with Coach Bates. Since Coach Bates was one of only two black teachers in the school, and since Jeremy was one of the 5% black student population, no one knew quite what to make of the way they behaved toward each other. Jeremy seemed to talk down to Coach Bates, saying "Yassah" and "Shore Boss" instead of "Yes Sir" like the other kids did. Coach Bates didn't seem to notice the antagonism at all. The white kids had to wonder if that was just the way that "negroes" talked to each other. Maybe Jeremy wasn't being disrespectful at all; it was hard to tell, yet, it influenced the team. It seemed that the athletes began to think of themselves as sharing equal status with the coach. Discipline was slipping and negative attitudes were manifesting.

Then Jeremy took his liberties a step too far.

The coach told Jeremy to set up some small hurdles. Jeremy answered loudly, as he jogged down the track, "Yassah, Master Bates." Dan was among the group of hurdlers doing stretching exercises, and they all overheard the comment. For a moment there was absolute silence as the huddle of adolescents evaluated the comment. For Dan, there was a temporary confusion. He didn't recognize any insult in the comment, but he was very aware of the sarcastic note in Jeremy's voice. Then, when a couple of the other boys began to snicker in that half-embarrassed, half-excited way that ninth graders do when the subject of sex is broached, Dan understood the implication and the insult.

The coach made no comment. The moment passed.

The second time Jeremy used the disguised slur toward the coach, the team had just finished a track meet. Jeremy had easily won the three events he had competed in. The rules limited each athlete to participating in three events, or else he would have won several more. He was feeling especially cocky and had been complaining again about not being able to compete with the varsity teams. The group of twenty-two had boarded the bus and they all had taken their seats except Jeremy. Jeremy was standing next to his seat explaining to a friend three rows behind him how his times would have put him in the top three had he competed with the varsity. The coach entered the bus and took a head count, while Jeremy continued his homily on the stupidity of the age requirement rule. Finally, the coach called out, "Jeremy, I need you to take your seat. We are ready to head home."

"Yassah, Master Bates," Jeremy called out. The snickers began immediately as Jeremy slid down the back of his seat.

Before Jeremy's bottom connected with the thick plastic seat cover, he found himself rising back to his feet. Dan had one hand gripping his outside elbow. Dan's other hand had reached behind Jeremy's back, lodged under his other arm, and gently slid him back up the bench seat. Jeremy reflexively righted himself and had been marched two steps up the bus aisle before he realized what was happening to him. Jeremy turned his head to Dan but saw no anger in his eyes. Jeremy was about to offer resistance when the two youths were even with Coach Bates' seat.

When the two teammates stood in front of their coach, Dan turned and confidently addressed the rest of the team.

"Jeremy is going to apologize to Coach Bates for being disrespectful. He is going to promise the coach that he will try to have better attitude, and I'm sure that Coach Bates will forgive him." Then, with no hesitation, yet with no hurry, Dan returned to his seat and sat down.

All eyes were on Jeremy. He gazed at his teammates, who were gazing at him. Then he thrust his hands in his pockets and stared down at his feet, watching himself elevate and descend to and from his tiptoes four or five times. No one could guess whether Jeremy's heart was softening or hardening in those moments.

"I ... I really am sorry, Coach Bates." His tone was firm, yet humble. No one questioned his sincerity.

"Thank you, Jeremy. And don't you worry about it, okay?"

"Okay."

Jeremy returned to his seat. The bus returned the team home. Respect and discipline returned to the team. Only Dan had nothing to return from. He had never left.

Jeremy eventually became known for having great athletic abilities and a remarkably coachable spirit. A full-ride football scholarship at the State University paved the way for an outstanding college career. His Junior year, Jeremy was runner-up in the voting for the Heisman Trophy. He opted out of his Senior year, was drafted high in the first round, and went on to have an outstanding career in the NFL. He became a hero to his hometown.

Dan's best friend was Ben Gates. Ben lived down the street, attended the same church, and played the same sports.

It had only been natural for Dan and Ben's parents to begin trading rides for their boys and become good friends. The friendship between Dan and Ben easily matched that of their parents. They were comfortable together. Ben was more outgoing and outspoken. Being a couple of months older, Ben was first to get his license, just like he had been first to kiss a girl, to break a bone, and to get a job. Dan followed Ben's lead without becoming a follower; Ben just seemed to do things first. Dan may have been a little smarter and better coordinated. Ben may have been a little taller and stronger. None of that really mattered to the boys. They were comfortable together.

So, the day when Ben's heart was broken for the first time, Dan was the one who heard about it. Crystal had broken up with Ben just before they returned from summer break to begin their Senior Year of high school. When the first day of school rolled around, Ben was not prepared for what came next.

Walking into school hand-in-hand were Crystal and Ben's friend, Doug. Either Doug had moved in quickly after Ben and Crystal had broken up, or else Crystal had broken up with Ben in order to date Doug. Neither option sat well with Ben. So, on this their first day of their Senior Year, Doug and Ben almost began a fight in the lunchroom.

Ben confronted Doug at the same table where they had so often sat together the year before. "A friend wouldn't do that to a friend," Ben began. Soon they were yelling at and threatening each other when Dan entered the room. With only a look at both of his friends, Dan moved between them, raising his arms.

Ben and Doug ceased their arguing and the onlookers

stopped talking to hear what Dan would say. Dan lowered his arms and looked back and forth at his two friends. But before Dan could say anything, Doug decided to take advantage of the fact that everyone knew that Dan and Ben were best friends.

"You shouldn't flip me off like that! Just because you two are friends doesn't mean that I am automatically in the wrong."

For a moment it seemed like Doug's accusation that Dan had flipped him off had succeeded in redirecting the situation. Dan's face turned red. He didn't know what to say. Then again, he didn't have to. Crystal witnessed the entire event.

"Doug, you know Dan would never flip off anyone for any reason. I can't believe you would say such a thing!" Crystal had taken control of the situation, and everyone knew it.

Someone from the crowd shouted, "Why would Dan flip you off?"

Sensing a possible way out, Doug replied, "Because Dan is in love with Crystal, too."

Once again, the situation had taken a whole new turn. Without pause he responded, "Yeah, I guess most of us guys are somewhat sweet on Crystal, but I still would never flip you off."

With the issue firmly in the open, Dan had provided Doug a way out. Doug said the only thing he could, "I know Dan, I'm sorry."

Having taken one right step, Doug pushed on to the next right step and turned to Ben. "And I'm sorry to you too, Ben."

Soon the boys fell back into easy chatter, sitting all together around Crystal. The only fallout from the incident was that no one asked Crystal for a date for the entire rest of the semester.

Meanwhile if something wasn't quite right in the life of Will Rogers High School in Spavinow, Iowa, someone would call on Dan. If someone needed help with his homework, he would look for Dan in the lunchroom and Dan would help if he could. If there was going to be a fight after school, someone would tell Dan about it. He would tell the combatants that there would be no fight and that they would have to work it out some other way, and they would. When his team lost a close game, Dan would congratulate the other team. His teammates would follow his example. When the guys talked dirty about a girl, he would tell them that they couldn't treat his friend that way. The disrespect and innuendo would end.

Dan never ran for any class office. He wasn't the most athletic, the smartest, or the most handsome, but there was a unique role that he played in his small high school. There was a general expectation that Dan would know what to do in most every circumstance, and he did. It was expected, and it seemed normal. Afterward no one made a big deal about it.

No, Dan hadn't been anyone's hero, but the world seemed a little gentler when he was around.

# CHAPTER 6
# DIVORCE

*"The individual's willingness to humble himself before God is the point upon which his claim to faith stands or falls."*

— TERRY EWING

Ben tells me that it was during the Christmas break of Dan's senior year in high school that Dan's life-story was shaken to its foundations.

Christmas had been rather anti-climatic. The family had attended the Christmas Eve service at church as usual. They had opened presents on Christmas morning after his dad had read the nativity story from the Gospel of Matthew, as usual. Mom had made a large brunch, as usual, but Dan knew that something wasn't right. His mom and dad were hardly looking at each other, much less smiling. Dan assumed they were upset over something with each other but hoped everything would soon be fine.

In fact, they continued to get worse. Finally, on New Year's Eve, Dan learned the awful truth.

Dan had planned on spending the evening with his friends at a youth group event hosted at the church. The event was scheduled to begin at 7 pm, and Dan was running late. He and Ben had been playing basketball and lost track of time. Ben came with Dan to clean up at his house. Ben jumped in the shower and Dan went downstairs to tell his parents what he was doing.

Dan found them standing in the kitchen. They were too focused on each other to notice his presence. He knew he should have let them know he was there, but the sad and angry looks on their faces told him he might be about to get some answers to the questions that had been in his mind for the last week.

"I used to believe your rules were just your way of leading us toward what you thought was best for us as a family," his mother said. "Now, I believe you both loved your rules and hid behind your rules. They were your way of not having to get close to Dan and me, to not have to really care about what we thought or what we felt. Well, you can have your rules and you can live with them all by yourself."

In the pause of their conversation, Dan's parents realized he was there. They both took a small step away from each other and focused on him, neither saying a word. As the silence hung in the air, Dan's mind raced with new understanding. In a matter of seconds, he had reinterpreted what he believed about his family. He realized with amazing clarity his mother's nurturing and father's strict discipline had been only the calm surface of a lake with dangerous undertow currents.

Married late in life and believing they would not be able to have children, Dan was born when his dad was forty-two and his mother was thirty-eight. Dan had been the glue that held two very different people together. They had never really learned to appreciate their differences and blend their personalities in loving bonds. Instead, they had partnered in raising their son and made the best of the rest.

Had there been fights? If so, Dan never heard them. Had there been disrespect or even infidelity? Dan didn't know. He would never ask. What he did know, in a flash of certainty, was that once he moved away to go to college his parents would divorce.

After long seconds of awkward silence, his mom turned

toward the sink of dishes, his dad walked silently into the living room, and Dan went upstairs. Dan took his shower, joined Ben in saying goodnight to his parents, and left with Ben to celebrate the dawning of a new year.

# CHAPTER 7
## COLLEGE

*C.S. Lewis claimed that it is safe to say that only the pure in heart will see God because only the pure in heart really want to.*

During the months of Dan's last semester of high school and the following summer, before he left for college, things returned to normal with his parents. They were making eye contact with each other. They spoke pleasantly with each other. They even smiled at each other from time to time. It was almost like normal. Except now Dan saw the sadness that formed an invisible wall between them. It seemed so real to him that he wondered how he had not seen it before.

It was the day after graduation that Dan and Ben sat together in Ben's bedroom comparing graduation gifts from the night before. Among the gifts, Ben's parents had given Dan a twenty-dollar gift certificate to J.C. Penney's, and Dan's parents had given Ben a twenty-dollar gift certificate to Sears. They laughed together over the coincidence. Then, Dan's face clouded.

"My parents are getting a divorce," he stated matter-of-factly.

"What?" When Dan offered no reply, Ben challenged the statement. "You can't mean it,"

"I've known it for a while now."

"Oh man, I am so sorry! What happened?" Ben's distress was comforting to Dan.

"Nothing … I guess that is the problem. Nothing really happens between them."

"I don't get it," Ben pressed. "Surely they told you why.

"No, they haven't even told me that they will divorce. I just know that they will. When we go to college they will file." Ben made one last attempt to understand. "I always thought, you know, that your parents were good together."

"I thought so too, but now ... I think they haven't been good together for a very long time."

Dan and Ben looked into each other's faces and made a silent vow to see each other through whatever would come. They had already made plans to dorm together at the University of Iowa. They had shared history, school, sports, church, friends, and secrets. They had shared clothes and cars. They had shared dreams and broken hearts. So, it only seemed natural for Ben to offer what he could.

"I've got some weed." Dan knew Ben's statement was an offer.

"No, I'll deal with it." Ben felt no judgment in Dan's declining his offer. He had offered and Dan had declined before. In truth, in ways the graduates didn't know how to communicate, the offer had been a question of how Dan was going to cope with the pain he felt. His answer was understood. Dan would be calm. He would love his parents. He wouldn't judge them. He would take it in his normal stride.

But something changed in Dan that day. The day he finally told his friend of the hurt he carried brought something unseen into his life. An anger Dan had never known before took up residence in a corner of his heart. Not even Ben could see it at the time, but Dan was different.

His parents had betrayed him. Dan had been able to honor, respect, and even love his parents' differences with each other. He was the walking, talking embodiment of the blend of both their personalities. For them to reject each other was a judgment against him.

It wasn't until years later that Dan could put these feelings into words. He felt like his mom could never really love the parts of him that were like his dad, and that his dad could never really love the parts of him that were like his mom. They loved him for what they saw of themselves in him and tolerated the other parts like they had tolerated each other all those years.

The University of Iowa was a different world for Dan. It was large. The classes were large. The dorms were always full of people and noises. He was a relative unknown.

He began his college career with an undeclared major. He attended the classes that comprised basic requirements, classes he found easy, and he finished his first semester with A's and B's, but without any stress.

Any intramural team Dan and Ben played on together was guaranteed to be successful. They played flag football, then basketball, then softball as the seasons turned.

They dated some, often going on double-dates. In short, they were enjoying their first year of college.

The summer after his first year of college would be the last that Dan would spend at home. As expected, his parents had divorced during his first semester. His dad had moved to another home. His mom had made frequent visits to campus, always bearing gifts of cookies, clothes, and toiletries. She would lavish affection on Dan, Ben, and any of their friends who got caught in her wake. She was always a welcome sight, never overstaying her welcome.

Meanwhile, Dan's dad had come to the big events (Parents' day, and the homecoming football game). He sent a one-page letter every other week, usually containing advice on maintaining his focus on his goals "during this very important time of life."

That summer at home brought some of Dan's changes into the light. The fact that he hadn't been going to church didn't seem significant until he was home for the summer. Then the changes were obvious. Not only did Dan have no desire to attend church for his own sake, but he didn't even have a desire to attend for his mother's sake. And, when Dan's dad suggested he might prefer to go with him to his church, he simply said, "No, thanks." No explanations. No compromise. It seemed Dan was neither concerned about his faith, nor his parents' feelings about his faith.

This was a very different Dan.

Dan spent most of the summer working the lawn care business he and Ben had begun together three years previously and hanging out with his friends. By the end of the summer, Dan had made some decisions. First, he and Ben agreed to sell their business trailer, equipment, and faithful customers to one of his present customers who planned to expand the business to provide year-round services. He and Ben both put a tidy sum into savings accounts.

Second, Dan determined to declare a major: Psychology. He told himself that he wanted to understand people better. Later he would admit that it seemed to draw attention to the blend of science (rules) and relationships (nurturing) that his parents had failed to accomplish. In one light, his decision to study Psychology could be viewed as showing respect to both of his parents' positive influences upon him. In the other light, it could be seen as his judgment against the incompleteness of each.

And finally, Dan determined that next summer he would

find a job on or near campus. He would not be coming home again.

Psychology was a thoroughly unsatisfying field of study for Dan, as most of his classes were purely academic: History of Psychology, General Theory, Systems Theory, Freud, Jung, Statistics, and, of course, numerous research papers. His favorite class had to do with testing the perceptions and receptiveness of the human mind. After exposing a volunteer to a "scene" (usually on video), they would ask questions to determine what details had been retained. Dan was amazed at how different the perspectives of the scene could be.

As psychology students are prone to do, Dan and others would subject themselves to these same experiments. Dan proved to be very good at accurately perceiving and recounting the scenes. This insight gave strength to his tendency to trust his own perceptions over those of others, whose own views may be biased for whatever reasons, while his were not.

Dan's Sophomore and Junior years were busy, and enjoyable, but also empty. He did not make many close friendships or date anyone for very long. He didn't attend church. He wasn't called upon to help others. He held his parents at arm's length. But Ben was aware of the change.

Ben noticed that Dan was not patient with people like he used to be. Dan was just as calm as always, but not quite as kind. Ben wasn't the worrying type, but he did notice a change in his best friend.

It was the first week of Dan's senior year, at 4 am on a Tuesday morning that Dan woke up Ben with the news. "Ben, you have to wake up. I've been lying here for over two hours, and I have to talk to you. Ben, are you awake?"

"Yeah ... give me a minute." As Ben regained focus, he

became startled. "Are you alright? Is there something wrong?"
"No, I just need you to listen to me. Please wake up and let me tell you my dream."

"You are waking me up to tell me a dream?"

"Yes, I need you to listen to me. This dream is important. Are you awake?"

"Yeah, I'm here. Tell me."

"Okay. First let me say that I'm not sure what it means, but I know it was important. I could tell every thought in Satan's mind and the thoughts of the condemned – uh-uh, don't stop me. I've already told myself the dream five or six times. Now I need to say it out loud with someone listening."

Ben held up his hand as if to say, "Go ahead."

Dan began the story of his dream: "Within the manifestation of the unholy…"

"Wait," Ben interrupted, despite Dan's request. "Did you say, 'within the manifestation of the unholy'? What the heck is that?"

"I told you not to interrupt. We can talk about it after I tell you everything."

"Okay, I'm really ready this time."

Dan took a calming sigh and began again. "Within the manifestation of the unholy is a realm of reality reserved for the meeting, communicating, and interacting of demon-beings. Within this realm, Satan has willed the ethereal forms of multiplied millions of condemned spirits to be knotted together in an intricate, painful fashion to form the floor, walls, and ceiling of a great throne room. The condemned retain forms that mimic the color and shape of their once flesh and blood bodies. These provide the medium for Satan's artistic genius."

Dan paused to see if Ben was really with him. Ben nodded

to the unasked question and Dan went on: "The weave of tormented souls created a four-dimensional picture. At first sight the walls and floors seemed embellished with huge mosaics depicting acts of human depravity and suffering. The mosaics seemed to be composed of subtle colors and stiff strokes. Upon closer observation, the three-dimensional woven forms of the condemned could be identified. Their souls had been captured in these forms and literally tied and knotted together to form the very substance of the wall. Their shapes and coloring dictated their place within the two-dimensional mosaics." Ben nodded again. Dan closed his eyes and continued.

"As twistedly brilliant as Satan had been in the creation of the repulsive mosaics, the few demons allowed the privilege of extended observation would never guess the depth of Satan's joy in the suffering he had created. The demons could delight in the perversions and sadism depicted two-dimensionally by the forms; they could even enjoy the obvious torture of the individual souls that made up the pictures. What they were not aware of was the subtle shifts that were taking place in the pictures due to an exactly measured gap in the density of the forms. Satan had allowed for just enough room for movement among the tapestry of the condemned for an escalation of their agony. When one soul-form used the minute space available to adjust its position to slightly ease its own suffering, the new position added to the intensity of suffering of the next soul-form. As the soul-forms made their series of adjustments, the effect was an eventual increase of agony for them all. Therefore, each soul-form resisted making the adjustment knowing that the short-term relief would facilitate greater torment."

Dan opened his eyes to receive another nod from Ben.

Closing his eyes again, he continued. "Occasionally, Satan would remind the soul-forms that the process could also be reversed. If a condemned soul chose to use the space available to intentionally increase its own sufferings, and if every other soul did the same, the overall effect would be a gradual relief. Satan even claimed that through this means they could eventually disentangle themselves altogether. But he also knew the condemned were utterly incapable of self-sacrifice or working together for the common good. The soul-forms blamed each other for their fate. They expressed their hatred vehemently. Their vulgar ravings are a calming music to his ears. Within this cube of total despair, hatred, self-serving, and degradation, Satan's usual constant agitation was somewhat abated. He savored the mental agony of the soul-forms."

Dan sat with his eyes closed. It was only seconds before Ben had to ask, "Then what?"

Dan opened his eyes as a tear rolls down his face. "Then… nothing. That was it. That was the dream."

"It is incredible. The way you described it, I think it almost has to be real. Do you think there really is such a place?"

"I don't know, but I don't think that is the point." "So, what is the point?"

As another tear ran down his cheek, Dan made the point he needed Ben to hear. "I haven't cared about the suffering of others for quite awhile. I've been caught up in managing my own hurts without concern for how I've been affecting others. I have to get back to being myself because God is calling me to be a pastor."

With absolute sincerity, Ben looked into Dan's eyes and said what he needed to say and what Dan needed to hear. "I believe that. Now that you say it, I think I have known that for a long time."

"What happens now?" he asked.

"Now, I wait 'til morning so I can call my parents and let them know."

Dear Reader, I need to interrupt my own narrative of Dan's life to offer an opinion. I must agree that the dream Dan shared with his best friend, Ben, was a call to ministry. It touched the core of Dan's lost sense of self and stirred him into reclaiming his true joyful identity. But, because I know of the events to come as Dan progressed through his life, I can't help but believe that the dream was something more; it was a warning to Dan concerning how he also might be drawn into the dark mosaic of Satan's designs. Dan's efforts to avoid conflict and legitimate suffering will result in growing conflict and the illegitimate suffering of those faithful to the beliefs and policies of the UMC.

# CHAPTER 8
# SEMINARY

*"He who marries the spirit of an age soon finds himself widowed.*
— W.R. INGLE

Dan's last year of college was a blur of activity, his return to assertiveness, you might say. He pursued a relationship with his parents. He renewed his relationship with God and the Church. He became the encourager and gentle exhorter that was such a natural part of his personality. He found interest in his studies and began dreaming of his future.

He was his old self again.

I haven't mentioned it yet, but you may have guessed that Dan and his family had always been members in the United Methodist Church. Therefore, when Dan began looking for a seminary, he only sought out UMC-approved seminaries. And, since Dan had no real understanding of the theological differences in the seminaries, his choice was quite easy. He chose the nearest one.

He took his Graduate Record Exams and made his application. The seminary granted him scholarships based on his GRE alone. He also discovered that his home church had an endowment funding scholarships for members who were pursuing ministry in the UMC. Since the local church had had only one other member apply for the scholarship, and that was over ten years previous, the money was quite significant.

In the summer after receiving his undergraduate degree, Dan was invited to preach at his home church. This was not just a pleasantry. The congregation was required to hear Dan preach and then vote on whether they would recommend him for candidacy for ordination in the UMC.

On the Sunday Dan preached, the congregation that averaged two hundred and fifty attendees grew to just shy of four hundred. They were there to hear "the young man we watched grow up." And they were not disappointed. Dan spoke about the First Beatitude: *"Blessed are the poor in spirit, for theirs is the Kingdom of God."* He claimed he had learned in studying for his degree in Psychology how incredibly difficult it seems to be for humans to really know themselves. Selfunderstanding and self-acceptance seem to be almost impossible to achieve. This, he argued, was only logical. "No one can begin to be humble enough to see himself clearly until he has humbled himself before his Creator."

The vote for recommendation was unanimous.

Less than a month later, Dan had his first meeting with the district board of ordained ministry. With his local pastor's recommendation and the vote of his home church, the board accepted him into candidacy for ordination as a deacon. They explained the requirements of his candidacy: Dan must meet annually with both the district board of ordained ministry and the conference board of ordained ministry. He would be required to fulfill the requirements of each, then, after finishing his second year of seminary, he could be recommended to the Executive Session of the Iowa Conference of the UMC for ordination. If he received a majority vote of the executive session (comprised of the ordained elders of the conference), then he would be ordained a deacon (an associate member of the conference, a minister in good standing, available to be appointed to a ministerial role by the bishop and cabinet of the conference). He would be required to attend a leadership seminar, take a battery of psychological tests, submit a life history, and formulate a first set of doctrinal statements.

The whole process was just steps in a familiar dance for Dan. He was among friends, and doing what came naturally. In the meantime, he loved being a seminarian. He was discovering that his mind and his heart loved theology, the history of the church, apologetics, hermeneutics, Greek, and Hebrew. Everything he learned seemed to have the scent of God, the thrill of His presence about it. Studying, discussing, writing, and even testing felt like a very intimate type of worship for Dan.

It was during a week set aside for researching his thesis paper that Dan had a second dream about the demonic realm. This time he shared the dream with his supervising professor, Sonny Pranger. Professor Pranger was a truly accomplished church historian and a gentleman who, it turns out, had been one of my good friends for years. "Prof" (Sonny's nickname) made a deal with me.

"If you want to know how Bishop Davidson thinks, read his thesis paper. Then come back and I will tell you about the dream he had. Put the two together and you will know how special the man really is."

So, I read his thesis paper, and while I'm sure that I didn't understand it all, what I did understand was amazing to me. To the best of my ability, I'll try to summarize it for you.

Dan's theory was that early in the sixth century B.C., a theological and philosophical change invaded the earth. Yes, "invaded," as if dumped upon the world by aliens from another world.

This was the time of Confucius (551-497 B.C.), of Lao Tse, founder of Taoism (approx. 604-517 B.C.), of Budda (563-480 B.C.), of Mahavira, founder of Jainism (599-527

B.C.), of Zoroaster (around 600 B.C.), and the Vedānta school of thought in Hinduism (around 500 B.C.). Throughout Greece, India, and China, new rationalistic religious philosophies were replacing their animistic and polytheistic predecessors. In short, across the world, simultaneously (in historical terms), rationalism was replacing mysticism of every stripe. The only unchanged religions were the Theist religions. Dan's task was to document this convergence of thought and to hypothesize its source.

While the rest of the world was moving speedily toward these rationalistic religions, God's people were in Babylonian captivity. There would be another "400 silent years" until the birth of Jesus. It was as if God stood aside and let men come up with their own answers.

Dan quoted Princeton scholar B.B. Warfield, who pointed out that mysticism easily transforms into rationalism: "Warm up a rationalist and you find yourself with a mystic in your hands. The history of thought illustrates repeatedly the passage from one to the other. Each centers himself in himself, and the human self is not so big that it makes any large difference where within yourself you take your center."

It made sense to me. Men, left to ourselves, vacillate between mysticism and rationalism. I got it. Even today, as Dan pointed out in his thesis, the natural evolutionists (rationalist) are losing ground to the quantum evolutionists (mystics). But this trend is too slow to be acknowledged and is limited in its geographical areas of exposure. Not at all like the shift that took place in the early sixth century B.C.

How do we account for such a global, simultaneous philosophical change? The answer Dan proposed was classically "Christian": Satan did it.

Satan was no longer content to be "one of the gods" in the minds of men, inferior to "Father God." He was laying the groundwork replacing the mythologies that could acknowledge a "Father of all gods" in favor of a humanistic rationalism in which evolution would be identified as mankind's creator and, therefore, their savior. Satan was laying a foundation for men's eventual acceptance of Naturalistic Evolutionary Theories.

Somehow Dan was able to make a case for this conclusion without seeming to be a "backwoods fundamentalist." He didn't quote anything from Genesis. He referenced patterns of philosophical developments among the "great religions" that continued and continues to mirror each other. He identified the "spirit of the various ages" and, finally, he proposed that the dynamics were too consistent to not be attributable to a single source. Only then did he mention Satan. Almost as an afterthought. Still, it was an incredibly bold way to end a thesis paper.

In typical Dan-like fashion, he calmly made his case and clearly communicated his personal conclusion with a minimum of defensive justifications. The Devil did it, and, having read his thesis paper, I was even more eager to hear about the dream Prof had promised to tell me.

Prof began by challenging my understanding of what I had read. "I imagine you saw the flaw in Dan's thesis?"

"No," I admitted, "I was just trying to understand it, not critique it."

"Sonny G., I know you couldn't help but critique it. What did you think?"

"His research was obviously very wide-reaching, but he laid it out well … and I can certainly go along with his conclusion."

"So, you didn't see the flaw?"

"No, Prof, I didn't see the flaw. So, educate me."

Prof was almost giddy over my curiosity and attention. He didn't draw it out but got right to the point. "Why would Satan suddenly want us to switch from mysticism to rationalism? Why would he wait 'til the sixth century B.C. before laying the groundwork for our eventual acceptance of the theory of evolution? You see, it doesn't make sense for Satan to be inconsistent like that."

Prof said all this with a sly smile on his face, so I knew there was still something he wasn't telling me. "Apparently, you have an answer for this riddle," I prodded him.

"Not me, the answer was in Dan's dream."

"But a dream is not sufficient to base an academic theory on." "True, but if the academician believes the dream, then he can't help but adjust his assumptions to it." This response from Prof surprised me, because I had never known him to let subjective data (like a dream) go unchallenged.

"So, Dan believed in his dream," I offered, and Prof smiled. "So, you allowed for the 'flaw' in his thesis paper?"

"I did," he affirmed with the same smile. "Because you believe in his dream also?" "I do," he said with an even wider smile.

"Okay already, tell me the dream," I demanded in mock combat.

"I will, but before I do I want you to know that I will have some questions for you afterwards."

"In his dream, Dan saw the same Satan (in corporeal form) he had seen in a dream once before, only he knew that this time was different. It was the early sixth century B.C.

He didn't know how he knew the date, but he was sure of it. He saw Satan standing before a lesser demon. Other demons stood apart from them, watching on. Satan was furious with the lesser demon and was blaming him for some terrible failure in Satan's plans. Then, on what seemed like an impulse born of pure rage, Satan grabbed the lesser demon and squeezed it against his chest. Satan intended to smash the lesser demon into mush. Instead, the lesser demon was absorbed into Satan himself. Satan and the surrounding demons registered surprise at this development. This was something new. Then Satan began to smile. 'I have his memories, his knowledge, and his strength,' Satan exclaimed. Meanwhile, the substance of the lesser demon began to reemerge in a puddle from Satan's backside. It was as if Satan shat the lesser demon out. The demon pulled itself together on the back side of Satan, totally drained of energy and knowledge, left with just a vague sense of fear and self-pity. Satan's form increased to the same degree that the lesser demon's form had decreased. Satan was amazed by his newfound ability. Had he always had this ability, or had he recently developed it and instinctively enacted it? Of course, it didn't matter. All that mattered was what this ability meant. It meant that Satan himself can grow, develop, *evolve*. Then, with a shout that shook the realm, Satan yelled out,

'SPREAD THE WORD: I HAVE EVOLVED.'" There was a long pause.

"That's it?" I asked. "'Spread the word: I have evolved.' Then what?"

"Then," Prof frowned at me like I had failed a test, "then, simultaneously, across the world, religions changed to reflect Satan's new awareness. He put us on the road to rationalism, which would inevitably lead to the theory of natural evolution

… And I believe it. It makes sense to me. Even without Dan's dream, I could believe in his theory. I would have explained it as a chess match between God and Satan, with Satan making a move to counter God's revelation of Himself to and through the Hebrews. But I have no problem believing that Satan reached a point of self-delusion and concluded that he will evolve beyond the limitations placed on him by his Creator. So, now let me ask you a couple of questions, Sonny G. First, do you believe in Dan's dream?"

# CHAPTER 9
## MY DREAM

*"There is no neutral ground in the universe: every square inch, every split second, is claimed by God and counterclaimed by Satan."* — C.S. LEWIS

"Do I believe in Dan's dream? Do I believe that Satan's rage led to a discovery that made him believe in evolution? I don't know. I guess it wouldn't surprise me that Satan would believe in evolution."

"Didn't you tell me that one of the reasons you chose to take on this case had to do with a dream you had?"

"I did. And now you want to hear my dream." I turned the question into a statement that Prof, again, declined to answer.

I had a dream involving Satan, and now I wondered if he looked the same in my dream as in Dan's. In my dream, I knew time was immediately following Jesus' death. Jesus was facing Satan and innumerable demons, who stood in front of a wall of brick-like cells. The wall was too high and too long for me to determine. And, within each cell, a human spirit was housed. Across the surface of each cell ran replays of innumerable moments of the captured spirits' lives. There were no flames or other torments. Just the replays ... and awaiting judgment.

For the three days Jesus was held in bondage to DEATH, he projected scenes of love and forgiveness into each and every cell. Every cell-bound spirit received unique messages directly from the Christ. After three days, Jesus shook off SATAN and DEATH and stood at the very gates of Hell, welcoming all who embraced His offer of forgiveness. Every cell-bound spirit was offered release to follow Jesus to be with His Father, but with one condition: if only the spirit would acknowledge that the "replays" were unbiased perspectives of who they really were, and they would accept they really deserved the sufferings Jesus endured on their behalf, then their cell would release them to follow Jesus to heaven.

When the moment came that Jesus turned and walked past DEATH and SATAN (who were powerless to stop him), my heart broke within me when only very few spirits stepped away from their crumbled cells and followed Jesus past the gates of Hell. I finished my story and looked up.

With tears in his eyes, Prof told me, "I believe in your dream, too. I don't know if the details were literally true or symbolic, but I trust that the message is true. Imagining all those human spirits who couldn't bring themselves to acknowledge their 'replays,' or to embrace the substitutionary atonement makes me want to scream."

"I've never known you to scream, Prof."

"I may be about to start." He paused and ran his hand over his face, looking as if he were holding back tears. With a deep sigh, he said, "Anyway, back to the point. Assuming your dream was from God, and I do, why did He show you your dream?"

"At the risk of sounding egotistical, I know what the dream means. I must do my best to bring truth to light. I've always had that drive, or gifting, or neurosis, whatever you want to call it. But my dream makes it clear to me that, while I might be used of God to pursue truth at all cost, it is never my right or role to judge the salvation of others. I'm good at what I do, but I must not get caught up in guessing or assuming what is happening in the spiritual depths of anyone else.

"I believe this case is the most important case of my career. I believe the truth is on my side. But that doesn't mean we will win. Each person involved will have to decide what the truths of this case mean to them. I can relax in to trying this case while leaving all judgments and all results to Jesus alone. He meant for me to take this case, win or lose."

Easing from his chair, Prof laid a hand on my shoulder and blessed me. "Go in peace, my friend."

I still have one more dream involving demons to share with you, but since the dream was not given to me or to Dan, I will share it with you later. I will tell you now that I believe all four dreams (the two Dan was given, the one I just shared, and one to come) were given to us by God. They were more than our subconsciousness working through some stress or confusion. These dreams were common ground for the primary players in what may prove to be the trial of the decade. The similarity of the content of our dreams seemed to affirm each other. Yet, it was a miracle that we (of all people) have had these dreams made known to us.

# CHAPTER 10
## THE WORST THING YOU EVER DID

*The ancient Didache begins, "Two ways there are, one of Life and one of Death, and there is a great difference between the two ways."*

Two weeks after Dan graduated seminary, the Iowa Annual Conference met. Dan eagerly awaited the announcement of his appointment. For weeks prior to the conference, the bishop and his cabinet, consisting of the eight district superintendents, met to decide which pastors would be assigned to which churches. With the average appointment lasting less than four years, 25% of the elders would typically be reassigned each year. Of course, only the smaller churches were considered for newly-placed pastors. When Dan was appointed to a smaller church in the largest district, it was considered quite a compliment.

It may seem naive of me to say, but Dan was a natural. His sermons were not just intelligent and engaging, but also inspiring. The atmosphere he created for the volunteer church workers was one of mutual admiration and appreciation. Within six months, the church that had been averaging seventy in attendance was rapidly moving toward one hundred. They had taken in nine new members and had begun discussing the possibility of hiring a youth director.

Yet, even more significant to Dan than the church growth was his new dating relationship with Sharon.

Dan was introduced to Sharon when she returned home

during Christmas break of her senior year. Dan was the new pastor of the church she had grown up in, and the athletic blonde decided to date him the first time she heard him preach. "It wasn't love at first sight," she later told her friends and family. "I just thought he deserved a chance." Her self-assurance appealed to Dan as much as Dan's did to her, and by the time they parted ways after church that Sunday, they had made plans.

Their first date was the last time either of them considered themselves single. Although neither had fallen in love before, they both seemed to know that they would be together. Sharon had spent more than a year with her previous boyfriend, but had broken it off when she realized she had no desire to marry him. Dan had dated casually throughout college but had never taken any of those relationships seriously. But, within two weeks of their first date, both thought of the other as their closest friend. Sharon moved back home to do her student teaching at the local high school. Dan began thinking more about covenant relationships.

"What is the worst thing you have ever done?" Sharon asked Dan on their third date.

"Why would you ask me that?" The way he asked was not defensive, but an honest question.

"I don't really care about any bad things you may have done. I just want to know what you consider to be the worst. You know what I mean?"

At some point they had positioned themselves to make it comfortable to hold hands and look into each other's eyes.

"You aren't asking how bad I've been, you're asking what I feel worst about."

"Yes … will you tell me?'

"Yeah, I'll tell you … I never talked to mom or dad about their divorce."

Sharon wasn't sure she understood his guilt. "What is it that you feel like you should have talked with them about?"

Surprising even himself, Dan felt tears forming in his eyes and a lump in his throat. Looking away to gather himself, Dan answered, "I could have told them that they could change, they could grow, and then, they really could love each other."

Sharon squeezed Dan's hand in hopes of communicating understanding and acceptance. Still, she felt like she needed (and he needed) to press a little farther.

Dan was obviously pushing himself, maybe thinking through some of his own feelings for the first time. Taking a deep breath he said, "Well, first, we just didn't talk like that. I think just trying to have such a conversation with them would be offensive to them. It wouldn't have done any good."

"You mean it just wasn't the kind of thing your family could talk about?" Dan nodded. "And, what's the other reason?"

Dan was obviously fighting with himself to not withdraw from the conversation. He realized he had pulled his hands away from Sharon's. Very intentionally he reached over to reconnect physically with Sharon. "They both seemed so sure of themselves. They knew it wouldn't work between them. Nothing I could say would change that."

Dan thought they had reached an end to this conversation, but Sharon was in the very middle of it. "Then why do you feel guilty for not asking them to change?"

Dan had seemingly forgotten how this conversation had begun. "I guess I just wish things had been different."

Sharon set her jaw and there was a fire in her eyes that Dan hadn't seen before. Before she spoke, Dan knew that she was not going to settle for his answer. Then, things got even worse. Sharon intentionally withdrew her hands from Dan's, crossing her arms on her chest.

"Dan, you are doing it again. The worst thing you've ever done and now you are doing it again." Their relationship was on the line and Dan didn't understand why.

Dan was feeling two things very new to him. He felt anger. He had always been accepted as the calm voice of reason. Of course, people had been angry at him and falsely accused him at times. And, he had been hurt by people from time to time. But this conversation was very different. Sharon was talking down to him. He was sharing his heart with her, and it wasn't good enough. If he had been in a counselor's office, surely the counselor would appreciate his honest struggle and affirm him for it. Sharon, however, seemed ready to walk out on him.

This scared Dan. He didn't want Sharon to leave. He wasn't even sure why she was so mad. He was scared that he might lose her, and he was scared to think through why she was so mad. He felt trapped. Think it through or lose her. He wasn't sure why he was desperate to hold on to this girl whom he had only known for a week. And he wasn't sure why he didn't want to think through "the worst thing he had ever done."

# CHAPTER 11
## KYLE'S DREAM

*"Only those who try to resist temptation know how strong it is …
You find out the strength of a wind by trying to walk against it
… "* — C.S. LEWIS

This may not seem like a good time to share with you
the fourth dream, but it is. You'll see why when I'm done. This
dream came to Kyle. He was the clergy representative in the
court case. You will get to know him well during the trial, but
in the meantime, his dream highlights the predicament Dan
was in during this conversation with Sharon.

Kyle was standing at the front of a large group of people. Between the group and a stream of attacking demons
stood two large angels defending the people with two shining
swords. The angels were fierce and terrible in their defense
of the group behind them. Their swings were vicious, if not
reckless, rending demon limbs and slicing demon torsos. The
stricken demons shrieked away as the next row of their allies
pressed in behind them.

Then, the unthinkable happened. A demon passed the
defenses of the angel on the right and gashed his leg, creating a terrible wound. Even as the first angel was falling to
the ground, the second had sidestepped in to the path of the
demon and cut his right wing from his form. Then, stepping up beside the fallen angel, the single angel continued its
defense of the group.

Meanwhile, the fallen angel's sword had clattered to the
ground at Kyle's feet. Without hesitation, Kyle picked it up.
Once the sword was in his hands, it became obvious to Kyle

what he must do. As strength surged from the sword into his body, Kyle ran to take his place on the other side of the fallen angel.

Kyle's defense against the demons was uninhibited by fear or compassion. With great two-handed swings, Kyle beat against the attacking demons. One after the other, the demons bounced away from the impact of his sword. Yet, to his dismay, the demons fell back as if struck with a baseball bat, recovered themselves and returned to the battle. No arms were severed, nor were there any deep cuts. Even as his muscles strained and sweat flew from his brow, Kyle knew that something was terribly wrong. Without an audible voice, but with a certainty beyond question, Kyle knew an explanation was offered to him: "You have to want it to cut."

Why did I tell you Kyle's dream in the middle of my account of the first crisis point in Dan's and Sharon's young relationship? This Is Crucial! I believe that this whole case comes down to everyone involved determining whether Dan wanted to beat his demons into submission, or to destroy them entirely.

And, dear reader, I would ask you the same question: "How radical do you want to be in your struggles with your personal demons?"

I believe we each must admit that one of the powers of our personal demons is to blind us to what it means to allow them to be destroyed. There is one character in this story who, as far as I know, always seemed content to confront her demons with a blade that cuts. Sharon is the true hero of this story.

Let me tell you now, I believe that for you to walk away from this book with a non-verdict in this case is an insult to your own humanity and spirituality. I'm not saying you need to reach the same conclusion I have. What I am telling you is that not to reach a verdict in this case is to join Dan in "the worst thing he ever did."

I realize that me challenging you like this may seem very grandiose and may break the rules for writing an account like this, but I told you up front about the way I am: I challenge people to struggle with themselves. And, rest assured, I struggle with myself, too.

Now I am challenging you to put yourself on the jury in this trial. Reach a conclusion. Not because your conclusion will affect others in any way, but because reaching a conclusion will clarify your own faith, character, and values. You and I, like Kyle and Dan, have demons to contend with. We do not have the power, nor do we have the skills, to win in our confrontations with our personal demons, but we do have a significant role that only we can fill. Our role is to determine who we choose to be.

# CHAPTER 12
# DAN IN LOVE

*"Only by knowing and ultimately accepting oneself can one enter into valid relationships with others."*
— BELLAH ET AL, *Habits of the Heart*

When Sharon asked Dan about the worst thing he had ever done, he had shared his guilt over not confronting his parents about their divorce. Then, when challenged by Sharon to identify his sin, Dan had withdrawn his confession and redefined his role as a morally-neutral bystander. Now, Sharon seemed ready to dump him, and he was trying to buy himself some time to win her back.

"I honestly don't know what you mean when you say that I'm doing it again. I'm not fighting with you. I just don't know what you want." He spread his hands out in supplication.

"I asked you to confess your sin. Are you honestly telling me that you don't know why you did the worst thing you ever did?" She still had her arms crossed, anger in her eyes.

"Give me a minute, okay? Just a minute." Sharon didn't answer, but neither did she leave.

Dan closed his eyes and began talking slowly and out loud. "The worst thing I ever did was to not tell my parents that they should have changed … And I didn't tell them because … they weren't used to talking about things like that… And, if I made them talk to me about how they could change … they could … maybe they would … leave me like they left each other. That's it … I couldn't risk not being loved by them. So, I just kept my mouth shut … and it was the worst thing I've ever done."

When he opened his eyes, he saw Sharon reaching out to take his hand. The anger in her eyes had been replaced by a look of love that made his heart flutter. "You couldn't risk not being loved by your parents," she repeated contemplatively. "Thank you. I can't tell you how much that means to me."

Dan was amazed at what had just happened to him. Sharon had done what he had failed to do with his parents. She had asked him to name his sin. What kind of woman was this? "Have you asked others this same question?"

With a sly smile she answered, "A couple." "Did they do better than me?'

"No … they wouldn't or couldn't answer me." "And?" he had to ask. "What happened next?" "And I knew we couldn't be more than friends."

Dan liked that answer. It sounded like a promise of things to come.

Was this what love was? Dan had to admit that not only did he feel more spiritually united, and more sexually attracted to Sharon after that conversation, but he simply, overall, admired her more than anyone else in his life. On the other hand, he didn't know if he could have those kinds of conversations very often. His mixed emotions kept him thinking of Sharon and wanting to be with her, while slightly afraid that he was going to be caught off guard again.

Sharon, for her part, seemed very satisfied. She seemed happy to be around him, and Dan gained confidence daily that she was as in love with him as he was with her. And his congregation was having fun watching the sweethearts fall in love.

Two major events were on the horizon for young pastor Davidson: the covenant of marriage and the covenant of ordination as an elder in the UMC.

Did Dan want the sword of the Lord to destroy the demons that had contributed to "the worst thing he had ever done," or did Dan just want to manage these demons?

Who can know? Sharon assumed that all was well. Was that also the nature of love?

Dan had faced his demons for the sake of love. Who could ask for more?

Remember, I was the prosecuting attorney. I had to make a case against Dan. He was the primary witness for the defense, the chosen representative of the denomination. Of course, I'm sharing things in this writing that I couldn't very well bring up at the trial. On the other hand, I loved the man, so the possibility exists that I am representing his character too positively.

Anyway, Sharon had made her choice. And, the fact that Dan loved her more after this may tell everything we need to know about him.

# CHAPTER 13
## ORDINATION AND MARRIAGE

*"'Finding oneself' is not something one does alone."*
— BELLAH ET AL., *Habits of the Heart*

The ordination service took place on Thursday during the last evening service of the Iowa Conference's annual conference. The week-long proceedings of each annual conference began with an executive session. This Monday morning session was only for the elders of the conference. It was generally a happy reunion of the more than four hundred elders in which a ritual of exhortations preceded the announcement of the Board of Ordained Ministry's recommendations of candidates for ordination.

Dan had completed all the requirements for ordination. There was really very little in this process that had changed for him over the last three years since his ordination as a deacon. He had graduated seminary and completed his first two years in full-time ministry, but none of his doctrinal statements had changed much. Nor were there any stressors or surprises in his continued meetings with either the district or conference boards. His interviews had always been friendly and enjoyable.

Still, this ordination seemed much more significant to Dan than he had anticipated. Maybe because it finalized the long process he had been through. Maybe it was important to him because after his ordination he would be an elder voting on the next class of candidates. Dan didn't think these accounted for his excitement, however. The process had been relatively easy for him and he was led to believe that the voting at executive session was just a formality (a rubber stamp).

No, Dan decided, his excitement was one of a sense of belonging. The bishop had met with the candidates the week before and exhorted them to carefully consider the covenant they were about to enter.

However, this ordination was not the only covenant on Dan's mind that week: he and Sharon had spent five weeks planning a wedding, which would be Saturday following his ordination. Both covenants were closely associated in Dan's mind. Not only were both ceremonies happening within forty-eight hours of each other, but the same pastor (Dan's district superintendent) would lay hands on Dan during the ordination and then perform the marriage ceremony for Dan and Sharon. Dan's family, friends, and congregation would be there for both. It was a wonderful community time. Covenants were firmly planted in Dan's heart as the most wonderful of life events.

It may seem as if Dan and Sharon were well on their way to living happily ever after, and it is true that their love was both bright and contagious. People were drawn to the couple, their love for each other was a powerful magnet that inspired others to love, as well. Of course, it all flowed from their love of God and the circle of love continued to lead them back to Him.

Still, they would face challenges, same as everyone else. The first challenge they faced could have forced them apart. Many strong marriages have dissolved over the years for much less. Indeed, things did get difficult for a spell.

By their third year of marriage, Dan and Sharon were ready to have children. After eight months of trying, they sought a doctor's help. It took another ten months before what they feared was confirmed: they would not be able to have children naturally.

When it became obvious that it was Sharon who was infertile, the two of them hit a very challenging time. Sharon felt guilty, like her infertility was her fault. They couldn't have children, and she was to blame.

Dan saw this and felt his own sense of guilt; as her husband, he should have been the one to bear this. It should have been *his* infertility, not hers. The worst part was that he didn't know how to help, and his attempts were met with silence. He thought it was shame on her part, he didn't know it, and thought she was mad at him for – in his mind – "leaving this on her." As a result, he began to withdraw, too, which she interpreted as confirmation that he blamed her.

The distance between them was becoming their comfort zone until an elderly parishioner, named Mabel Huntsworth, noticed the change and asked Sharon over for a cup of tea. Like many in the congregation, Mabel had prayed diligently over the previous months when Dan and Sharon had shared their prayer request with the congregation. She and her husband had been through a similar situation.

"Have you grieved?" she asked as soon as they sat down. Mabel Huntsworth was nothing if not direct.

Sharon blinked her eyes in surprise. "Of course," she said once she had regained herself. "I've been grieving ever since the doctor told me."

"Us," Mabel corrected.

"I'm sorry?"

"Us," she repeated. "You and Pastor Dan. The doctor told both of you, and this is affecting both of you."

"Of course, it -

"So, I will ask again: have you grieved … together?"

Sharon sat back, understanding flooding her mind.

Without any warning, or the ability to stop them, tears filled her eyes and rolled down her cheeks. "I've been so stupid," she said, burying her face in her hands.

"Yes." Mabel said.

Sharon laughed. "I can count on you to be honest, can't I?"

"We have nothing, if not integrity," she said. Then, in a surprising show of warmth, Mabel took Sharon's hand in her own. "Talk to him. He is losing part of his future too, and if you don't address this together, your love won't survive."

That night, Sharon broached the subject. I won't go into the details of their conversation – that is not for our eyes or ears – but, suffice it to say, it was uncomfortable. But it was much needed. Their shared sadness drew Dan and Sharon even closer. Soon, after more prayer and conversation, they felt they could claim that neither fertility options nor adoption was God's will for them. The time and energy they might have otherwise directed toward their children would be spent showing love to their church members, friends, and family all the more.

This commitment may have exacerbated yet another challenge that Dan and Sharon would face.

It is almost cliché to note that the pastor's wife must learn how to deal with the expectations of the congregation. The wives are expected to be an example of church leadership (in submission to their husbands, of course) and service. The problem was that Sharon didn't seem to struggle with these expectations at all; she simply ignored them. Her call to ministry would not take place through any of normal activities, roles, or offices of the church, but through relationships and invitations to share her home, her cooking, and shame-free intimate conversations.

# CHAPTER 14
## SHARON'S BOUNDARIES

*"Walk into most churches in America, have a look around, and ask yourself this question: What is a Christian woman? Again, don't listen to what is being said, look at what you find there. There is no doubt about it. You'd have to admit a Christian woman is ... tired. All we've offered the feminine soul is the pressure to be 'a good servant.' No one is fighting for her heart; there is no grand adventure to be swept up in; and every woman doubts very much that she has any beauty to unveil."*

— JOHN ELDREDGE

In Dan's first church, Sharon's home church, her firm boundaries were not much of an issue. Dan had served as a single man for the first two years of his six-year ministry there. Everyone knew Sharon and already appreciated who she was and what she did. So, when Dan and Sharon were appointed to their second charge, Sharon made no changes at all in her style.

Dan's second appointment was considered a promotion. Although the church membership's average age was older, and the attendance numbers had been declining steadily for over a decade, it was in a larger city, was a larger church, and was wealthier. It seemed the congregation's expectations of Sharon were more, too. Their expectations of Sharon rose again when they learned that she had no children and they rose again when she determined to not seek a teaching job in their new community. Many of the older women seemed intent on grooming Sharon to become the perfect minister's wife. The problem was Sharon's boundaries were far too healthy: she simply smiled and said "No"… repeatedly.

No, she would not serve on the Education Committee, or the Outreach Committee, or the Welcoming Committee. No, she would not teach a youth Sunday School class, serve in the nursery, or sing in the choir. No, she would not be president, vice president, secretary, or parliamentarian for the United Methodist Women's group.

There were murmurs and rumors of complaints circulating for the first two years or so. Then the expectations seemed to adjust as Sharon won the friendship of people just by being her encouraging self, for Sharon was a very busy person and a hard worker. She made hospital visits and shut-in visits as if she were on staff. She hosted dinners at the parsonage as an act of friendship (not ministry) at least twice a week. So, although she declined every role offered her, she was still engaged in the lives of almost every member of the church.

In their third year of ministry, Sharon's style became ingrained through a crisis. This particular crisis began the day Sharon stopped by the house of a friend who had earlier declined a lunch invitation, claiming sickness. Sharon had picked up some soup and juice, intending to drop them off on her way to her next stop. When her friend, Beth Meyers, came to the door, Sharon instinctively knew that something was wrong. Beth met Sharon at the door with her head down, refusing to make eye contact, her hair obscuring her face.

"Please," Sharon said gently, "won't you look at me?" In the short time it took for Beth to make a quick glance up, Sharon knew the truth. Beth had been beaten. "Is he home?" Sharon asked.

Beth shook her head. "May I come in?"

"I don't think it is a good idea," Beth answered quietly.

"I need to make sure you don't need medical attention." Beth's head shot up, her eyes wide. "Oh! No! No!" She shook her head. "I – I can't."

Sharon masked her horror at her friend's face, and instead put on as sympathetic a look as she could muster. "How about just letting me listen? I won't judge you."

Beth considered this briefly, then slowly stepped back and opened the door wider. Sharon entered, and soon they were sitting on Beth's sofa, the story spilling out. Kent's abuse had become progressively worse over the three years of their marriage. This last episode had been triggered by Beth's request that they visit other churches. She thought her husband, Kent, was much too dependent on his parents (especially his dad). Kent worked for his dad, leased their home from his dad, attended the same church, and sought his advice on every decision.

Since Kent's dad, Bob Meyers, was a leader in the church, a successful businessman, and had a marriage that had lasted over thirty-five years, he might have seemed a good person to take advice from. But the truth was that Kent's dad had ruled his wife with an iron hand. And when Kent had told his dad about some of their marriage problems, the men had agreed Beth was totally at fault.

Before Dan had made it home from work that afternoon, Sharon had moved Beth into their guest room and had taken photos of her injuries.

Dan was supportive of Sharon's choices and ready to do whatever it took to keep Beth safe, no matter what the consequences. Dan and Sharon were operating as a team. Together, and with Beth's consent, they scheduled a meeting with Kent and both of his parents.

Dan took the lead as the meeting began. With chairs drawn together in a tight circle, Dan was able to look each participant in the eyes as he confronted them as directly (but as gently) as possible.

"The facts, as I understand them, are these. First, Sharon and I are fully prepared to call the police. The law no longer requires that the victim press charges. We can press charges on her behalf. That is fact number one. Fact number two is that unless everyone here agrees to our terms, we will do exactly that; we will call the police tonight.

Kent stood up, knocking his chair over, glaring at Beth. "You little –"

Dan reached for the rotary phone on the desk next to him. "Or I can call right now," he said.

Kent turned his glare on Dan, paused, retrieved his chair, and sat back down.

"Our requirements," Dan continued, "are that Beth stay here with us for the next four months, at a minimum. Kent will be allowed supervised visits only. They will both enter counseling. Kent will also begin anger management counseling. As will you, Bob," he said, nodding to Kent's dad. "In fact, Bob, you and Gale will also begin marriage counseling. Gale, you will attend a co-dependency group. In addition, Kent, Bob, and Gale will resign any and all positions of leadership at the church until I am convinced that you have all grown and healed to my satisfaction.

"These are the facts, any questions?"

Bob was quick to respond, an attack focused on Sharon. He accused her of meddling, not knowing the full story, misleading her husband, encouraging Beth's lack of submission, and jeopardizing a marriage.

Though Sharon seemed unfazed, Dan's anger flashed. His eyes grew steely, and he slowly stood. "You will leave my wife out of this," he said, "or the police will be arresting an unconscious man."

When Bob realized that his actions only increased Dan's convictions, he took a new tactic. This time he expressed his disappointment in Dan, disappointment that their pastor was under his wife's thumb, that he was attempting to blackmail Bob and his father, and disappointment for jeopardizing the best interests of the church.

Kent, for his part, sat back in his chair with an open-mouthed amazement at his dad's inability to shake Dan and Sharon's resolve and escape their ultimatum. Gale sat quietly with an occasional tear running down her face.

When Bob finally paused, Sharon was first to respond. "Dan, I think we have overlooked an important part of this situation." Bob smirked. Apparently, he thought Sharon was about to make some concession. Kent took a short, relieved breath. Father and son both thought Sharon was about to back down. They didn't know her very well.

Reaching her hand out to Gale, Sharon continued, "We have two guest rooms. I think Gale may need a safe place as much as Beth does."

The silence in the room emphasized the significance of the moment (the presence of the Holy Spirit) as, after only a short pause, Gale took Sharon's hand.

I can tell you how it worked out for the couples of both generations by a single phrase: the Meyers family became Dan and Sharon's great friends and biggest supporters. But that is not my point. I just wanted you to see what a great match Dan and Sharon were together.

I can honestly tell you that, to me, this is the most amazing of the "Dan stories." I am not amazed that Dan would be this kind of leader, that he could act with such commitment, intelligence, and love. What amazes me was the ability of Dan and Sharon to know and trust each other well enough to team up so effectively during a crisis.

I have heard of other couples being able to work through their perspectives to reach agreements as to how to respond in such difficult circumstance. But I don't think I've ever known a couple to partner so well together on the spur of a moment. I have to say, when I heard this story, I envied Dan his marriage.

# CHAPTER 15
# A SLIGHT DISAGREEMENT

*"Somehow the human species has an extraordinary knack for taking the best teaching and turning it to the worst ends. Nothing can put people into bondage like religion, and nothing in religion has done more to manipulate and destroy people than a deficient teaching on submission."* — RICHARD FOSTER

After another six-year stay, Dan and Sharon were relocated again.

They were not looking to be moved, because the church was experiencing growth and, critical for stability in church ministry, the church staff was happy and supportive. Dan was a shining star among the clergy in his conference. He served consistently and well on conference boards and committees. His church grew, so the church budget grew, so the apportionment allocations – the money a local church paid into the district and conference budgets – grew.

Dan was great at presenting apportionments, not as an obligation or a burden on the church, but as an amazing opportunity to support ministries much too big for a local church. Because he truly loved these ministries, his churches grew excited and celebrated paying their apportionments.

The week before annual conference, Dan received a call from his district superintendent. "Dan, I know this is last minute notice, but we will need to announce a move for you next week. We are still in cabinet meetings, so I can't tell you where we want to move you yet, but rest assured, this is a very good move for you. I'll call you back tomorrow to fill you in on the details."

Dan was barely able to get a response in. When he did, he sounded more agreeable than he was feeling; "How will my church deal with this?" "Your church has done very well over the past six years. They are in great shape. They will be proud of the move we have in mind for you. Don't worry. Call a special meeting of the Pastor-Parish Committee for this Sunday afternoon and I will be there. I'll explain our need of you and give them details on who their new pastor will be. I'll call back tomorrow with more details."

As soon as he hung up, Dan called Sharon. He explained what had happened and asked her to come to his office to talk about it some more. Fifteen minutes later, Sharon entered Dan's office. Without a word, they both knew the other would need some encouragement and they fell into a long hug.

"What do you think about all this?" Dan asked, letting her go.

"I think there may be a mistake. I'm not at all sure we should move." Sharon's innocent response hit Dan like a glass full of cold water in his face.

"Sharon, we aren't in a position to make that decision. The bishop and the cabinet make that decision." It was her turn to experience the cold water in the face.

After a pause, she said slowly, "Surely they would need to talk to us and to the church *before* they could make a decision." "Apparently, they are in a difficult situation and are having to make adjustments at the last minute. They probably haven't had time to go through all their normal steps." Then, trying to redirect, Dan pushed on. "The D.S. said it would be a good move for us. There aren't that many churches that are considered 'better' than here."

Sharon would not be sidestepped. Returning to her concern, she pleaded with Dan, "Can't we spend some time in prayer, asking God what He wants us to do?"

Her plea touched Dan's heart and he softened toward her, but not toward her plea. "Babe, if you are asking if God will tell us His will, He already has. When I was ordained, I committed to go wherever the bishop and the cabinet send me. And when we married, you committed to following me wherever God sends me. Even if we don't like it, we don't get to change the deal now."

"I'm not asking to change the deal," Sharon protested. "I'm just asking to pray to see if God might want us to say something to the people making decisions about our lives. And, even if we are committed to abiding by their decisions, it may serve us well to know that we could be subject to things God didn't intend for us."

Ignoring the heart of her plea, Dan responded as if she just needed some encouragement. Hugging her again, he assured her, "It's going to be alright. This kind of thing happens to someone almost every year. They would only move us like this if they absolutely needed to and knew it was the right thing to do."

Sharon let him hug her. She let him make the decision for them both. She would miss the people here and she would love the people in the next church. But in her heart and mind, she knew that she had been disrespected, not by the bishop and the cabinet, but by Dan. She didn't need Dan's reassurances. She needed to hear from God. Dan had acted so certain of what God would say but refused to join her in seeking His voice.

Over the years Sharon tried to explain her feelings about this event several times, but each time, Dan felt like she was questioning his commitment to the church. She returned to the subject as often as she did in hopes of clarifying her thoughts and feelings. This may have been the first time they simply could not come to understand each other.

# CHAPTER 16
## MORE OF THE SAME

*"Like the nation, America's churches breathe the atmosphere of self-protection and self-aggrandizement. They run after the same things the world does. The church is not free for the Kingdom."*
— HOWARD A. SNYDER

The next day, it wasn't Dan's district superintendent who called, but the bishop. "Dan, I want to express my gratitude for making this untimely move. Our confidence in you is very high. We are moving you to the third-largest church in our conference. We are asking that you allow Reverend Petree time to announce his retirement on Sunday morning before you announce your move to your Pastor-Parish Committee on Sunday afternoon. He has been advised by his doctor not to put off his retirement any longer."

"How do you think his congregation will take this?" Dan asked.

The bishop sighed. "Reverend Petree has served there for the last eighteen years. He is dearly loved and will be sorely missed. We ask that you simply be yourself and be patient with a congregation that is unprepared for this change. We have spoken to the staff there and they are committed to helping you maintain and advance the proud history of this great congregation. But," he continued, "there will be some resistance from those who don't like changes. Be aware of that."

All went as planned. When the moves were announced the next week at the annual conference, Dan was repeatedly congratulated. Some pastors looked at him as if he had won the lottery. Others wondered aloud if the congregation would feel slighted by the appointment of a thirty-six-year-old senior pastor. Dan guessed that some of the pastors felt slighted themselves for being passed over for a younger minister.

The new parsonage was representative of Dan's and Sharon's new social standing. The 3,500-square-foot manse's kitchen was newly remodeled with industrial-quality appliances. The dining and living rooms were expensively furnished and could easily host a dozen guests. Each of the three bedrooms had their own bathrooms and walk-in closets and the garage was made to house four cars, tool cabinets, and lawn equipment.

Reverend Petree's wife had left a notebook of details concerning the maintenance of the house, from how to operate the sprinkler system to which companies provided their landscaping services.

Within a few days, Dan and Sharon had all of their boxes unpacked and were settled in. Then Sharon hosted Dan's first meeting with the staff, which consisted of three associate ministers, the youth director, the children's minister, and the worship leader. Dan would meet the other employees, five secretaries and four janitors, later. This first meeting was intended to lay a relational foundation, as well as address a rather pressing issue.

With the surprise retirement of Reverend Petree, the church schedule had been sabotaged. The sermon series was interrupted, the members who were scheduled for weddings and the anticipated funerals would most likely be uncomfortable with a pastor they didn't know, and many members were hoping to honor the Petree's with a retirement party.

Dan, who was never one to micromanage his staff, took this in stride. He intended to empower his staff, including the employees and part-time staff, with authority in their areas of responsibility. During that first meeting, when asked what he thought should happen in any given situation, he typically responded with, "You tell me. You know more about that than I do. What do you suggest?"

As a result, Dan and Sharon's first year at their new parish was a happy one. The one exception to the rule was an associate pastor who seemed most concerned with "being respected" than being respectful. It soon became apparent that this associate was also the one least capable of managing his responsibilities well. Dan had one quiet conversation with his superintendent, and the following summer this associate was reassigned to a position in another church. Dan determined that his position was not necessary to the function of the church, and no one was assigned to take his place. To those who knew and understood such dynamics, Dan was considered a very firm leader indeed.

Then the honeymoon year ended.

Sharon's boundaries were causing problems again. She said "no" to all the same things. But this time the murmuring was not quiet. This larger church boasted members who were accustomed to others being accountable to them. Their leadership positions and successes in their own fields of business created an expectation that their opinions would carry a lot of weight in the church. Part of the culture of this larger church was an unwritten rule that the senior pastor be shown proper respect. But, for some reason, this rule did not seem to apply to his spouse. Why should it, when the spouse didn't even feel the need to at least explain herself to those whose expectations were not being met?

Sharon said "no" to all requests for her to serve in church

roles, in order to be free give her time and energy to hosting people in her home and developing relationships with them.

In a paradoxical way, Sharon's freedom to show love and concern, and to meet needs as she encountered them, worked against her. Staff and members alike would share their struggles with Sharon, who became known as an encourager and great keeper-of-secrets. But even though she was great at pointing people toward the highest good, her involvement in the squabbles of the church was used against her.

The more those she ministered to loved and respected her, the more some seemed offended by her. By the beginning of their fifth year there, Sharon had become a divisive issue. When those who loved her heard the criticisms against her, a backlash against Sharon's critics began. Like yeast in dough, the controversy grew and spread. The sides formed along age-group lines. The thirtythrough fifty-year olds seemed to consider Sharon the "patron saint" of the younger leaders. Whereas those fifty and older tended to demonize Sharon, calling her "unappreciative of the opportunities her gifted husband had created for her."

Truth be told, the rumors of war in a church does a lot to increase attendance and giving as each side makes efforts to increase their influence. So, from the outside, the church seemed stronger than ever.

For a long time, the nature of the controversy was hard to identify. Dan and Sharon were told stories about what one group was saying about the other, and vice versa. It seemed that everyone was waiting to see what Dan would do about it all. Meanwhile, Sharon felt like God had a plan. She was willing to meet individually and privately with certain leaders in the older group. She would give them as much honest praise as she possibly could. She would try to win their friendship and ask them to use their influence to end the rumors and gossiping. However, the constant bickering and increasing bitterness between the groups discouraged her.

Dan asked her to give it some more time. He suggested using that time to build friendships with some influential older members.

The longer Sharon followed this advice, the more convinced she became that she needed to directly address the issue with the older members. As the months passed, the hostility between the sides increased, and had less to do with Sharon's boundaries. The Nomination Committee became the principal battlefield. Debates broke out as one side argued that new members should be given positions of responsibility to encourage and develop their leadership for the future. The other side argued that members already known for their faithfulness and their leadership skills should be placed in the positions of greatest responsibility.

It took all the patience and calm authority Dan could muster to navigate the nominations to a peaceful conclusion. Although the sides were more clearly defined, the war was temporarily avoided.

For over two years, Sharon waited on Dan to agree with her on addressing the issue directly. Dan's avoidance seemed new and different to Sharon. Dan called it "not being drawn in" and "putting the burden on God," which Sharon respected, but the problem was that Sharon felt like God was leading her to a more direct approach. So, it seemed to her that Dan's alternative approach indicated a lack of trust in her to relate well to her critics. Dan did not dispute that assessment, but continued to say, simply, "Let's give it time." It turned out that, in the course of time, Sharon did bring a conclusion to the hostilities, just not in the way she had anticipated.

Sharon's dad had been diagnosed with stage three inoperable cancer. He was told he could pass within a month. Sharon's parents needed her comfort and help. Still, she didn't leave Dan and the church until she met with the staff and asked for their prayers. That move alone began to turn some hearts, and after she left for her parents', Dan was faithful to give updates and ask for continued prayer while Sharon was away. The expected lifespan of one month ended up being closer to four months as her dad spent most of his days in a painkiller-induced sleep. When he passed, it was due to pneumonia.

The church sent wonderful bouquets and cards from every Sunday School class, and by the time Sharon returned home, she was treated with respect by all. For her part, she continued caring for individuals and avoiding serving in "roles." Dan continued to be the dynamic preacher and calm leader he had always been.

Still, there was a growing sense of individuality in how Dan and Sharon went about their ministries. Opportunities to partner together in addressing situations were bypassed as one or the other cared for the matter. They would talk of events afterwards, but not with as much detail as they had before.

Their ministry at this church lasted twelve years, at which time Dan was appointed one of the youngest district superintendents the conference ever had. At forty-eight years old, Dan was being talked about across the conference as someone who would be a bishop someday.

For those reading this book, you may observe that the "give-it-time" approach that Dan recommended served them well; the sides faded away in time and in the face of the circumstances of life. Some could call it Providence, but I believe God's purposes are those of redemption and sanctification, not just a passive well-being. Who knows what wonderful growth might have come from Sharon's willingness to talk openly and directly with the older church members?

Don't forget that I am challenging you, dear reader, to not be a passive recipient of this story, but to find your place in it. As I chronicle the dynamics of Dan's and Sharon's relationship as objectively as I can, it is important to ask yourself if you can value their differences equally or if one or the other was twisting away from the purity of their former characters. Were they both simply maturing in different ways, or was one of them regressing?

# CHAPTER 17
## MORE OF MORE OF THE SAME

*"Pseudocommunity is an apt name because it is a false community something that looks like a community but isn't. Gather a group of people together for virtually any purpose and they will begin by pretending that they are already a community. The basic pretense is that there are no significant differences between them. And when our differences are forced to the surface one way or another the group will immediately degenerate into the stage of chaos. Occasionally, the members do succeed in 'stuffing' their differences so as to regress into an even stronger form of pseudocommunity or cult."* — M. SCOTT PECK

I'm telling a story based on the stories I've been told. I don't know if the stories I've heard are the most important stories of Dan and Sharon's lives, but I do know that while these are important stories (meaning, lots of people seem to know about them), the most important stories of our lives are often the smaller, more intimate ones. And, though the stories I've heard – and told to you – certainly propelled us to the unfortunate end, I am certain it was more of the little, unknown stories that really brought them to the place where I first met Dan.

I might as well tell you now: not long after this point in the story, Sharon is going to divorce Dan. Knowing now what neither Dan nor Sharon would have even considered divorce at this point in the story gives us a way of considering each detail of their relationship pessimistically. So I might be telling some of their stories with a twist that wasn't there at the time. But the conclusion of their stories is not in doubt: their marriage will not survive.

It is probably not surprising that the first big sign (in hindsight) of marriage problems for Dan and Sharon came when Sharon's freedom to represent herself collided with Dan's role in the denomination.

As the wife of a district superintendent, it was expected that Sharon would participate in the bi-annual "ministers' spouse meetings." Sharon was successful in avoiding any elected positions at the district level by expressing a desire to avoid any conflict of interest, because her husband would be required to make decisions that directly affected the lives of the ministry spouses. But when the wives of other district superintendents nominated her for the honor of serving as president of the Annual Conference Spouses Committee, Sharon knew she couldn't decline.

You see, Sharon was not being nominated because the spouses needed someone to fill a nominal role. Sharon was nominated because the Spouses Committee had become a stage on which the "theological diversity" of the denomination would be on trial. It seemed the ministers' spouses had more freedom in expressing their opinions about the theological conflicts in the denomination than the ministers did, and the controversy resulted in the sides taking stands and representing themselves publicly.

What this all boiled down to was George Gibbs had also been nominated for the position of President of the Spouses Committee. George was the husband of a female clergy member of the conference, and those who supported him made strong declarations of how biased it would be for anyone to challenge his nomination just because he was male.

This put the more conservative ministers' spouses in a

difficult position because their objection to George was not that he was male, but that he himself was an ordained minister in the Unitarian Church. In their eyes, this created a huge conflict of interest, which raised very legitimate questions: How could a man who was a minister in one denomination be making decisions for a completely different denomination? How could they encourage each other in the faith if they held different faiths? How could they worship together if they didn't share the same Gospel?

Dan was shocked when Sharon told him that, in her short candidate's speech, she intended to raise these questions, and his first response avoided the whole issue of theology. "Sharon, you have always avoided roles like this. I know you don't want to serve as president of any committee."

"No, I don't," she admitted. "But this isn't a matter of a role on a committee. It is simply recognizing a reality. Our denomination is not Unitarian. We do not believe in Universalism, and those who do have another denomination that they can go to."

Sharon had entered this conversation expecting to have Dan's understanding and support. Instead, she soon realized, he was determined to try to avoid having Sharon involved in the conflict.

"Sharon, the Spouses Committee is not the place for theological discussions. You have dinner meetings. They sing some hymns, listen to an encouraging speaker, and socialize. *That's all.*"

"That would be all, Dan, if a Universalist weren't nominated to be our president."

"At the spouses committee, George is not a universalist or a conservative. He is just the husband of a clergy member of the conference. That's all."

There was a pause, while Sharon adjusted her thinking. "So we can just sing some hymns, like we always do, as long as the hymns don't mention that Jesus is our Savior … *that's all.* We can listen to an inspirational speaker, like we always do, as long as the speaker doesn't mention that Jesus is our Savior… *that's all.*"

Although Sharon was speaking softly, he recognized the sarcasm directed against him. Again, trying to avoid the issue, Dan addressed the sarcasm. "I am not the enemy here. I believe just like you do. Your sarcasm only hurts us both."

Dan was used to being able to direct conversations. Since childhood, he had been able to circumvent conflicts and direct people to peaceful resolutions. This role came naturally to him. However, in Sharon he had met his match. While they had certainly had similar arguments before, he was not used to being condescended to. He briefly pondered the irony of it: her ability to represent herself and set healthy boundaries had always made her attractive to Dan but was now putting them at odds with each other.

"Dan, you can't ask me to pretend I don't see the bigger picture here. The conservative spouses are being sent a very direct message. They are being told, in no uncertain terms, to stop speaking out concerning the theological controversies in the denomination. Am I supposed to sit by and let that message win?"

Without pause Dan responded, "Yes, please. The committee is not the place for controversy. We have a hundred other ways of addressing our theological issues. Nothing good can come from fighting such causes through the spouses committee, of all places! Please don't be a part of exacerbating such a futile conflict."

Sharon took a moment to process Dan's request. "Okay, Dan, I will decline the nomination. But there are two things I need to ask you first."

Dan was visibly relieved and nodded to Sharon to continue.

"First, will you tell me that you understand that the conservative spouses are in no way responsible for this conflict? The others nominated George for no other reason than to make their own theological statement. Do you understand that?"

"Yes, of course I do," Dan stated calmly and deliberately. "Okay, then, I need you to understand I can let this controversy go only because I believe that you are using all your talents and influence to address these controversies in those other ways that you mentioned. I am trusting you to do all you can to keep situations like this from happening again in the future."

When Dan responded, "You know I will," Sharon was surprised to realize that she really didn't know that he would.

# CHAPTER 18
# BISHOP DAN DAVIDSON

*"When held up next to our ministry, this episode in Acts 5 reveals our deceit. We say we tolerate Ananias and Sapphira because we love them, because we are called to a ministry of service and compassion, even when people are wealthy liars. In other words, we have more love than Peter had in Acts. In truth, we deceive ourselves. We do not believe in Ananias and Sapphira as much as Peter believed in them."*

— RESIDENT ALIENS, HAUERWAS AND WILLIMON

After serving four years as a district superintendent, Dan was nominated and elected to serve as a bishop in the United Methodist Church. Dan's role as bishop left Sharon in a difficult position that she had not anticipated until she got there.

Sharon had anticipated becoming active in one of the sixteen local United Methodist Churches in the state capital (home to the conference headquarters). Since Dan would be speaking in other churches on a regular basis, she anticipated visiting and selecting a church based upon God's leading. As was becoming more common, this issue led to another argument.

Dan shared his preaching itinerary for the first three months with Sharon and asked her to travel with him on five of the weekends. Sharon readily agreed, then proceeded to share her plans for visiting churches on the other weekends he was away.

Knowing that this subject would be a difficult one, Dan began in compassionate tones. "Sharon, I hope this doesn't upset you, but it is not a good policy for the bishop's wife to visit churches in order to pick one to attend. Every pastor would be very sensitive to not being picked. That is one of the reasons why it is customary for the bishop and his wife to attend First UMC whenever one or both of them are in town. You can see why that is. I hope you are not disappointed. I really believe you will love First Church. I've met their pastor and he is a very fine man."

Sharon had listened with a growing sense of surprise. It had never occurred to her that her home church would have already been picked for her. She stood in silent contemplation for so long that Dan eventually reached out to her and took her hand. "Every church would love to have you," he assured her. "I'm sure you will feel right at home in no time." He spoke as if her agreement were a foregone conclusion.

Instead of feeling comforted, Sharon felt cornered. Still, her voice was calm as she tried to identify the boundary needed to represent herself clearly.

"Okay, let's slow down. Dan, I haven't agreed to anything yet."

Dan shouldn't have been surprised. This was Sharon, after all. So, changing his expression to one of reconciliation, Dan pressed on. "Of course. I'm sorry we didn't talk about this sooner. It just came up right now. So, tell me what you are thinking."

"I'm thinking that God might have plans outside the 'norm' for where I go to church. I may not fit in at First Church, or He may want me somewhere else."

"Sharon, I know my new role as bishop puts lots of burdens on you. I'm sorry if there are disappointments, but it seems to me that God's will is clear. We've been honored with the highest position of trust the denomination has to offer, and I never could have done it without you. You are the best wife any minister ever had. So," he smiled mischievously, "some of these burdens are your fault for making me look so good."

Sharon accepted the compliment but remained unconvinced. She loved Dan and didn't want to be hard on him, but decided to think and pray about the issue before returning to the discussion. She would attend First Church without a fuss and give God the option of confirming her decision. If it didn't work out that way, she could raise the issue again later. Unfortunately, as much as she had hoped it wouldn't happen, Sharon was soon convinced that she had no business being anywhere near First Church.

Sharon's first visit was conducted under the close supervision of the senior pastor's wife. Helen was twelve years younger than her sixty-two-year-old husband. Her husband was a dynamic preacher whose friendly personality complimented his sincere faith. His first marriage had ended in divorce, and he spent the next eight years – well into his thirties – as a happy bachelor. When he recognized his singleness was raising some concerns among his congregation, he decided to look for a new wife. He was handsome, personable, and successful. Helen was beautiful and interested. Before long, they were married and they moved together to their next appointment, a step up to a larger church.

Helen, alone in her thinking, found leadership deficiencies in her husband and had determined to help him manage the staff and programs of the church. Unconsciously, she depended on her "get-away-face" (pretty enough to get away with minor offenses) to get her way. Nevertheless, life was good for several years. Then, the power struggle began.

Helen's husband was made aware, through the repeated complaints of others, of his wife's high-handedness. When he finally confronted her about it, Helen told him directly that he could not afford another divorce so he could damn well get used to the idea that she was her own person.

That had been over twenty years earlier and Helen's husband had followed that advice ever since. In the meantime, he had found comfort in food. He had gained sixty pounds, but it didn't detract from his appearance that much. Helen had gained forty pounds herself, and every pound she gained went directly and only into her hips, rump, and face. She looked like an entirely different person. Without her physical attractiveness, her unattractive personality seemed so much more obvious. People began to pity Helen's husband for being stuck with her.

And, although Helen was totally unwilling to change, she was aware of how she was perceived. She placed the blame for others' negative perception of her on the unrealistic expectations the laity had for their clergy spouses. She also justified her abrasive behavior by pointing out her husband's passiveness, saying, "Someone has to be brave and take charge."

When Helen met Sharon, it was hate-at-first-sight. Sharon and Helen first met in the parlor of the church.

They had chosen the time and place during a prior phone call.

Helen's first words to Sharon were, "Don't you just love it? I oversaw all the new remodeling and decorating in this room."

Sharon had to pause to find the word "interesting" to replace the honest answer that screamed in her head: "GAUDY."

"I had to fight tooth and nail to convince everyone that the parlor should be the one place, if there could be no others, where we show some refinement."

Sharon concluded that Helen's idea of refinement must be limited to anything expensive, because that was the only thing she could see that the furnishings of the parlor had in common with each other.

Sharon committed herself to pleasantness and moved the conversation from one topic to the other. Their limited time together, before the worship service began, was an exercise in diplomacy for Sharon. Without offering Helen false compliments or praise, Sharon showed a lively interest in whatever seemed to interest Helen, but Helen was smart enough to see through Sharon's tactics and thoroughly resented her for it. After attending First Church four or five times, and being inescapably escorted by Helen each time, Sharon was beginning to feel trapped.

The trap was sprung through an e-mail.

*Sharon, I know that being the bishop's wife tends to isolate you from consequences of your actions. You probably are not used to being critiqued, but as your friend and sister in Christ....*

The e-mail accused Sharon of being a flirt with men (*"unintentionally showing off your figure"*) and being a snob toward women (*"ignoring the valuable contributions of the wives of less successful husbands"*). Helen's complaints about Sharon's "distractedness," "distancing," and even "delusions of superiority" were offered as truths spoken in love. The two-and-a half-page e-mail must have taken hours to write. The concluding paragraphs held out the hope for building upon this foundation of honest discourse.

Sharon printed the e-mail and showed it to Dan. This

e-mail became the context for their most devastating argument up until that point.

"Oh, Honey, I am so sorry," Dan offered. "I would not have believed that Helen could be so hurtful."

"Thanks," she replied, "but I really am not in the least bit hurt. I am very angry, but not hurt. She is simply out-of-control. I would say that she is psychotic, but I believe she knows exactly what she is doing."

"Okay, well, what is it you think she is doing?"

"She wants me to become a fan of hers, drooling over everything she says and does, or else she wants me to go away. She feels threatened by me and is trying to gain dominance over me."

Still with concerned and supportive tones, Dan asked, "Do you really think she is smart enough to do all that?"

"No, but she thinks she is."

"What I mean is, don't you think that she is probably insecure and hurting and just needs some assurance from you that you see value in her?"

"Maybe, but the way she chooses to act out of her 'insecurity' is to be controlling and mean. Not just with me. I've seen her be that way with her husband and I know she is walking all over people at the church."

Having become a little agitated by his inability to calm his wife, Dan challenged her. "Once you have time to get beyond your anger, I bet we can find a way to be helpful in this situation."

"I already know what I need to see happen here. I think Helen could benefit from counseling. Maybe it should be couple's counseling with her husband. Whatever, she needs to be in counseling."

"That is probably true, but I doubt it will happen. She probably doesn't believe she needs counseling."

"Then maybe you should let her know."

"I don't know about that. It could be seen as a 'power play' on our part. That would be catastrophic, especially if Helen already feels threatened by you."

"Well, fine. If there is nothing I can do, I certainly will not subject myself to her presence again if I can help it. I will find another church to attend."

"Sharon, we have already had the discussion about visiting other churches. You do remember the complications I told you it would create?"

"I do remember. I'm sorry if my choice creates problems for you, but I will not be returning to First Church. And don't you forget to find a way to get Helen the help she needs before she does more damage to the church than her husband can manage."

Dan didn't know how to proceed. Sharon had made it clear that she had made her own decision regardless of his perspective. He groped for some solid ground to stand on, unwilling to accept Sharon's decision.

"I can't believe you would be so cold and selfish," Dan told her. "I've never known you to be so uncaring."

Sharon's eyes filled with tears. "Sharon, you must consider the bigger picture. All you are seeing right now is your own hurt feelings. Would you please be patient and pray about this before you make things worse than they already are?"

It only took a few seconds for anger to dry her tears. "No, Dan, I will not give this another thought! Now my thoughts are on something entirely different. Now I am thinking that you don't know me very well and I certainly do not know you. I do need some time to think, not about attending First Church, but about our relationship. I think I need to go spend the next week or two with my mother. I think we need some time apart."

With his mask of sad calmness firmly in place, Dan said the only thing left to say, "If that is what you feel you need, then I understand."

After a full minute of looking each other in the eyes, each hoping the other would back away from the edge of this cliff, they both turned and walked away. Sharon began her packing, and Dan returned to his office.

# CHAPTER 19

# AN INTERVENTION:

*"Consciousness brings more pain, but it also brings more joy. Because as you go further into the desert – if you go far enough – you will begin to discover little patches of green, little oases that you had never seen before. And if you go still further, you may even discover some streams of living water underneath the sand, or if you go further still, you may even be able to fulfill your own ultimate destiny."* — M. SCOTT PECK

What you and I know, from our objective perspectives, is that Dan and Sharon needed someone to intervene for the two of them in the same way they had intervened for others in the past. They needed a friend, a counselor, or even a family member to sit down with them and help them confront the growing hurts and disconnections in their relationship. But it is very difficult for the leaders and healers to ask someone to lead them and help them. So, it seems to me that God found a different way to intervene. He put Dan in the spotlight of a statewide moral and political issue.

The governor and a majority of the state legislature were promoting a state vote to legalize casino gambling and lotteries in the state. A portion of the proceeds from the gambling would be designated to supplement the state's education budget. The issue was being promoted on two fronts: 1) keeping the state competitive with other states that had already legalized gambling, and 2) doing it for the children. The "Vote Yes" campaign was being underwritten by the Teacher's Union and by out-of-state casino owners who hoped to expand their businesses.

It was on the third night of their separation that Dan was asked to be chairman of the "Vote No" campaign. Dan called Sharon and asked for her help. She agreed and returned home the next day.

Sharon took Dan's decision to lead the campaign as a desire and a commitment on his part to return to his role of standing up for what was right. She thought that his request for help was his way of admitting that he trusted her to stand beside him.

Over the next six months, Sharon felt like she had her husband back again. This was the man she loved. Standing against all odds, with a budget one-fifth that of the opposition, Dan was the voice of reason and concern in the midst of a political and moral whirlwind. In speech after speech, Dan avoided the attacks claiming he was trying to legislate morality and gain religious power over state government issues. Instead, Dan spoke directly and persuasively of the negative consequences faced by states that had passed similar legislation. He quoted statistics about how very little money the gambling industries had generated for the states and about how devastating the consequences for the states had been: increases in gambling addictions, increases in bankruptcy filings, and increases in divorce rates. Not to mention the other crime that comes when people are broke and desperate.

Yet these statistics were not the heart of his message. Instead, his unique take on the situation caught the media and the opposing campaign totally by surprise, and drew more attention than ever to Dan. His main message was that if a majority of the state's population thought that legalizing gambling was in their best interest then they should vote for such legislation. But not this legislation. He explained that the current proposed legislation made the government a promoter of gambling and made the education system dependent on an ever-increasing amount of gambling. Dan effectively dissected the elements of the proposed legislation and showed the harmful dynamics of every part.

The effect of Dan's pointed, engaging, humorous, and challenging speeches earned him the love and support of a fast-growing segment of the population of the state. Meanwhile, an equal but opposite effect was that Dan became the target of attacks. The media called him a "religionist," the council of bishops warned him that he should be seen as a representative of all perspectives within the UMC, and he began receiving threatening and hateful letters and phone calls.

Meanwhile, Dan and Sharon were doing wonderfully together. They were sharing life together intimately. They researched the issues together, planned his speeches together, critiqued each new development together. And when the threats became reality, it drew them even closer.

Dan and Sharon were at the Holiday Inn in the county seat town where a debate had been held that evening when they received the phone call telling them that their home had burned to the ground. Yes, it was arson. No, there were no suspects. No, they would not be able to recover any clothes, furniture, or personal items. Yet, as Dan and Sharon cried together over the news, they may never have felt closer to each other.

Their relationship was restored. Even after the majority of voters approved the new gambling laws, Dan and Sharon never second-guessed the rightness of their stand and never begrudged the price they had paid.

# CHAPTER 20
# A SPIRITUAL HOME

*"Jesus led his disciples to a place that for generations had been known as 'the gates of hell,' a place where various religions over the ages had practiced rituals including cutting themselves, orgies, rape, and murder of the innocent (including infants). This was a place that Jesus' disciples would never go near if Jesus hadn't led them there. It was there that Peter proclaimed that Jesus was the Messiah. It was there that Jesus proclaimed, 'Upon this rock I shall build my church.' There is some confusion whether Jesus' reference to this rock was intended to refer to Peter (which carries the meaning of 'little rock'), or to Peter's confession that Jesus is the Messiah (the theological foundation of the church), or to the rock that served as an altar in this place he had brought his disciples to. But there should be no confusion about Jesus' next statement concerning the church, 'And the gates of hell shall not prevail against it.'*

*Clearly, Jesus was proclaiming His church would be established within the very shade of the gates of hell and it would be assaulted by a brilliant and practiced evil, yet His church would not be overcome."* — TERRY EWING

During the months of campaigning, Sharon had visited and then joined St. Paul's, where Kyle Fedder was pastoring. Dan, being busy with his duties in other churches, never once attended with her, but neither did Dan protest that Sharon had chosen a smaller local church as her church home.

Sharon's first visit to St. Paul's was a combination of two divergent yet wonderful feelings for her. Sharon described it as "a new adventure" and a "loving homecoming" rolled into one. Sharon entered the sanctuary quietly and only introduced herself as Sharon to the greeters and those sitting near her. No one seemed to recognize her as "the bishop's wife."

The service began when Kyle stepped into center stage and two other church leaders spaced themselves horizontally across the stage. Simultaneously, the three raised their outspread hands and the congregation grew silent and bowed their heads. Together, the three recited the Aaronic blessing over the congregation: *"The Lord bless you and keep you, The Lord make his face to shine upon you and be gracious unto you, The Lord lift up His countenance upon you and give you peace."* Then, as the worship team took the stage, one of the leaders proceeded to welcome the congregation. "Thank you for joining our community this morning! Whatever faith you profess, whatever life you lead, whatever wounds you bear, and whatever motivations brought you here this morning, please know that your presence is a gift to us and we are glad you are here!"

Without pause, the musicians began an instrumental introduction to their first song as the leader continued. "We begin our service with an open altar invitation to prayer for anyone other than yourself. Feel free to come to the altar to pray for those you love, for those in need of miracles, or wisdom, or comfort, or guidance, or strength! God loves your intercessory prayers. A time for prayers for your personal needs will come after the sermon, but, for now, we open the altar for intercessory prayers."

Sharon was surprised, but not sure why she should be. After all, shouldn't such prayers be expected among every body of believers? She quickly relaxed as the worship team began a series of songs and the congregation joined in. Before long, Sharon realized that something special was happening.

As people knelt at the altar, their friends and family members would come kneel with them or stand behind them with their hands on their shoulders. The fact that people were praying for others as she sang added a profound sense of expectation, appreciation, and depth to the words she sang. And Sharon could tell that those praying could feel the encouragement and empathy of those who were singing. The words she sang were not just to God or about God but, it seemed, as if God, the singers, and those in prayer had entered a holy partnership. The service had just begun, and Sharon was already feeling bonded with these believers.

The sense of bonding was expanded when the worship leader invited the congregation to "join with their fellow believers across time and across the world as we declare the essentials of our faith as expressed in the Apostle's Creed.

"'*I believe in God, The Father Almighty, creator of heaven and earth*

*And in Jesus Christ, His only son, our Lord:*

*Who was conceived by the Holy Spirit,*

*Born of the Virgin Mary, suffered under Pontius Pilate,*

*Was crucified, died, and was buried, He descended into Hell'...*"

At the words, "He descended into Hell," Sharon stumbled. Those words had not been apart of what she had been taught and had recited throughout her lifetime. Then, she quickly continued:

"*The third day he rose again from the dead; He ascended into heaven, is seated at the right hand of God, the Father Almighty,*

*From thence he shall come to judge the living and the dead.*

*I believe in the Holy Spirit,*

*The Holy catholic church,*
*The Communion of the saints,*
*The resurrection of the body,*
*And the life everlasting. Amen."*


As soon as the statement of faith was completed, Sharon began making notes on her phone about what she had experienced so far.

When Kyle began to speak, it took Sharon a moment to recognize him as the senior pastor and that he had begun his sermon. He didn't stand in the pulpit or wear a robe. He was dressed casually and was speaking casually. It took her a moment to catch up to what Kyle was saying. She continued typing in her notes more quickly. She was captivated by what Kyle was saying.

"What if I told you that the whole idea that God *commands* us to *obey* Him is all wrong? What if God never intended us to think that He ever said, 'Do as I say'? I know this may sound like I've lost my mind, but today I want to convince you that the 'do-as-I-say' idea is not Biblical at all."

Kyle's audience was patiently waiting for him to make his case for this wild idea. He began by giving an example of a parent who insists that his child should "do as he/she says" and the parent who wants the child to "listen intently," "consider," and "conspire" with them to live in peace together. Which parent is more likely to viewed by the child as being loving and respectful? Which child is more likely to learn how to be loving and respectful?

Then he began telling Bible stories. The first story was chosen because it was the first time the Hebrew word sha'ma,' translated "obey," was used (Gen. 27:8). It is the story of Isaac tricking his father, Jacob, into giving him the blessing of the first-born instead of giving it to his twin, Esau. Jacob's mom, Rebekah, wanted the same and said to him, *'Now, my son, listen (sha 'ma') carefully and do what I tell you to do.'*

"They were conspiring together. Jacob and his mom were pursuing a common goal. He was listening intently and considering. Surely, it would be wrong to say that Jacob tricked his dad because his mom 'told him to.' Obviously, they conspired together for a cause that they both believed in. So it seems to me that when we use the word 'obey,' we mean that we don't really want to do what God is telling us to, but we are obligated to do so despite our real desires. But I believe God has never intended that we just act like he wants us to. I believe that God wants to conspire with those who share His heart. To share a deep delight in each other's highest hopes and dreams. He invites us to join together in practicing all the characteristics of God: justice, peace, love, and mercy. He offers us nothing less than being joined in heart together.

"God invites us to join with Him in His purposes. Some may say He 'commands' us to join Him. But again, we find a word we commonly read is not what we've been led to believe. The translation given us, 'command,' is a shallow and misleading interpretation of an invitation to join God in His purposes. The word actually means 'to enjoin.'

"When we use the words 'command' and 'obey' instead of the words 'enjoin with' and 'conspire together,' we are seeing ourselves as servants of God rather than friends of God.

"This is why Paul called himself a bond servant of Christ. A bond servant was one who chose to stay and serve in a home even after their debt had been paid.

"This is why St. Augustine could elaborate on scripture

by writing, 'Love the Lord your God with all your heart, mind, soul, and strength, then do whatever you want.'

"This is why Jesus said, 'I no longer call you servants, but friends.'

"This is why it is inappropriate to say the most frequent command in scripture is 'fear not.' You can't stop entertaining a legitimate fear because someone tells you to. In fact, such a command would make me more fearful of the one giving such an absurd command. Instead, we know that God is speaking to us encouragingly when He says, 'fear not.' He is comforting us, not reprimanding us. When we think of such exhortations as 'commands,' it turns a joy bond with God into a fear bond with God. Just the opposite of His intentions.

"This is why I will never preach a sermon telling you that you should give your time, money, or talents to God. I don't have to tell any Christian that they should do any of those things. Christians want to do those things. And if you don't want to do any of those things, I want to encourage you not to. I will not ask you to 'obey' some 'command' of God. Please, do not act like a Christian when you really don't want to. Instead, I will tell you the good news that God can give you a new heart that rejoices over His willingness to 'enjoin' with you in 'conspiring' to live out all the highest virtues. I invite you to accept that Jesus has paid any debt you ever owed to God so that you can consider yourself his bond servant and his friend.

"Then, when your 'spirit is willing, but your flesh is weak,' when you 'do the very thing you don't want to do,' when you 'don't do the thing you want to do' … you can say, 'I remain a bond servant to all the nature of God,' and, 'I never need be ashamed,' for 'there is no condemnation for those who are in Christ Jesus.' For we will constantly fail in living out the very character of God, but we won't change our hearts. We will always desire to be a part of what is highest and best. We will always need His forgiveness and His strength. We will rejoice in being a part of His conspiracy!"

The service ended with an invitation to receive communion or to be met at the altar for any personal prayer needs, including salvation. Sharon, who usually loved to receive communion, remained glued to her seat, pondering all she had seen and heard, enjoying the atmosphere, and praying (at a distance) for those kneeling at the rails. She was nurturing a conviction that she had found a spiritual home.

Dear Reader, a shiver of joy went down my spine as Sharon described the bond she felt with Kyle and every believer. She and I agreed that we didn't want or need religious people obeying some commands. We want to be members of one body, those whose heart rejoice to conspire with God in the fulfillment of His purposes.

# CHAPTER 21
# SHARON'S SPIRITUAL FAMILY

*"For of course, religious people – that is, people who are being religious – are not interested in religion. Men who have gods worship these gods; it is the spectators who describe this as 'religion'.... The moment a man seriously accepts a deity his interest in 'religion' is at an end."* — C.S. LEWIS

As soon as the service concluded, Jenny Whitaker approached Sharon and introduced herself. When Jenny learned this was Sharon's first time attending their church, she enthusiastically invited her to join her family for lunch. Before she could answer or tell Jenny who she was, Jenny was calling her husband and children over to greet Sharon. Sharon quickly decided that the Whitaker family was delightful.

During lunch, Sharon let the Whitakers know she was the bishop's wife and was looking for a home church. Jenny assured her they loved this church, and explained they were so wounded and needy when they moved their membership to St. Paul's from another United Methodist Church where, so she said, "they had been cast out."

Jenny couldn't hide the sadness that came over her when she said that. Fred stepped in to lighten the mood. "I wondered if we might not be cast out of St. Paul's a few weeks back," he said with a smile on his face. Sharon recognized the redirection and went with it.

As if she had known them for years, she asked, "What did you do this time?"

Jenny looked to see her children occupied at a video game on the far wall of the restaurant, took on a smile, and nodded to her husband.

"Well, it was like this," Fred continued with a sly look. "Often on our way to church we will take turns sharing our favorite songs with each other. That particular week it was Jenny's turn. She played a song by Jason Mraz on her cell phone, and we all liked it so much that we listened to it three times. Mraz is famous for his plays on words. This song was about an airplane ride that started too quickly and ended too soon, so he takes the next flight also.

"As we pulled into the church parking lot, Jenny began laughing so hard we all wondered why. She told us she just figured out what the song was really about and, of course, we all wanted to know. Well, our practice with our kids is to have a 'family only' talk when we discuss sensitive subjects. Jenny said this was one of those times. Which just made us all the more curious. We all agreed this would be a 'family only' talk. "Jenny informed us that the song was about premature ejaculations. We took a little time to answer the kid's questions about it. Peter is fifteen and we've had a few sex talks before. The subject was a little newer to Patty at only twelve. "Then we all went into church and to our different

Sunday School classes. It was about ten minutes later when Patty's teacher waved me out of my class and said that Patty needed to talk to me about an incident. I found Patty standing in the hall outside her classroom with her arms crossed and a frown on her face. She preceded to tell me that the teacher was making a big deal out of nothing. One of her friends had been telling the class that her parents were upset with each other. The dad had been ready to go and eager to get to church before the mom was ready and they had quarreled about it. Patty proclaimed, 'I wasn't talking about it, I just told them that it wasn't that rare a thing. It's called premature ejaculation.'"

Sharon couldn't help but laugh.

"I clarified for Patty that the term only applies to a sexual relationship. Then she understood that maybe it was a mistake. I assured her that she was not in any trouble and that it was an honest mistake. We all went back to our classes and had a great morning. However, we didn't realize that we had upset some parents of the youth who had heard Jenny's statement and later asked their parents about it.

"Thank goodness, Kyle heard about it and gave us a call. He laughed about it too and assured us that the concerned parents could use the incident to have a healthy conversation with their own kids, or, if they had placed inappropriate judgements on it all, they could just get over themselves. We worried about it a little bit, but never have heard anything about it since."

Sharon expressed how impressed she was with the Whitakers and with Kyle for how they had made the most of that incident. She couldn't help but imagine how the situation might have been handled by more inhibited, less healthy parents and their pastor. The story made Sharon feel so comfortable with the couple that she let herself explore with them her impressions of the worship service they had just participated in.

"I'm sad to say that I have never experienced anything quite like it. The two altar calls to prayer were so wonderful. During the sermon I was so happy to hear thoughts expressed that I think I've known but haven't heard explained Biblically. It also made me sad and maybe mad that I've been a Christian all these years and am just now hearing what I immediately felt was true. And," she continued excitedly, "there was that phrase in the Apostle's Creed that I hadn't heard before either. The one about Jesus descending into hell. Was that really a part of the original creed? If so, why haven't I heard about it before now?"

"I know," Fred jumped in. "That was a surprise to us our first Sunday as well. We asked Kyle about it and he confirmed that it was a part of the original creed that the denomination decided to leave out because it raised too many questions. He explained that some denominations soften the statement by substituting that Jesus descended to the dead. Apparently, that is not a wrong interpretation of the statement theologically. The several words translated 'hell' may have different theological implications. Jesus used different terms which have been interpreted to mean 'the place of the dead,' 'the garbage heap,' 'the place reserved for Satan,' or, simply, 'hell.'"

"I'm not sure what to think about that," Sharon stated. "We're not either," continued Fred. "We don't know if the statement means that Jesus experienced a kind of dreamless sleep until the resurrection. Or if he experienced a kind of purgatory the Catholics believe in. Or if he experienced other souls in the afterlife – some happy and some so unhappy as to be analogous to weeping and gnashing of their teeth in a fiery torment. Or if he experienced an actual place of fire and brimstone."

"So," asked Sharon, "what does Kyle think was Jesus' actual experience of hell?"

"He says he is content to not know. He believes that within the big box that our essential beliefs define are a lot of doctrines we can theologize and debate about. He believes that such doctrines serve us best when we hold them loosely.

When we asked about it, he gave us an analogy related to a study he read. It seems that a study was conducted in which a large playground was developed without any fences around it and another playground, of equal size, was given a high fence around it. One thing that was noted was that in the playground without a fence the children played almost exclusively in the middle of the area, whereas, on the playground with a fence the children consistently played all over the area.

"Kyle says that a firm orthodoxy is a helpful fence around the doctrinal differences amongst Christians. Within the safety of orthodoxy, we are free to 'play,' as he calls it, with all the doctrines Christians have disagreed about over the last two thousand years."

"And one statement of orthodoxy is the Apostle's Creed," Sharon stated as a fact.

"Exactly! And I agree with Kyle that it would be arrogant and presumptuous to change the creed just because we can't make it support just one theological interpretation or doctrine. But that is just what the United Methodist Church took upon itself to do. We at St. Paul's have just returned to the original creed."

"I have another, less important, question," Sharon continued. "Why did we start the service with a benediction? I recognized the High Priestly Prayer, but I've always heard it used in services as a benediction, not as an opening prayer."

Jenny fielded this one. "In Old Testament times, the priests would begin by proclaiming the blessing over the people. All the priests would wash their hands, hurry to their designated spots around the people, spread their fingers apart as far as they could and bless the people. The blessing was a prayer for every individual to experience God in the specific personal and intimate way that they needed during the rest of their worship and rituals. At all other times, the people prayed with their eyes open. When the priests prayed this blessing over them, they would cover their faces and close their eyes. It was that personal.

"You may not have noticed, but all the other times we prayed during the service most of us kept our eyes open. When we pray for each other, or when we pray corporate prayers like The Lord's Prayer, we are usually looking at each other the whole time. For me, it feels like we are all connecting as a body of believers just a little bit more when we pray with our eyes open."

Sharon left the Whitakers and St. Paul's eager to meet again next week and eager to talk with Dan about everything.

# CHAPTER 22
## TO COME CRASHING DOWN

*"When a minister 'consecrates' a marriage or a communion wafer, it is understood that he is merely proclaiming a reality that God has already consecrated. This is an authorized use of human consecration. When a human being tries to consecrate what God has never consecrated, it is not a genuine act of consecration. It is an act of desecration. It is an act of idolatry."* — R.C. SPROUL

As it turned out, Dan preempted Sharon sharing her day by telling her of his own. This conversation would not go well for them.

Sharon had always been willing to think the best of Dan. She had never burdened herself with jealousy over any of the women who sometimes went to great efforts to gain her husband's attention, or whose attractions to him were thinly veiled. She trusted Dan. Dan had the same trust in Sharon. The same was true concerning the management of their money. Neither had strong desires for material possessions, and their income always exceeded their needs. Neither had complaints about the other's willingness to perform the chores associated with maintaining their home, cars, clothes, etc. They had both always been energetic and, without children to sometimes overwhelm them, they had always gladly partnered in fulfilling the to-dos. Furthermore, neither had ever been prone to angry fits or verbal attacks of any kind. There had never been a hint of verbal abuse, let alone any fear of physical abuse. It simply was not in their natures.

Therefore, although they disappointed and frustrated each other on occasion, they had never had reason to divorce.

They were not only best friends, but their standing as religious and community leaders would also seem to prohibit the possibility of a divorce. After all, they had been married for over thirty-five years by this point.

Yet, as I told you before, they were destined to divorce. The divorce may be blamed on the fact that, having become so close through the trials of the vote to legalize gambling, Dan actually shared too much of his thinking with Sharon. Specifically, Dan told Sharon all about the complicated decisions he was constantly making as a bishop in the UMC. Sharon, believing she had implicit and explicit agreements with Dan on how he would perform as a bishop, made her thinking known freely and intimately. Most of the time, they reached agreement in what and how things should be done, which drew them closer. At other times, when they simply could not agree together, they still had a bond in their ability and willingness to understand and support each other.

So, when there came times when they simply could not even understand where the other was coming from and felt they could not offer each other any support in what one of them had determined to do, it was a crisis for them. Or at least it was to Sharon.

Dan's first mistake was telling Sharon that the cabinet, he and the eight district superintendents, had determined that it was time to move Jim Sheridan and his wife Helen to another church. It seemed that Helen had gotten crosswise with the worship leader of the church and had been demanding that he be fired. Everyone seemed to agree that the problem was Helen, but her husband remained unwilling to deny his wife what she demanded of him. The district superintendent heard about the dilemma and suggested the move.

When Dan told Sharon they planned to move Jim and Helen to a church of equal stature, she was shocked.

"Surely, you mean you hope to be able to make an appointment for Jim after he and Helen have completed a course of counseling? You can't mean to simply ship a known problem over to another church?"

Knowing this conversation with Sharon would be difficult, Dan had mentally prepared himself. He invited her to sit. "It is not as bad as you think. I've talked with Jim. He knows why we are moving him. He admitted attempting to fire his worship leader was the wrong way to handle the situation. I let him know it had been necessary for every member of the cabinet to know the reason for his move. Obviously, he was embarrassed. I am hopeful he will be able to stand up to his wife in the future."

"Dan, how can you believe that?" Sharon responded. "Jim can't control Helen, and Helen can't keep from causing problems. You are just moving the problem, not doing anything to solve it."

"There is nothing for us to do to solve it. We can't require Helen to go for counseling. She isn't employed by the church, her husband is. And Jim is a good pastor. We can't punish him because he can't control his wife."

"Isn't there anything you can do?"

"If there is, I certainly don't know what it would be." The conversation ended there, but Sharon's thoughts did not. What she thought, but did not allow herself to say was, "If you cared more about the church and less about the denomination, you could figure out something to do." She didn't say it because she really didn't know if it was true. Nevertheless, the feeling was still there.

The feeling. The feeling. What was the feeling? Not anger – disagreements are normal and healthy. Not sadness – the events weren't happenstance, but they were caused by someone. Not guilt – Sharon was confident in her actions and attitudes. It was mistrust. She finally named it, and she hated it, but it was true. Sharon wasn't sure that she could trust Dan. His decisions didn't seem honest to her. Maybe he wasn't being honest with her about his decisions. Or maybe he wasn't being honest with himself.

Sharon had ignored her feelings of mistrust so often in the past.

When the dean of the Wesleyan College was invited to speak at a district meeting and claimed, "The simple articles of Faith that grounded our forefathers are no longer complex enough to engage a diverse society," Dan had said nothing to him or to the district superintendent who had issued the invitation. When Sharon had asked him if he was concerned the dean was misrepresenting the faith, Dan had commented he doubted if there were more than five people at the meeting who even understood what the dean was saying.

When a group of ministers began a petition to subsidize abortions through the conference counseling center, Dan assured Sharon that the petition stood no chance of being adopted. Sharon wasn't satisfied with that answer and questioned Dan about what could be done about the ministers who supported the petition. Dan's passive response was that he, "Wouldn't be surprised if a couple of them took their defeat so hard that they will resign their ordinations."

Now that she had acknowledged her feeling, Sharon couldn't help but make a new start on their old conversations. Although she tried to be as understanding of Dan as she could make herself be, Sharon's questions became more assertive until she finally asked him, "Dan, what would it take for you to file charges against one of your pastors?" When he responded the system was set up with a large number of checks and balances that made such aggressive actions unnecessary, Sharon finally voiced her feeling about him.

"I hope I am wrong. I pray that I am wrong. But the truth is, I don't trust you. I have seen you ignore so many offenses against what is right morally and what is true Biblically that I don't think I can trust you anymore."

Without raising their voices, speaking over each other, or being intentionally hurtful, Dan and Sharon continued this conversation for well over two hours. There was no conclusion, no apologies, no new commitments. The tension between them continued day after day and week after week; waiting upon the next circumstance that would either allow them to move toward reconciliation or further distancing.

They didn't have long to wait.

The next Sunday, Sharon had asked for time to meet with Kyle and get to know him better. He readily agreed and they met in his office the following Wednesday before the scheduled evening classes.

Since Kyle had met her before, he knew Sharon as 'the bishop's wife.' As such, Kyle felt he needed to further his relationship with Sharon based upon openness and honesty. Therefore, Kyle needed to confess to her his plans to make a challenge of the Board of Ordained Ministry's report at Executive session that he anticipated would upset Bishop Davidson considerably.

Annual conference was two weeks away and Kyle had already submitted the petition he intended to present to the executive session (the first meeting of each annual conference). Kyle's petition was a challenge to the board of ordained ministry's recommendation for ordination of a candidate that Kyle knew was apostate. I would make this petition, along with the one Kyle presented at the next executive session a year later, a significant part of the trial to come. For now, our concern is the effect of Kyle's first petition on Dan and Sharon's already wounded relationship.

Kyle confided in Sharon that, since he had made vows at his ordination to protect the church from apostates, he couldn't imagine not making his knowledge of a recommended candidate's apostasy known. Sharon kept the surprise and angst of knowing that Dan must have already known about Kyle's petition and had chosen not to talk with her about it. At the moment, all Sharon could do was to wholeheartedly encourage Kyle.

It seems that Kyle and Sharon were equally concerned and rejoiced in finding a kindred spirit with each other.

Dan maintained his calm demeanor when Sharon confronted him about the petition Kyle would present the next day. "Please," Sharon had said to him, "I need you to be strong at this executive session. I want to be able to trust you."

Dan responded, "I don't want to fight with you, Sharon, but you can't hold me responsible for what other people do. I will do what I have always done, the best I know how, for everyone concerned. But I have a request of you. Please, don't make church issues a problem for us. You don't even know or understand all the complexities of these church issues that you seem so upset about. Can't you let our relationship just be about us?"

Sharon responded, "The church issues are about us. You

promised me if I would not get involved in church politics, you would do all within your power to stand for the truth. I've kept my side of the agreement. I really don't think you have." After having cemented his character through years of testing and trials, Bishop Dan Davidson was not about to change his approach to life's challenges. He knew the events of this day would cause some commotion and some longterm consequences. He knew that allowing a first-year elder to challenge the nomination of the board was an exercise in futility for all involved. He was convinced nothing good could come of it. Yet, he also knew that to deny the young elder his say would be to compromise himself and the stated purpose of the session. So, he would go through the trial. He would lead by example. He would show respect to all sides involved and expect them to show respect to each other during the session and thereafter.

"If the board has recommended her for ordination, you can't possibly give any credence to the objections of an elder participating in his very first session. Good Heavens, man! No one has challenged a recommendation in the thirty-two years I've been serving in this conference, and I've never heard of it happening in any other conference."

Bishop Davidson's calm was unshaken. He had already anticipated every word Reverend Pierce was now voicing. At sixty years of age, Reverend Pierces's 6'2", 190-pound frame still exuded a relaxed athleticism. His intense blue eyes projected a practiced concentration. The bishop could not only have predicted what the unofficial leader of the theologically moderate pastors would say, but also the order of his arguments. He knew Pierce, his friend and confidential advisor, was a "company man." He knew he fiercely believed and would evangelically promote the principle that the unity of the denomination must be protected from any extremist positions that threatened it. The bishop recognized in the aggressive posture and gestures of his theologically moderate advisor an extremism in Reverend Pierce. Dan could recognize how defensive and controlling his friend's ideas were, as well as Reverend Pierce's utter inability to recognize it about himself. "It is an insult to Reverend Cliff, every member of the board, and even to you." Pierce's eyes slightly watered and his words were heavy with sympathy. The advisor had reached his closing arguments to the jury of one, moving from righteous indignation to grieving over the victims. His oval face, with deep-set eyes, was downcast, the smoothness of his long forehead beckoning others to bow their heads also.

"You have been so diligent in counseling the ordinands. I have been so moved by your exhortations to consider the seriousness of the vows they will take. You have been a stern, but loving father to them in their journey toward ordination as elders. The board has required much of them, and only about half of those who began the process have completed it. It took a minimum of five years for each ordinand to reach this moment of ordination. They have been required to complete a ninety-two-hour Master's degree program, serve two years of full-time service in a local church, undergo a battery of psychological testing, submit and defend exhaustive theological statements, and win the approval of their local church, their district superintendent, the board of ordained ministry, and you, their bishop."

The advisor's face grew red and tight as his emotions turned again toward righteous indignation.

"This executive session should be a time in which the

six-hundred plus elders of our conference welcome them and celebrate their diligence and their success. You can't allow some misguided youth to turn such a sacred moment into a circus of futility. You know as well as I that the majority of the executive session will certainly confirm everyone nominated by the board of ordained ministry. The only thing that can possibly become of this debacle is hurt feelings and animosity." Then, with a final whisper, Reverend Pierce concluded, "The Board of Ordained Ministry deserve better, the ordinands deserve better, and you, dear Bishop Davidson, deserve better. Don't let the young man take the floor at this session."

Bishop Davidson was surprised to feel himself so deeply moved. He had anticipated every word that his advisor had spoken, and yet the pastor's delivery had impacted him. The bishop had a new sense of understanding and appreciation for how this man of little ability for analytical thinking or theological consistency had been able to lead one congregation after another, throughout his years of ministry, into numeric and financial growth. It wasn't due to what the pastor had to say, but the way in which he said it. He made his listener *feel* as though what he was saying was true and right regardless of the absence of any logical or Biblical foundations.

The bishop's calm pervaded the room as the silence between the two men lingered. Now, it was Reverend Pierce's turn to be the bishop's audience and he waited with an anticipation verging on anxiousness for the silence to be broken. He remembered how proud he had felt watching the television ads of Bishop Davidson explaining to the world why his denomination opposed the legislation legalizing gambling. Afterwards, there had been a firestorm of accusations from all sides. Anonymous individuals sent threatening letters and the media labeled Dan a "legalist" with a "holier-than-thou" attitude. One newspaper had unwittingly found the bishop's most sensitive nerve: they had referred to him as a "religionist." Those who knew him best, as did Reverend Pierce, knew the implication that Dan's faith served as a backdrop for a profession rather than the foundation of his calling, had infuriated him. Nevertheless, Dan's calm had never been shaken, and that calmness had eventually won him the respect and support of other religious leaders and the members of his denomination. His calmness had always served him well. He trusted it, and today he believed that any event could work for the good (as he perceived it) so long as he maintained his calmness.

"No," Dan asserted, "I won't deny Kyle the opportunity to follow his conscience. I agree that there is nothing to be gained in this situation. The pastors will vote to uphold the recommendations of the board of ordained ministry. Few of them even know who Kyle is. They will see him as young and idealistic. Those who will resent him for upsetting Teresa Moss will offer comfort to her and will eventually forgive Kyle. We have both seen this kind of dispute come and go."

Dear Reader, now is a time for us to reflect.

Once I get to my narrative of the trial, you will be viewing this story from my perspective. Of course, I was not present with Dan and Kyle in this executive session, which would ultimately mean so very much to each of their futures. I can tell you that Dan would come to recognize this event was the tipping point in his marriage, as Kyle would come to recognize it as the tipping point in his career in the UMC. You and I are seeing this event through hindsight. Neither Dan nor Kyle could know the full significance of what was about to take place.

I am pushing this point because I want you to reflect on the possibility that Dan thought he was taking a strong stand for truth by allowing Kyle to address the executive session. It is in hindsight that we will come to recognize that Dan is about to betray Sharon's trust again. Dan did not know that Teresa Moss would take encouragement from the conflict to publicly disclose her apostasy in years to come. He didn't know the problems he would be passing on to the bishop who would follow him in leadership of the conference. He couldn't have predicted the behind-the-scenes negotiations that would eventually lead to Teresa Moss quietly resigning her ordination and leaving the denomination.

Dan may have truly believed that Kyle's actions would not be held against him by the district superintendents who would decide the course of his career in the UMC. He may not have known that his passiveness in this event was, in effect, choosing to encourage the apostates and punish those who would resist them. But, in hindsight, we know that this is all true. Nevertheless, I am asking that you give Dan the benefit of the doubt as I describe the crisis that was this year's executive session.

# CHAPTER 23
## WHAT IS THIS FEELING?

*"If we consider churches in their role as institutions, they exemplify the common ailment of institutional failure in a declining society. Families fail to nurture, governments fail to provide justice, schools fail to educate, and so churches fail to represent Christ."*
— HERBERT SCHLOSSBERG, *Idols for Destruction*

Kyle once told me a story about a professor of Greek at his seminary.

A guest preacher was speaking before the entire university student body at a mandatory chapel service. The preacher was expounding upon a certain verse and reached a dubious conclusion based upon his interpretation of the Greek manuscript. He promoted this conclusion with great enthusiasm, even though it referred to a very controversial subject and could be applied to young people's lives with disastrous results. The preacher was driving his point home and calling for support, shouting, "Do you believe it? Do you believe it?" Then, interrupting the momentum of the preacher and stunning everyone in the service, this professor stood to his feet and called back, "No, no, I don't believe it."

You can only imagine the thoughts and feelings that followed: embarrassment, anger, confusion. The professor stood his ground as the university officials dismissed the chapel service and met to determine an appropriate response to the professor's offense to their guest speaker, and to the students who had witnessed the event.

Kyle never knew what (if any) discipline had been handed out to the professor. The professor was not fired. An apology was published from the university to the guest speaker. Then, "officially" nothing more was said about it.

The event had so impressed Kyle that he took every class he could with this professor as his respect for the man continued to grow.

So, you can imagine Kyle's relief when it was this same professor who came to his rescue at the executive session.

The executive session had been conducted according to tradition and ritual. The attending elders, numbering more than six hundred, had sung together and prayed together. They had been exhorted to remember their vows to protect the church from apostasy and to, in effect, "speak now or forever hold your peace." The candidates for ordination as deacons had been introduced. They were universally and unanimously approved without any discussion. When the candidates for ordination as elders had been introduced, however, Kyle rose.

He read a prepared statement, copied and distributed, which assured them he had personal knowledge that Teresa Moss confessed to not believe in the historical, physical resurrection of Jesus Christ. He asked them to deny her nomination to become an elder.

Then, Kyle was attacked.

The first elder to respond to Kyle's statement stated that the session should consider the possibility that Kyle was personally or theologically prejudiced against women. The second confessed he couldn't imagine Kyle's audacity in questioning the board of ordained ministry and his disrespect for the celebration to which these candidates were rightly entitled. A third speaker stated, "If Reverend Fedder's concerns are not put in their place today, we might find this sacred time of fellowship turned into a personal gripe session for every misguided youth cocky enough to draw attention to themselves year after year."

That was when the Greek professor rose to Kyle's defense. The mild-mannered professor was hot. For a moment he just looked around at his peers. "Kyle has done only what we have all been directed to do. He spoke without rancor and with no unnecessary words. You people, on the other hand...."

That is when Dan interrupted the professor. "It is true that Reverend Fedder was totally within his rights to present his petition at this time and place. So, let us vote."

Then, without any discussion of the issues presented in Kyle's petition, and without a single question to Teresa Moss or the board, the vote was taken. Hands were raised for and against. The bishop determined that Kyle's petition was defeated.

The executive session completed the ritual ceremony and was dismissed.

Dan didn't make it home until almost 10:00 that night. It had been a long and trying day.

Although his responsibilities throughout the day prevented him from having discussions concerning the executive session, he had been repeatedly thanked for how he had managed the "Kyle Fedder issue." Although Dan determined to put it aside for now, all the following day's events seemed colored by it. Every word spoken in the worship service that night seemed to intimate support for or antagonism against the vote of the executive session. Although the content of the service had been crafted long ago, each song, responsive reading, and scripture quoted seemed selected to justify or confront 'the elephant in the room".

Dan was not prepared to discuss the matter with Sharon.

Nevertheless, Sharon had heard all the details of the meeting from her network of friends throughout the conference and was not going to be denied the opportunity to confront Dan about it.

Years before, Dan and Sharon had begun referencing a phrase from the movie *Hook*.

At one point in the movie, elderly Mary speaks to the grown-up Peter Pan (who has become a lawyer) saying, "Why, Peter, you've become a pirate."

Instead, Sharon might say, "Why, Dan, you've become an old man," the term they used to describe a man who had stopped pursuing his wife. Or Dan might joke with her by saying, "Why Sharon, you've become a race-car driver," if she accelerated too fast.

So, when Sharon began their conversation by saying, "Why Dan, you've become a religionist," he should have known she had picked the hill she was willing to die on. He knew she had intentionally used the one phrase that would hurt him the most.

Still, Dan did not take her nearly seriously enough. He was tired. He didn't think he could explain the way the institution works that would satisfy her. So, he said the same thing he had so many times before: "I'm sorry you feel that way."

If his past ability at self-awareness had not been slowly but steadily devolving, Dan might have recognized he was responding to his wife like his dad had responded to his mother's pleas for emotional and spiritual connections. He did realize that Sharon would be disappointed. He had prepared himself to remain calm and make his usual response when she was "acting out" toward him. Apparently, she had been preparing herself for such a moment as this for quite some time.

"Are you entirely sure that this is how you want to leave things between you and me?"

A little taken aback, he asked, "How do you mean?"

"I've just expressed my profound disappointment in you, and you've put the issue back on me, like it is just a feeling I have, rather than that I'm pointing out a huge transition I've seen you make. I know you better than anyone in the world, and I'm telling you I think you have betrayed something very important to your soul. And you tell me, 'I'm sorry you feel that way'? Is that how you want to leave this between us?"

Dan responded, "Yes, for now... I think that's best." Tears began to form in Sharon's eyes. They continued to face each other, no words, no backing down; the tears brimmed over and ran down her cheeks. Dan still gave no response.

"Dan, I need you to listen carefully to what I am about to say. I need you to feel very anxious and very upset. I need you to be anxious and upset about what you are becoming. I need you to stop being calm about some things. I want you to not be calm about your role in ordaining an apostate. I want you to not be calm about how rote our marriage has become. I want you to be anxious and upset that our life is about to change. You are going to have to take a whole new approach to being a bishop in a denomination that is becoming increasingly apostate and a whole new approach to our marriage OR ..." she paused to let the gravity of what she was about to say sink in, "... I will divorce you."

As Dan watched his wife walk away, he felt like he was transported to another dimension where he could watch himself from outside himself. He felt frozen in place, but could still feel adrenaline spreading through his body and mind. Then, in a blink, he saw himself as a teenager listening to his mom telling his dad she wanted a divorce.

With a clarity of thought that surprised him, Dan remembered hearing his mother ask his dad to give up his rules in the same way Sharon had just asked him to give up his calm. He realized he was the same age his dad had been when he had heard similar words. For just a moment, he had a sense of déjà vu that made Sharon's threat of divorce seem not only possible but unavoidable. Then, the moment was gone.

He knew his marriage was so different, so much better, than his parent's had been. Even though he knew Sharon was famous and infamous for representing herself accurately and intentionally, he simply could not (would not) believe that she would do it. Shaking himself free of his introspection, Dan followed Sharon into their bedroom. "For now," he said gently, "for now, I need you to be patient with me. I don't know what to say. I don't know what to do."

Sharon was looking into his eyes as a tear inched down his cheek. Taking this as a good sign, she took his hand and said, "I know you dread what has to be done, but you are one of the very few men I have ever known who has the wisdom and grace to be able to make this right."

Dan wasn't sure what Sharon was suggesting. His mind and body had gone numb with relief when she had taken his hand. He wanted to ask her what it was she thought he was supposed to do but couldn't bring himself back into focus. She had given him a reprieve and he took it. He nodded to her, squeezed her hand, and began preparing for bed.

The next day was the first full day of annual conference. Presentations by boards, committees, ministries, and conference staff were scheduled for all day for the next four days, followed by worship services each night. The evening of the first night the worship service featured the presentation of the candidates for ordination (voted on the day before). Before the service began, Sharon knocked gently on the door of the small office Dan had set aside to eat meals and to refresh himself between sessions of the conference.

Dan opened the door and expected her to follow him to the chairs as he went to sit down. He had been prayerfully considering what to say to her when he had the chance. He wanted to tell her that he loved her, that he wanted to make things right with her, that he knew they needed to set aside a long weekend together to talk things through. He didn't get the chance to say any of these things.

Sharon stood in his doorway, looking as beautiful as she had when they first met. The gray in her hair looked to him like highlights other women would pay big bucks to a fancy hairdresser to have styled into their hair. Dan thought of the few wrinkles on her face as "laugh lines" and "wisdom marks" that were as attractive in their own way as her smoother skin had been years ago. Her posture was the same as always: straight and open. Her hands hung near her hips where she would rotate her palms up and down, in and out as she spoke. Her eyes were direct and focused on his, with the same touch of gentleness that rarely left her. She was the same as always, except that she remained standing in the doorway.

Without giving Dan a chance to set the tone, Sharon spoke. "Dan, you have an opportunity to set right what you allowed to transpire yesterday. When you were ordained an elder and again when you were ordained as bishop, you made vows to God and to this denomination to protect this church from apostasy and to uphold the doctrine and policy as recorded in *The Book of Discipline*. Furthermore, you have repeatedly promised me that if I would not use my lesser roles in the church to confront the apostacies and injustices I've encountered, you would certainly use your greater roles in the church to do so.

"Dan, yesterday you failed your vows and promises. I think you have been failing your vows and promises for some time now, but what happened yesterday is beyond my ability to understand in you. Tonight, you have the opportunity to make an executive decision to decline the recommendation of Teresa Moss. She may be a very fine person in every way, but she is also an apostate. "I know that if you should choose to fulfill your vows and promises in the service tonight, that all hell will break loose in this conference and probably throughout this denomination. I also know there are very few men who could represent God and themselves as lovingly and as wisely as you. You can stand your ground and offer others refuge when chaos is all about us. I know you and I can find strength in God and in each other. I also know if you chose to ignore this crisis, I will not be able to remain with you. I need you to know I would never threaten you or try to manipulate you. I am asking you to risk creating a crisis to stand up for what is right. And right now, I am doing the same thing. I am risking losing the man I love, the church I believe in, and the life of ministry that I excel in."

Then she turned and walked away.

That couldn't be right. She didn't even give Dan a chance to make sure he understood her or to challenge her thinking. She just turned the world upside-down and inside-out, and walked away from the scene of the crime as if nothing had happened.

Dan felt a shaking in his legs, stomach, and chest. He

realized if he hadn't been sitting down, he would have fallen to the ground. Taking a deep breath and letting it out slowly, Dan felt control returning to his limbs. In an effort to regain rational control of the moment, Dan asked himself, "What, exactly, am I feeling?" He thought that by putting a name to his feelings he could manage them better.

"I am feeling exposed. The door is wide open, and I am just sitting here." The next natural step was for Dan to shut the door and then return to his chair. "Am I feeling shocked, or numb? Held in God's arms in the midst of a storm? Calm? What does it matter what I call it?"

Dan had once heard a lecture on "transpositions." Transpositions are our unconscious choices in what name we give to our feelings. If our body manifests an accelerated heartbeat, a queasy stomach, and some muscle tensions, we may have come to believe that the proper name for such physical experiences is "excitement," or we may believe that it is "anxiety." If, somewhere along the way, we learned to call such feelings "excitement," we will feel empowered and focused to take on the task at hand. If, on the other hand, we call these feelings "anxiety," we will be weakened and distracted. He had benefited from this knowledge in the past. He believed that it really did matter what he called his various physical responses to events.

From the depths of his soul, Dan heard a voice that he knew was not his own. "It matters. It matters what you call this feeling. Beware what you call this feeling!"

The voice was clear, but it was not an answer. Dan needed to move forward. The service would be starting soon. The next step was to put on his robe, adjust his stole, and meet the worship leaders. His feelings didn't change the fact that people were waiting on him. So, Dan did what he had to do: find his place behind the children carrying the banners and the candelabras, walk down the aisle of the sanctuary, and take his seat next to the elevated pulpit. Others would be responsible for the service until he either intervened or until he pronounced the benediction at the end of the service.

At the close of the first hymn, Reverend Cliff was afforded the great privilege of introducing the candidates for ordination to this sacred assembly.

Dan determined that if he was going to intervene that the most appropriate time to do so would be immediately following the introductions. He could step up beside Reverend Cliff and ask to be allowed to say a word. He wasn't sure what he would say. Would he apologize for the disruption of the service, and especially to Teresa Moss, in that he needed to withdraw her name from the ranks of the candidates for ordination? Maybe he could be somewhat vague in order to limit the embarrassment to Teresa as much as possible. Even though the clergy members would quickly understand that the bishop had withdrawn his support of her ordination on the grounds of her apostasy, most of the laity would have to guess for now and ask their clergy members about it later. Dan had unconsciously chosen, many years ago, to trust his words. If he had the words to say that rang true to him, he believed God was encouraging him to speak out. If he didn't have the words, he believed he was not the one who God intended to speak out in a situation.

As Reverend Cliff read their names, the candidates stood to their feet for a moment until the next candidate was introduced. There were small groups of family and friends who would quietly applaud as their loved one stood. When

Reverend Cliff read Teresa Moss' name, a large group of clergy members stood and applauded, almost as if she were a celebrity receiving an award.

For Bishop Dan Davidson, the support expressed to Teresa Moss set in motion a series of considerations about his responsibility at this moment in the life of the church. Any way he looked at it, it seemed to him every policy had been followed and all the checks and balances of the system had already determined to allow Ms. Moss to be ordained. As much as it ran counter to his beliefs and feelings, it was not his place to arbitrarily disrupt the process when it was all but completed. He would have to allow the process to be bigger than his personal issues with it. Sharon would be upset, but she would eventually accept it, and maybe even understand that it was for the best.

Bishop Dan Davidson stayed in his seat until it was time to offer the benediction.

# CHAPTER 24
## THE DIVORCE

*"It would, no doubt, have been possible for God to remove by miracle the results of the first sin ever committed by a human being; but this would not have been much good unless He was prepared to remove the results of the second sin, and of the third, and so on forever."* — C.S. LEWIS

Dan left the conference immediately following the benediction. He knew he needed to be with Sharon as soon as possible. All other concerns would have to wait. She was more important to him than anyone's interpretation of why he left so quickly.

It only took Dan a couple of moments to find the note Sharon had left on the kitchen cabinet next to where they always placed their keys. The note simply read, "I am on my way to Mom's. I will call you on Saturday."

This was bad. Dan didn't need to look in the bathroom. He knew she would pack her makeup regardless of how long she planned to be gone. He went directly to the closet. Her side of the closet was completely empty. His mind had time for one more complete thought before that feeling came over him again, his body began shaking, and he dropped to the carpet. *She didn't have time to do this after the service. She packed before she met me there.*

Twenty, thirty, forty minutes passed before Dan was able to begin his deep breathing and calm his body. He didn't cry. He didn't move. He was not sure how long he has been there, but the Voice had returned. It seemed to him that he knew what the Voice would say before he heard it. Maybe the Voice had been speaking the same things over and over for a while. "What is the worst thing you've ever done? … What do you call this feeling?"

Dan started with the second question.

"Am I feeling shocked? Or numb? Or held in God's arms in the midst of a storm? calm?

"I don't know. What I do know is I must be at the Cabinet meeting with the district superintendents at 6am. I must get some sleep. The conference will continue through noon on Friday. Sharon is going to call me on Saturday. I know what I need to do now." Feeling his mind grind to a halt, Dan slowly began preparing for bed.

The conference ended on Friday morning by celebrating their retiring pastors. This session was always an inspiring celebration of faithful, lifetime ministries. Each retiring pastor was given ten minutes (but usually took at least fifteen) to address the conference. You could always count on most of these "elderly elders" to exhort their younger peers with humor, tall tales, and genuine humble gratitude. This session had been among the funniest and most God-glorifying Dan could recall. Dan had been even more blessed in that several of the retirees had spoken directly to him about how they had grown to love and appreciate him. Dan soaked up every moment of encouragement he could. He knew he needed all the faith he could muster, and all the grace God could give to keep him going through the motions until he could finally talk with Sharon.

Dan had determined to do whatever it took to get right with Sharon. He had been calling Ben regularly since Sharon left. Together they had prepared for Dan's Saturday phone call from Sharon. Dan had determined to ask for forgiveness, to ask for marriage counseling, to offer to retire, and to over-whelm her with love. It was the right thing to do. It was what he wanted to do.

Dan had contacted and fully updated all those on his short list of best friends and asked them all to be in prayer for the two of them on Saturday. He was beginning to feel some hope. He was beginning to be able to think of Sharon without that other feeling coming over him. When the phone rang that Saturday morning, he still had no idea that this would be their last in-depth conversation ever.

"Dan, I'm sorry I couldn't talk to you earlier. I wanted to take some time to determine what I need to say, and I didn't want to take you away from the work the annual conference requires of you."

"Sharon, honey, I want to hear everything you have to say, but is it okay if I say some things first?"

During the short pause that followed, Dan could feel that feeling surfacing in him again. "Okay." She sounded gentle, which encouraged Dan.

"Sharon, I have been praying, talking with our friends, and remembering all the times I asked you to try to understand my perspective concerning the church. I thought my perspective was at least a little better than yours because I'm the one most directly involved. I'm the one who dealt with the realities of the churches, the ministers, and the people every day. I really believed that, if you were in my shoes, you would come to the same conclusions I did. And, because I believed that, I mean I really, really believed that, I didn't accept what you were telling me, that you needed to stand up for our Faith, and you needed me to support you in that.

"Sharon, I am so sorry that I have been hurting you like

that for so long. I want you to know that I love everything about you. I don't want you to change in any way. I want to be your husband first and foremost, before the denomination and before my career. I want us to be life-partners, like we always used to be, and I will do anything to make that possible. Anything. Really."

Dan could hear Sharon softly crying. He waited while she processed what he had confessed to her. "I believe you, Dan. I really do, but there is more I need to tell you that I don't think you have really heard yet."

"Okay, I want to," Dan couldn't stop himself from interjecting.

"This is what I have discovered about myself. Dan, I feel like a mother. I feel like a mother to the United Methodist Church, not just to certain churches or certain pastors, but to the whole denomination. You and I chose not to adopt children, not because either one of us wouldn't have been good parents, but because we believed God was directing our time and energy toward this work. For me, the church became my children." He started to speak, but she cut him off.

"Listen to me now. I need you to hear this: In lots of ways, I saw you as a father to the church. You were a kind leader, with clear insight and wisdom into what was highest and best for your children. But our child, the denomination, developed an addiction. The United Methodist Church became addicted to grace. The denomination lost its ability to deal with the harsh reality of sin and apostasy. Instead, the denomination demanded more and more grace from those who wanted to end the addiction.

"And, Dan, I know I haven't said this as well as I had hoped, but I want you to understand me. I see you as a co-dependent facilitator of our child's addiction. I picture God asking you and me to conduct interventions. He gave us opportunity time and again, but you wouldn't do it. You refused to join in the ultimatums we had to give for the interventions to be successful. So, together, we watched our child sink further and further into the addiction.

"This last episode was our final, and maybe our greatest opportunity, to conduct an intervention that might have made the difference for our child. If you had stood up to the board, the whole denomination would have heard about it. Everyone who heard about it would have to decide if they thought you had done the right thing. I know it would have caused a crisis for the whole denomination, but that is what an intervention is: a crisis. But without that crisis the child is left to the demands of the addiction.

"That is the choice I have watched you make over and over. I am sick over it. I am angry about it. I don't trust you to ever change. I cannot partner with you anymore."

"I – I don't . . don't understand," he stammered.

She sighed. "I know if you had embraced your opportunities to intervene in the sickness of our church, the denomination may have just rolled right over both of us and continued on its way. If you had stood up, at least we could have been together. We could grieve our loss and embrace the other good things life has for us. We could still have each other. But you didn't, and we don't – no I'm not finished.

"Dan, I know there are a thousand things we could say to each other, but none of them would help. I want you to know that I have filed for divorce. I have asked that you be served papers on Monday at the house. I know that we will have no problem agreeing to terms. The money isn't important to either of us, and we don't have any children.

"I wish you well. Please respect my wishes in this. Please don't try to talk me out of it. You know how I am." The phone clicked.

Like all the other times, lately, it was over, and she was gone before Dan could even fully register what was happening.

# CHAPTER 25
## THE DELAYED RESPONSE

*"About a year before I actually went into psychotherapy, I had decided that this would be a good thing for me to do. I was then a psychiatrist-in-training in the armed forces and I knew a therapist who was on the faculty of my hospital who seemed like a hip guy and would be obligated to see me for free. But when I brought up the idea to him, he asked me why I wanted to do it. So I told him, "Well, I've got a little bit of anxiety over here and a little bit of anxiety over there. It would be a useful educational experience and it would look good on my curriculum vitae." He said, "You are not ready yet," and refused to treat me. I stormed out of his office, furious at him, but of course, he was quite right." —* M. SCOTT PECK

It took Dan over two hours to shake off the fog that took his brain captive the moment Sharon hung up the phone. He had some awareness of hearing those same words that he knew were not his own. Eventually, he had come to himself. He demanded focus from himself, and asked, "What is the next right step?"

He needed to call Ben.

Dan talked through every detail of the phone call. Their discussion of it took almost four hours. Ben offered no opinions and no judgments. He asked questions about Sharon's tone of voice and about the intervention opportunities. He was a sounding board. Dan needed to think it through out loud. Ben encouraged Dan's reflections, memories, and tentative conclusions. When they finished, nothing had been concluded, but Dan could begin to accept the reality of it all.

They would discuss it all again several times in the days and weeks to come.

Over the next couple of weeks, as the divorce proceedings began, Dan reached one firm conclusion: he needed to resign as a presiding bishop. Maybe he could move to another conference and serve a small church in his semi-retirement. Maybe he could travel to Africa to witness and find a role for himself in the fast-growing United Methodist churches there. He had always delighted in his indirect involvement in the wonderful missions of his denomination. He might ask for a commission to survey them all as a visiting bishop.

What soon caught his attention was an opportunity several semi-retired bishops had practiced before him; he could become a "bishop in residence" at one of the denomination's universities. He could remain active on the council of bishops and teach any master level course that interested him. It was perfect for him. Nevertheless, it took another three years before the right opportunity presented itself and he made the transition.

His new life fell into place quickly and naturally. He loved to teach, and the students loved him as a teacher. It was a new life, in a new place, among people who had never met his ex-wife. It was challenging and rewarding, and he remained in a position of leadership in his beloved church. At times, Dan felt surprised and humbled to realize that life did indeed go on. Indeed, life was often good.

As the distance between his current and former lives grew, Dan felt like his perspective of it all had become more objective. He was able to admit that he would never marry again; he still did and probably always would love Sharon. He reflected on his part in the breakup of his marriage. In his mind, he would return again and again to their last conversation, and he convinced himself that he had done what he could to make the healing of the marriage possible.

He had acknowledged their different perspectives and admitted to himself he had not only failed to fully value her convictions, but had actively sabotaged her opportunities to follow through on them. He had asked her to subjugate her perspective to his. He was glad he had come to his senses at the end and asked for her forgiveness. He had confessed his role in breaking down their marriage. And maybe his self-awareness had come too late, but he still believed there could have been hope if she had been willing to embrace the middle ground of each being supportive of the other in their convictions and actions.

Most importantly, he had been able to answer the two questions the voice repeatedly asked of him. He knew that he had not appropriately valued and protected his partnership with Sharon. He had taken it for granted. He hadn't committed himself to partnering with her in the fulfillment of her convictions in the same way she had been dedicated to partnering with him in his calling.

As for that feeling that had nearly overwhelmed him, it was the feeling of dread that came with hearing her boundaries too late. It was the subconscious knowledge he had lost her forcing itself to his conscious. He had resisted it, but he couldn't avoid it indefinitely.

But, to his way of thinking, Sharon had ended up taking an extreme position that would have required him to subjugate his thinking to hers. In the end, her solution was to demand a role reversal where she would dismiss his perspective and demand he endorse hers, a perspective that was clouded by hurt. Yes, it was hurt he had caused, but it was still extreme and clouded. The whole analogy of the church being a child addicted to grace and unable to resolve their differences and disagreements just didn't hold up.

Given the time and the right circumstances, Dan was convinced that he could have explained to Sharon the reasons he had always been able to leave all results and all judgments to God. Dan was free to teach and preach and live the conservative, historical faith without needing to judge the hearts of others or theological understanding of God. He would argue that the need to judge and control the faith and beliefs of others was due to our own hurts, hang-ups, or misunderstandings of The Gospel.

Dan had forgiven himself for having done the very thing to Sharon that he believed Sharon was now doing to him. By not supporting her in the unique giftings and callings of her relationship with God, she had now become unable to support him in his. He understood it. He regretted it. But, by God's grace, life does indeed go on.

Dan continued to value his perspective without recognizing his betrayal of his own faith. Without fully realizing it, he had long ago begun framing the disagreements between himself and Sharon as her jealousy for his other covenant relationship: his relationship with the denomination. The denomination had affirmed him, needed him, depended on him. Sharon … less and less so. He had begun to resent Sharon's demands upon him. He had decided that her expectations were unreasonable. She was co-dependent. She was obstinate. She was self-righteous.

He never explained, even to himself, how Sharon was wrong in her expectations.

He believed she was insensitive to the needs of the denomination.

And, he resented her independence. In some vague way, he expected her to be able to make the sacrifices for the sake of the marriage that he knew his fellow pastors were unwilling to make for the sake of the faith. He never admitted these thoughts and feelings to himself, but he certainly acted upon them.

At the next year's executive session following the divorce, Kyle had presented a petition asking that the BOM be directed to provide all elders access to the written doctrinal statements required in their candidacy process. Although the *Book of Discipline* clearly and repeatedly recorded the right of all elders to have access to these statements, Dan found cause to help prevent it (more about this will be presented during my account of the civil trial to come).

And, the following year, Dan 'reluctantly' accepted Kyle's resignation from the denomination when Dan informed him that he would not allow any further petitions or interruptions to take place at the upcoming executive session.

The year after that, Dan let himself believe that it was evidence of his personal emotional, relational, and spiritual growth when he was nominated by the Council of Bishops to be their representative and liaison to the class action lawsuit that was being brought against the UMC. He felt that the Council was expressing understanding and acceptance of his divorce and appreciation for his lifetime of service to the denomination.

Dear Reader, you must understand that I think Dan has deluded himself. I won't state what I think is obvious by detailing how I would answer the Voice's questions for him.

Oh, hell ... yes, I will. In truth, I want to yell it in Dan's face. The worst thing he ever did is the same thing he did with his parents. He failed to speak the truth to them because he was afraid of losing their love, and he did the same thing with the UMC. And the feeling he had was panic. He was afraid that God would require him to risk offending the denomination and lose its love. But he was always able to shut the feeling down and find a self-deluding answer to the "worstthing" question.

Still, God is patient, and He perseveres. It is not a coincidence that Dan has been given this role in the lawsuit. I hope you don't think I'm being arrogant when I say, I may be God's last and best chance for getting through to Dan.

Or maybe you think Dan knows better what is happening in his own mind and spirit. Maybe you think I have organized these facts to suit my own delusions. Well, maybe. I won't say it's impossible. But I will recommit myself to reporting the details of the trial with as much honesty and objectivity as I can muster.

# CHAPTER 26
# THE REBELS FIGHT BACK

Imagine that you and your sister belong to a small, loving congregation of believers. The congregation has been through good times and bad times together. They have developed faith in and respect for each other. This is a congregation of people you love, led by people you trust.

Several people within the congregation have noticed the special attention your sister is receiving from an elder's son, John. John is a young man whom the congregation has watched grow and mature with great pride. He is not only handsome and athletic, but also intelligent, personable, and seems committed to the teaching of the church. He has shown himself to be a capable leader in the youth group and a consistent witness for God at school.

It is no surprise that some within the congregation have made comments about how compatible John and your sister seem to be. After all, your sister is absolutely angelic. She is so beautiful, inside and out, that others can't help but be mildly intimidated by her. No one can say how she might change for the better. Their friends find ways to encourage John and your sister to be together: they are asked to teach an elementary class together and seem to always be side-by-side when singing in the choir. When John finally asks your sister for a date and she accepts, the whole congregation seems to have an investment in their courtship. You have never really been able to think of them as *a couple,* but have no real objections to their dating one another.

After dating John for three months, your sister tells you that she had made it very clear to John that she is no longer interested in dating him. You become concerned when you realize that John continues to show up wherever your sister happens to be. You know there is a problem when a fellow member of the church tells you that John is saying that he and your sister are in love. You plan on talking to your sister about it, but soon find out that it's already too late – the tragedy has occurred. Your sister comes running up the stairs to your bedroom screaming and, hysterical, she falls in a heap into your arms. As she weeps uncontrollably, you notice that she is quite disheveled. Almost afraid to ask what happened, you ask anyway. "Is it John? What has he done to you? Has he raped you?" After calming your sister and taking care of her needs, you call the police and arrange for your sister to file charges for John's arrest. The whole time you are barely able to contain your anger. Your sister needs you desperately, so you must stay in control. You stay by her side all that day and the next.

By evening of the second day, the church has become aware of what has happened. John's father, an elder in the church, has met with the other leaders of the church. Now the pastor has asked to meet with you.

The pastor begins by telling you how very sorry he is for both you and your sister, and how shocked he is that John could do such a thing. Then, he gets to the point – the elders have discussed it and they asked you to convince your sister to drop the charges against John and allow the church to take disciplinary measures regarding John and the situation. He quotes you the appropriate chapter and verse, assuring you of honorable intentions to "follow through with this matter to the fullest extent possible."

Trusting the pastor, and (despite your anger) really wanting the best for John, you agree to talk to your sister about it. Your sister is devastated by the rape and totally unable to process the whole situation. She decides to leave the decision to you. You decide to drop the charges and allow the church to intercede.

The next Sunday the entire worship service is committed to facing this issue. You and your sister take a seat on the front row as various members offer words of comfort and assurance. The pastor stands before the congregation and states the matter plainly and factually. He turns to John and asks, "John, do you love her?"

"Yes, of course I love her," he pleads in an apologetic tone.

John, would you be willing to marry her?"

"Oh, yes, yes!" John (looking over the congregation) assures them all.

"What is this?" Not yet able to believe what appears to be happening here, your voice is small.

The pastor turns to your sister and asks, "Isn't it true that you and John have been sexually active?"

"Yes … I mean, no … I mean…." she stammers, confused, and starts to cry.

"It is the decision of the elders that the appropriate thing to do, considering the circumstances, is that the two of you marry," the pastor says. John is surprised yet obviously delighted. Your mind is spinning, trying to fathom what is happening. Your sister faints, crumbling to the floor.

As the people in the congregation begin mingling around and making some attempt to rearrange the sanctuary, a judge within the congregation, contacted earlier in the week, steps forward and hands the pastor the required marriage license for a marriage ceremony. It's finally becoming frighteningly clear to you that the decision of the elders and the congregation is that this situation is to be immediately rectified by seeing to it that a wedding take place that very hour.

Everyone there is disregarding you and you are unable to get the attention of anyone in authority. When you return your attention to your sister, you notice everyone scurrying to get back into their seats, while two of your long-time friends are dragging your half-conscious sister to the altar. As everything inside you wants to scream, you hear the pastor clear his throat, and boldly ask, "Who brings this woman to be married to this man?"

"We do, on behalf of the whole church," the friends supporting your sister reply with the most respectful tone.

Finally, you can't stand it another minute as your mind regains control of your voice, and you yell out loud and clear, "Stop it! Stop all this right this minute!"

Members of the congregation turn on you and begin accusing you of being judgmental, uncaring, and hypocritical. "None of us objected at your wedding," they accuse. "We know you haven't loved your mate perfectly either. You really didn't have any idea what you were doing when you made your own wedding vows. Besides, you agreed to submit to the church's decision on behalf of your sister! Who are you to judge anyway? Are you God? Do you know better than the elders what is best?"

Your objections are being put down faster than a train can rumble down the tracks. As you are "helped" to your seat, the ceremony continues....

This is the end of our emotional word picture, but this scenario is a representation as true as life and so congruent with the reality many of us live with. You see, the truth is that we all do have a sister who has been raped, manipulated by those she trusted, and offered in marriage against her will.

Our beautiful sister's name is Orthodoxy; she is the "essentials of our faith," the "gospel of Jesus Christ," the "plan of salvation." And in many mainline denominations, she is being married off against her will in ordination services where those who don't believe in the literal, historical truths of the Gospel are being anointed to serve as pastors."

When Kyle's resignation was made known to the St. Paul's congregation, many of the members, including the Whitakers and Sharon, also withdrew their membership from the United Methodist Church. They left the building and all the assets associated with the church to the denomination, including the parsonage, buses, and savings accounts.

Over the next several months, several meetings were held amongst the "rebels." They began a new non-denominational local church. They had virtual meetings with leaders of the African conferences of the United Methodist Church. Then, they formally met with me. It was decided that we would file a civil suit against the denomination. I'll be honest with you. Our hope is to win a big enough judgement to bankrupt the United Methodist Church before it can fulfill its plan of dividing into two denominations. It was determined that any money gained beyond the expenses of prosecuting the case would all go to a trust fund for the African United Methodist churches after they disaffiliated from the denomination also.

# CHAPTER 27
## JURY SELECTION

*"Abundant Life" is more of the peaks and valleys, joys and sorrows, victories and failures, than you ever thought was possible for your life. You will need a greater capacity to love, give, hurt, and strive than you could ever possibly muster within your own strength. You will be given more opportunities to die to self so that Christ may live in you than you intended when you prayed for it. You will be made terribly aware of your weaknesses, in order that the Holy Spirit's strength might be gloriously revealed in you.*

Judge Brown had conducted a preliminary *voir dire* of prospective jurors. Each prospective juror had answered a list of questions that the defense and I had agreed upon, and the judge had added several she determined were important. Before we even saw the candidates for the jury, five or six have already been released due to personal needs that conflicted with a prolonged case. Two more had been dismissed due to "health complications," and the remaining candidates were excused when the defense attorney or I exercise our peremptory challenges.

As the potential jurist entered the court room, I smiled at each one and gave a satisfied nod at the good fortune I had in having drawn such a great set of prospects. As they entered, I paid no attention to their age, or their race, or how they were dressed. What I did do was note whether or not I could make eye contact with them sometime during the first three minutes they were in the courtroom. I didn't care if they were smiling or frowning. I just wanted to lock eyes with them. If, in the first three minutes, I was successful in this one thing, then I was confident the foundation had been laid for acquiring a good juror. Our eye contact would communicate that being there at that moment was creating all kinds of mixed emotions in me (which was true), and that I understood they were experiencing their own set of mixed emotions. We were together in this!

My second goal was to make each juror think I was especially glad they were on the jury. I wanted them to feel like we were partners in this adventure. I would let each of them know, in some unique way, I was trusting in their intellect, character, intuition, or whatever gift I could identify in them. I would let the defense team try to screen out those with religious prejudices or loyalties. I wanted Bob Chaney to be seen as the one who may not accept them, may not affirm them as worthy of this endeavor. Even as the prospective jurist tried to earn Bob's confidence, they would find reasons to discredit him (in case he should end up excusing them). Meanwhile, my questions of the jury would give each of them a chance to shine. I invited them to brag on themselves and then affirm what they had to say.

The first juror was a short, plump white woman with a worried look. Her purse was shaped like a dog. "Mrs. Greer," I said, smiling warmly, "you look a little worried. I was wondering if maybe you have a pet at home?" She was a little guarded but admitted to having two cats and a dog. "If you are chosen for this jury, will you be able to find someone to care for your pets?" Although this may have been the least of her worries, she visibly relaxed. *Voila*, that's all it takes. Juror number one felt like she and I were in this adventure together. I wanted her on the jury.

Bob Chaney asked her some questions about her religious beliefs and history. He found no problem with her. Still, Mrs. Greer knew that Bob was the threat to her placement (not me), and the other potential jurors knew it too. Already, the jury saw Bob as someone to be wary of. We were off to a good start.

Juror Number Two was a large older man who had recently retired as a railroad engineer. I asked him about how many towns he traveled through on the trains he ran. He proudly estimated that he had been through over two hundred towns and cities. I didn't know if that was a number a railroad engineer should be proud of but I nevertheless paused and gave him a surprised look. I even gave a low whistle. He was still beaming as I asked a few more inconsequential questions. Mission accomplished.

So it went. The third juror carried a romance novel: "Do you do a lot of reading?" "This trial will require jurors who have open minds, can focus, and can follow themes." I left her with the impression that I had somehow divined she had all these abilities.

Juror Number Four was a thin, male college student. His hair was long and his jeans were tight. I could see sinewy muscles in his arms that extended beyond his short-sleeve button-up shirt (his effort at dressing up). I asked about his extracurricular interests and he claimed to be a competitive skateboarder. "Have you ever injured yourself?"

He answered modestly, "Too many times." I laughed. We connected, and I was already thinking about Juror Number Five.

Yes, I asked each juror some pertinent questions, but not until after I had connected with them, not until they seemed relaxed with me. I've found when someone relaxes, he is more likely to show any quirks of perspective or character or personality. I'm not afraid of the atheist, or the homosexual, or the patriot, or the social warrior, or the devout Catholic. I was not trying to weed out any potential juror based upon his predisposition to agree or disagree with my most important arguments or my witnesses. I was only hoping to weed out those that are emotionally or relationally dysfunctional in some way. I've been around long enough to know the case will be best served by jurors who can relate to each other. Therefore, I figured if they had some resistance to connecting with me (an expert at connecting, if I do say so myself), then there is probably something wrong with them. I'm not a psychologist, and I wouldn't assign any diagnosis to anyone, but if the prospective juror didn't connect with me, I didn't want them on my jury. Not just because I wanted the advantage over the defense counsel of establishing a bond with the jurors, but also because I didn't want the jurors to have problems with each other. I wanted them focused on the facts of the case, not on a personality conflict with a fellow juror.

Juror Number Seven was average looking enough: a middle-aged, middle-sized man. I noticed him before I even finished with juror number five. He seemed unaware of his own facial expressions. When Bob and I were interviewing the jurors before him, Juror Number Seven would be nodding or shaking his head as if he were answering the questions himself. It seemed to me that he was desperate to prepare himself to give the expected answers and be placed on the jury.

"Mr. Carr, how are you today?" "Fine, thanks."

"Good! That's fantastic! Tell me," I said, borrowing from one of Bob's standard questions, "have you ever been employed by a religious institution?"

"No, not that I know of." He meant his indefinite statement to be a cordial response, but I intentionally misrepresented it as confusion on his part.

"Yeah, sometimes it is hard to know what is and isn't a religious institution," I said, putting finger quotations in the air. Now Juror Seven really was a little confused and didn't know what to say. If he agreed with me, it might have seemed he was discrediting the question he had already heard the defense counsel asking other jurors. His face reddened as he replied, "I'm not sure."

While this conversation was couched in the same tones and expressions of acceptance as my earlier conversations had been, my intention was very different. "So, help me with this, Mr. Carr, give me your definition of a religious institution." He stammered a little and I jumped in the gap with my friendly smile. "Are you one who segregates the holy and the secular, or do you see them as overlapping?"

His expression became blank. "I'm not sure."

I pressed on. "After all, we are in a court of secular law, yet this case will be based upon several matters that are held sacred by those I represent." This was more or less a nonsense statement that I made just to confuse the issue. I gave him my friendship smile and left the statement hanging. Mr. Carr looked down at his hands then back at me. His eyes showed a pleading for me to give him a clue as to how I wanted him to answer me. He looked down and back twice more, slower each time. I continued waiting patiently. After his fourth long look at his hands, he looked back up at me and said that he was not feeling well and asked to be excused. I sympathized with him and directed him to the hallway restrooms. As he left, we moved on to Juror Number 8.

Juror Number Eight turned out to be a great card (an Ace?) in the deck. I had to decide whether I could risk allowing her in the deck (unsure whether she would end up in my hand). Her name was Jane Morris, and she was an active member of the United Methodist Church (indicated on the self-disclosure form each panelist had completed prior to being seated as a potential juror in this trial). She was forty-ish, slim, attractive, and seemed attentive and intelligent. Bob had asked her all his usual vetting questions, except the one about her faith and church involvement. I liked the eye contact she gave to each of us and her calm deliberative answers. I asked her a couple of questions about her education (and gave her approving nods as she detailed her degrees). I determined to let her stay in the deck. I expected that she would become the foreperson should the jury enter deliberations.

After our acceptance of the next juror, we had our eight jurors who would be seated for the trial. Then Judge Browne took a moment to state some pragmatic details. We expected the trial to last two weeks: they would not be sequestered unless it became necessary. Finally, Judge Browne asked if any of the eight jurors had reason to believe that they were not fit for serving in this capacity.

Jane raised her hand. "None of the things you mentioned, Your Honor, but I thought you might need to know that I am a faithful member of First UMC on Twelfth Street. Neither of the attorneys have asked me that question."

Judge Browne looked to me to dismiss Jane for cause. I held Jane's gaze for a comfortable moment then said, "We would like to keep this juror, Your Honor."

I didn't look, but I would have guessed that Bob Chaney, the judge, and some of the jurors had startled looks on their faces. I was sure I had surprised them all with this unexpected turn. I doubt I know any other attorney who would think keeping Jane on the jury would be a good thing for my case.

I didn't care. I knew my case. I knew my clients. And Jane had shown herself to be an honest person. My case was based on the presumption that the average member of the church did not know how the hierarchy of the denomination had conspired to thwart accountability to *The Book of Discipline.* The average lay person had been led to believe that the controversial issues in the denomination were being debated every four years at General Conference, but that *The Book of Discipline* was authoritative in the church's practice and doctrine. If Jane's faith tended toward the conservative perspective, she would be alarmed to learn that the doctrine and polity of the denomination were being regularly and intentionally subverted. If Jane's faith tended toward the liberal perspective, she would still be appalled to discover how my clients had been manipulated into serving a church that has consistently and intentionally misrepresented itself to them, and at the systemic racism the apostates has employed to safeguard their positions and their agendas.

My decision to keep Jane on the jury solidified my presentation of myself as the attorney who was confident in my case, confident in this jury, and unafraid of the truth!

# CHAPTER 28
## Instructing the Jurors

*"To the materialist things like nations, classes, civilizations, must be more important than individuals because the individuals live only seventy odd years each and the group may live for centuries. But to the Christian, individuals are more important, for they live eternally; and races, civilizations and the like are in comparison the creatures of a day."* — C.S. LEWIS

After having confirmed the eight jury members and four alternates, Judge Browne addressed all the jurors. Standing between the counsel tables on the floor of the courtroom she welcomed them to "this place where legal issues are disputed." With a pride of place and purpose she described the history of the courtroom: when it was constructed, why it was laid out as it was, and when she first came to work there. She introduced her deputy and her clerk. She bragged on them a little. "If this trial takes as long as we anticipate it will, you will come to know and trust these good people, just like I do."

I couldn't help but feel some fatherly pride for Judge Browne as she represented herself, the court, and our trial. I could see the jurors relaxing as she spoke.

"This is my workplace. This is the place I have been given the responsibility of guarding the legal boundaries in which two sides will present their cases. The lawyers are responsible for presenting their cases to the very best of their abilities. They will devote the best of their intelligence, their personalities, and their talents to convincing a jury their side has the best arguments. They will not be arguing about whether one side or the other has broken the law, because this is not a criminal trial. They will not be arguing for or against someone going to jail. You are responsible for paying close attention to details. Take notes if you like. Do not reach a conclusion until all evidence and testimonies are concluded. Soon you will need to choose a chairperson who will represent your needs, guide your deliberation discussions, and eventually, represent your decision to this court.

"I thank you in advance for respecting my authority as I direct you and the attorneys in following the guidelines of the law. Together, we will accomplish a task that relatively few nations and people have experienced over the course of history, a trial by a jury of peers. It is an amazing gift our forefathers handed down to us. I feel very privileged to share this moment in history with each of you."

Judge Browne was relaxed, yet serious. Her words were accompanied with eye contact and significant pauses. Her admonitions were direct, short, and clear.

"Finally, in a civil trial the burden of proof is not the same as in a criminal trial. In a criminal trial you, the jury, must be convinced 'beyond a reasonable doubt' before someone could be convicted. In a civil trial we ask that you give a verdict based upon 'your best judgment'; the legal term is "the preponderance of the evidence". You don't have to be 100% convinced of your verdict. We simply ask you to determine what seems true to you as an objective observer. You must work hard at hearing everything both sides have to say equally. This is a daunting responsibility we are entrusting you with. God bless your efforts!"

As many times as I have heard a judge give pre-trial directives, I had never heard it done better. I wanted to clap for her. I wanted to stand up and clap. I guess I really am sold on the miracle of our judicial system. Our system truly is unique in the history of mankind and, as many faults as I can sometimes find in it, I believe it is the best judicial system this world has ever seen.

At moments like this, I feel the excitement of the starter's gun being fired – the race begun. I feel the honor of being entrusted with representing my clients to a jury composed of people I have already come to respect. I feel a little anxiety that something may go wrong, of course, but mostly, I feel confident this is where I belong and what I am supposed to be doing. Win or lose, what could be better than that?

# CHAPTER 29
## OPENING STATEMENTS

Elements of Breach of Contract:

Plaintiff is required to prove by the greater weight of the evidence the following in order to recover on the claim of breach of contract against the defendant:

- Formation of a contract between plaintiff and defendant
- Defendant breached the contract by (state the way in which the plaintiff claims the breach occurred)
- Plaintiff suffered damages as a direct result of the breach

The courtroom was set up like any other courtroom. The trial drew huge publicity in the first days of preliminary trial motions. This warm and beautiful Monday morning, the back rows and aisles of the courtroom were filled with cameras and reporters.

I intended to ignore them, and I will ignore them in the narrative. I don't know how they covered the trial, whether positively or negatively. I assume each reporter twisted his or her account of the trial, and picked excerpts from the testimonies that supported the political orientation of their networks.

No, I do not believe that any news organization is concerned with objective reporting. If I thought this trial was represented objectively by any other source, I would probably have talked myself out of offering this book.

I realize you may be thinking, "How objective can one of the attorneys actually be about a case?" I don't know. I can tell you that I'm trying. I've told you how I am devoted to the truth. This book may be my test to see how honest with myself I really can be.

Anyway, the press was there. I won't mention them again. Witnesses were sequestered until they were called upon to give testimony. After each witness testified, he was re-sequestered due to the possibility that he would be called upon later as a rebuttal witness.

When it was time to present my opening statement, I moved from behind our table to stand approximately five feet in front of the witness box. This is where I intended to stand every time I present to the jury. I wouldn't be pacing back in forth, or making grand arm and hand gestures, or even dramatically varying my voice tone. I wanted the jury to know what to expect from me. I would either hold their attention by what I had to say, or not at all. I wouldn't try to engage their attention. I expected them to give me, and the witnesses, the attention we deserved. I simply had to make sure that my words deserved their attention. Taking a brief moment to look each of them in the eye, I began.

"Don't raise your hands or answer this question out loud, but have any of you ever been swindled? Have any of you ever been conned?

"If so, I'm sorry and I hope you weren't taken for too much.

"But, if you have been swindled, you might imagine how my clients felt when they learned the church they belonged to was not what they had been told it was. You can imagine how it feels to slowly begin to realize you have been manipulated. You may remember the humiliation you felt.

"Okay, here it is: My case is based on the premise that this book –" I held it up "–known as *The Book of Discipline. The Book of Discipline* is how the United Methodist Church represents its Doctrine and Polity. 'Doctrine' is what they believe, and 'polity' is how they are structured. The polity part of *The Book of Discipline* is their means of preserving and presenting their doctrine. Our whole case comes down to whether those I represent had a right to believe that the church would adhere to *The Book of Discipline*. In other words, those I represent are claiming that by not adhering to *The Book of Discipline*, the United Methodist denomination is liable for breach of contract.

"Those I represent gave years of service, their money, and lots of love to their local churches and the denomination based on what they had been taught to believe were covenant agreements. They were taught 'covenant agreements' are sacred and that these agreements were specified in this book. This book is the product of the entire history of the denomination.

"This case can easily be resolved based upon just a few quotes from *The Book of Discipline*. From Paragraph 67: *as doctrinal standards that shall not be revoked, altered, or changed*
. . .

*Christ did truly rise from the dead, and took again his body....*"

"I will stop with just those two statements, because they are enough for you to determine what my clients had a right to believe they were committing to when they joined the church. When they were told that no article of religion, as found in this book, would or could be revoked, altered or changed, I think they had every right to expect that those ordained into the church would believe in those articles. And when my clients were told that one article stated that Jesus was truly risen from the dead and took again his body, were they warranted in believing that this doctrine defined their common understanding? Or were they supposed to think it was okay if the Constitution was ignored and their essential doctrines were only accepted as analogies for life and truth, rather than actual historical events?

"If you can look at these statements and determine my clients were wrong or naïve to expect them to be honored, then we will have lost our case. But, if these statements seem concrete and declarative enough that my clients had reason to believe they would be determinative in who would or would not be ordained, and in what they and their children would or would not be taught, then we will have won our case.

"So, for the sake of these opening statements, let me summarize my main points. It is our contention, that first, men and women who do not believe in the denomination's traditional doctrinal statements are being ordained as ministers nonetheless. Second, the boards, who know those who don't hold the required beliefs, are recommending them anyway, and third, because the constitution of the denomination does not allow for any changes to their articles of faith, these false ministers are attacking the social principles of the church without being held accountable for the apostacies that underly the changes they try to make.

"Furthermore, often these false ministers do not even let the members of the local churches they are leading know what they really do and do not believe. For example, if someone were to directly ask one of these false ministers if they believe in the resurrection of Jesus, they say, 'Yes.' What they don't tell their lay members is that they don't really believe that Jesus was literally, historically, physically raised from the dead. They don't explain that they only believe that Jesus is alive today to the extent that we remember Him, honor Him, and embrace

His teachings. And that is how they preach their sermons. When they say "Jesus is Alive," the members of their congregation think the false ministers mean that Jesus really is alive. The false ministers hide their true meaning. The whole time they are really making small steps toward teaching their congregations to accept their false gospel.

"Now, this is not, ladies and gentlemen of the jury, about what you personally believe – accept the Resurrection, reject it, it doesn't matter. What is important is the fact that these ministers are willingly and knowingly misleading their congregations.

"And, worst of all, the vast majority of all the ordained ministers in the United Methodist Church in the USA know this is happening and have not put a stop to it. Even the so-called conservative pastors know this is happening. They talk about it. They write about it. It is easy to prove. I will give you lots of evidence of it. Yes, the conservative pastors who have remained in the denomination know this is happening, BUT they will not do what they can to change it! So, when the honest pastors try to do something about it, the institution turns against them. One by one the honest pastors are run off. When the lay person tries to do something about it, they are labeled 'troublemakers.' One by one they are run off also.

"This travesty extends all the way to the organizations that claim to be protecting the denomination from the false ministers. They hold conferences and publish newsletters detailing what the false ministers are doing. These 'reform' organizations give the average lay person hope that something will be done about the false ministers so the lay people stay on as members of the local churches they love. But, year after year, even decade after decade, these reform movements make their protests, but they don't do the things that really could change the situation. They give the lay people a false hope. This allows conservative pastors to keep the lay people in the pews. Meanwhile, the denomination is ordaining more and more false ministers.

"I represent a small portion of the lay people and true ministers of the faith who have given up or been run off one by one. The one hundred and forty ex-pastors and over two thousand ex-lay members I represent in this court today are but a small fraction of those who have suffered this same fate over the years.

"If I can prove all that I have just claimed to your satisfaction, then I will ask you to tell the United Methodist Church that what they are doing is not okay. Technically, it is 'breach of contract,' what you may call 'a con game,' 'religious abuse,' and the 'manipulation and humiliation of people of good faith.' It is all those things. And, when I prove it to you, I want you to send a message to the United Methodist Church in the only terms that you will have available to you. You won't be able to hold these false ministers accountable. I'm sorry, I wish you could. You won't be able to restore the years of service my clients have given or to heal the hurt feelings they have suffered. I wish you could. But what you can do is demand that the denomination return a portion of the money my clients gave to them under the false assumption that the contract between themselves and the denomination, who represents themselves through this book, *The Discipline*, would be honored. It has not been. I can prove it. And you can make the denomination give my clients some of their money back. Thank you."

At the table next to me, Chaney slowly stood, looking down and shaking his head. His face conveyed the idea that I had missed the point.

Raising his head and eyes to the jury, he gave them a big smile. He was ready to address the false charges against his client, but first he must follow the proper etiquette. "Ladies and gentlemen of the jury, let me take a moment to thank you for being here. The case you are about to hear is one based on very strong feelings and profound religious convictions. It will be a difficult case to hear and judge unemotionally. I know you will be steadfast in your responsibilities. I thank you now for your efforts to embrace justice."

He paused, stepped away from his table, toward the jury. He was ready to set the story straight. "My job is not so hard. In order to persuade you to rule in favor of the United Methodist Church in this trial, all I need do is remind you of one thing: The United Methodist Church is a very large organization. As such, the denomination is made up of people who don't all think alike. Even with the faith that unites them, the members of this denomination live all over the world, in hundreds of different cultures and with just as many different personality types, perspectives, and life experiences. In short, they will not all get along with each other. In any organization involving millions of people, there are going to be those who eventually discover that they just don't fit in, for whatever reasons.

"Please hear me, I am not saying the reason someone may not fit is because of something good about them or bad about them. I'm not saying they don't fit in because they are smarter or dumber than the rest of the group. And, I am certainly not saying they don't fit in because they are better or worse

Christians than the others. I am simply stating the obvious: in an organization the size of the United Methodist Church, not everyone is going to get along."

Bob began pacing. His steps were slow and deliberate, as if we were all taking a walk with him, joining his movements and embracing his thoughts.

"Religion is a very sensitive issue for people. Faith is very important, and we each take pride in our search for truth and justice. That's why religion is often compared to politics. Politics can also represent our search for truth and justice. So, let me make this comparison: In the United States our political beliefs are represented by two primary parties, the Democrats and the Republicans. If you are a Democrat, I will bet my last dollar that you don't agree with everything our last Democratic president has done during his term so far. And, if you are a Republican, I will bet that same last dollar that you didn't agree with everything our last Republican president did, either."

Bob stopped his pacing and posed for the jury with slightly raised eyebrows and slightly raised shoulders and hands, as if to say, "What could be more obvious?" He resumed pacing.

"I won't tell you which political party I usually vote for, because it isn't relevant to what we are doing here, today. Still, I can tell you for sure I am not always happy with what my party does. I will go even farther than that and tell you that sometimes I agree more with what the other political party wants to do.

"That's how it is with big organizations. They can't please all their people all the time, can they? Religious institutions are also organizations. One of them is the United Methodist Church. People who share some thoughts in common and who are similar in some ways still may think very differently on some subjects and can be very different from each other. For a while, one person might rise to leadership in a big organization who is different from the last person who was leading before him or her. And the next leader to come along will be a little different from the one leading now. That is the way it goes in big organizations.

"So, if I get upset with my political party, the one I have worked hard for, the one I have given my money to, and I go over to the other political party or maybe even drop out of politics altogether," he paused, "I couldn't ask the party to give me back the money I gave them in the past. For one thing, I know that money is long gone. They used the money I gave them as fast as I gave it to them. And, when my political party changes a little one way or the other, it doesn't mean that I was swindled or conned. These changes are a natural part of the process. I'm invited to get even more involved and work to move the organization the way I want it to go."

Bob stopped his pacing, this time squaring himself before the jury. "The same is true of the United Methodist Church. Yes, the organization changes a little this way and that way. All big organizations do. No, these changes do not mean that anyone has been swindled or conned. And, certainly whatever money was given to the denomination has already been spent. The money was spent on so many wonderful ministries that I can't begin to even count them. This is all it takes to rule in favor of the United Methodist Church in this case; you must simply recognize that it is a large organization functioning like every other large organization does.

"Nevertheless, let me give you one more illustration of what you must find in favor of the United Methodist Church.

This illustration is not about a large organization. It is about the smallest organization there is. Do you know what I'm referring to? The smallest organization is formed when people get married. Together, the two of them form the smallest organization: a couple. Of course, you know where I am going with this. The people have some wonderful reasons for getting married: They love each other, and each think the other person is great. But then they begin to live together. They begin to learn how different they are. They try to resolve their differences. Still, roughly half of marriages in the United States end in divorce, don't they?

"This state is a 'no-fault' divorce state. That doesn't mean that neither person was at fault for the marriage failing. It just means that the courts don't try to figure out who is at fault, or who is more to blame. The reason so many states are

'no-fault' divorce states is because the courts learned a long time ago that marriages are just too complicated for the court to figure out. Maybe a marriage counselor could tell us if the man is more to blame or if it was more the woman's fault, but the courts realized that they couldn't figure it out. And here is my point. If the courts can't figure out who is more to blame when something goes wrong for the smallest of organizations, how can we possibly say that we know who is more to blame when someone leaves one of the largest organizations in the world?

"I know the plaintiffs think they can make their case, but I will be here to remind you that no matter what they say, the matter is more complicated than we can know. We will only be able to see tiny slices of an organization that is world-wide and over two hundred years old. Whatever stories we hear can only be anecdotes: one person's perspective of what happened to him. But just like in the smallest of organizations involving only two people, and just like in other large organizations, not everyone is going to get along with everyone else. Sad, but true, yet, certainly not reason for a trial against an organization that is trying its best to do as much good as possible, for as many people as possible."

I had to give him credit. Bob's opening statement had neutralized my own. He painted us as objects of pity, the social misfits that couldn't understand why people didn't like us. I saw a couple of jurors nodding when he made his points. His approach was working. For now.

I didn't mind: it wouldn't hold up. Before we were through, the jury would see that Bob was the true social misfit. He has himself in the same role that the denominational hierarchy had taken toward my clients. He had not disputed their claim concerning *The Book of Discipline*: he had simply dismissed them, ignoring our claims as if they were irrelevant. But that tactic only works when one is in power. In control. That was not the case here, as Bob and the denomination, would soon discover. I would emphasize that there is a truth that is easily understood, and that I can't imagine why Bob (and by extension, the entire United Methodist Church hierarchy) couldn't acknowledge the simple truths of this case.

# CHAPTER 30
## THE FIRST WITNESS

*"Every preference to a small good to a great or a partial good to a total good involves the loss of the small or partial good for which the good was made. You can't get second things by putting them first; you can only get second things by putting first things first."*
— C.S. LEWIS

The first witness the jury heard from was William Capps Jr., a lifelong United Methodist who had written five books on the history of the United Methodist Church: one on John Wesley, one on Francis Asbury, one on John and Charles Wesley, one on the role of the denomination in the Great Awakenings emphasizing their ardent opposition to slavery, and one on the 1968 creation of the United Methodist Church through the merging of the Methodist Church and the United Brethren.

My first impression of William Capps, when I had met him for depositions, was a positive one, but he quickly proved me wrong. He was younger than I expected, walked with energy, dressed in chic-casual jeans, tee, and sweater vest. He was average height and sat in the witness chair casually. He smiled as he was sworn in. Then, the terrible reality was revealed. Unlike during depositions, once on the stand our expert historian chose his words so carefully that his slow speech began tranquilizing all who heard him within the first five minutes of his testimony.

By the time Junior had answered the second of twelve prepared questions (six apiece from myself and the defense team) I was ready to break my conviction against energy-drinks. I couldn't keep myself from yawning while he answered questions.

Yawning, as you know, is contagious, and it seemed the only thing that kept some life in the courtroom was that the jury began smiling at each other's efforts not to yawn too obviously. Judge Browne, measuring the capacity of the jury to maintain their focus, called a break after the fourth question and dismissed for the day after the eighth, almost an hour early.

Not a good day for my team.

The jury probably did not hear some of the points supporting our case that Junior had, ever so slowly, verbalized. Even my most important questions, concerning how the hierarchy of the denomination had conspired to limit the proportional representation of the African churches, were answered in such neutral terms and tones that the jury may not have registered the heinous nature of this part of the denomination's history.

Therefore, the last well-presented thoughts they had heard were those in the opening statement of the defense and, I imagine, the jury went home dreading the next morning.

On day two, the jury was seated, and Junior returned to the stand. The jury was rested enough to focus on the testimony, but I could tell they were really having to work at it. By the time Junior finally finished and the jury was dismissed for lunch, here is what was said that really needed to be heard: First, the denomination began as a reform movement within the Anglican Church. The movement stayed in submission to the Anglican Church until their differences became too pronounced and the Methodists continued on their own. In other words, when their reforms were not accepted, they went their own way. They did not attempt to take over the hierarchy or pretend they belonged when they didn't. They did not try to deceive or manipulate the established church. They accepted the differences and continued their work on their own, raising up leaders as the needs required. They first published the *Book of Discipline* in 1784.

Second, Junior affirmed that one of the central articles of incorporation stated that all properties are to be held in the name of the denomination in order to safeguard against apostates leading a congregation away and transferring ownership of the property. I would have other witnesses emphasize how this article was now being used against local churches who recognized problems within the hierarchy. Recently, the local church choosing to withdraw from the denomination because its members expected the *Book of Discipline* to be followed lost the properties and buildings that some had spent a lifetime planning and funding.

These points carried the playing card values of a nine and a ten respectively. They were not face cards that would win the case, but they definitely carried value. The last point, the property clause, would gain in value as the case went on. I was hoping the first time the jury heard this concept it would register as a nine. Then, as I applied it again and again through different witnesses, it would gain the value of a jack and maybe even a queen. As it was, I think this point got lost amidst the tedium of dates and principles having to do with changes in the *Book of Discipline* as the denomination grew from a local to an international organization and as the Methodist Church became the United Methodist Church through its 1969 merger with the United Brethren Church.

Junior made it all sound like tedious historical details.

How anyone who loves history can present history as a dry record of events is something I will never understand. As such, I will not claim that this witness should be scored as a win for the plaintiffs, but rather as a win for the defense.

I doubt the jury heard the upside-down realities of a denomination on fire against slavery and racism becoming possibly the most blatant practitioner of systemic racism currently active in American Christianity, or how the creative ways the denomination's founders put in place to safeguard against apostasy in their ranks had been subverted to force the orthodox believers to forfeit their properties and assets when they disaffiliated.

In any case, Bob finished the cross-exam and we were dismissed for lunch. I ate my lunch with enthusiasm because I knew what was to come. After the lunch break, I would call a better witness: I would put an ace into play.

# CHAPTER 31
## KYLE TAKES THE STAND

*"The most deeply compelled action is also the freest action. By that I mean, no part of you is outside the action."* — C.S. Lewis

The court was called to order and Judge Browne directed me to call my first witness.

I was hoping that the jury remembered the defense's opening statements about people who are just unable to get along. In my opinion, my witness was among the most likeable people I have ever known, and his charisma really shone even as he took the stand. Kyle Fedder smiled as he was sworn in and took his seat. He was obviously eager to make his statements. He seemed to be enjoying himself.

"Reverend Fedder, before you tell the jury your history with the United Methodist Church will you state your reason for being here as a witness against the denomination?"

Turning to face the jury, Kyle began, "I am a first-hand witness to the ordination to elder of a person who does not believe in the basics of the Methodist doctrine."

Kyle paused momentarily, then continued, "The first year after I was ordained an elder in the United Methodist Church, I presented a petition at the executive session opposing the ordination of a candidate who had represented a lack of faith in the physical resurrection of Jesus. I was shocked and amazed when I was attacked and the majority of the over six hundred pastors voted to ordain her as an elder anyway.

"I have known other apostate clergy members who taught their apostasies at youth camps, knowing the children wouldn't question what they were being taught. I have known apostate clergy members who worked diligently to word their sermons in such a way as to keep their congregations from knowing of their apostasy. I have been threatened by leaders of the conference in which I served that my career would be very limited unless I stopped making stands against the apostasies I encountered."

Kyle made these statements in a "can-you-believe-it?" tone.

"Kyle, let me interrupt," I injected. "You have repeatedly used the term 'apostasy.' What does this term mean?"

"Apostasy is the lack of faith in the basic truths of Christianity, specifically by those who are expected to promote and protect those truths," he responded.

"Okay, and second, I want to ask you to clarify something else for me. Did you go looking for opportunities to take stands against these apostates?"

Kyle smiled. "No. I am not the personality type that goes looking for an argument. I'm the type that must really challenge myself to risk embarrassment and conflict."

By now, Kyle and I had established an easy rhythm. In order to showcase his attractive nature, I decided to enjoy the moment with him. "So, you might say that you and I are a lot alike?"

Slyly, Kyle retorts, "I've sworn to tell the truth, so you may want to withdraw that question." The jury is leaning in toward us, enjoying the banter.

"I withdraw the question and thank you for giving me a diplomatic way out." I paused to allow the attitude of the conversation to transition to a more serious tone. "So, before I ask you to elaborate on these encounters, would you tell of some of your history with the United Methodist Church?"

Kyle nodded. "I loved being a pastor in the UMC. I was raised in the United Methodist Church. I was probably the youngest pastor serving in our conference when I first began pastoring. Just before my twentieth birthday, I had the great privilege of being appointed as a student pastor while I completed my undergraduate degree. After four years in my first church, I was moved closer to the seminary I attended and served for three years in my second church. After graduating seminary, I was asked to start a new church. After three years there, I was moved again. I served for four years in my final appointment before withdrawing from the denomination. My family and I had wonderful experiences in each of the four local churches in which I served. It was heartbreaking to give up on the denomination.

"The average member of a local United Methodist Church is much more conservative than the average pastor. Only the clergy seem to work hard to hide that fact."

"OBJECTION!" the defense called out. "Hearsay." "The objection is sustained," the judge calmly stated. Before I could ask my witness another question, Kyle looked directly at Bob and said, "You're right. I'm sorry."

I had never seen an apology to one of the attorneys in court before. Apparently, Bob hadn't either. Before he could catch himself, he had given a genuine smile to my witness. He began to say, "That's alright," but stopped himself before the second word and looked down at the papers on his table.

I watched the exchange from my spot, the spot I stood in to make my opening statement and the same I occupied every time I engaged a witness. I turned my head to the spiral notebook I held in my hand to let the jury know that I was proceeding according to plan. The spiral notebook I use in all my cases serves one major purpose: it contains bullet-points of the issues I intend to address. These are written in large, bold letters. If a juror happened to look at my notes, which occasionally I will hold at an angle that permits them to do so, he or she will see my notes, worded the way that serves my case best and communicating (once again) that I have nothing to hide.

"Reverend Fedder, will you give us an example of the deception the liberal clergy allegedly practice?"

"Yes. For instance, I attended a seminar hosted by Phillips seminary. It was titled 'Theological Integrity in an age of Diversity.' This seminar had been conducted annually for the previous four or five years. The seminar consisted of presentations by four United Methodist pastors: one represented himself as theologically conservative, one charismatic, the third was moderate, and the fourth was liberal. Each one gave an overview of their theology and why they chose to identify with the UMC. The seminar was concluded with a Q & A. So, I asked the presenters if there was one theological statement they could all agree on, including the definition of their terms. The presenters took some time, but eventually admitted that they could not. I then asked them how, with integrity, they could represent themselves as belonging to the same denomination when they didn't share the same basic faith. The moderator said they would have to address that question later. We had lunch, and afterwards, the seminar was dismissed with no new discussion. That seminar was never held again."

"For the sake of clarity," I say to Kyle, "what exactly did this event communicate to you?"

"That, within the closed door of a seminar attended only by clergy, everyone was obviously aware of the apostasy being held by clergy members of the United Methodist Church," Kyle responded. "And that we were all expected to ignore the absurdity of the seminar. It was assumed that none of us who attended the seminar were supposed to notice the emperor was wearing no clothes."

"How did you feel afterwards?" "Cold, tired, a little sick."

By sticking to my spot, I hoped to send the message that I didn't feel like an especially important point had been made. I continued in the same tone of voice, "Did you feel like you had won the debate?"

"No, there were no winners. There was nothing to win." I lowered my head to reflect my true compassion for Kyle and sympathy for the state of the denomination. Then, as if we were both examining the sad scene of a funeral in progress, I pressed on: "Can you give us another example?"

Kyle again nodded sadly. "I can give you a dozen or more."

"I know you can. One more, for now?"

"I can tell you about when Dr. Kirk promoted the creation of a Conference Director of Evangelism position."

I gave Kyle a slight nod, telling him to go ahead.

"Dr. Kirk was the pastor of the largest church in our conference. He was very conservative. He had been the dean of the seminary I attended. He was a leader in the renewal movements. I had a great deal of respect for him."

"Something happened to change your perspective of him?"

"Objection, he is leading the witness." Bob made the words sound as if he were more tired and bored than irritated. "Sustained," the judge's voice was crisp and clear, but showed no indication of rebuke toward me.

"I'll rephrase. How did you feel about Dr. Kirk, initially?" "I admired him greatly," Kyle began again.

"Can you tell us what changed?"

"Dr. Kirk was chairman of the Conference Committee on Evangelism. His committee had decided to create a new position in the Conference called the Director of Evangelism. Dr. Kirk was told by the bishop that if he could raise the money needed to underwrite this position, then the Conference would approve it. To raise the money, Dr. Kirk spoke at district conferences, where he shared his vision. He presented a job description in which the new conference employee would go from church to church, leading revivals and teaching about evangelism. Dr. Kirk was very inspiring, and easily raised the money. After he had spoken at my district conference, I asked to speak with him privately for a minute. He agreed, we stood in a nook, and I asked him, "'Won't it be the bishop and the cabinet who will appoint someone to this new position, and not the COE?' He agreed, so I pressed on. 'Don't you think it is very likely that a theological moderate will be appointed to this position?' Dr. Kirk admitted that it was possible. 'Don't you think that you should have told those giving the money for this position that your vision is only a hopeful one, that they may be financing just another conference job for moderates and liberals?' Dr. Kirk told me I was being too pessimistic, and our conversation ended. Within the year, the bishop and the cabinet assigned a pastor who confessed a conservative faith, but who ended up fulfilling very little of the evangelistic vision Dr. Kirk had promoted."

"And what did you learn from that experience?"

"I had two thoughts confirmed to me. First, that the conference can pervert the best of intentions. Second, that even our leaders in the conservative renewal movement were unwilling to be honest with the lay people about the state of our denomination."

Kyle had made these statements so matter-of-factly that I was concerned that the jury may have missed the importance of what he had said. "Are you saying that Dr. Kirk intentionally misled the lay people? Why would he do that?"

As if speaking the eulogy at the funeral we had all been attending, Kyle stated, "I don't know if he was fooling the lay people or just fooling himself."

I was still unwilling to let the jury reach their own conclusions. I needed them to see the effects such events had upon Kyle. I wanted them to expand these examples by the over two thousand clients I was representing in this trial. "If, and we surely don't know, but if Dr. Kirk did intentionally mislead the lay people, what motive could he have had to do so?"

"His motive could have been to offer a false encouragement to the conservative lay people, so they wouldn't give up and leave the denomination."

"And, Dr. Kirk, who pastored the largest and one of the most conservative local churches, would have a lot of motivation to keep the conservatives in his congregation hopeful about the United Methodist Church?"

I could see that Bob wanted to object to this question. It was practically a statement of testimony by me. I was leading the witness. Bob didn't object. I assume he didn't object because it would change the attitude of boredom that he was trying to project.

"Yes."

"And you don't know if Dr. Kirk was fooling himself or fooling the lay people?"

"Yes."

"But, either way, you lost respect for Dr. Kirk?" I made the same statement that Bob had objected to earlier. I was testing his resolve in maintaining his act of boredom. He raised his eyebrows but said nothing.

"Yes," Kyle answered again.

Since Bob had decided to keep to his act, I decided to make him pay for it by continuing to ask leading questions. "And is it fair to say, that you lost trust in the renewal movements?

"Yes. At the time, Dr. Kirk was the only member of the Conserve our Faith Coalition that I knew personally."

"Had you begun to lose faith in the Conserve our Faith Coalition prior to Dr. Kirk's success at establishing a so-called Director of Evangelism position in your conference?" I was really rubbing Bob's nose in his decision to appear bored.

"Yes, definitely."

"Would you tell us why?"

Kyle took a deep breath, let it out slowly, then made a statement that struck at the heart of our case. "In my own mind I had determined that there were only three things the renewal movement could do to safeguard the denomination from those who ignore the directives of the Discipline: 1) they could encourage all the conservative churches to withhold their apportionments, 2) they could prepare for a division of all assets and let each local church decide if they would become an independent church or identify with another denomination, or 3) they could insist on their rights under the *Discipline*, they could vote against the ordination of apostates, they could file charges against the bishops and elders who promote teachings contrary to the *Discipline*, they could refuse to stop rehashing the same issues every four years at General Conference, and stop just hoping that the theologically liberal would finally give up and quietly go away."

In my semi-challenging tone of voice, I asked, "Aren't the reform groups telling the truth to their constituents?"

"Yes, but they were not honest about their will to lead a reform. Therefore, they were offering their constituents a false hope for reform. They played a bait and switch con-game. They offered reform, but traded any hope for reform for loyalty to the local church while the institution went on the same as always. They said we must maintain a tone of civility. We don't like being called 'homophobic', 'sexist,' or 'racists,' so we should not call others 'apostate,' 'heretical,' or 'subversive' by those who won't engage in an honest conversation or debate with us. It doesn't seem to matter to them that we are not racists, homophobic, or sexist. It doesn't seem to matter that the liberals truly are apostate, heretical, and subversive. They said, we still must maintain a civil tone. So, they didn't talk about separating, or pressing charges, or using their majority to stop the repeated petitions to change the *Discipline*. They sat back and ignored the powers *The Book of Discipline* gave them, while more apostates were ordained, and more conservatives who attempted to enact appropriate accountability, like myself, finally gave up and moved on."

"So, Reverend Fedder, because you gave up on the leadership being accountable to *The Book of Discipline*, you left the denomination?"

"I did. I reached the conclusion there was no hope for appropriate accountability or reform in the United Methodist Church."

"And why have you agreed to be a party to this lawsuit

against the United Methodist Church?"

"Well, for several reasons: First, because the lay members of the church deserve to know the truth and I hope the attention this case is bringing will bring the truth to light. Second, I am a part of this lawsuit because I still love the denomination and the members of the denomination, so I still want to call for accountability and reform even if I must do it from the outside."

"Reverend, I noticed that you spoke of the reform movements as con games in the past tense. Has something changed since you withdrew from the denomination?"

"Yes, the growth of the African churches has changed the balance of power in the General Conference. Even though their membership is not allowed proportional representation, their conservative faith stands in direct opposition to the apostates in the U.S. Conferences. They have forced the issue of following *The Book of Discipline* and are advocating removing the apostates from their ministry and leadership positions, or facilitating a separation with the denomination."

"So, the African Conferences, churches, and membership want to separate from the denomination?"

"No, they really desire to stay and see *The Book of Discipline* appropriately enforced. At the last General Conference, they supported 'The Traditional Plan.' This plan would have provided the apostate leaders and any local churches that chose to, the ability to disaffiliate from the denomination and allow those local churches to keep their properties and assets. Even though The Traditional Plan gained the majority vote of the General Conference, the plan has been cast out by the same manipulations and deceits the apostates regularly use to avoid following the dictates of its own policies and procedures. And the systemic racism that keeps the African delegation from getting its proportional representation will prohibit them from moving forward the proposals they support at the next General Conference."

I could tell that Kyle's use of the term "systemic racism" was frustrating Bob, but what could he do? This was the third time the idea of systemic racism had been presented to the jury. The first time was in my opening statement, and Bob couldn't raise objections there. The second time was during Junior's testimony. Bob didn't raise any objection then because he was hopeful (probably rightfully so) that Junior's testimony was so blah (yes, "blah" is a technical, legal term) that Bob wouldn't have wanted to draw any special attention to anything Junior said that wasn't helpful to his case. So now, he couldn't suddenly object to something he had ignored previously without raising questions among the jury. Nevertheless, I expected that Bob would want to nullify this part of Kyle's testimony during his cross-examination.

I pressed on and gave Bob something he couldn't resist objecting to.

"Are you saying that the growth of the African churches and their support of the Traditional Plan somehow forced the Conserve Our Faith members to also support a plan of accountability and reform?"

"Objection, Your Honor. The plaintiff is leading his witness!"

"Sustained."

"My apologies, Your Honor. I'll rephrase. Reverend Fedder, what effect did the African delegations support of the Traditional Plan have on the members of the Conserve Our Faith member delegates?"

Of course, Kyle can't know for sure what the effect was, but because our jury strategy agreement stipulated that each of our limited witnesses were to be considered expert witnesses, their personal views and conclusions could not be challenged by the attorneys through objections. An expert witness's testimony can only be challenged by clarification questions during cross-examination or by other witnesses' testimony. "The Traditional Plan was approved by the 2019

General Conference, but the Conserve our Faith Coalition began getting negative coverage for being the ones who were wanting to establish a new denomination they referred to as The Global Methodist Church. As had always been their pattern, the Coalition showed no fortitude for exercising the power they have been given. When the Judicial Council, the Council of U.S. Bishops, and other agencies of the church began ruling against the provisions of the Traditional Plan, the Coalition began meeting with so-called 'Progressives' and

'Centrists' to create new, less combative proposals for the next General Conferences consideration."

"Let me make sure I'm understanding what you're telling us," I address Kyle. "Are you saying that instead of standing up for the Traditional Plan that was passed in 2019, the Conserve Our Faith Coalition leaders immediately began redirecting their support away from this adopted plan supported by the African Churches and began working to create a compromise plan?"

"That's exactly what I'm saying," Kyle said in a low tone. "Did the Coalition explain why they would abandon The Traditional Plan?" I asked, raising my voice with incredulity. "I heard from an African delegate friend of mine that although it seemed that the victory had been won at the 2019 General

Conference, Coalition delegates explained to them that their protests to entertaining new proposals didn't recognize the complexities of the church's governing boards, and for some reason, spent a large portion of the time they had together explaining *Robert's Rules of Order*, as if they were ignorant of these things."

Once again, I could see that Bob wanted to object to Kyle's statement. Normally, the 'hearsay' objection would apply when a witness states what they were told by someone else, but, again, our accepted court strategy that limits our number of witnesses means that he can't object. Bob can try to break down Kyle's testimony in his cross-examination or rebut it with his own witnesses. But he cannot object at this moment.

To take full advantage of this moment, I press in by asking, "So, your friend on the African delegation felt talked down to?"

"Yes, but much worse than that. He realized that the Coalition was withdrawing its support of The Traditional Plan and would be working to replace it. Once again, the clear intentions of the majority were set aside through interpretations of *The Book of Discipline* that ignored the clear meaning and intent of the constitution of the church and insisted that it was not clear enough to support many of the provisions of The Traditional Plan. It was the same old con game that has been working in the denomination for the last forty years.

"Of course, the African churches wouldn't even need the support of the coalition pastors if they were given proportional representation. Yet, these same leaders sabotaged the clear intent of *The Book of Discipline* by finding ways to limit the number of representatives that the African churches could send to General Conference."

I repeat Kyle's statement, just for clarity. "'The same old con game that has been working in the denomination for the last forty years'…. I have no more questions for this witness at this time, Your Honor."

I didn't want to have Kyle elaborate on the experiences which were most impactful to him, because I wanted to save these details for my cross-examination of the defenses' witnesses.

Plus, it felt right to end with that last statement. The emotional impact was high, and I wanted the jury to feel it.

Judge Browne suggested that this was a good point at which to recess for the day and begin the next morning's session with the defense's cross-examination.

That afternoon I had won my hand. I had introduced the jury to Kyle. He was an ace. Maybe, because he was such a contrast to Junior, the jurors gave him their full attention and seemed to really enjoy him. He set the attitude for our case. His demeanor was relaxed. He wasn't angry. He was working to make himself understood, but not emotionally manipulate anyone. He was a great witness, and I trusted his connection with the jury.

Tomorrow, it would be Bob's chance to play his own hand against this ace. Bob believed that he could lessen Kyle's influence over the jury. I was betting that he could not. Bob's entire case rested on the premise that my clients are discontents who just couldn't adjust to the dynamics of a large corporation. He thought of himself as the ace and Kyle as a lesser card. I was betting the jury would see things differently.

# CHAPTER 32
# KYLE'S CROSS EXAMINATION

*"The universal problem for all partnerships was not getting closer;*
*it was preserving self in a close relationship."*
— EDWIN H. FRIEDMAN, *A Failure of Nerve*

The jury was ushered into their seats and Kyle returned to the stand. I noticed the jury members seemed comfortably alert. It was nine-thirty. They had been instructed to expect a break for lunch before noon. They seemed glad to see us all. Kyle was his usual affable self: comfortable, focused, leaning forward on the edge of the witness stand toward the microphone.

I was happy to lean back and watch the show.

I will tell you now, I already knew this was not going to be a good day for the defense. If I were him, I would get Kyle off the stand as quickly as possible. But I doubted if Bob would be willing to let Kyle go until he had scored some points for the defense. That would be a mistake.

"Yesterday, you said that you don't like being called a whole list of names, including homophobic. Can we talk about that?"

Kyle paused before answering. I could almost read Kyle's mind. He was trying to decide whether to correct Bob. Instead, he leaned back a little, smiled, and answered, "Sure." "Did being called derogatory names have something to do with why you left the UMC.?"

With a sly smile, Kyle answered, "No, I don't mind being called names."

"Really?" Bob asserted. "I don't think I would like it."

Taking the blame on himself for Bob's misrepresentation of him, Kyle responded, "I didn't mean to confuse you with the issue of being called names. What I don't like is people redirecting away from what I am saying by accusing me of racism or sexism or homophobia. What I don't like is when a legitimate issue is deflected by personal attacks."

Bob clearly wasn't expecting this and didn't like the peacemaker role that Kyle was demonstrating. I watched him collect himself and redirect his line of questioning. "So, I guess we need to be very clear about this. Are there circumstances in which others might consider you to be homophobic?"

Without pause Kyle took the conversation to a deeper level, "Sure, depending on their definition, I could be considered homophobic."

I have had these kinds of conversations with Kyle before. I understand that when discussing difficult issues, he would be brutally honest and expect others to follow his detailed explanations of his own thinking. I hoped the jury was willing and able to follow him. It was a risk, but I felt we would be okay.

Bob continued smoothly, "Well I think a common definition of homophobia is when someone fears that they may become homosexual. Do you think that you might become a homosexual if you are exposed to too many of them?"

Kyle gave Bob a perfectly earnest look. He was in his comfort zone and ready to really converse. "I am sorry. I would really like to answer your question, but I don't think you and I are talking the same language."

Bob was ready to make it sound as if Kyle was being obstinate. With an angry tone, Bob asserted, "But, you know what I am asking you?"

"I think you are asking whether I think it is possible that I might develop or discover some same gender sexual attraction within myself, given the right circumstances. And, I think, you are asking whether or not that possibility is frightening to me."

Still intent on trying to make Kyle seem combative, Bob replied, "In spite of us speaking different languages, it appears you have understood me perfectly. Would you please answer the question?"

"Yes, we agreed that there were two questions involved: One, could I develop same gender sexual attractions, given the right circumstances? Two, does that prospect scare me?"

After a sigh meant to show that he was being patient with Kyle, he said, "Okay, would you please give an answer?" Leaning into the conversation and looking back and forth from Bob to the jury, Kyle answered, "Yes, I think it is possible to develop or discover same gender sexual attractions within myself. And, no, that prospect does not frighten me." Characterizing Kyle's clarifications as defensiveness on his part, Bob pressed on, "So, I have to say that you seem to enjoy confusing us." Bob turned to the jury with his eyebrows raised as if he expected them to be frowning at Kyle in agreement. What he saw instead was looks of interest toward Kyle, and frowns toward himself. The jury wanted to hear Kyle's explanation. Bob knew it and I knew it.

Bob turned back to Kyle and asked, in a gentler tone, "So, you do think, in the right circumstances, you might develop same-sex attractions?"

"I might develop or discover some same-gender sexual attractions."

Bob, who was embarrassed a moment ago, tried to regain his ground by sighing again in infinite patience. His tone was condescending, "Isn't that what I said?"

Kyle realized that Bob was upset but was determined to answer the question honestly. Reluctantly. "No sir, you said same-sex attractions. And, you said develop, not develop or discover."

"And, of course, you think those are important clarifications to make?"

Kyle answered in a gentle tone, "Yes sir, if we want to understand each other."

Bob tried to regain ground by matching Kyle's tone. "Reverend Fedder, I have to admit, I am not sure of what you are trying to get me to understand about the possibility of you becoming a homosexual."

Kyle sat forward in his chair and spoke passionately. "I want you to understand that I would hope to never classify anyone by their sexual preferences. I don't refer to people as 'homosexuals.' I believe they are people with same-gender sexual attractions. I want you to understand that identifying a group of people by their sexual orientation is neither accurate nor productive. I want you to understand that sexual attractions can be acknowledged without changing the more important aspects of a human being. I believe that the development of sexual attractions is a complex process that needs the safeguards against premature exposure to sexual stimulation, molestations, and lack of gender-specific affirmations."

Kyle's response was thoughtful and articulate and was well-received by the jury. So Bob raised his hand and began speaking over Kyle. If I thought that Kyle needed my help at all, I would have objected that the defense should let the witness fully answer the question.

Bob interrupted Kyle by stuttering, shaking his head and

speaking as if Kyle had been going on for ages. "Okay, let's not get caught up in the theoretical. I think the jury would be benefitted by understanding any issues you may have with the UMC concerning homosexuality. So please stop avoiding the question. What do you really believe about the practice of homosexuality?"

Kyle was clearly caught off guard by the interruption and by the charge that he was not answering the question. He paused and decided to let Bob be in control. He looked to the jury, who seemed to be silently rooting for him, and stated, "I believe that the practice of same gender sexual intercourse is emotionally, relationally, and spiritually unhealthy."

Bob waved his arm as if Kyle had been avoiding his question until now. "Okay, so there we have it. You are against homosexuality." He paused as if he had asked a question.

"I am against the practice of homosexuality in the same way that I am against the practice of adultery or fornication, and for the same reasons."

"Really, Reverend Fedder? So you think that homosexuals are just another group of sinners that need 'big brother' telling them what to do? And you left the UMC because the authorities were not direct enough in telling the homosexuals what was best for them?"

Kyle's face reddened and I saw Bob smirk. He clearly assumed that Kyle was embarrassed. I knew that Kyle was angry.

"I believe that I need, you need, we all need a God who is wiser than we are, who loves us dearly, and wants to guide us toward what is best for us. One of the reasons I left the UMC is because instead of people trying to carry on an honest conversation about important issues, they resorted to intentionally misrepresenting what I said and characterized me as anti-something instead of truly caring about the people involved."

I suppressed a smile. It wouldn't do for the jury to see me laughing at Bob. He had just succeeded in becoming those whom he was defending. He was modeling the exact behavior that had driven so many good people away from the Methodist Church. I may have overestimated him by saying he is a jack.

Realizing the jury was following this exchange even more closely than he wanted them to, Bob tried to return to his theme of legitimate differences.

"You think I am trying to misrepresent you? Couldn't it be that we just honestly disagree?"

Kyle quickly released his anger. He obviously wanted to resume this conversation in a productive way. "I don't know if you and I disagree; I don't know what you believe. Yes, I think you are trying to misrepresent me. It is your job. I can respect that."

Bob, perhaps fearing that he had been outclassed during his own cross, resumed the role of the long-suffering honest inquirer. "Okay, let's make this conversation more practical. Since, as we have just experienced, homosexuality can be a complex and difficult subject to talk about, maybe you will understand why the United States military has adopted a 'don't ask, don't tell' policy? Would you have been happier in the UMC if *The Book of Discipline's* social statements were more like the military's?"

Kyle paused to contemplate this new avenue of conversation. He had not heard Bob's opening statements and didn't know why he had moved the subject to the dynamics of a secular organization. Nevertheless, having redirected his thinking,

Kyle looked to the jury. "I believe that people with same-gender sexual attractions should be shown the same respect that all people deserve. I don't think any of the proposals that are currently in place, or are being discussed, offer people in the military who have same-gender sexual attractions the respect that others are offered."

Once again trying to couch Kyle's answer in the worst possible light, Bob exclaimed, "You don't think it matters if homosexuals are given the same right to serve their country that everyone one else has?"

Bob must have thought he had scored some point against Kyle and continued, "Now, you have confused me again. I can't seem to get a straight answer from you." He let out a big grin. "No pun intended."

I didn't see a single jurist who seemed to care about the pun. The jury was waiting to hear Kyle go on with his explanation.

"I'm sorry." Kyle, again, took responsibility for the confusion and continued, "What I mean is that no one should have to bunk and bathe with others that they are sexually attracted to. Unless the U.S. military is willing to provide every individual who has same-gender sexual attractions his or her own private bath and bedroom, those with same-gender sexual attractions are being adamantly disrespected."

Kyle's reply took Bob by surprise. He hadn't anticipated Kyle's ability to adjust to the change-up question. However, it was too late to change approaches. He could only hope that someone in the jury was defensive concerning homosexuality and would appreciate his attempts to put Kyle in his place.

"So, your idea of respecting homosexuals is to secure them away from everyone else?"

"Only for their bathing and bunking."

Bob saw an opening and took it. "It seems obvious to me that your line of thinking would create an unworkable situation for homosexuals in the military."

Kyle was again in his comfort zone. "I have nothing to do with creating any kind of situation for the military. You may be right that private beds and baths for those with same-gender sexual attractions won't work in the military. I don't know that it couldn't be done. I just know that every other soldier is given the respect of not having to share a shower room or a bunk room with those they are sexually attracted to. I wouldn't want to have to share a shower room or bunk room with healthy young ladies."

With nowhere else to go, Bob asserted, "You are saying that you are afraid that your base sexual urges would be incited beyond your control."

With no hesitation and somewhat enthusiastically Kyle answered, "Yes, sir!" The jury gave the reserved but honest laughter that Bob had sought for himself earlier. "My libido would drive me crazy. Eventually, it would get to me. I imagine that you are the same way." The jury was openly looking at each other and laughing. Bob knew that the laughter was directed at him. To what I imagine was his lasting regret, he ignored the jury's response and barreled forward.

Avoiding Kyle's reference to himself, Bob asserted, "Once again, it seems that there are no practical alternatives that you can live with. So, here we have another American institution that you, Mr. Fedder, would have problems with."

"I wouldn't personally have a problem with it. I just realize how disrespectful such a situation is for those with same-gender sexual attractions." Kyle had shown himself to be the kinder and gentler debater. If the jury had to vote one of the debaters off the island, it would be Bob. I thought, "Stop now, Bob; you can only make it worse for yourself." But Bob was nothing if not persistent and confident. So, he continued. "Couldn't you let the homosexuals decide that for themselves?

With a nod of his head, Kyle responded, "Yes, sir, I most certainly could and would."

It was almost noon, and I could have asked for a lunch break, but I preferred to let this cross-examination continue. The jury did not look fatigued at all.

# CHAPTER 33
# KYLE'S CROSS EXAMINATION CONTINUED:

*"Blessed are the merciful, for they shall receive mercy!"* — JESUS

Hoping that the jury missed how lopsided this cross-examination had been, Bob maintained his poise and spoke as if his points had been successful.

"Are there other occasions where you have had conflict with others over the issue of homosexuality?"

I couldn't help but snort in amusement. He was clearly grasping at straws. It also meant that Bob knew he had been thoroughly defeated. The cardinal rule for lawyers is "Never ask a question you don't know the answer to," but he had done it. He would have to ride it out.

Kyle answered, "There was one I can think of right now." Hoping for a way out, Bob asked, "Did that situation occur in the UMC?"

"Yes, Mr. Chaney, it occurred in a local United Methodist Church."

Still hoping to back away from the slippery slope he felt himself on, Bob asked, "Did you initiate this conflict?"

"No sir. I was asked, by her parents, to talk to a fifteen-year-old girl who was experiencing same-gender sexual attractions. She had told her youth pastor about her same-gender sexual attractions. The youth pastor set up a meeting with her and her parents to talk to their pastor. Their pastor referred her to me. After meeting with her and her parents once a week for a couple of months, we realized that her father had played a big role in the development of her same-gender sexual attractions."

Bob's eyebrows raised. "How so?" he asked.

"The father had maintained his sobriety for the previous two years after a tragic history of his alcoholism had left his daughter with a fear and anger toward men. Being a more passive personality, when her sexual motivations emerged it was natural for her subconscious to direct her desires toward the – in her mind – 'safer' gender."

Interrupting Kyle's narrative, Bob asserted, "You seem confident in your psychological analysis. Are you really qualified to speak so authoritatively?"

Unflustered, Kyle responded, "Only in hindsight. As the story played out it made some of these conclusions more obvious."

Trying to head off Kyle's telling of the story, Bob concluded for him. "I think we got it. You helped her forgive her father and her homosexuality went away. "

Kyle seemed to think that Bob's attempt at oversimplifying was actually helpful. "Yes, Mr. Chaney, that is exactly what happened. After she forgave her father and their relationship was restored, she was free to begin considering males as sexually attractive."

Returning to what Bob was still hoping was a point he could win, he pressed on, "So, what was the conflict with the church?"

"The youth director decided it was not good for the youth group for this young lady to be in any leadership positions, so he removed her from the praise team and from leading a small group. I asked for another meeting with the pastors and the family. I asked the senior pastor to overrule the decision of the youth pastor. I asked them to have faith in a young woman who was humble enough to confess her struggles and to seek healing. I urged them to let the youth group see God's love and healing at work. The senior pastor felt like he was obligated to support the youth director's convictions, although he didn't share them. I advised the family to move to another church. Which they did."

Bob was eager to characterize this revelation and jumped in with his own conclusion. "So not only did you walk away from a denomination you were pledged to, but you also encourage others to do so?"

Again, Bob had underestimated Kyle. His response was worth gold to me. "I did. I was very sorry to have to do it, but I couldn't really see another option. The church had broken faith with my fifteen-year-old friend."

Asserting his own conclusion, Bob closed with, "Thank you for that example, Mr. Fedder. I think the jury finally got a good perspective on your tendency to break your denominational loyalty and to encourage others to do the same. No further questions at this time."

Judge Browne suggested then would be a good time to adjourn for lunch. I asked the court to indulge me in a short re-direct of my witness. Most judges recognize the need for prompt re-directs. Judge Browne answered, "Of course. I think we can survive."

I really think I saw heads nodding in the jury! "Reverend Fedder, I also thank you for that last example and for your very valuable insights into the social implications of living with same-gender sexual attractions. I do have a couple more questions that the defense counsel failed to bring up concerning your conflicting views with the UMC about those with same-gender sexual attractions.

"First, do you agree with *The Discipline* when it forbids the ordination to the roles of deacon and elder to those who are, and these are the exact words, 'self-avowed, practicing homosexuals?'"

"Yes, I agree with *The Book of Discipline*."

"And, Kyle, do you know for sure there have been self-favowed practicing homosexuals who have been ordained as deacons or elders?"

He gave a long pause before answering, and when he did, his voice was soft. "Yes, I do."

I let that tone hang in the air a moment before I continued. "And, do you agree with *The Book of Discipline* when it forbids the performing of marriage rites for same-gender couples by UM clergy"

"Yes, Sir, I agree with *The Book of Discipline*."

"Do you know for sure that there have been marriage rites for same-gender couples performed by UM clergy?"

"Yes Mr. Richards, I do."

"Do you know what happens to those clergy who ignore *The Book of Discipline* and perform same-gender marriage rites?"

Kyle looked to the jury. "In June of 2011, the Reverend Amy DeLong was tried by a church court for both the offenses you just mentioned. During the trial, she chose not to make her confession as to being a 'self-avowed, practicing homosexual' on the grounds that she shouldn't be asked if she were practicing or not. The court found her innocent of this charge. Reverend DeLong was found guilty of performing marriage rites for same-gender couples. The court penalized her by placing her on suspension of ministerial duties for twenty days. She was unwilling to say that she would not repeat the offense, and the court did not require her to do so."

I asked sympathetically, "Kyle, does it surprise you the court let Reverend DeLong off without even a slap on the hand?"

"No, Sir. That was what I had learned to expect. The only thing that surprised me is the court was willing to hear the case at all. My friends and I all expected that nothing would come of it."

"For those who are presently still a member of the denomination, and still expect *The Book of Discipline* to be honored, what do you think the situation with Reverend DeLong represents to them?"

"I think it represents a clear breach of contract between those sincere members and the hierarchy that betrayed them."

"No more questions, Your Honor."

"Mr. Chaney, would you like to cross-examine?" Bob stood. "Um, no, Your Honor, I would not." "Reverend Fedder, the Court would like to thank you for your testimony today. You are free to step down."

Once the witness had been dismissed, Judge Browne stated, "We are overdue for a break. I suggest that we all return from lunch break at 2:00."

Bob and I answered in unison, "Agreed, your honor."

# CHAPTER 34
# FRED WHITAKER TAKES
# THE STAND

*"We never doubted that the unorthodox opinions were honestly held: what we complain of is your continuing your ministry after you have come to hold them."* — C.S. LEWIS

"Your Honor, I call Fred Whitaker as my next witness." Fred was one of those guys who is hard to describe.

When I tell you that his nose is too big, his chin too small, his hairline receding, and his shoulders slouch forward, you may tend to guess that he is unattractive. Somehow, that is not the case. With his brown hair cut short, his blue eyes sparkling, and his suit accenting his muscular frame, it all seems to come together for him. His speech is slow (though not Junior-slow), clear and full. His manner can be too direct at times.

Fred, at times, referred to himself as a "professional learner." During his career as a book editor for a major publisher, Fred had specialized in non-fiction books. He enjoyed learning, as he edited works related to sociology, history, philosophy, psychology, and theology. For someone without a Ph.D., he was one of the most highly educated people I've known. Obviously, I like him a lot, but others may not. I have estimated that, within this context, his card value is a king or queen.

"Mr. Whitaker, will you tell the jury your history with the United Methodist Church?"

Fred directed his answer to the jury. "I was raised in the

UMC. My mom had been a member before she and Dad married. They joined the closest UMC each of the three times we moved to a new city. I was confirmed as a teenager, and I was a member of the denomination until we withdrew our membership about two years ago. My wife and I were married by a United Methodist minister, our two children were raised in the denomination, and we served the church in many different capacities over the years."

"How old were you when you withdrew from the UMC?" "I was forty."

"And how old were your children?"

"My son was sixteen and my daughter was thirteen." "How were each of your family members affected by the change of churches?" I asked about his family because I knew that they would be central characters in the testimony to come.

"Well, we all had friends in the UMC. My children left behind some friends they had known all their lives. My wife and I were very upset about leaving friends also. But the biggest effect was how heartbroken were over watching a denomination practice apostasy with no accountability."

"Objection, Your Honor." He must have prepared himself for the next time one of my witnesses used the word apostasy, because his argument was more sophisticated than his earlier endeavors. "Apostasy is a theological term whose definition has not been adequately established in this court. Moreover, the claim of no accountability is very subjective indeed."

"The inability of the United Methodist Church to define what is and is not apostasy is one of the key points of our case," I countered. "The denomination's unwillingness to hold its members accountable to their stated doctrines and policies may be the primary issue being adjudicated in this trial, Your Honor. The right of my client to make this statement is what we are asking the jury to decide."

Without looking up from the papers on her desk, Judge Browne answered, "Overruled. You may continue, Mr. Richards."

"Mr. Whitaker, would you give the jury a couple of illustrations of what you mean when you say that the UMC practiced apostasy without accountability?"

"Yes. The Conserve our Faith Coalition distributes a newsletter every quarter that documents all kinds of examples: bishops ordaining self-avowed practicing homosexuals, our agencies funneling money to abortion rights groups, things like that."

"Could you give us a couple of examples of how you have been directly affected?"

"Okay," Fred began. "The first time I really remember having a problem with the apostasy came when my wife and I committed to a two-year course of Bible study using a curriculum created by our denomination. We kept that commitment. We finished the course. But we kept coming across things in the curriculum that concerned us. Along with the rest of our group, we found lots of questions being raised by the curriculum writers that they never answered. For instance, the curriculum spoke of natural evolution as if it were a fact instead of a theory. Our group couldn't decide if we were supposed to believe that, or if the authors were just showing how God could have used that process. When I pointed out that natural evolution theory has been rejected by most secular scientist in favor of quantum physics, our pastor seemed upset with me.

"There were references that seemed to support

Universalism and the position that the miracle stories were not really miracles, but just analogies about the love of God. The studies never came right out and said miracles didn't really happen and Jesus was not really physically raised from the dead. It just said what was important was the meanings, not the events.

"My wife and I grew more and more troubled and sometimes made a point of saying to our group things like, 'If the miracle didn't really happen, then there wouldn't be any meanings to be gained.' And we would ask, 'Is this saying there is no such thing as a real demon?' Before we were done, we realized that our pastor never answered us directly. He would ask others to share what they thought, and he would emphasize where we did agree, but he wouldn't really answer our questions. After one of our discussions, our pastor preached a sermon on the dangers of 'putting God in a box' and of 'not being open to the thinking and experiences of others.' My wife and I felt like he was trying to make a point with us, but again, he didn't come right out and say it."

"Did your pastor ever tell you directly he disagreed with your theology?"

"No, though I wish he would have said one way or the other, but even when things got really bad, he never would tell us what he believed. And that didn't seem right to me. Why would a pastor be so careful about not telling us what he believes? I would think a pastor would look for good opportunities to share his faith."

"You said that things got really bad. Would you tell us about that?"

"It was when I served as a counselor at the District Church Camp that my children were attending. It was the summer before we moved our memberships to St. Paul's, where Kyle Fedder was the pastor." Fred paused, looked upward as if viewing the past, and continued. "Well, there was what happened at the camp and what happened after the camp." Another pause, still looking upward. "I took a week off work to go to camp with my kids. I was told that we would be studying the Bible and experiencing God through nature with our children. I still am not sure what they were really trying to do. The teachers never talked about God as 'creator,' but only as a fellow 'lover of earth.' They provided yoga classes where the kids were encouraged to 'empty themselves and connect with nature and its spirits.' The third day was supposed to be a vegetarian day in which no meat would be served in the meals. If the kids had to have some meat products, the kitchen would provide it, but each child had to talk with the camp dean before they would be served any meat on that day. That morning, of the third day, communion was served. The kids were told that communion was about celebrating nature. When communion was served the song *Love on the Rocks* by Neil Diamond was being played. I always have kind of liked that song, but for the life of me I couldn't figure out what that had to do with communion. That was when it occurred to me that if I couldn't make any sense out of what was being taught at that camp, then the kids must be even more confused. So, I took our kids aside and asked them if they wanted to go home."

"When you say, 'our kids,' do you mean your two children or all the children from your church?"

"All the children from our church. There were fourteen in all."

I watched the jury to see how many details I could solicit

from Fred without losing their interest. They were with us so far. "What did the kids want to do?"

"They were ready to go home. During the breaks, I had been talking with them about what was going on. The kids knew I had spoken with the camp dean and I was being treated by him and other camp leaders like I was some kind of troublemaker."

"How had you caused trouble?"

"Obviously I don't think I did anything that caused a problem, but I know the dean was frustrated with me for going with several of our kids to talk with him about eating meat that day, instead of the kids going one at a time."

"What did the dean say when the group of you showed up together to talk with him?"

"He said that he really didn't have the time needed for a group discussion and told us to just go tell the cook he said it was okay for them to be served some meat. Then, when other kids saw us lining up to be served some meat, almost the whole camp full of kids lined up behind us and wanted to be served meat. The cooks hadn't made that much meat, so they made some more, and lunch took much longer than was scheduled. I could tell the camp dean and his group of leaders were upset with me. Three different times that afternoon, members of the leadership group made sarcastic comments to me about 'sabotaging' the camp. I thought it was because my actions were seen as encouraging all the campers to ignore the challenge to not eat any meat that day. I thought I was also being blamed for the disruption of the schedule. Later, I believe, I learned what they were really upset about."

"Oh?"

"When most of the campers had decided not to embrace

the challenge to be vegetarians that day, the worship leaders had to change some of the liturgy planned for service that night. The liturgy the leaders had prepared for the communion service included references to our 'unity to all nature and brotherhood with all creatures.'"

"Let me make sure I understand you," I replied. "The liturgy they meant to use talked about mankind's 'brotherhood' with animals?"

"Yes."

I paused and rubbed my chin before asking, "And what was this 'brotherhood' with animals was all about?"

"I'm not sure, but it was obvious that 'brotherhood' implied that mankind should not be eating animals."

"Objection!" Bob called. I could have seen that coming.

"Speculation!"

"Sustained," Judge Browne said. "I would ask the jury to disregard that last statement. Richards, you may continue."

"Thank you, Your Honor." I turned back to Fred. "So this was the worship service that evening after the morning communion where the Neil Diamond song was played?" I was making sure the jury followed the flow of the story.

"Yes."

Ready to sum up this narrative and make our point, I asked, "And, in your opinion, what was the point of this worship service?"

Fred leaned forward with honest frustration. "That's the point. I was raised in a Christian home, was saved at the age of eight, and have sought to learn and grow almost every day since, but I must tell you I don't know what that service was about at all. I can only guess the service was supposed to make the campers feel sad and maybe think that they had been lied to in the past."

"Lied to about what?"

"I really don't know. I asked the camp dean about the song and the service. He said the whole service had been recommended by the conference camps' curriculum design team. Finally, he admitted he was part of the curriculum design team, but he didn't tell me anymore about what they hoped to communicate in the service."

Knowing Fred's story was a long one, I was hoping to draw attention to major points. "Let me get this straight: the camp dean helped create the curriculum for the camp, but couldn't tell you what this service was meant to communicate to the kids?"

"Right. He acted like it was the most natural thing in the world, and I was being antagonistic just for asking about it."

"He acted like you were being antagonistic?"

"Right. He kept saying that the curriculum committee had worked very hard to create a positive experience for the kids. That was the only answer he would give me."

"After the communion service and your talk with the camp dean, what did you do?"

"Every night before bed the youth would meet together with the counselors from their local churches. When we met with our kids, they were upset because they felt like our church group was being blamed for messing up the camp. We talked about what they were being taught in their small groups. Some of the kids said they were being taught they hadn't been doing enough to save our environment and to connect with nature. They didn't think they were learning about the Bible or Christianity. They felt confused. We talked about packing up and going home. Turns out, they were eager to go home.

They didn't want to go to their small groups or to any more worship services at the camp. The kids were convinced that what they were being taught was not Christian."

"Did all fourteen of the kids want to go home?" I had to ask, or Bob would.

"Some felt strongly about it, some didn't want to stay if others were leaving. By that time, it was after eleven. We decided to go to bed and leave the next morning. The kids were going to call their parents and let them know what was going on. I called our pastor and told him what was happening. He said he would drive to the camp and meet with us all at breakfast. The next morning our pastor was there, having driven all night. We all ate breakfast together at the same table. The pastor said he knew the camp dean and the other leaders. He said he knew they meant well and were very hurt that we were not open to some of their ideas. He offered to stay for the last two days of camp with anyone who was willing to stay. He thought it would be offensive and hurtful for us to leave. He said we would be sending a very negative message to all the other kids at the camp if we left.

"I told the pastor that I wouldn't stay and that my two children would be coming home with me. I told the kids each of them could make up their minds what they thought was best. All the kids said they were ready to go home. So, we all loaded up on the bus and went home."

By now I knew Bob was feeling good about his defense premise: that my clients were people who couldn't get along within a large and diverse organization. I could imagine him shaking his head and frowning at Fred throughout his testimony. I never so much as glanced his way, but I could picture his satisfied look.

That's okay. Fred's story represented hundreds and hundreds of others. The jury would have to decide where the fault lay. I would not avoid this complicated story. Most real-life stories really are this complicated. I was content to proceed. "Was that the end of this situation?"

"Oh, no. Once we got home there were meetings with parents and the pastor almost every other day for two weeks or more."

"What was the nature of those meetings?"

"Some of the parents couldn't understand what the problems had been at camp. Some of them didn't think I had set a good example for the kids while I was at camp, and several thought I should have supported the pastor more."

"What was the end result of these meetings?"

"It got to where the parents who supported my actions and those who didn't were taking sides against each other. None of the parents really disagreed with the concerns I had while at the camp, but some thought I should have supported the pastor's recommendation that we stay and finish the week of camp. I decided to resign as a youth group sponsor. I thought that would be the end of it."

"That was not the end of it?"

"No. The next thing I knew, our kids came home from a youth group meeting and told us that the guest speaker that night had encouraged them to support 'women's rights over their own bodies.' They were being taught that a woman should always have the right to end a pregnancy 'legally and safely.' It turns out that the guest speaker was a member of our Church and Society staff at our conference headquarters."

"Fred, let me stop you for a moment. I need you to tell the jury what *The Book of Discipline* says about abortion."

"*The Book of Discipline* says, 'We cannot affirm abortion as an acceptable means of birth control'."

"Now, Mr. Whitaker, is that a direct quote or just your wording?"

"That is a direct quote. 'We cannot affirm abortion as an acceptable means of birth control.'"

"And you are telling this jury a paid member of the staff of the conference headquarters was teaching abortion is an acceptable means of birth control. That the woman has a right to choose abortion as a method of birth control."

"Right." Fred turned to the jury. "That is what I am saying."

I paused momentarily to let this sink in before asking, "Is that when you left the church?"

"No. You may think I am rather dense, but I still thought our pastor would want to know about what had happened and would do something about it, so my wife and I met with the pastor. He told us he thought we were too easily offended. He encouraged us to teach our children all sides of an issue and let them make up their own minds." Fred paused and dropped his head. "He asked us to consider why it was we felt the need to cause controversy and divisions in the church. He said we might be well served to consider seeing a marriage counselor, or family therapist."

You could have heard a pin drop in the courtroom. Fred's demeanor was not angry or defensive, but sadly factual. When he said his pastor had suggested he and his wife get counseling, every juror seemed to realize they would have to take sides in a very personal issue. They were not being asked to make a decision concerning legal issues only. The legal issues would require they make a judgment concerning the emotional and relational health of a large group of plaintiffs, as represented by Kyle and Fred.

I had selected this jury based upon this one guideline: could this jury understand the emotional and relational dynamics that led to my clients giving up and withdrawing from the denomination? I was trusting that they could.

"Mr. Whitaker, let me clarify a few things." I knew where Bob was going to go with this, and I wanted to cut him off at the pass. "Are you saying your issue is that you cannot get along with people who support abortion?"

"No, no. Not at all. I may not personally support it, but I've never cut people out of my life just because we disagree. If I did that, I wouldn't have any friends or family left."

The jury chuckled, and I offered a brief smile. "Indeed, Mr. Whitaker. Indeed. Why, then were you so upset about this speaker?"

"Well, the biggest issue was the speaker was going directly against our denominational policy and stance. And, I think what was worse was that our pastor didn't care. In fact, he was angry at *us* for being upset."

In sympathetic tones, I asked Fred, "So, is this when you left the church?"

"Well, at first, I thought my family and I would just withdraw for a little while. But the more we talked about it the more foolish we felt."

"Why did you feel foolish?"

"You know, it was like we were Germans living during the holocaust, denying that our government could be so wrong. We surrounded ourselves with people who believed in the United Methodist Church. We couldn't believe good Christian people like us were part of an apostate denomination. We read about the things taking place in other conferences, but we hadn't understood the same things were happening in our district and even in our local church."

Turning to the jury with an urgency to be understood, he added, "I won't say that our pastor was apostate, because I never heard him deny the basics of our faith. I can say he talked in circles. But I finally had to admit that if I couldn't even say for certain what my pastor believed, then I was in the wrong church. I felt foolish because I never even considered what strange teachings my children might be exposed to at our church camp. If I hadn't been there, I wouldn't have believed it. And then, when our pastor wanted to pretend everything was fine at the camp, I began to feel foolish. And, at that last meeting, there was nothing I could say. He thought I was limiting my children's understanding of the world they live in, and I don't know what else. I didn't try to talk him out of it. I figured he had already made up his mind about my wife and me, so we just thanked him for meeting with us and walked away kind of stunned-like.

"Even then, we did not want to give up on the denomination. We transferred our membership to St.Paul's, as I said earlier. We were active there for another two years before Kyle resigned his ordination and left the denomination. That is when we officially left."

"Thank you. No further questions, Your Honor."

"Let's take a quick recess, and begin cross-examination after lunch."

# CHAPTER 35
## FRED WHITAKER'S CROSS-EXAMINATION

*"If we return only what can be justified by standards of prudence and convenience at the bar of enlightened common sense, then we exchange revelation for that old wraith Natural Religion."*

— C.S. LEWIS

After recess, we returned to the courtroom, where Fred once more took the stand. Judge Browne reminded him that he was under oath and, looking to Bob, told him he may proceed.

"I first want to address your views about abortion," Bob announced. "You do know that abortion is legal in most states in our United States of America, don't you Mr. Whitaker?"

"Yes, I do."

"And, am I correct in assuming you would like to see restrictions placed on a woman's right to choose her reproductive options and to maintain control over what happens to her own body?"

"Some restrictions, yes."

"Would you elaborate for the court what kind of restrictions you would support placing upon women's rights?"

The conversation had almost seemed academic and business-like to this point, but Fred was obviously unwilling to discuss this subject convivially. Taking a deep breath and turning to face the jury, Fred said with conviction, "I would like to restrict anyone from stopping the delivery of a baby once its head has crowned, just before the fully formed baby would fully exit its mother's womb, then sticking a sharp hook up its neck and into its brain, cutting the baby's brain to pieces. That is one of the restrictions I would support."

Bob had not been prepared for Fred's tone to become aggressive, but this behavior fit into the scenario Bob was trying to promote. Therefore, Bob used the opportunity to focus on Fred's anger.

"Mr. Whitaker, you sound like a very bitter man."

It wasn't really a question, but Fred responded anyway. "Yes, I think I am."

Once again, Bob was taken back by the honesty. You would think he would have learned by now my clients were not defensive about their beliefs or their emotions. And, again, Bob still believed he could use my clients' transparency against them.

"Have you stopped to consider, Mr. Whitaker, that your bitterness may be the reason others don't want to hear what you have to say?"

"Yes sir, I understand that, but I also believe it is a sin to not be angry about barbarism, or lack of humanity, especially toward evil."

"So, Mr. Whitaker, are you directly stating to this court that a woman claiming her reproductive rights and control over her own body is evil?"

"I am saying that those who approve of what has come to be known as 'partial birth abortions' are either exceptionally naïve as to what they are doing or, yes, they are evil."

"Mr. Whitaker, do you know your legalistic judgment makes you a minority in this country?"

"No. I do not know that. I believe there are multiple current surveys demonstrating that the American public views partial-birth abortions as unacceptable."

Each time Bob seemed to think he had won a significant point, Fred doubled-down, raised the stakes, and pressed on.

Bob, on the other hand, was not ready to go all-in on this hand. Trying to lessen the stakes while still characterizing Fred as the agitator, Bob continued, "I am not sure why you have decided to drag this court through the issue of partial-birth abortion, Mr. Whitaker. The issue of partial-birth abortion has never been one that the United Methodist Church has made direct rulings about, has it?"

"No, Mr. Chaney, not directly, which is part of the –"

"Excuse me, Mr. Whitaker," Bob interrupted, "would you please just answer yes or no?"

Bob must have been terribly flustered to have made such a mistake.

I stood halfway, which was more assertive than this jury had seen me be before, "Your Honor, please direct the defense attorney to allow the witness to answer the question."

Judge Brown calmly stated, "Mr. Whitaker, you may answer the question."

"Thank you." Looking to the jury, Fred continued, "I wish the denomination would directly address the issue of partial-birth abortion. I am always in favor of people being honest about what they believe about such important issues. But to answer your question, Mr. Chaney, what has happened in the denomination is, despite *The Book of Discipline* claiming that abortion is not an acceptable means of birth control, the denomination continues to support other social agencies that promote the availability of all forms of abortion. Last year alone the General Board of Church and Society gave over five million dollars in donations to radical pro-abortion groups."

"Mr. Whitaker, your bitterness may be getting the best of you. Would you tell us what you mean by 'radical pro-abortion groups'?"

"Yes. I would categorize any group who promotes the legality of partial birth abortions as radical. I would categorize any group that resists legislation requiring abortion providers to offer their clients fully-informed choices by giving women relevant information concerning their choice 'radical.' I would call any organization 'radical' that refuses to acknowledge scientific facts concerning the infant in the womb."

"Thank you, Mr. Whitaker," Bob stated smugly, as if he had just made a point. I made a note to ask Fred about the 'scientific facts' in my redirect to come. Bob quickly redirected away from Fred's last statement by raising a new issue.

"So, is it fair to say, Mr. Whitaker, you believe you know what is best for young women who find themselves with an unwanted pregnancy?"

"If you are asking if I think, once more, that abortion is wrong, the answer is 'yes.' But that is not the point."

Bob looked bemused. "Then what, pray tell, is the point?"

"The point is that the Methodist Church has a clear doctrine on abortion, and its leadership was violating that doctrine, and attempting to hide its violations by claiming 'understanding.' That is, in my opinion, dishonest."

I watched as Bob shuffled his papers. Once again, he was shaking his head and sighing as if Fred had confessed his sin. "No further questions, Your Honor.'"

"Very good, thank you, Mr. Chaney. Mr. Richards, would you like to redirect?"

"I would, Your Honor."

"Very good. Let's take a fifteen-minute break, and come back for redirect." She banged her gavel, we all rose as she left and the jury filed out, and I took a few minutes to reflect.

I wasn't sure how to judge who won this encounter. Bob was thrown off course and never got back on track. Fred answered Bob's questions authoritatively, but I was not at all sure the jury saw through Bob's attempt to make the issue about Fred's belief, rather than the Church's handling of it. So, maybe a draw. But a draw is a loss for the lawyer doing the questioning. The lawyer must make his case with every question he raises. Bob certainly failed to do that. The best he was hoping for was to paint Fred as an arrogant bigot. The jury would have to decide if Fred was being arrogant, or was just heartbroken over the lies and deception.

# CHAPTER 36
# THE REDIRECT OF
# FRED WHITAKER

*"Be sure there is something inside you which, unless it is altered, will put it out of God's power to prevent you being eternally miserable."* — C.S. LEWIS

Standing in my usual spot, holding a tablet filled with notes, I began my redirect. "Mr. Whitaker, you stated that you, and I quote, 'would call any organization "radical" that refuses to acknowledge scientific facts concerning the infant in the womb.' Is that an accurate quote?"

"Yes, it is."

"And, Mr. Whitaker, do you know for a fact that part of the money you gave to your local United Methodist Church was channeled into some of these radical organizations?"

"Yes, I do."

"Objection! Lacking foundation."

"Sustained. Richards, please establish a foundation."

"Whitaker, how do you know that your money was being funneled to these organizations, despite the official statements in *The Book of Discipline?*"

"Because I was also on the funds appropriation committee."

"And you were aware of the list of organizations that received church funds?"

"Yes, I was."

"Would you tell this court how you feel about the money you gave being used to support these radical organizations?"

"Shocked, angered, betrayed. I can't imagine any religious organization that claims to value life being so willing to betray their own statements. My church took a stance I agreed with, but behind my back, they were undermining that stance." Fred's "rant" was stated calmly and clearly, but he couldn't keep his voice from cracking as he finished his last sentence. Unashamedly, he looked at me with tears in his eyes.

I let the pause linger while I consulted my notes.

Fred took the moment to wipe his eyes and clear his throat with a drink of water.

Dear reader, I know how hard it can be to not be drawn into your own personal discourse with Fred as you read. You may agree or disagree. You may challenge his "facts" or share his tears. But I want to redirect YOU to the purpose of this writing. I am not asking you to determine if Fred is right in what he believes. I am only making the point that he genuinely believes what he says he does, and that he had reason to expect that the denomination to which he belonged supported him in what he believes. I want you to believe that his feelings of shock, anger, and betrayal are real and appropriate *for him* and every member of the United Methodist Church who expected *The Book of Discipline* would actually be followed by the denominational leaders (as each had made vows to do).

"Okay, so let me close with one last question. I want to go back to when your pastor stated that 'You were limiting your children's understandings of the world they live in.' and that 'you should go for counseling.' What did you feel"?

"I felt like he had slapped me. The pastor and I, along with our wives, had been through Bible Studies together, served on committees together, and attended dozens of youth events and social events together. I always showed him respect.

He knew my wife and kids. He knew how I study issues and discuss them with my family and friends.

"I am not bragging, but my kids have been leaders in the church for years. They are joyful, curious, adventurous kids, with a string of successes and recognitions I could bore you all to death with." During his pause I could hear a few chuckles from the jury. "And, my wife, whether this makes her sane or insane, loves me. We are best friends even though, in some ways, we are as different as night and day.

"No, I have to say, I think the pastor said what he said just to let me know that he did not want me back at church. He couldn't say it directly, of course. He – apparently – couldn't even talk about his religious beliefs directly, but I thought the message was loud and clear. He would rather us not be active in the church."

My timing was impeccable. After the perfect pause and with just the right tone of sarcasm, I stated, "No further questions, Your Honor."

Judge Browne asked Bob if he intended to re-cross Mr. Whitaker.

"Not at this time," Bob said, "but I would like to reserve the right to recall him later."

She nodded then asked me, "Do you rest your case?" This was a moment I had been preparing for. "No, your

Honor, I would like to call Mr. Marshall Carr as an adverse witness and Bishop Dan Davidson to follow."

Bob's response was immediate. "May we approached the bench your Honor?"

Judge Browne dismissed the jury for the day and invited all four of the attorneys to meet in her chambers.

Four chairs were placed in front of the Judge's desk. Bob

and I sat next to each other with our associates seated at out sides. Bob put forth a valiant effort at holding in his anger as his associate argued I shouldn't be allowed to call "his" witnesses and I should be required to wait for my opportunity to cross-examine them after the defense had questioned them. I sat looking as innocent as I knew how, while my associate, William Evers, argued against the motion being made by Kenton Webb.

"Mr. Carr and Bishop Davidson are listed as witnesses for the defense," Mr. Webb argued. We agreed to a very limited number of witnesses so that both sides could find the best representatives out of very many that could be called upon from both sides. We submitted the names of our witnesses, and they submitted theirs. Now, the plaintiffs want to change the agreements we made."

"Not true, Your Honor," Kenton retorted. "Our agreements never stated that witnesses could not be called by either side at any time. Our agreements simply limited the number of witnesses to those specifically named by each side. We agreed to include Mr. Carr and Bishop Davidson in the witness list. We never agreed to not call upon them."

This encounter only served for the defense to make objections (letting their frustration out) without the jury hearing. Judge Browne showed her patience with the defense team when Mr. Webb insisted that we recover and read the verbiage of the court strategy agreement we had made, but eventually stated, "I have no legal reason to deny the plaintiffs any witness the agreement lists."

By calling Marshal Carr and Bishop Dan Davidson as my witnesses, I could stand to gain a lot: 1) I could send a message to the jury that I was not afraid of anything these men have to say, 2) I would get to question them first, and redirect them after Bob had his turn with them, and 3) I would get to leave Reverend Tom Jenkins, the chairman of the Conserve our Faith Coalition, as the only witness Bob gets to call. This would leave jury with the impression that Tom was strictly a witness for the defense – their only witness, in fact.

Bob had chosen not to cross-examine my two witnesses on any other subjects. His only goal had been to depict them as "unable to fit into a large organization." But the fact was that if the jury had to reach a verdict with only what they had heard so far, they could not be against my clients. But neither would they award significant damages for my clients unless I could accomplish the difficult task of showing the denomination, and their chosen witnesses in proxy, as having intentionally betrayed their sworn contracts with my clients.

It is not enough that the jury like and appreciate my clients. To some serious extent, the jury must dislike the witnesses for the defense. It was the only way to assure a judgment awarding us the huge amount of money I was seeking.

So, this was a new card game. Any wins gained so far just earned us the right to continue into this next game.

# CHAPTER 37
# Marshall Carr Takes the Stand

*"You must show that a man is wrong before your start explaining why he is wrong. The modern method is to assume without discussion that he is wrong and then distract attention from this (the only real issue) by busily explaining how he became so silly. In the course of the last fifteen years, I have found this vice so common that I have had to invent a name for it. I call it Bullverism."*

— C.S. LEWIS

After Mr. Carr was sworn in, I returned to my usual place. It was easy to tell he wasn't too happy about being called as my witness, which made sense. He and Bob had rehearsed his testimony and I had disrupted that. Another benefit to my strategy.

I began my questioning as gently as I could. "Mr. Carr, thank you for your willingness to offer your testimony. Could you begin by telling this jury a little bit about yourself?"

Offering the jury a smile he hadn't offered me, he began, "I'm Ohio born and raised. My wife and I married just before I earned my engineering degree. I've worked as an engineer for the Ford Motor Company for the last twenty years. We have two married daughters, and five grandchildren so far. My wife and I are ardent basketball fans and love to travel to NBA games."

"Mr. Carr, how long have you been a member of the UMC?"

"Since I was twelve years old. I am fifty-seven now, so,

for forty-five years."

"And you've been an active member of the denomination?" "Yes, I have served in just about every role there is in the local church. I am a certified lay speaker, I have been a Sunday School teacher, Sunday School superintendent, chairman of the administrative board, and a dozen other positions in the local church. I have also served on several district and conference boards and committees. I have been a delegate to our annual conference nine times, and a delegate to general conference twice."

"Am I right in saying you have to be elected by the other delegates of the annual conference to become a delegate to the general conference?"

"Yes."

"So, that would indicate you are held in high regard by the other lay delegates to your annual conference?"

"I believe so."

Marshall Carr was an attractive gentleman. His hair was more white than gray. He looked healthy but not formidable, neither over nor underweight. He had light blue eyes that made me want to look directly at them. His hands were resting in his lap. He seemed steady and capable.

If Mr. Carr expected me to be an unfriendly adversary, he was mistaken. I intended to show him as much respect as I possibly could.

"Mr. Carr, can you tell us a little bit about your faith?"

"I can give a pretty good summary by making two statements. My faith is reflected in the Apostle's Creed, and the phrase used by John Wesley, 'unity in the essentials, diversity in the non-essentials.'"

"Am I correct in understanding the Apostle's Creed states

the essentials of your faith?"

"Yes, Sir, it surely does." It was the first time he called me "Sir". That was progress.

"Mr. Carr, I would like the court to hear the Apostle's Creed, but I am not sure I would say it all correctly. Would you recite it with me to help me out?"

"Objection!" Bob's voice rang out. "Relevance?"

"It is relevant, Your Honor, because we are establishing Mr. Carr's faith and the basis of his faith." "Overruled."

"Thank you. Carr, would you proceed?"

"Surely." With a clear, confident voice he recited: "'I believe in God the Father Almighty, Maker of heaven and earth, and in Jesus Christ, his only begotten Son, our Lord: who was conceived by the Holy Ghost, born of the Virgin Mary, suffered under Pontius Pilate; was crucified, dead and buried. He descended into hell. The third day he rose again from the dead. He ascended into heaven and sits at the right hand of God the Father Almighty, from thence He shall come to judge the quick and the dead. I believe in the Holy Ghost. I believe in the holy catholic church, the communion of saints, the forgiveness of sins, the resurrection of the body, and the life everlasting. Amen.'"

"Thank you, Mr. Carr. That was beautiful. Now, would you agree that *The Book of Discipline* is the standard for the profession and practice of faith for United Methodists?"

"Yes."

"But *The Discipline* is subject to change every four years at the General Conference?"

"Yes."

"Is it true that, as of now, *The Book of Discipline* reflects conservative positions on controversial issues, such as abortion and the ordination of self-avowed practicing homosexuals?"

"Yes, Mr. Richards, that is correct."

"Are you concerned that those positions might be changed at some future conference?"

"I really doubt it. If that happened, then it would be time for the conservatives to leave the church."

"Mr. Carr, do you ever consider leaving when these controversial issues are being discussed and debated?"

"No, Sir. I think it is good to discuss the best ways for people of faith to address the needs of our culture."

"What are your thoughts about those who share your faith, but have left the church?" He looked a little confused, as if he was searching for a trap, some way I would trip him up or discredit him.

"I don't understand them. The big issues are about abortion and the ordination of self-avowed practicing homosexuals. Like we just said, *The Book of Discipline* statements are as conservative as they can be. Even though there are motions to modify those statements every four years at general conference, the statements are always affirmed, and the proposed changes are rejected. What more could those people ask for?" "So, you are telling this jury the denomination has repeatedly affirmed the conservative position on these controversial issues?"

"Yes, every time."

"So, why would a conservative, who supports *The Book of Discipline* as it now stands, leave the denomination?"

"I don't know, but I could guess." I imagined that Bob had instructed Marshall that he would not be allowed to conjecture as to what others may think, and here I was inviting him to do so.

"What is your guess?" I wondered if Bob would object, thinking that I was setting Mr. Carr up so I could discredit him. I wasn't, and he didn't.

"I think those who have left the church want to control things. Even though *The Book of Discipline* says exactly what they would hope for, it is not good enough for some people. It seems to me they want to monitor and police everyone else. Well, we have a system that has worked for millions of people. The system has allowed us to develop amazing ministries literally all over the world. We've cared for people and proclaimed the gospel for over two hundred years. But I guess that is not good enough for them. They want everyone to think and believe exactly the same or they are upset. Every member, past and present, made a vow to support the church with their prayers, their presence, their gifts, and their service. Those who left the church have broken their vow. I don't understand why."

"Mr. Carr, I hear your passion and I not only understand it, but I really do appreciate it. So, maybe you understand the passion my clients have for this case. If you personally knew that apostates, who don't believe in The Apostle's Creed as literal, historic truth are being ordained as elders, would you feel betrayed?"

"Let me state, Mr. Richards, as directly as I can, that I do not know of any apostates being ordained into the United Methodist Church." He paused and seemed to think I was about to interrupt him. I nodded for him to continue. "But, if that were to happen, I have confidence that when that person began preaching and teaching in a local church, the leaders of that church would do something about it. They could notify their district superintendent or go directly to the bishop of their conference. Since I was asked to testify at this trial, I have studied *The Book of Discipline* even more than I had in the past. And, if it is okay with you, counselor, I would like to point something out."

"Please do," I said, gesturing toward him.

"There is a whole section in *The Book of Discipline* that has to do with bringing charges against the clergy. Among the list of charges that can be brought are, and I quote, for 'disobedience to the Order and Discipline of The United Methodist Church,' or for 'dissemination of doctrines contrary to the established standards of doctrine of the Church.' Anyone can bring charges against any pastor at any time. A trial will be conducted according to guidelines clearly stated in *The Book of Discipline*."

"Thank you, Mr. Carr, that is a very good observation. As a matter of fact, are you aware that such charges have been made many times in the past ten years?"

"Yes, Sir."

"And, over the last ten years, how many charges of apostasy have reached church trial?"

"I am not aware of any, although several charges of disobedience to the Order and Discipline of the Church have made it to trial."

"I may need to explore with you and before this jury the cases that made it to trial, but for now, you are stating, as far as you know, no cases involving the charge of 'disseminating false doctrines' have reached the level of a church trial?"

"Yes, as far as I know."

"Am I right in understanding that, if a charge is brought against a clergy member, a Committee on Investigation consisting of seven other clergy members is convened and that at least five votes are required before any charge will be presented for trial?"

"Yes, that is the case." He seemed a little surprised that I knew such details from *The Book of Disciple*.

"And who chooses which seven clergy members are on the investigations committee?"

"The bishop of the conference in which the charge was made."

"I'm sure you have had the opportunity to meet Bishop Dan Davidson, who will be testifying before this court soon." "Yes, I have."

By this time in his testimony, Mr. Carr was visibly relaxing. I continued inquiring. "If a charge had been brought against a clergy member in the conference he was serving, he would have been the one to choose which seven clergy members would be on the Committee of Investigations?"

"Correct, if charges are brought by the Committee of Investigations."

"Then, before a trial is convened, doesn't the issue get referred to the chairperson of the BOM, and then to the Joint Review Committee? So there is a trial only if it is recommended by the Committee of Investigations, then the Board of Ordained Ministry, and the Joint Revue Committee? Am I getting that right?"

"Yes, I think that is the case. The process is meant to hopefully dismiss the charge or correct the behaviors or beliefs of the clergy member being charged before engaging in a trial."

"So, hopefully, a trial wouldn't be necessary?"

"Of course. A trial is a very last resort."

"Mr. Carr, I want the jury to understand this process. Am I right in saying that the charge first goes to a committee of seven clergy members appointed by the bishop?"

"Right."

"Then it is referred to the chairman of the Board of Ordained Ministry?"

"Yes, if there seems to be merit to the charges."

"Then the charges would be forwarded to a joint committee consisting of one district superintendent nominated by the bishop, two board of ordained ministry members nominated by the chairperson, and three clergy members, one nominated by the bishop and two by the chairman of the board of ordained ministry. Correct?"

"I believe that is correct."

"So, everyone involved in this comprehensive process prior to an actual trial is nominated by either the bishop or the chairman of the board of ordained ministry. Correct?"

"Correct."

"Now, Mr. Carr, I have a very important question about all this. Let's imagine that the pastor being charged was a person whom the bishop had previously ordained and the chairperson of the board of ordained ministry was the same person who had recommended that the person be ordained? Would that bishop or that chairperson be required to recuse himself from the proceedings?"

"Not that I know of."

"So, if one of my clients were to press charges of apostasy against a member of the clergy, they would have to trust the same bishop who ordained that clergy member, and the same chairman who recommended that clergy member be ordained in the first place? Wouldn't those filing the charges have to trust that the bishop or chairperson reviewing the charges would be open to the idea that they had made a terrible mistake in supporting the clergyperson's ordination in the first place?"

"Yes, they would have to trust the bishop and the chairperson."

"Because, obviously, the bishop or the chairperson could divert the process away from a trial at several points along the line, couldn't they?"

"I guess they could."

I had been asking lots of leading questions, but Bob hadn't objected. I think he knew that the Judge would allow me some leeway with, what was technically, an adverse witness. I think he also recognized that neither Mr. Carr nor the jury would appreciate him for it. I continued. "You recognize that there would be some conflict of interest in that both the bishop and the chairperson had already read his or her doctrinal statements and conducted their interviews and approved the person once before, and now were being asked to decide if that appointment were correct?"

"Yes."

"You recognize that these two people, maybe more than any others, are aware of the theological leanings within their conference and the controversies between the more conservative and more liberal of their members?"

"Yes."

"And you recognize that these two people, the bishop and the chairman of the board of ordained ministry, are given extraordinary influence over this complex process leading up to a possible trial?"

"Yes."

"So, isn't it true that the bishop and the chairman of the board are expected to use the power and influence of their positions to make sure that a charge doesn't result in a trial? Between them, they are given no less than four mandated opportunities to see if the issues can be resolved without the necessity a trial. Correct? After all, *The Book of Discipline* states 'church trials are to be regarded as an expedient of last resort.' Correct?"

"That is correct, yes."

"Okay. Mr. Carr, I need you to make a declarative statement for this court, if, and only if, you absolutely believe it is true. Would you say the bishop and the chairperson of the board of ordained ministry have significant opportunities and significant pressures to keep a charge from reaching the final step of going to trial?"

A pause of honest consideration preceded Mr. Carr's response. "Yes, I believe that is true." After another pause of consideration, Marshall stated, "I believe it is true the bishop and chairperson who manage charges of apostasy against one of their clergy members have significant opportunities, significant influence, and significant pressure to resolve the issue prior to it reaching a church trial."

"Thank you, Mr. Carr. I will tell you now, I would like to use that exact statement in my closing argument to this jury."

"Fine."

"Thank you. Now, I want to point out that you expected to be called as a witness for the defense in this case. Correct?"

"Correct."

"And, to this moment, you believe the jury, despite the statement you just made, should find the United Methodist Church not liable for breach of contract with my clients?"

"Yes, I do."

"Can you tell the jury why, in light of the opportunities

and pressures placed on the bishop and chairperson to keep a charge from resulting in a trial, my clients are wrong, in your opinion, to have given up on the denomination?"

"Gladly, Mr. Richards. The reason is easy enough. I think the bishop and chairperson of the board of ordained ministry are trustworthy. I know the people in these positions throughout the denomination are those who have earned the trust of their peers over many years of faithful service. They have come to these positions due to the trust that their peers have in their integrity. They are trustworthy."

"That, Mr. Carr, is a very good reason. I see the logic in how you reached it. It is a persuasive reason, and it does deserve the attention of this jury. I would even go as far as to say that not every bishop and every chairperson must be trusted, but that if there are more that can be trusted than those who cannot, then the process should still be able to safeguard the denomination against the established practice of tolerating apostates as clergy members. Would you agree?" "I hadn't thought it through that far, but yes, I agree." Marshall and I are being very serious with each other, not as adversaries, but as fellow deliberators thinking this subject through.

"Now, Mr. Carr, I don't want to put words in your mouth, but am I correct in saying you have a pretty firm confidence that the majority of bishops and chairpersons would not cave into the pressures of avoiding a trial?"

"I would like to say that, but obviously, I don't know very many bishops or chairpersons of the boards of ordained ministry."

"Right. So, I really didn't ask a totally fair question." "Not totally fair, no."

"Okay. I want to make the question a fair one, so let's go

with a bishop you do know and who will soon be introduced to this court: Bishop Dan Davidson. Would you trust Bishop Dan Davidson to stand against the pressures of avoiding a trial?"

"Yes, I certainly would."

"So, if I were to demonstrate to you that Bishop Dan Davidson could not be trusted to stand against the pressures of avoiding a trial, would you think my clients were right to give up hope for the denomination?"

"Objection! Calls for speculation!" "Sustained."

Dear reader, I want you to consider that this entire course of questioning has been leading to this moment. Both Marshall Carr and I had proceeded in polite, conversational tones. We never even raised an issue which put the two of us at odds with each other.

But then, Marshall had realized I planned on putting the entire weight of my case on the shoulders of Bishop Davidson. Marshall knew I intended to show the bishop to be untrustworthy. So, not only would his answer influence the jury to place all this weight on the Bishop's testimony, but Marshall would be committing himself to agree with the verdict should the jury rule against the church. I needed to get him to this point, but I needed to switch tactics.

"Mr. Carr, do you believe a covenant is important?""Yes, I do."

"What, in your opinion, are some of the most important covenants?"

"Well, there's the covenant of marriage between a husband and a wife. There are business covenants – although we call them agreements. And there's a covenant that God makes with men who trust Him."

I slowly nodded. "Yes, those are important covenants. Now, you're a businessman, correct?"

"I am."

"Would you tell the court what you do for a living? We've heard your very impressive church record, but what do you do for a living?"

"I am a general manager for a concrete company. We handle concrete for construction projects."

"How long have you been doing that?" "Fifteen years."

"So, you've had a lot of business agreements – covenants – correct?"

I saw Bob jump up out of the corner of my eye. "Objection! Relevance!"

"Your Honor, I'm establishing Mr. Carr's authority to speak on the issue of agreements and covenants, which is central to this case."

"Overruled. You may proceed, Mr. Richards."

"Thank you. So, you've had lots of business contracts, correct?"

"Yes. I've dealt with hundreds, maybe even thousands." "Now, tell the court what types of agreements you make with your clients."

"We set up delivery agreements: how much concrete, date and time of delivery, location, price, that sort of thing."

"And this agreement is a type of covenant, correct?" "Yes, I would say so."

I pause in order to think. "A few moments ago, you said that the United Methodist Church has upheld its end of the covenant made with members because its doctrines are spelled out clearly in The Book of Discipline. Let me see if I can quote you –" I consult my notes "– there: '*The Book of*

*Discipline* statements are as conservative as they can be.' Were those your words?"

"As I recall, yes."

"So, because the *Discipline* has not been changed or altered, the covenant remains strong?"

"Yes, I would say so."

"Allow me, for a moment, to offer a hypothetical. Let's say you agree to deliver so many tons of concrete to a particular location, on a particular day, at a particular time. That normal?"

"Yes, perfectly."

"Now let's say that day and time arrive, but you only deliver half of what was promised, but for the same price. Would you say, in your professional business opinion, that you were upholding the contract?"

"No, I would not."

"Why not? The contract was in writing, was it not?"

"It was, but both parties have to actually act on the agreement. If one of them fails to do as promised, or fails to keep his or her word, then the contract has been violated."

I remain friendly and amicable, but I am suppressing a large grin that is threatening to spread over my face. "So, an agreement is more than words, it is also actions?"

"Yes, that is correct."

"Are you familiar with the official Church doctrine on abortion?"

"Yes, the United Methodist Church does not endorse abortion at any level."

"As stated in the *Discipline*?"

"Yes, that is my understanding," I say, nodding slowly. "Now, you weren't here yesterday, but we heard testimony that, not only did a speaker come into a United Methodist Church and tell the listeners that a good Methodist would support abortion, but the church leadership also supported that speaker. Let me get those notes for you." I turned to my partner, who handed me the stenography notes from Fred Whitaker's testimony. I handed Mr. Carr a copy. "Would you please read, aloud, lines fifteen through twenty-six?"

Marshall cleared his throat. "Certainly, but some of the names are redacted."

"That's fine. Just read what you can."

He nodded and began: "Mr. Richards: 'And you are telling this jury a paid member of the staff of the conference headquarters was teaching abortion is an acceptable means of birth control. That the woman has a right to choose abortion as a method of birth control.'

"It's redacted. 'Right. That is what I am saying.' "Mr. Richards: 'Is that when you left the church?' "Again, redacted. 'No. You may think I am rather dense, but I still thought our pastor would want to know about what had happened and would do something about it, so my wife and I met with the pastor. He told us he thought we were too easily offended. He encouraged us to teach our children all sides of an issue and let them make up their own minds. He asked us to consider why it was we felt the need to cause controversy and divisions in the church. He said we might be well served to consider seeing a marriage counselor, or family therapist.'" Marshall stopped and looked up. He blinked rapidly. "That is from a former member of the UMC. Would you, again in your professional opinion, consider this a breach of contract if it had taken place in the business world?"

Marshall Carr swallowed hard. His eyes darted back and

forth, between me and Bob. He swallowed again, and blinked several more times, his eyes large behind his horn-rimmed glasses. "Was disciplinary action taken?"

"No, though the bishop was made aware."

Again, Marshall blinked rapidly, but this time he licked his lips. "I – I, uh ... yes, I would."

"No further questions, Your Honor."

Rather than cross-examine, Bob asked to approach the bench. The judge called us forth and Bob offered his proposal: "It is time for lunch. I will waive my cross if Mr. Richards will agree to postpone calling his next witness until Monday morning."

"Well?" she asked me.

I agreed. I had the weekend to pour over all the sources of information I had concerning Dan. Bob, conversely, had the weekend to prepare "my" witness for his testimony.

# CHAPTER 38
# BISHOP DAN DAVIDSON
# TAKES THE STAND

*"I cannot understand how a man can appear in print claiming to disbelieve everything that he presupposes when he puts on the surplice. I feel it is a form of prostitution."* — C.S. LEWIS

Bishop Dan Davidson, my friend, my role model in many ways, was sworn in and took the stand. I intended to hit him with everything I had.

"Bishop Davidson, for the sake of the jury, will you tell us your history of ministry in the United Methodist Church?" He gave his attention to the jury as he went through his resume. He didn't elaborate on the details, but shared enough that the jury was impressed. He ended with, "And now, I have been honored with the responsibility of representing the denomination and, more specifically, the Council of Bishops of the United Methodist Church in this trial."

"Thank you, Bishop Davidson. I want to begin by exploring the opportunities you have had to offer some encouragement or discouragement to my clients. Many of them have looked to your example for many years to help them determine if it made sense for them to hold out hope for the denomination...."

"Objection," Bob stated, "The counsel is testifying." Judge Browne sustained the objection and I changed my approach.

"Okay, let's start with an event that happened on January 16th, 1999. Dan, do you have personal knowledge that on that date ninety-five United Methodist ministers gathered in Sacramento, California to bless the union of a lesbian couple?" "Yes, I am aware of that."

"Is it also true that seventy-one more United Methodist clergy lent their name to this ceremony *in absentia?*"

"Yes, that is also true."

"Of course, there were charges filed against these ministers."

"Yes."

"Will you tell this court what became of those charges?" "The Investigative Committee dismissed the charges." "Did the Investigative Committee dismiss the charges because the charges were proven false?"

"No, the charges were dismissed because the committee determined the charge against the ministers was not a proper charge for trial."

"Okay, so the committee found the charges they were given were not proper for trial."

"Yes."

"Isn't it true the charges they were given were not the original charges filed against these one hundred and sixty-six ministers?"

"Yes, that is true."

"So, what happened to the original charges?"

"Bishop Talbert and his cabinet designed and substituted their own set of charges."

"Bishop Talbert was the bishop over the California Conference where this event took place?" "Yes."

"Could you tell this jury why the bishop and his cabinet would change the charges that were being brought against these one hundred and sixty-one pastors?"

"No, I really can't. I was not present for those discussions." "I understand, but I guess Bishop Talbert was within his rights to change the charges. He had that authority according to *The Book of Discipline*?"

"Yes."

"Am I right in assuming Bishop Talbert would have known, even before the investigative committee ruled, that the charges he substituted for the original charges would not qualify for trial?"

"I can't say what Bishop Talbert knew."

"Okay. That is fair. Bishop Davidson, if I were to look up 'chargeable offenses' in the index of *The Book of Discipline* and find that it directed me to Paragraph 2623, how long do you think it would take me to read the single paragraph that details the chargeable offenses that can be brought against a clergy member of the denomination?"

"I doubt that it would take you more than five minutes." "So, isn't it reasonable for us to conclude Bishop Talbert, or at least one member of his cabinet, knew what would and would not be accepted as a chargeable offense for trial?"

"Objection! Calls for speculation!"

"Your Honor, Bishop Davidson is more than qualified to testify as to what kind of knowledge bishops should and should not have."

"Overruled. Bishop Davidson, you may proceed." "Yes. That is a reasonable conclusion," Dan said.

"Right, of course it is. Why do you think the bishop intentionally changed the charge?"

"I have no first-hand knowledge."

"Okay. And here is where I bring this event back to you and your first-hand knowledge: Would you tell this jury what actions you or the council of bishops took in response to this obvious subversion of the *Discipline?*"

"We wrote an open letter to the members of the denomination stating our affirmation of *The Book of Discipline*."

"You wrote a letter … to the members of the church … but what about Bishop Tobert? What about the one hundred and sixty-one pastors who had defied the policy of the church? What did you do about them?" I suddenly realized I was clenching my fists, and made a concentrated effort to unclench them.

Regathering myself, I continued. "Did you or the council of bishops take any action in response to the obvious subversion of the *Discipline* by Bishop Tobert?"

"No. We did not."

"I know you can't speak for the entire council of bishops, so I am just going to ask you to speak for yourself. Bishop Davidson, why didn't you file charges against Bishop Talbert?" "I was elected to the bishopric in 1998. I hoped to learn the ropes and earn my place among the council." "That was not the question I asked."

"I didn't want to overstep my bounds," he said resignedly. "Overstep your bounds? Okay. I want to understand this. I have been led to believe that bishops are bishops for life, unless dismissed by trial or by their own resignation, correct?"

"Yes."

"So, you didn't have to worry about somehow being kicked off the council?"

"No."

"So, maybe you disagree with *The Book of Discipline* concerning same-gender marriages?"

"No. I agree with *The Book of Discipline*, but what those

one hundred and sixty-one ministers were performing was not a marriage, it was a blessing of their union. At least that was the vocabulary which was used. So, the charge of a direct disobedience to the *Discipline* was debatable. There was room for disagreement."

"So, what you are telling this court is, it depends on what the definition of 'is' is?"

"Objection, your Honor! Badgering the witness."

I wasn't doing very well at holding my attitude in check. Bob got me.

"Sustained," said Judge Browne (although I must point out that she said it gently).

"I apologize Your Honor, and to you, Bishop Davidson."
"I understand." Of course, the jury couldn't help but like Dan. He hadn't been anything but cooperative so far. I still had to convince them he was not to be trusted. So, I went for it.

"So, you wrote a letter to try to encourage the members of the denomination not to assume that *The Book of Discipline* was being intentional subverted?"

"Yes."

"But you didn't mention Bishop Tobert and the one hundred and sixty-one pastors had just gotten away with a fast one, did you?"

"No, we did not. I assumed the message did get across though."

"But, Dan, what if the exception becomes the rule? What if those disobedient to the *Discipline* always seem to find a way around it? At what point does the denomination lose its integrity and become a façade?"

"I don't know." Dan made this statement in a tone I find hard to describe, even now, all these years later. It was spoken with honesty and with regret, yet I still felt it held something sinister.

"Dan, I have one final question about this incident. In your mind, would you consider it understandable if those who originally filed the charges against Bishop Tobert and one-hundred and sixty-one pastors, resolved that the contract they held with the United Methodist Church had been breached?"

Knowing the significance of this question, Dan answered, "No, not technically. We were very clear about our intentions to uphold the *Discipline*."

"Okay. Let's look at another incident, but before we do, I move for adjourning for lunch break, Your Honor."

Judge Browne agreed and off we went. You see, I was trying to keep these events clear in the jury's mind even as I piled one on top of the other.

I considered this session a draw, which was good for me. It would help keep the jury engaged, giving them time to live with the growing sense of despair I would present them with, just like the process my clients went through.

# CHAPTER 39
## EXAMPLE NUMBER 2

*"Our business is to present that which is timeless (the same yester-day, today, and tomorrow) in the particular language of our own age. The bad preacher does exactly the opposite: he takes the ideas of our own age and tricks them out in the traditional language of Christianity."* — C.S. LEWIS

"Bishop Davidson, the next event I want to ask you about directly involved you. I am referring to the events at the 2000 General Conference. Would you set the stage for the jury by explaining the nature of a general conference and your role in the exceptional occurrence that took place that year?"

Dan nodded. "The General Conference is held once every four years," he explained. "A group of delegates is chosen by their respective annual conferences so all our conferences, across the globe, are equally represented. Only at the General Conference may *The Book of Discipline* be amended. Different bishops are asked to preside over different sessions of the conference. During the session in which I was presiding, significant events occurred which, I assume, are the ones Mr. Richards is referring to."

"Yes, it is. Thank you. I will summarize the petition that was debated, but please clarify for me if I misstate it. In the session over which you presided, the petition to change the prohibition against the ordination of self-avowed practicing homosexuals and the performing of marriages for same-gender couples was being debated, correct?"

"Yes."

"When it seemed likely the petition was going to be

defeated, a group of protestors disrupted the conference, true?"

"Yes."

"Fifteen bishops joined in the pre-planned demonstration, right?"

"Right." "Fifteen?"

"Yes," Dan replied patiently.

"And here I have a copy of the Denver Post article written about this event, holding it up. Would you read aloud the highlighted portion to the jury?"

Dan read clearly and steadily:

*"One distraught woman nearly toppled from a balcony to the convention floor. People grabbed the woman, Jeanne Smiley from California, afraid she planned to jump from the balcony during the debate on the burning issues of gay ordinations and same-sex unions. Meanwhile, twenty-seven more protesters were arrested Thursday after disrupting the conference.*

*Bishop Davidson and others talked to the protestors for almost half an hour before an agreement was reached that they could remain in the aisle during the convention. But the agreement broke down when they lost a vote on gay unions and the protestors went to the stage and refused to leave."*

He stopped reading and looked up.

"Thank you, Bishop. Is this article accurate, as far as you remember?"

"Yes, it is."

"After the petition failed, the protestors failed to keep their agreement and they returned to the stage. Of the fifteen bishops who joined the protest, do you know how many of them broke their agreement with you and returned to the stage?"

"I was not trying to keep count."

"Okay, but we do know there were at least two bishops who broke their agreement with you and returned to the stage, because two bishops were part of the group that got arrested. So, at least two, right?"

"Yes."

"Is it also true that a representative from Africa stood in the midst of the protesters who had crowded around the microphone and pleaded with the other members not to 'kill the church in Africa' by supporting the amendments to change the wording of *The Book of Discipline*?"

"Yes. That is true."

Trying to move Dan into statements he wouldn't feel so comfortable saying, I tried to lead him by matching his calmness. "Do you know why the African delegate would proclaim that a change in the wording of *The Book of Discipline* concerning the ordination or marriage ceremonies for self-avowed practicing homosexuals would kill the church in Africa?'

"I think I do," Dan stated, all too calmly it seemed to me. "Would you explain to the jury why such a change could kill the United Methodist Churches in Africa?"

"First, let me say that I don't necessarily agree that the change would have such drastic consequences for the African churches."

I quickly jumped on this statement because I wanted the jury to note the first signs of Dan being defensive. "Nevertheless, you do know why a member and representative of the African churches would make such a claim?"

"Yes."

"Please tell the jury why that would be."

Looking at me instead of the jury, Dan hesitantly explained, "The United Methodist Churches in Africa are theologically and culturally unprepared to embrace such changes in *The Book of Discipline*. The representative quoted in the article had reached the conclusion that if such a change was made, the members of the African United Methodist Churches would leave the denomination."

"Why do you feel the African representative was overreacting?"

"I can't say he is wrong about the possibility," Dan said calmly, "but I'm certainly not convinced his fears were valid."

"Okay, but why? Why don't you think his concerns were valid?"

"I did say it was possible."

I had him. He was refusing to answer my direct question. "Your Honor, I would like to register the witness as non-responsive."

"Noted," Judge Browne said smoothly. "Move on."

"Okay, Bishop Davidson, this leads me to an important part of my clients' complaint against the United Methodist Church which you have not been present in the courtroom to hear yet. My clients have asserted systemic racism as a contributing factor to losing faith in the denomination. They claim that the African church receives less than half the representation to general conference that their over six million members deserve. Why did a delegate have to beg forty-nine percent of the membership of the denomination to not make a change that would be catastrophic for fifty-one percent of the membership of the denomination? Can you help us understand why the African church composes fifty-one percent of the membership of the United Methodist Church, but only has twenty-four percent of the delegates at general conferences?"

Dan showed no defensiveness or surprise at the question. "Each of our annual conferences is appointed equal representation. The African churches have organized such that their annual conferences are, on average, over twice as large as the average membership of the other annual conferences around the world."

"So, correct me if I'm wrong, but what I hear you saying is that the African churches became a victim of their own success by growing their membership more than the rest of the denomination?"

"Yes, I think you could phrase it that way."

"Did there ever come a time when the African churches recognized that having annual conferences with over twice the average memberships of the annual conferences limited their representation to the general conference and attempted to restructure themselves by forming more but smaller annual conferences?"

"There have been discussions along that line," Dan admits.

"Can you explain why those discussions have yet to lead to a reorganization of the African churches so that they gain proportional representation at general conference?"

"I was made aware of some of such conversations, but I understand it would be a complicated process that I was never fully up to date concerning." Dan has returned his attention to the jury and seems to expect them to accept this obfuscation as a difficult, sad, and unavoidable reality, but I won't have it!

"Isn't it true that one reason the African churches have

not reorganized is that the council of bishops has made it known that they would not approve the expenses of establishing so many new conferences in Africa?"

"I have never seen a formal statement from the council of bishops to that effect," Dan answered.

"The lack of a formal statement does not mean that such a statement has not been made, maybe even behind the scenes, does it?" I've raised my voice a notch.

Dan is nothing but honest, even if he is obfuscating. "I have no knowledge of that."

"Do you have any reason to doubt that the council of bishops would resist the reorganization of the African churches and reference finances as one of their reasons?"

Dan seemed to pause to dissect my question to find a way to avoid a direct answer, but ended up saying, "I don't have any reason to doubt that."

"And, isn't it true that if the African church were to reorganize, they open themselves up to the council of bishops assigning apostate bishops from another continent to oversee one or more of the new conferences?" I've raised my voice another notch.

Dan shows some indignation toward me by slightly raising his voice and proclaiming, "I've not agreed to your accusation that there are any apostate bishops in the United Methodist Church!"

I lower my voice and offer a moderating statement. "No, you're right. I suppose you haven't, have you?" I flip through my notes briefly. "I want to look deeper into the events of the particular day on which you were chairing the session of the general conference in 2000. Did you personally hear any protesters make provocative threats that they would stage Sunday morning protests against any pastor who spoke out in support of the traditional UM position on human sexuality?"

"Yes. I heard some threats being made."

"Were any of those threats being made by any of the bishops who were part of the demonstration?"

"I can say that I definitively heard one of the bishops make threats."

"Did any of the bishops who were part of the demonstration try, in any way, to stop the threats or to distance themselves from them?"

"Not that I know of."

"So, and correct me if I'm wrong, we know there were fifteen bishops who originally joined in the demonstration, and at least two of them directly broke their agreement with you and disrupted the conference until they were arrested, correct?"

"Correct."

"And the two who were arrested were guilty of a crime, another chargeable offense, correct?"

"The seventeen who were arrested were originally charged with a misdemeanor, but soon all charges were dropped."

"So, maybe, the two bishops who were arrested were not technically guilty of a crime?"

"Correct."

"Or maybe, even in the civil courts, those who were in position to press charges against the protestors declined to?"

"Correct."

"And, if it came down to one person whose position it was to press the civil charges, wouldn't it have fallen to the bishop who was presiding over the conference at that time?"

"That is correct."

"Which would have been you, correct?" "Yes,"

"But you declined to press charges against those who had to be hauled out of the conference by the police?" I allowed my voice to take on a touch of incredulity.

"No. It didn't come to that. After the lawyers got involved, a letter was drafted to the courts in which we declined to press charges."

"Lawyers for whom? What are you referring to?" I was firing questions at Dan.

"Lawyers for the United Methodist Church drafted the letter to the courts the very night of the arrests."

"Oh, I see," I replied in a tone that I hoped communicated to the jury that this action reflected even more negatively on the denomination. However, I didn't elaborate on that point because I didn't want to take the focus off of Dan's individual role in the general conference session.

"Now Dan, as the presiding bishop of this session of the general conference, it was you who chose not to stop the demonstration when it was initiated. You could have insisted it stop right then and there, or the police, who were already present, could have been asked to escort the demonstrators out right away, correct?"

"Yes. I chose to give the demonstrators a little time to make their protest."

"And, as the presiding bishop, it was you who allowed the demonstrators to remain in the session while the debates concluded and the votes were taken?"

"Yes, that was my decision."

"The demonstrators remained in the aisles where they could take note of who voted for them and who voted against them, after the threats had already been made, correct? So, the bullies were allowed to watch and see who voted against them?"

"I didn't think the threats were serious. They were just emotional outbursts."

"You didn't think the threats were serious, but can you tell us today that the duly-elected representatives who held sincere beliefs against the ordination of self-avowed practicing homosexuals and the marriage of same-gender partners felt the same way? Can you tell us that they didn't take the threats seriously?"

"No, I cannot."

"You allowed the bullies to watch the vote, which was taken by the raising of hands?"

"That is correct."

"As the presiding bishop of this session, it fell to you to bring charges for church discipline against the bishops who helped stage the demonstration, correct?"

"I do acknowledge that I would be the most likely candidate, but any of the delegates could have brought the charges."

"But you were the most likely candidate, and when you didn't do it, what kind of message did you think you were sending to others who felt charges should have been brought?"

"I had other avenues of addressing this issue. I had relationships with several of those bishops. I made my frustration and disappointment with them clear, privately and individually. I thought I had the most influence that way."

"Dan, let me repeat my question; When you, the most likely candidate to press charges, didn't do it, what kind of message did that send? Remember, we are talking about bringing charges against bishops!"

"I can't know what message, if any, was perceived by my

choices. I won't try to make guesses."

"I understand that, Bishop Davidson, but wouldn't you agree that the way you managed that session in 2000 is still affecting general conferences today?"

"How do you mean?"

"I am thinking of the 2012 session of general conference. Isn't it true that the 2012 General Conference was a slightly less volatile, but still anxiety-ridden, repeat of the session you presided over in 2000?"

"Yes. There have been petitions made to change our statements concerning abortion and homosexuality in every general conference I have attended."

"I have an article that summarizes the 2012 session by saying that the proposed amendment was that *'United Methodists disagree on whether homosexual practice is contrary to God's will," indicating all sides of the issue choose to remain unified and coexist. This would have essentially made all the current language moot. The amendment was defeated by a vote of 441 to 507. Following the vote, a group of those in support of the amendment began a demonstration that effectively shut the conference down until after the lunch break that day. Despite the efforts of the presiding Bishop, Bishop Coyner of Indiana, to call the session to order.'*

"Does this article sound accurate to you? "Yes, it does." "Don't you think that, if you had been more assertive during the 2000 General Conference, and even pressed the civil charges or the church discipline charges you could have against the demonstrators, maybe the faithful and true delegates to the conference would not be subjected to these dramas every four years?"

"Objection! Calls for speculation!" To be honest, I had

forgotten Bob was even there.

"I withdraw the question," I stated before Judge Browne could rule against me. "Bishop Davidson, don't you know of conservative members of the church who have repeatedly attended general conferences, who grew weary of being treated to threats and demonstrations and stopped seeking to be elected as representatives to general conference now?"

"I don't know any who have said that would be their only reason or the determinative reason for them not to go." He was obfuscating again.

"Bishop," I asked slowly and directly, but without angry tones or volume, "how could any of my clients who participated in the events where you were the designated authority ever trust you to uphold *The Book of Discipline* during any other controversial situation you found yourself in?"

"I did not act in contraction to *The Book of Discipline* at any time you just mentioned," Dan responded with the same voice I had employed, looking me in the eyes.

"No," I said, "you just failed to stand up for the principles of the denomination and for any others who supported them."

"Objection! Badgering the witness, again, Your Honor," Bob stated as he slowly stood up. "Sustained," stated Judge Browne, and she sounded upset at me, "Mr. Richards, I expect better behavior from you. Let's adjourn for the day." She punished me by leaving her reprimand to me the last thing the jury heard that day.

It wasn't until that moment I realized we had gone well beyond the time we usually adjourned for the day.

# CHAPTER 40

# Example Number 3

*"Dear friends, although I was very eager to write to you about the salvation we share, I felt I had to write and urge you to contend for the faith that was once for all entrusted to the saints. For certain men, whose condemnation was written about long ago have secretly slipped in among you."* — JUDE

"Good morning, Bishop Davidson. Let's pick up where we left off. Since the event in 1999 when one hundred and sixty-one pastors blessed the union of a same-gender couple and the disruption of the General Conference in 2000, have other UM pastors performed blessings of the unions of same-gender couples?"

"Yes. Many."

"And, did these 'blessings' serve as a wedding ceremonies?" "Yes."

"And, have all the ministers in these events been charged with disobedience of the Order and Discipline of the denomination?"

"A few have."

"And have any of these pastors been found guilty?" "Yes. A couple have."

"Of those found guilty, have any been forced to surrender their ordinations, been refused future appointments, or been removed from membership in the denomination?"

"No. Though some have chosen to withdraw their membership."

"Okay. With that background, let me ask you about an incident in 2005 involving Reverend Edward Johnson. Do you remember the case?"

"Yes."

"Would you tell this jury about it?"

"Reverend Edward Johnson refused to accept an individual into membership in the local church he served because the individual was a self-avowed practicing homosexual."

"Was there a charge brought against Rev. Johnson?"
"There was."

"By whom?"

"By Bishop Charlene Prammer, who presided over the conference that included South Hill, Virginia, where Reverend Johnson's church is located."

"What was the charge?"

"I think the charge was 'failure to perform the work of the ministry.'"

"That is one of the chargeable offenses listed in Paragraph 2623 of *The Book of Discipline*. Do you think it applied to Reverend Johnson?"

Dan made a slight pause before answering, but gave his honest opinion. "No. It did not."

"Nevertheless, the reverend was placed on involuntary leave of absence, correct?"

"Yes." "Do you think there was any hope of Reverend Johnson being reinstated to ministry in that conference as long as Bishop Prammer was presiding there?"

"Objection! Calls for speculation."

"Your Honor," I countered, "I am asking for Bishop Davidson's professional opinion."

"Objection sustained," the judge answered. "Please move on.

This was a blow to my hand that I didn't need, but I had

no choice, so I continued.

"Is this another example of a bishop twisting the meaning of the words of the *Discipline* to fulfill her own liberal theological agenda?"

"I can't know that for sure."

"That is fair, but let's bring this back to you. As a bishop, couldn't you have filed charges against Bishop Prammer for disobedience to the Order and Discipline of the church?

"Yes, I could have filed charges. I don't know that the charges would have held up."

"So, why didn't you file charges?"

"I didn't think it would be productive."

"So, a pastor who is faithful and true gets kicked out of his own church, and you have nothing to say about it? But a bishop who acts out of order is not even reprimanded?"

"I can speak my mind, and I did, but I didn't think it would help to file charges against Bishop Prammer."

"I see. Now, Dan, I want to tell you why I am asking again about you filing charges against one of these clergy members who blatantly disregard or manipulate the Discipline and Order of the United Methodist Church. I am raising this issue with you because you are the standard bearer, the one chosen by the council of bishops to represent them. I assume they chose you because you best embody the character of the denomination. You are a conservative believer, correct?"

"Correct."

"You probably agree with Mr. Carr, the other chosen representative of the UMC, that the Apostle's Creed is literally and historically true."

"I do."

"And, you have expressed to me your conviction that all

Christians should share 'unity in the essentials and diversity in the non-essentials.'"

"I have."

"So, my clients, who are also conservative believers, share a common faith with you and Mr. Carr."

"I believe that is true."

"But, Bishop Davidson, here is the problem. My clients have given up hope that the UMC intends to enforce the terms of agreement set forth in contract form in the document known as *The Book of Discipline*. When Mr. Carr and I discussed this problem, he said it came down to a matter of trust in leaders like you. As a matter of fact, since you are the representative chosen by the denomination the issue becomes even more focused –"

Bob interrupted, "Your Honor, is Mr. Richards conducting his closing argument now?"

I don't blame him. I haven't left him much to do.

"This is a necessary part of my question, Your Honor."

"Get to the question, Mr. Richards." Again, I have to say she sounded frustrated with me.

"The question, Dan, is can we trust you to follow the Order and Discipline of the denomination? Are you, personally, guilty of sabotaging those who would try to hold the apostate and disobedient pastors accountable to *The Book of Discipline*?"

Looking me in the eye, Dan stated, "I am not prepared to admit or deny that. I can say that in the examples you have asked me about so far, I am in no way guilty of disobedience to the Discipline and Order of the UMC. I understand that your clients may wish I had done things differently, but I have followed my conscience and applaud all other parties for doing the same."

In tones of reconciliation, I pressed in. "I don't doubt that you have followed your conscience. I understand that your reputation for honesty and integrity has been earned over the many years of your ministry. So, I need to ask you if your unwillingness to file charges against those individuals involved in abusing their roles of authority and the Discipline and Order of the denomination in the situations we've discussed yesterday and this morning ... does that represent you also gave up on the denomination long ago?"

"Not at all," Dan asserted. "I always believed people of good faith would eventually be able to find our way together." "Are you describing the bishops who threatened delegates at General Conference, and the bishop who removed a faithful pastor from his church, as people of good faith?"

"As far as I know. I can't know another person's heart. I know those bishops were raised to their positions of service in the denomination for good reasons."

"Are you now telling us that you still expect they and you will be able to find your way together in the same denomination?"

"Yes! That is my expectation!" Dan proclaimed. I have to admit that this answer caught me off guard. Remember the maxim about not asking a question you don't know the answer to? This time it was me who had committed the unforgivable folly. I tried hard not to show my surprise and hoped to find a way forward with my questions. But, in my delay to respond, Dan jumped in with further comments. "I'm sure you and the jury are aware of the recent revival events at Asbury University! Asbury is a United Methodist university, as I'm sure you know! Videos of the events went viral on the internet. The whole Christian community in the United States have been encouraged and inspired. I've always believed such revival was possible, and I'm not going to stop believing for revival now. I won't ever believe that division in the United Methodist Church is inevitable until it has actually happened," Dan boldly proclaimed.

So, I asked another question I didn't know the answer to but that I would need to know in my prosecution of this case. Letting my voice take on a stunned tone, I asked, "Bishop Davidson, are there other bishops who share your belief that the United Methodist Church will not divide?"

"Yes, there are others," he offered. Then, anticipating my next question, Dan added, "But I couldn't tell you how many." Dear Reader, I know I've represented myself as an Ace in the card game we're playing, but at this moment I found myself performing with a card value of a two or three. In hindsight, I know that I stood in my usual spot with my hands at my side and face frozen in dumbfounded, lock-jawed, stupidity. My mind was racing to catch up with what I had just heard. I had assumed there was some form of agreement between the powers that be in the denomination that there would be a new denomination formed, already initiated and named The Global Methodist Church, that the conservative pastors and churches would be able to move their membership into with the blessing of the remaining United Methodist Church. I had believed there was a commitment from those who would remain to help those forming the new denomination with twenty-five million dollars a year for the first four years of the formation of The Global Methodist Church. I believed it was settled that the pastors who waited until the split was formalized would be allowed to keep the entirety of their retirement accounts.

I knew it was the common understanding among the pastors and churches who remained in the United Methodist Church that it could be a testament to their godly intentions if they remained until such a peaceful and loving separation could be orchestrated. Now it was dawning on me the con-game among the powers-that-be may have risen to a new level. Not only had the apostates found a way to sidetrack a majority vote of the general conference for "The Traditional Plan," but were now positioning themselves to win a general conference vote to prohibit more disaffiliations from the denomination unless the local congregations were willing to surrender their buildings and assets. They had allowed the most verbal pastors and congregations to disaffiliate, while maintaining their properties and assets, just long enough to get rid of the leaders who would oppose them at general conference and the local churches who could afford to challenge them in civil courts.

I couldn't let myself continue contemplating all that at the moment. I needed to reengage with the jury. I couldn't let the jury leave for lunch with Dan's proclamation ringing in their ears. I jarred myself back into action. Though now I admit my next statements were ill-considered, I glared at Dan and stated, "I guess I will need to bring up the events where you were the actual perpetrator of violating *The Book of Discipline*. I think the jury will agree you gave up on the denomination years ago."

This time, Bob objected with the tones and volume expected to represent his disgust with me, "Your Honor, Mr. Richards is testifying, badgering the witness, and...."

"Sustained," Judge Browne stated in her own exasperation. "Members of the Jury, I instruct you to disregard Mr.

Richard's last statement. And, Mr. Richards, I am prepared to hold you in contempt if you continue this conduct."

All I could say was, "I understand, Your Honor."

Over the next hour and a half I walked Bishop Davidson through a litany of historic events. After each reference I asked him if there was any hope in any of the events being reviewed, overturned, or otherwise used for the establishment of accountability to *The Book of Discipline*.

I asked if Bishop Davidson could give us a reason to hope based upon the 2007 dismissal of the president of Asbury seminary in Kentucky even though there was nothing immoral, unethical, or illegal charged against him. He was dismissed for being "too conservatively based". "I'm not at liberty to address that situation," he claimed. "There were some details of the actions that are subject to non-disclosure agreements."

I raised the issue of the resolution passed in the 2008 California-Pacific Annual Conference stating that, *"while we recognize we are governed by the Book of Discipline ... we support those pastors who conscientiously respond to the needs of their parishes by celebrating same-gender marriages...."*

"Does this statement make any legal sense to you?" I asked him. But, he wasn't shaken and answered calmly that it did not, but that he couldn't represent the intentions of those who wrote it.

I asked him about a 2008 statement within the Conserve our Faith newsletter that stated, "When the Conserve our Faith Movement was called into being in 1994 ...we did not then and have never since, had the open support of our active orthodox United Methodist Bishops ... all active Bishops have kept a safe distance from the Conserve our Faith Movement and all other renewal organizations."

"Did this statement misstate your involvement or support of the Conserve our Faith Movement?"

"I've never felt like the Movement has needed or solicited my direct involvement," he stated.

As with the other examples, Bishop Davidson calmly dismissed any accountability for the rise of apostasy and ordained apostates in the denomination. He didn't seem disturbed by the events, and he didn't seem to let them diminish the hope he had for the UMC.

All these examples, and a dozen others I could have provided, were about what Dan had not done (sins of omission). I felt the need to go directly to testimony about what he had done (sins of commission). But I was unwilling to pretend he had any justification for failing to defend the Doctrine and Polity of the denomination. I certainly would not fail to point out the examples of when he, personally, had been guilty of disobedience. He had to know the examples I planned to bring. He knew Kyle Fedder was one of my witnesses, and he could not have forgotten the role he played in sabotaging Kyle's initiatives. Well, it was time to stop being passive; it was time to go for broke.

# CHAPTER 41
## SINS OF COMMISSION

*"These men are blemishes at your love feasts, eating with you without the slightest qualm."* — JUDE

"Bishop Davidson, would you describe to this court the purpose and the procedure of an executive session?"

"The executive session is for full members of the conference only, those ordained as elders. It is the first session of every annual conference. The board of ordained ministry presents the candidates they are recommending for ordination as elders. The order of service includes an exhortation to the elders to be aware of their duty in voting conscientiously. The candidates are presented, and the votes are taken."

"Is it accurate to say that during an executive session the bishop follows a prescribed ritual of inviting any elder of the conference to challenge a recommendation of the board of ordained ministry? Every bishop in every conference reads the same exhortation?"

"That is correct."

"Have you ever personally witnessed an elder challenge a recommendation of the board?"

"I have."

"Who issued that challenge?"

"That would have been Reverend Fedder."

"Is it true that copies of Mr. Fedder's petition had been distributed to all the members of the executive session?"

"Yes. That is true."

"And, at the appropriate time, Mr. Fedder read his petition word for word before the executive session?"

"Yes."

Turning to Judge Browne, I declared, "Document was entered into evidence as 'plaintiff document number seven.'" Redirecting myself to Dan, I continued, "We have presented this court with that very petition and it is being handed out to each of the jury members. As they silently read along with you, would you read aloud the petition put before you and the Executive Session by Kyle Fedder?"

After patiently waiting for the copies to be distributed, Dan read the petition aloud in a calm and clear voice:

*Fellow Elders of the Okla. Conference of the United Methodist Church, I come before you this afternoon to express my opposition to the Board of Ordained Ministry's recommendation of Teresa Moss to ordination as an Elder.*

*I have limited this opposition statement to two primary concerns: the first is theological, the second questions Teresa's commitment to this covenant community. Each of these concerns are based upon a face-to-face discussion between Ms. Moss and me.*

*The first of two statements that Ms. Moss made in response to my efforts to discuss her theology was that she does not believe in bodily resurrection of Jesus. Despite the fact that the apostle Paul proclaimed, 'If Christ be not raised from the dead, then our preaching is in vain and so is your faith,' Ms. Moss stated that she does not accept that Paul believed in the physical resurrection of Jesus.*

*Although this is the only theological statement by Ms. Moss that I can claim first-hand knowledge of, I believe it is more than sufficient cause for this covenant community to reject the Board of Ordained Ministry's recommendation of her. The second statement Ms. Moss was willing to make was that she had been approved by the board; recommended for ordination, and 'encouraged to continue to be a representative of radical theology.'*

*What is this 'radical theology?'*

*I don't know. Teresa refused to discuss it and has denied the board of ordained ministry permission to release the doctrinal statements submitted to them. Refusing to cooperate with appropriate and responsible theological inquiry is not indicative of an appreciation for, or a commitment, to covenant community.*

*My initial concerns over Ms. Moss' Christology and Soteriology have never been addressed. Other than her rejection of the Bodily Resurrection of Jesus, I cannot claim a direct knowledge of Ms. Moss' theology for one reason only: Ms. Moss has not allowed her beliefs to be made known, even for the expressed purpose of properly representing her theology to this assembly. Teresa Moss' actions are an avoidance of covenant community. We should acknowledge them as such and deny the recommendation for her ordination.*

*I understand that this opposition to Ms. Moss' ordination to elder is not an action against her personally, but is an inquiry into the ministry's recommendation of her. Therefore, I request that the board elaborate on their recommendation to this executive session. Specifically, I request answers to the following questions:*

*Was the board of ordained ministry aware of Ms. Moss' rejection of the Bodily Resurrection of Jesus?*

*What doctrinal statements could have been referred to when the board of ordained ministry encouraged Ms. Moss (in her words) to 'continue to be a representative of radical theology'? and Can the board of ordained ministry assure this executive session that Ms. Moss' Christology is not pantheistic, and can you clarify for us her Doctrine of Soteriology?*

*I do not question Ms. Moss' character, gifts, or minis-*

*try abilities. However, in view of her rejection of Jesus' Bodily Resurrection, and her questionable commitment to covenant community, I oppose the board of ordained ministry's recommendation of Ms. Moss for ordination as an elder.*

"Thank you, Bishop Davidson. Would you tell us what happened after Kyle finished the reading of this petition?"

"There was some discussion then the vote was taken. Reverend Moss was approved for ordination."

"How was the vote taken?" "By a show of hands."

"And, since a three-fourths vote is required for approving a candidate, I assume over three-fourths of the vote was against Kyle's petition?"

"At least three-fourths of the vote was in favor of Reverend Moss' ordination," Dan rephrased my statement.

"Dan, can you tell us what the vote count actually was?" "We didn't make a formal count of the vote."

"So, who determined that at least three-fourths of the hands were raised in support of Ms. Moss' ordination?"

"I did."

"Now, Bishop Davidson, I have sworn testimony from over a dozen pastors present at that executive session who all agree that Kyle's petition received at least twenty percent support. Does that sound accurate to you?"

"I wouldn't doubt that."

"So, Dan, are you prepared to state before this court that you were able to tell the difference between at least twenty percent support and the needed twenty-five percent vote among over six hundred pastors without an actual count?"

"I felt confident at the time."

"Okay. Let's say you were able to tell the difference

between at least twenty percent and less than twenty-five percent of the vote. Let's change the subject for a moment. It seems to me that Kyle's primary concern regarding Ms. Moss was her theology concerning the resurrection of Jesus, correct?"

"Yes."

"And is it true that one of the questions Ms. Moss was required to answer as part of her written doctrinal statements was 'What is your understanding of the Resurrection?'"

"Yes."

"So. Kyle's concern could easily have been addressed simply by reading the answer Ms. Moss had given in her doctrinal statement?"

"Possibly."

"This is important, so help us with this. Even though Ms. Moss answered the question, it is possible that the reading of that answer wouldn't solve the issue, how is that?"

"In the world of theology, words can be used and interpreted in nuanced ways. In her doctrinal statement, Reverend Moss may not have directly answered the question the way Kyle proposed it."

"Oh, I see. Reverend Fedder asked if Ms. Moss believed in the bodily resurrection of Jesus?"

"Yes."

"Whereas, Ms. Moss was only asked about her understanding of the resurrection, not if she actually believed in the bodily resurrection – a literal historical resurrection of Jesus?"

"Yes."

"So, Reverend Fedder's question was a legitimate question?"

"Yes."

"Do you agree that if Ms. Moss did not believe in the literal historical bodily resurrection of Jesus, she is apostate, and she should not be ordained as a minister of any Christian denomination?"

"Yes, I agree with that."

"Isn't it true if you knew beforehand that Ms. Moss was apostate, you could have removed her name from the list of candidates by your own authority?"

"Yes. That is true."

"Did you ever ask that question directly?" "No, I did not."

"But Reverend Fedder did, true?" "True."

"But the question wasn't answered at executive session that day, was it?"

"No."

"Whose responsibility was it to make certain that question was answered?"

"That would have fallen to me." "But you didn't, did you?"

"No, I didn't."

"And, following Kyle Fedder's presentation of the petition challenging Ms. Moss' ordination, you said that there was some discussion, followed by a vote. Would you please elaborate? What was the nature of the discussion?"

"To the best of my memory, there were questions as to why Reverend Fedder would do what he had done."

"Let me get this straight. Please stop me if I misrepresent anything," I stated while looking at Judge Browne. I was trying to communicate to the jury that I was working hard to control myself. "First, you, as presiding bishop, reminded the elders of their responsibilities to carefully consider the candidates qualifications, then, even though Kyle Fedder had been denied access to doctrinal statements – statements which *The Book of Discipline* assured his right to – when the elders were asked for objections, Reverend Fedder read his carefully prepared statement."

"That is correct."

"And Reverend Fedder's statement that had been printed and distributed to all the elders in attendance, giving them access to his questions and concerns, correct?"

"That is correct."

"And after all that, the discussion that followed was about why Reverend Fedder had the audacity to do what he did, correct?"

"Yes."

"Was there any discussion about Ms. Moss' lack of orthodox faith?"

"No."

"Was there any discussion about Ms. Moss' unwillingness for her Doctrinal Statement to be made available to the executive session?"

"No."

"Was there any response from the board of ordained ministry? Did anyone try to answer any of the questions Reverend Fedder raised?"

"No."

"So, in effect, the discussion was solely about his motivation, not his actual concerns?"

"Yes."

"And what was decided?"

"I addressed the session. I told them that Reverend Fedder had the right to raise his concerns and then I called for the vote."

"Excuse me, Bishop Davidson, but you said Kyle Fedder had 'the right' to raise his concerns?"

"Yes"

"The right? Isn't it true that, according to *The Book of Discipline,* which you and he and every other elder had taken a solemn vow to uphold, that Kyle Fedder had not 'the right,' but the responsibility and the duty to make his concerns known?"

"Yes, that is true."

"Yet, you merely affirmed his right and redirected the session toward an immediate vote, without any of the items of his petition being discussed at all?"

He was calm and collected in a way that seriously disturbed me. "Yes."

"Then you determined that the hand vote reflected more than twenty percent, but less than twenty-five percent, of support for Kyle's petition?" "Objection, Your Honor. This question has been asked and answered. Mr. Richards is dangerously close to badgering the witness again." Bob had had enough. He hoped to distract the jury from Dan's obvious sabotaging of Kyle's petition. I was willing to change my course of questioning, but I didn't try to hide my contempt for Dan's actions.

I let myself run the risk of sounding condescending to Dan when I asked, "As a man who confesses an orthodox faith, did it surprise you over four hundred and fifty of the six hundred pastors you had oversight of were not willing to fulfill the vows of their ordinations by protecting the denomination from apostasy?"

Dan didn't seem to notice my anger and answered calmly,

"Kyle's accusations of apostasy were not substantiated beyond his statements. The elders making their votes didn't know if the accusations were true."

Angrier than before, I burst out, "Was it not your job to explore those accusations?"

"Objection! Asked and answered!" "Sustained.

Richards, I'm looking at the time here, and we're about fifteen minutes over. How much more do you have?"

"Quite a bit more, Your Honor."

"Then we will adjourn for the day, and resume tomorrow morning at 9:30."

Was I badgering Dan? Maybe. His calm demeanor was upsetting to me. I needed to pray about what attitude I would allow myself the next day. Did it help for the jury to see my frustration? I am not sure. On one hand, showing my frustration could have made Bob's case for him, that my clients and I just can't get along with others (even Judge Browne). On the other hand, not showing frustration would seem to indicate that nothing significantly wrong was being discussed.

# CHAPTER 4 2
## SINS OF COMMISSION
## – CONTINUED

*"They are clouds without rain, blown along by the wind, autumn trees without fruit and uprooted – twice dead."* — JUDE

I had decided that I would seem insincere if I didn't let my frustration with Dan show to the jury. Dear reader, you must understand, I gave you Dan's history. You know about his proven character as well as his failures. You know of his intellect and charisma. If Dan choose to be passive on the stand, I couldn't make him look better than he was. In fact, I had to challenge his passiveness, to reveal it as more of a moral failure it seemed.

"Bishop Davidson, is it true in the year following his petition in opposition of Ms. Moss' recommendation by the board of ordained ministry, Kyle Fedder submitted another petition to the executive session and that, again, this session was under your supervision and authority?"

"Yes."

"What was that nature of this second petition?"

"He was asking that the board be directed to develop a process by which the doctrinal statements of recommended candidates be made available to any elder of the conference who requested it."

"Bishop Davidson, did you, and do you, consider Reverend Fedder's request to be a reasonable one?" "Yes, I did, and I do."

"Please explain why."

"Each elder was being asked to vote. It is reasonable for them to want to know about the theology of those they are being asked to vote on."

"Now, Bishop Davidson, is it true that Kyle Fedder had copies of his petition distributed to the members of the executive session?"

"Yes."

"Then, at the appropriate time, did Kyle read his petition aloud to the session?"

"No."

"No? Why not?"

"I thought it would be redundant. The members had a copy of the petition in their hands."

"Bishop Davidson, would you give this court the respect you denied Reverend Fedder that day and participate in an actual reading of the petition he presented?"

Bob was alert and prepared. "Objection, your Honor. Mr. Richards is badgering the witness ... again."

He was correct, and I owned it without remorse. "I will rephrase the question. Bishop Davidson, would you begin reading the petition aloud and allow me to make questions along the way?"

Dan began without any preamble: "'Petition to the executive session....'" Dan looked up and I indicate he should continue. "'...regarding the right of any full member of the conference to obtain the doctrinal statements of any candidate for ordination prior to executive session in which the board of ordained ministry's recommendation of the candidate is to be considered and voted upon.'" Another look up; I nod for him to continue.

"'Whereas: Each person voting is expected to vote prayerfully based on his/her personal judgment of the applicant's gifts, evidence of God's grace, and promise of future usefulness for the mission of the church....'" Again, Dan looked to me and I asked him to read the reference listed.

"'...from paragraph 412, 3 of the 1992 *Book of Discipline.*'"

"Now, Bishop Davidson, am I right in saying that *The Book of Discipline* is presented as the authoritative guide to the doctrine and practice within the UMC?

"Yes."

"And am I right in saying that a voting elder would need to know a candidate's beliefs in order to follow this *Book of Discipline* directive?"

"Yes."

"Thank you, please continue."

"'Whereas: Only those shall be elected to full membership who are of unquestionable moral character and genuine piety, sound in the fundamental doctrines of Christianity and faithful in the discharge of their duties' from Paragraph 422."

"Okay. Bishop Davidson, am I right in saying that a voting elder would need to know a candidate's beliefs to follow this *Book of Discipline* directive also?"

"Yes."

"Would it be reasonable to say that those who choose not to know the theology of a candidate, and vote for them anyway, are in violation of the practice you just read?"

"The common practice is to trust that the board of ordained ministry has fulfilled the needed oversight."

"That is not what I asked, but please continue reading."

"'Whereas: Members in full connection shall ... have sole responsibility for all matters of ordination, character, and conference relations of clergy. This responsibility shall not be limited by the recommendation or lack of recommendation by the board of ordained ministry' from Paragraph 423."

"Again, Bishop Davidson, am I right in saying that a voting elder would need to know a candidates' beliefs to follow this *Book of Discipline* directive?"

"Yes."

"And, again, Bishop Davidson, would it be reasonable to say that those who choose not to know the theology of a candidate, and vote for them anyway, are in violation of the practice you just read?"

"Yes."

"Therefore, you are telling this jury, it was your common practice to facilitate a violation of the *Discipline* in every executive session you facilitated?"

Without batting an eye, changing his tone of voice, or blushing, Dan gave the same answer, as if we weren't discussing a moral failure and breach of contract practiced regularly by himself. "Yes."

"Could you tell this jury why your duplicitous practice does not constitute breach of contract with my client, Kyle Fedder?"

Again, with no change in his demeanor, Dan answered, "That is for the jury to decide."

I paused to let his statement resonate with the jury, then asked, "Can you continue?"

Dan continued as if the only meaning to my question concerned his physical capacity to read out loud.

"'Whereas: It is the right of the executive session of the clergy members in full connection with an annual conference to receive all pertinent information, confidential or otherwise, related to the qualifications and/or character of any candidate or clergy member of the conference,' from Paragraph 733, L." Dan paused, correctly assuming I would want to ask my next question. I didn't disappoint him. After a suitable dramatic pause, and with a real look of confusion on my face, I begin louder than before, "Bishop Davidson, I'm confused. Was this policy in effect the year before when Kyle Fedder requested a copy of Ms. Teresa Moss' doctrinal statement?"

"Yes."

"And you were the presiding bishop?" "Yes."

"Yet, Reverend Fedder, an ordained elder, was denied access to Ms. Moss' doctrinal statements?"

"Yes."

When I had prepared to ask these questions, I anticipated that Dan would elaborate on his answers. I was prepared to try to overcome any ambiguity his answers might create in the mind of the jurors. But Dan offered no defense, explanation, or elaboration. You might think I would be happy with these unequivocal admissions. I wasn't. I wanted Dan to offer some ambiguity or defense for two reasons.

First, I wanted to understand how this man I had come to respect could have so blatantly ignored his own convictions and responsibilities. Throughout all our time together in the depositions and personal conversations, Dan had never defended himself to me. I believed he must have had some rationalization for blatantly setting aside the guidelines of *The Book of Discipline*. It seemed so out of character for him. Dan's decision to sabotage Kyle's efforts to hold the board accountable for its recommendations seemed contrary to everything I knew about Dan's personal history. From what I thought I knew about Dan I expected him to be Kyle's biggest fan, not his adversary. There had to be some explanation.

Dan not only impeded Kyle's efforts, but he did so while Sharon was begging him to reconsider. You know all about that event, dear reader, even if the jury did not. At some point, Dan became painfully aware his marriage was dependent upon him "doing the right thing." Still, he had officially undermined Kyle. I wanted to know why. I was ready to challenge any justification Dan would offer, yet, at the same time, I wanted to understand. I just could not believe Dan gave in to the "pressures of his office" or "betrayed his convictions." There had to be some deeply heart-felt conviction which explained Dan's actions.

I couldn't imagine what it might be.

Second, I felt Dan's passive answers were sending a message to the jury: "It was no big deal. All this fuss was exaggerated and unnecessary." I couldn't let that message stand. Even after I had made my points with the jury, I pressed on.

"So, because you denied Kyle the rights stated in this paragraph of *The Book of Discipline,* the following year Kyle was forced to create this petition to request your conference to follow policy already in place and fully authoritative over you?"

"Yes."

I knew Bob wanted to protest I was badgering the witness, but he wouldn't; the jury would have seen it as protection Dan didn't deserve.

"Bishop Davidson, we have not completed the reading of Reverend Kyle's petition, but I must ask you, why did he even need to present such a petition?"

"Because I failed to uphold the directives of *The Book of Discipline* during the executive session the previous year."

There it was. A clear indictment. But the subdued way he said it seemed to deny just how significant a confession this was. I needed to press on.

"Do you have any justification for your failure?" "I decided to let the situation play itself out."

"And how did it play out? When Kyle petitioned for a procedure to be put in place that would allow elders access to the doctrinal statements *The Book of Discipline* already guaranteed, was there much discussion about that petition?"

"No, after the petition was seconded, there was only one elder who spoke against the petition."

"Bishop Davidson," I said with incredulity, "only one elder had anything to say about this petition?"

"Other elders were moving toward the microphones, but I determined our time was short, and I called for the vote." "You only allowed one member of the session to speak concerning the petition? Bishop Davidson, do you have a clear memory of why the one elder was opposed to having the doctrinal statements made available to the voting elders?" "I remember the elder was concerned that the executive session would become a battleground."

"And Kyle Fedder's petition was voted down?" "Yes."

"What was the vote count?"

"There was no vote count. I determined the vote by a show of hands."

"You looked out over the session and determined that more hands were raised in opposition to the petition than in favor of it?"

"Yes."

"The petition only needed a 50% plus one vote to pass?" "Yes."

"Now, Bishop Davidson, I'm sorry but I need to be very clear about this. Tell me again what happened when Kyle Fedder challenged Ms. Moss's ordination the year before."

"There was a vote taken, and Ms. Moss was approved for ordination."

"Yes, but before the vote was taken, there was a discussion, correct?

"Yes."

"And that discussion was not about Ms. Moss or about the board of ordained ministry?"

"No"

Again, I knew that Bob wanted to protest that these questions had already been asked and answered, but knew that a bail-out now would be judged as a total retreat of the defense by the jury. He was right.

"That discussion was not about anything Kyle Fedder had written or read?"

"No."

"That discussion was about Kyle Fedder?" "Yes."

"About how audacious he was?" "Some."

"About who the hell he thought he was? Excuse me, Your Honor. About why he would say anything at all?" "Yes."

"And then, a year later, the reverend came back with another petition to this same group of ministers in executive session, and you called for a hand vote? A vote where all the conference leaders could see who would stand with the guy that got his butt kicked – excuse me again, Your Honor – You called for a hand vote where you, all the district superintendents, and all the other conference leaders could see who voted to facilitate, what the only elder allowed to speak, depicted as an invitation to fight?" "Yes."

"Did it occur to you that some elders might be intimidated to be seen voting for Kyle's petition?"

"No, the elders were mature leaders. They were not easily intimidated."

This was the closest I had gotten to eliciting an explanation from Dan. He expected the elders to vote their conscience. He didn't seem to notice he himself had manipulated the circumstances by not allowing debate and prematurely calling for a vote. He took no responsibility for the messages he was sending to the elders over whom he presided. My heart sunk within me as I considered that maybe I didn't really know this man at all. My feelings at that moment must have reflected Sharon's feelings as she had watched these scenes unfold.

Giving up on my hope Dan might be able to somewhat redeem himself, I pressed on, though I was unable to hide the sadness in my voice. "So, these voting elders would not be intimidated by the possibility of offending you or the district superintendents who regularly exercise the authority of moving any elder to serve any church, large or small, as you determine?"

"No, I don't think so."

"Would it surprise you to know that Reverend Fedder's district superintendent told him he had made himself unacceptable to other district superintendents? That he would not be considered to serve churches in their districts?"

"No, I was told about those conversations."

"So, Bishop Davidson," I said, my volume escalating again, "even after his career possibilities had been directly threatened . . ." I struggled to remain calm and, taking a moment to gather myself, quietly asked, "Do you think the reverend was being threatened when his district superintendent said his petitions before the executive session had made him unappointable in certain districts?"

"He was being made aware of the reality that a number of district superintendents would not consider him for appointment in their districts."

"Would you consider that a threat to Reverend Fedder's career?"

"It was a reality that had developed." Now Dan's calmness was coming across as distant and cold.

"Not a threat?"

"No. It was accurate information." He was parsing words. A quick glance at the jury told me they didn't appreciate it.

"Okay. So, let me ask you, Bishop Davidson, how did you expect Reverend Fedder to respond to this information?"

"That was totally up to Mr. Fedder."

"Did you think maybe Kyle would apologize for fulfilling his vows and for asking you and the conference leaders to follow the denominational standards as represented in *The Book of Discipline*?" My tone was sarcastic, intentionally.

"I didn't think he would do that."

"Did you think that maybe he would just sit down, shut up, and stop rocking the boat?"

"Yes, I thought he might take that course, but I wouldn't characterize it in those words."

"So, you thought Reverend Fedder might just lay low and let the controversies die down or go on without him further jeopardizing his career?"

"Possibly."

"Did you think maybe before he would give up his own integrity, he might give up on you, give up on the conference leadership, give up on the United Methodist Church and walk away?"

"I knew that was a possibility. His decision was between God and himself."

"And, one last question, Bishop Davidson. Prior to this case being filed, did anyone ever talk to you about the possibility of the denomination being sued for what you were doing to people like Reverend Fedder?"

"No."

"So, when Mr. Fedder was facing damage to and loss of his career, the denomination had nothing to worry about?"

"No. I didn't think we had any legal or financial concerns involved."

There it was. His chief concern had been legal and financial trouble. Not doctrine. Not a man's career. Not even heresy. "I have no more questions for this witness at this time, Your Honor."

Bob announced that he would not cross Bishop Davidson. I told the judge and jury the plaintiffs rested their case. Bob gave a big sigh, as if I had done everyone a favor, and asked to call his first witness following the break.

I had been prepared for Bob try to help redeem Dan under cross-examination. My redirect would have been brutal. Instead, Bob wanted to put another witness between my questioning of Dan and our closing remarks. I would have done the same if I were him.

The only witness left to call was Tom Jenkins of the Conserve our Faith Coalition. I hoped for an opportunity to recall either Kyle or Dan as rebuttal witnesses to Mr. Jenkins. I wanted the juror's last impression to be of one of them.

Dear reader, I was still reeling from the realization Dan really was not going to offer any justification for himself. I was really willing to risk losing this case just to hear Dan's motivations. Instead, all I could manage to get from this man I had come to admire was cold indifference.

# CHAPTER 43
## TOM JENKINS TAKES THE STAND

*"These men are grumblers and faultfinders; they follow their own evil desires; they boast about themselves, and flatter others for their own advantage."* — JUDE

Pastor Jenkins stood before the witness stand, ready to be sworn in.

I don't think I had ever seen anyone so happy to be sworn in to testify. As he was asked to tell the truth, the whole truth, and nothing but the truth, he didn't just answer "yes," but restated the vow all the way through and added, "so help me God," with a smile on his face.

He made me a little nervous. I would have thought that he was the witness with least to gain in this case. No matter how he testified, he was sure to offend either the denomination or the supporters of his coalition.

Pastor Jenkins had a smile for me, the judge, the jury, and for Bob as he positioned himself on the witness stand. At a younger-looking fifty-two years old, Tom was dressed expensively and wore it well. His suit was tailored. His shoes were shined. His hair was styled, and his face was tan. I almost expected him to begin his testimony by sharing, "While I was completing my daily routine of running five miles at under seven minutes per mile, I was saying to myself…."

Okay, obviously I'm prejudiced, but the way he was smiling really did concern me.

Bob, whose time in front of the jury had not been long or successful up until now, was enjoying his moment also.

"How are you this afternoon, Reverend Jenkins?"

"Doing very well, thank you."

"Reverend Jenkins, you have been called to testify before this court as a representative of the Conserve our Faith Coalition, of which you are the current chairperson. Would you introduce yourself to this jury before you describe the nature of the coalition? Could you give us a history of your career in the United Methodist Church?"

Tom was able to work into his description of a remarkably accomplished career, including references to his Doctorate degree (although he failed to mention it was bestowed as an

'honorary Doctorate') that the oldest of his four children was currently completing his Doctorate program at Denver University, "just up the road from here."

Bob asked Tom about his faith. He was happy to say his faith was "the same conservative faith represented by *The Book of Discipline* and a faith shared by both Bishop Davidson and Kyle Fedder," whom he considered to be personal friends of his.

Tom described the history of the Conserve our Faith Coalition as "having begun in 1994. Now," he proudly added, "our supporters include over 1500 churches, 7,000 clergy, and 700,000 individuals." He reported the coalition's purpose statement to be: "We exist to enable the United Methodist Church to retrieve its classical doctrinal identity, and to live it out as disciples of Christ." His definition of "classical doctrinal identity" was explained using the same statement of "unity in the essentials, diversity in the non-essentials" the other witnesses had referenced.

Tom explained, somewhat mournfully, why such unity and diversity is a hard balance to maintain. The members of the Conserve our Faith Coalition, according to Tom, were those who were more concerned about maintaining unity in the essentials, whereas other organizations within the denomination focused on protecting diversity in the non-essentials. He elaborated on the need for both sides and the inevitability of consistent frustration between the two schools of thought. He shared with the jury his personal grieving that the balance had been lost and the denomination was anticipating a long-delayed split at the upcoming 2024 General Conference. Despite the frustrations this lack of balance had resulted in over the years, he believed he was very blessed to have been a part of the UMC and looked forward, after the split, to being a part of the newly forming Global Methodist Church.

When asked if these "frustrations" had ever impacted the progress of his career within the denomination, Tom assured the jury they had not. He claimed the leaders across the theological spectrum were able to recognize the abilities and integrity of the others. "My career within the UMC has been more than I hoped for so far. I consider myself blessed and honored to serve within this great denomination." Then with the appropriate emotional quiver in his voice, "This denomination is my theological mother, and my spiritual home. I am proud of her and plan in the future to continue to enjoy all the best traditions of the UMC in the Global Methodist Church." Finally, Bob went in for the kill shot: "But, Reverend Jenkins, you know this case is about those who have decided they could no longer stay in the denomination and are not planning to be a part of Global Methodist Church even though the newly developing denomination will encompass all the elements they say they believe in and value so much. I want to ask your thoughts about their dilemma. You recognize many, if not most, of Mr. Richard's clients were once members of the

Conserve our Faith Coalition?"

"They were, and we were glad to have them."

"Yet, they chose to leave the denomination. Now, Reverend Jenkins, I want to begin by talking about the clergy members who left the denomination. You have been devoted to the denomination, but they left. What can you tell me about why some stay and some do not?"

"Well, it is not so hard to figure. When people get frustrated with each other over long periods of time, some people, from both sides, are going to give up and leave. People from both sides are going to feel hurt, neglected, or even abused. We can only hope that the relationships we have built with each other and our common causes in the service of Christ will serve to keep us moving forward with each other. Of course, denominational loyalty has become a somewhat old-fashioned notion. There are other good denominations where sincere people of faith can go to worship at any time. I have found sufficient reason to remain faithful to one denomination all my life and believe the Global Methodist Church is just an extension of that faithfulness, but I do not judge those who determine it is better for them to move on."

So far, Tom was singing harmony to Bob's opening statements song: The UMC is a big organization that some can't navigate or appropriately appreciate; it's understandable if some choose to leave. Although the denomination will almost certainly be splitting soon, Bob sees both sides as staying faithful to their beliefs and to their commitments.

Bob and Tom were talking mostly to each other, only occasionally directing themselves to the jury. They seemed to have formed a mutual admiration society, smiling at each other as they went about this enjoyable conversation. Tom appeared very pleasant and very rational as he made Bob's case about how my clients were good people who just didn't find the right fit in the UMC.

If I challenged Tom too directly, I would also fall into the category of another good person who just couldn't get along with a pleasant and rational person. That's okay. Despite the moments I had been upset with Dan, I would show that I could be pleasant when I wanted to.

Bob pressed in by asking, "Tom, do you think it would be right for this jury to find the United Methodist Church in breach of contract with Mr. Richard's clients?"

"Honestly, I do not. The Conserve our Faith Coalition is accepted by the denomination as a beneficial, functioning organization that is directly involved in representing almost three-quarters of a million members of the denomination, and that our current plans to have a gracious and peaceful separation allow those of both convictions to move forward. That speaks to the integrity of the denomination. As an ordained elder in the UMC, I could not serve as the full-time chairman of the Coalition without my bishop's permission and support. As conservative Christians, we are given a voice and respect. But, maybe the most important reason I believe the denomination has kept faith with me is that the orthodox faith continues to be safe-guarded and promoted in every aspect of *The Book of Discipline*. The denomination continues to require orthodox faith and practice. Even our social statements are predominantly conservative. I must believe the Conserve our Faith Coalition has been instrumental in this history and will continue to do so through the Global Methodist Church following our split.

"Although there have been and will continue to be

challenges to the conservative perspectives, the influence of the Conserve our Faith Coalition and millions of faithful Christians around the world have kept the denomination orthodox and faithful."

Tom's testimony had been carefully crafted and rehearsed. Following their practiced script and beaming a smile that stretched from ear to ear, Bob looked to the jury. "Thank you Reverend Jenkins! I think that explanation was quite helpful. But I do have a concern. Mr. Richards has presented witnesses who represent the conservative theological leanings of the denomination to be under attack and at risk. Would you agree?"

"No sir, I do not. Even though we anticipate forming two different denominations soon, we are working on proposals to facilitate a responsible and peaceful divide. Although there is opposition to some of the current statements contained in *The Book of Discipline*, I would not characterize our faith or principles as being 'under attack,' and they certainly are not 'at risk.' Every believer is free to choose his or her place of worship. Currently, we anticipate the formation of a Global Methodist Church to be an alternative for those who choose to withdraw from the United Methodist Church. When the time comes, I will identify with the Global Methodist Church. Even then, I will acknowledge the unity both denominations will maintain with our Wesleyan heritage.

"Meanwhile, leaders who share our conservative faith, like Bishop Davidson, can afford to be gracious toward the efforts of opposition leaders precisely because the conservative perspective is the majority and not at all likely to ever lose that majority. As a matter of fact, the growth of the United Methodist Church in Africa is dynamic. There is really no threat that the *Book of Discipline* will be changed anytime in the foreseeable future."

"So, Reverend Jenkins, you are telling this jury that because of the effectiveness of your organization and the growth of the denomination in Africa, the conservatives are the ones in the position of strength?"

"Yes."

"And you are testifying that the conservatives are not in danger of losing that position of strength as you negotiate the separation?"

"That is true."

"And, finally, you are testifying that if the denomination seems gracious toward those seeking balance, it is because they can afford to be gracious because the position of power is not at risk for the conservatives?"

"That is correct."

Bob meandered casually back to his table and sat down before saying anything else. He was savoring the moment and wanted everyone in the courtroom to know it. "I have no further questions for this witness at this time, Your Honor."

# CHAPTER 44
## CROSS-EXAMINATION OF PASTOR JENKINS

*"Be merciful to those who doubt, snatch others from the fire and save them; to others show mercy mixed with fear."* — JUDE

If the jury had grown tired of day after day of testimony, they wouldn't be tired for long. I intended to wake them up.

Bob thought he had scored some points with Tom Jenkin's testimony yesterday, but he would soon find out the minor hands he had won would serve me well. I was about to score some major points.

Yes, I was calm and confident, but I was not happy. I don't like the idea of destroying a man, yet that was exactly what I intend to do. Tom Jenkins was deluded. He had justified his sins so thoroughly he may not have even realized the sins he had committed. He may have been a good man; I don't know. But I do know he was deluded, and I was about to point out his sins to everyone in the courtroom.

Pastor Jenkins took the stand. He offered his smile to the judge, the jury, and then to me as I moved to my questioning spot.

"Pastor Jenkins, I believe you are an honest man, and I am going to be honest with you. For me to make my case, I am going to have to show this jury you function as a con artist. I don't think you think of yourself that way or would act that way if you knew what you were doing. Nevertheless, as the chairman of the Conserve our Faith Coalition, you function as a bait and switch charlatan."

I had spoken these words directly and without emotion, pausing to let my accusation settle into Tom's consciousness. He had made it clear he was accustomed to being treated with respect. Over the years, I had come to recognize what form "organizational respect" (as I have termed it) often takes. Organizational respect requires all the participants to assume the best about each other, no matter how disrespectfully and counter-productively the participants might act. They come together to protect their organization, not through peacemaking roles, but by peacekeeping – often at the expense of truth.

In short, Pastor Jenkins had never been spoken to the way I had just spoken to him. He was visibly confused. His smile was gone. He wanted to be nice to me, but realized I was about to become very un-nice to him. He didn't know what to say.

"Pastor Jenkins, can you tell this jury about the trust clause?"

"The trust clause states that all local church properties belong to the denomination under the supervision of whichever annual conference the local church is a part of."

"So, the church building does not belong to the local church?"

"No, it belongs to the conference."

"How about the parsonage the pastor lives in?" "It belongs to the conference."

"What if one of my clients bought a bus for their local church?"

"It belongs to the conference." "What if he used his own money?"

"It would still belong to the conference."

"Now, Pastor Jenkins, would you please read aloud to the

jury Paragraph 103 of the *Discipline of the United Methodist Church* to the court?" "The very reason for the trust clause in deeds is to protect the doctrinal standards, not the conference, and the conference only insofar as it protects the doctrinal standards.'"

"Thank you, Pastor Jenkins. Now, have you known of, and documented in your Conserve our Faith newsletter, examples of local churches with conservative pastors and congregations who have withdrawn from the denomination and had to leave all their church properties behind?"

"Yes. We have documented several such events."

"And, Pastor Jenkins, have you known of and ever documented a time when an apostate pastor or a liberal congregation has been told they were no longer welcome to use the church properties they have?"

"No. Not that I know of."

"So, Pastor Jenkins, do you think the trust clause anticipated the need to kick conservatives out of their church properties, or to kick apostates out of theirs?"

With a false confidence, Tom asserted, "Obviously, the trust clause anticipated protecting the doctrines of the church from the apostate, which does not apply to all those with a more liberal perspective. But, as I said earlier, the conservatives are in the position of power; the trust clause is an illustration of that."

I was writing on my note pad, while standing in my spot. I nodded. "Yes, you have said conservatives are in the position of power. I want to notify the court I would like to recall Kyle Fedder as a rebuttal witness to that statement shortly. But first, I want to ask you about this second statement. You said that the trust clause obviously applies to the apostate, not the conservatives?"

"Yes."

"But you also say the trust clause has cost many conservative congregations all their church properties, but it hasn't been applied to liberal congregations?"

"As I said," Tom said with some frustration in his voice, "liberal is not synonymous with apostate."

"Okay. Let me try to be more specific. Should a pastor who supports abortion rights be considered apostate?"

"Most definitely not."

"Why not? It is in contradiction to the social policy of the denomination as stated in *The Book of Discipline.*"

"Yes," his words were slow and deliberate, almost as if he were speaking to an unruly child, "it is in contradiction to the social policy of the church, but it is not in contradiction to the doctrine of the church."

"So, Pastor Jenkins, you would say that a pastor can be supportive of abortion rights but not be apostate?"

"Of course." Kyle and I had discussed this issue extensively and I had asked him exhaustive questions about this subject in his depositions. I was prepared to press Tom on his statement.

"Isn't it true that when abortion is addressed in the United Methodist Church, it is addressed as a social issue, or a political issue, or maybe even as a moral issue. But for the pastor, who is Seminary trained, abortion, or rather the belief that life begins before the baby is delivered, is a theological issue directly related to belief in the Incarnation of Jesus. Theologically and philosophically, is there any way to separate the belief in life beginning before birth from belief in the Incarnation of Jesus?"

"I would have to think about that before commenting," Jenkins calmly stated.

I don't think he was prepared for me to pursue the issue further. I was ready to push deeply into it. "So, let's take some time to think about it together. Okay? Wouldn't a seminary trained pastor have to believe life begins before birth if they are to believe in the Incarnation of Jesus?" "There may be other theologians more able to address the issue than I am," Pastor Jenkins insisted.

"According to scripture, Jesus was recognized as alive during the very earliest months of Mary's pregnancy by Mary, by Joseph, by angels, by the mother of John the Baptist, and by John the Baptist himself from within his mother's womb. To dismiss the references to the Virgin conception and the recognition of the life of Jesus beginning within his mother's womb, or the life of John the Baptist within his mother's womb, is to mythologize the doctrine of the Incarnation of Christ. Correct?"

"Correct, but I can't speak for those who may have been able to reconcile the Incarnation and abortion rights in their own minds." Tom made this statement as if he were proud of his lack of judgement against others.

"I'm not asking you to speak for others. I'm asking you as a seminary trained theologian: Is the belief in the literal historical incarnation of Jesus philosophically and theologically antithetical to the practice of abortion?"

"Yes," Tom admitted reluctantly. "I believe it is."

"So, Pastor Jenkins, doesn't that lead us to the conclusion that you believe those who support abortion rights are apostate?"

"I have my faith and convictions, and I represent them,"

Tom stated. "I believe in the literal historical incarnation, and I believe in the sanctity of life, even life in the womb. I promote and defend that faith."

"Well, that is the question, isn't it? Do you really defend your faith like you have vowed to do? Have you filed charges against the apostate pastors that are supporting abortion rights?"

Tom had lost patience with me. He was not used to being challenged. He represented himself and assumed I would be content with how he had represented himself. He could not see the glaring contradictions between his statements. "Richards, I do not know that pastors who support abortion rights are apostate."

"I want to be fair with you Pastor Jenkins. Is it fair to say that you have decided not to reach any conclusion about the theological and philosophical inconsistency between those who support abortion rights and also claim to believe in the literal historical incarnation?"

"I don't know what their thinking is on this matter." "Right. So, it is fair to say that you are content to not reach any conclusion for yourself in this matter?"

"Mr. Richards, I don't know what you are trying to get me to say."

The more upset Tom became, the more calming my tone became. It was my turn to be condescending. "What I am asking is if you are willfully ignorant, or are you lying to this jury, or is there a third option?"

"I am not lying. I just can't assume pastors who support abortion rights are apostate."

"Why not? Aren't you, as well as every other UMC pastor, required to have theological training?"

"Yes, but there is lots of diversity out there. Theologically, philosophically, sociologically, and in every other field of study you can mention. We are not required to be experts in them all."

"So, Pastor Jenkins, for the sake of this jury, we have arrived at the reason for the accusation I raised against you. I've claimed that you serve or are used as a bait and switch con man: a man given leadership in a reform movement who can't decide what needs to be reformed. Are you now admitting to the jury that I have accurately labeled you?" Obstinately clinging to the role that had served him well throughout his United Methodist career, Tom asserted, "I'm saying that I am not an expert in philosophy or sociology. I am open to learn from others."

"Indeed," I affirmed. "Are you representing to this jury that you have not learned from the education you've received and the debate that has been ongoing in the UMC for decades that orthodox faith and pro-choice beliefs are antithetical?"

Tom seemed somewhat shocked that his testimony had become so contentious, when he had been determined to represent a pleasant demeanor. Tom looked to Bob then looked down at his hands lying in his lap. Bob could object that I was badgering the witness, but I had made it clear to the court that I intended to treat Tom as a hostile witness when I originally declared him to be a part of the con-game being played in the UMC. Nevertheless, Bob had placed his palms on the table, ready to rise and object. Since I had more evidence to confront Tom with, I quickly changed the subject.

"Okay. Pastor Jenkins, we can come back to that after I ask you about another way in which I think you have been conning your constituents. You testified earlier you are confident the conservatives will remain in power due to the growth of the Church in Africa?"

"Yes," Tom answered with a wariness in his voice.

"Pastor Jenkins, are you aware of the on-going efforts of the Worldwide Nature of the Church Study Committee to change the structure of the church?"

"Yes. I am aware. We have reported on this initiative often in our newsletter."

"Would you tell this jury what effect the proposed restructure would have on the voting power of the growing African UMC?"

"The last petition presented would have separated the overseas churches from the church in the United States to a large degree."

"And is it true that limiting the growing influence of the African churches on the denomination as a whole would protect the liberals in the United States from the African delegates who are widely acknowledged to be much more conservative than the rest of the denomination?"

"That may be too broad a statement."

"How so? Isn't it true that approximately ninety-five percent of the delegates in Africa rejected the restructuring amendments?"

"Yes."

"Isn't it also true, Pastor Jenkins, that the presiding bishop at the 2008 General Conference allowed only two one-minute speeches for and against the amendment?"

"That's correct."

"And, there was no time allowed to discuss the actual agenda behind the amendment?"

"Yes."

"And, the amendment was originally sponsored by a group called 'Breaking the Silence,' an organization advocating on behalf of 'the gay, lesbian, bisexual, transgendered, and queer' communities?" "Yes. I believe that is all true."

"So, Pastor Jenkins, doesn't it seem true to you that the presiding bishop at this session of the general conference was staging the debate in a way that would give the restructuring amendment the greatest opportunity to pass?"

"I don't know."

"You don't know? Don't you think such a massive change in the structure of the denomination deserves more than just two minutes of debate?"

"I don't know! Most delegates have decided how they are going to vote long before any debate takes place."

"I see. So no debate was necessary?" "You could say that."

"Other witnesses in this case have referred to this and other practices as evidence of 'systemic racism' in the UMC. Can you tell this jury that the whole attempt at restructuring should not be considered evidence of systemic racism?"

Slowing to consider his response, Tom conceded, "I cannot."

"Can you remember even one time when these obscenities were ever referred to as evidence of systemic racism in the coalition newsletters?"

"No."

"Why do you think such an obvious observation was never referred to in your newsletter?"

Tom hesitated before he answered, "I don't know."

"Yet another example of something critical to actual reform in the denomination that you, somehow, know nothing about. Pastor Jenkins, please tell this jury why they shouldn't consider you and your organization unwitting contributors to a con game with hopes of fooling believers into staying in a denomination that continually breaks their trust."

I made this last statement loudly and quickly, knowing that Bob would raise an objection. As soon as he did, I commented, "I don't need a response, thank you, Pastor Jenkins." "Mr. Richards," Judge Browne interrupted, "how much more do you have?"

I checked my notepad. "Possibly another hour with this witness, Your Honor."

"Then, this would be a good time to adjourn for lunch, as we are already fifteen minutes past. Court will be adjourned until 1:15." She banged the gavel and left the room.

I determined that this session had ended on a necessary note for us. I did not respect the "out" that Pastor Jenkins had given himself. It seemed cowardly and dishonest. And, since the jury was required to reach a conclusion (where Tom did not), I assumed they would think of him as cowardly and dishonest as well.

You may determine that I haven't correctly represented the events under consideration, or you may decide that you too are not required to reach conclusions about theological, philosophical, and social issues. You may believe these issues are too complicated to be considered in this context. But I want to challenge you to deny yourself an easy out. If you need more information, get it. If you need more feedback, talk to people you respect.

Don't you be cowardly or dishonest with yourselves.

# CHAPTER 45
# CONTINUING THE CROSS-EXAMINATION OF TOM JENKINS

*"Now to him who is able to keep you from falling and to present you before His glorious presence without fault and with great joy – to the only God our Savior be glory, majesty, power, and authority, through Jesus Christ our Lord, before all ages, now and forever more. Amen"* — JUDE

When Tom took the stand following the lunch break, his face was pale beneath the tan. He knew my agenda was to make him look the fool used by the institution or a traitor to his faith. I wished I knew which he dreaded most so I could attack him where it hurt the worst.

"Pastor Jenkins, the Conserve our Faith Coalition was begun in 1994?"

"Yes."

"Do you consider the Good News organization to be your organization's predecessor?"

"Yes."

"And before Good News there was a similar effort called The Memphis Declaration, and before that, another effort called The Houston Declaration?"

"Yes."

"So, there has been a lot of bumping and bruising going on between conservatives and liberals in the denomination before your organization began?"

"I guess you could say that."

"In 1995, your organization created a confessional

statement?"

"Yes."

"I want to hand you and the jury a copy of one of those statements made in 1995. Will you read it aloud to the court?" "The United Methodist Church is incapable of confessing with one voice the orthodox Trinitarian faith, particularly Jesus Christ as the Son of God, the Savior of the world, and the Lord of history and the Church.'"

"Thank you, Pastor Jenkins. Are you aware some pastors took that statement seriously and that the 1998 proposal by the Evangelical Renewal Fellowship to the CaliforniaNevada Annual Conference requested the development of 'a just way in which we might allow evangelical pastors and congregations the choice to separate from the Annual Conference'?"

"Yes." Tom answered somewhat hesitantly. "Are you aware that the proposal was adopted by a 74-1 vote?"

"I think that is correct."

"Did your organization offer support to this effort?"

"We supported the right of the pastors to make the proposal."

"That is not quite the same as supporting the proposal, is it?"

"It was a local proposal, not a national one." "And that makes a big difference, does it?" "I'm not sure what you mean."

"If it had been a national proposal, would your organization have supported it?"

"I don't know. I wasn't in leadership with the organization at that time."

"So, the short answer is 'No. The Conserve our Faith Coalition did not support the proposal by the California/Nevada Evangelical Renewal Fellowship in 1995.' Correct?"

"Correct."

"Do you know what became of those seventy-four pastors in California who supported the proposal?"

"I know a number of them left the denomination."

"Yes. A number of them left the denomination. We accepted some of those lay people and clergy as members of this class-action lawsuit. And isn't it true that entire congregations left the denomination with them?"

"Several churches lost the majority of their members."

"You may not be aware of how almost every church was anonymous in their choice to disaffiliate. Nevertheless," I continued, "isn't it true the pastors who left and the congregations that left with them, left behind the church buildings and all the local church properties, including parsonages, buses, and even savings accounts?"

"Yes, that is true."

"So, why didn't your coalition stand with these pastors and their congregations?"

"We published their stories to let the rest of the denomination know what was happening there."

"Again, that is not quite the same as supporting those pastors, is it?"

"I don't know." I answered for him, "It is not the same."

"Pastor Jenkins, the issue of developing a separation plan for those wishing to leave the denomination didn't go away, did it? I am handing out copies of another statement from a 2004 Conserve our Faith newsletter, part of an article your organization published by renowned pastor and professor, Maxie Dunnam. Would you read this statement to the court?"

Tom read, "Many have come to believe, I among them, that a deliberate amicable separation, worked out by all responsible people involved is a far more Kingdom-like approach than the division which has taken place and continues to divert us from mission and ministry.'"

"Yet," I continued, "in a recent May-June edition of your newsletter, the front page was filled by an article by Dr. Ira Galloway. Would you read to this court the highlighted portion of this article?"

"'*We would make a plea to all our supporters that you would "stay the course." If you leave the UMC, we are weakened. If you stay on as an active member of your local church and live out a vigorous apostolic faith, continuing your support of The Conserve our Faith Coalition, we are stronger and God will bless our witness.*'"

"So, Pastor Jenkins, which is it? Should conservative believers stay in the denomination, or should they go?"

"Obviously, the Conserve our Faith Coalition hopes for one of two outcomes: either we maintain our position of strength and allow the liberals to exhaust their hopes of changing our doctrine and policy, or an amicable separation agreement is devised."

"Yes. Now this is important, Pastor Jenkins. If the conservatives have the position of power, why is an amicable separation agreement needed? You already have the right, the authority, and even the responsibility to remove these apostate pastors from the denomination. But if you have decided it is unfair to just kick them out, why not just draft and push through your own separation petition? Surely, you don't believe any such petition will be amicable. Why not just make it happen?"

"It may come to that, but for now, we are willing to wait."

Armed with the startling confession that Bishop

Davidson made, that the expected split in the denomination would not happen, I began leading Tom into facing that possibility also. "You are willing to wait. Why is that? Why are you willing to wait while hundreds of conservative pastors and thousands of conservative members of the denomination are being forced out of the church? Why wait?"

"Because, we have been working to provide a just and loving separation through the forming of a new denomination: The Global Methodist Church," Pastor Jenkins stated confidently. I heard legitimate victory in his voice.

Dear Reader, poor Tom Jenkins was about to find out that he may be a victim of the bait and switch con game himself. Had he and his coalition been coerced? Bribed? Manipulated? Deceived? I didn't know which. They had been offered a new denomination they could transfer their ordinations, their retirement accounts, and their guaranteed appointments to. They were told that local churches would be allowed to vote to join the new denomination and transfer their buildings and assets into the trusted oversight of conservative leaders. I was convinced he would be surprised to know Bishop Davidson, for one, was not convinced this split would happen.

I take a sympathetic tone. "Pastor Jenkins, I have said you may be an unwitting participant in the con games my clients and I accuse the United Methodist Church of. Now, I'm wondering if you may become a victim of the same dynamics revealed to this jury so far in this trial. I must tell you, in Bishop Davidson's testimony to this court, he stated he is not willing to believe that there will be a split. He is not willing to believe there will be the transfer of the ordinations and retirement accounts of pastors to a new denomination. He is not willing to believe congregations who have yet to disaffiliate will be allowed to transfer ownership of their property and assets to a new denomination."

I paused and allowed the jury to note Pastor Jenkin's response. His hands were on the rail in front of him as he leaned toward me. He seemed ready for anything: to argue, deny or cry. I let the moment linger, then continued. "Pastor Jenkins, what if the apostates in the denomination no longer need the cooperation of any conservative pastors? What if they allowed the most vocal conservative pastors to disaffiliate? Who will replace those representatives to general conference who have disaffiliated? The larger congregations and the more vocal conservative pastors won't be at the next general conference, will they? The African church representatives have been limited to only twenty-four percent at the next general conference, right? What is to stop the next general conference from simply deciding to continue as is?"

As I proposed my question, Pastor Jenkins leaned back and slumped down in his chair. Nevertheless, he offered as strong a denial as he could, "I just can't imagine the bishops and other representatives would do that to us?"

"You can't imagine it? Bishop Davidson has testified to this jury that he wouldn't support a separation agreement. I'm guessing you are surprised to know that." I continued in a more confrontive tone, "Pastor Jenkins, hasn't your monthly newsletter reported such unethical behaviors by numerous bishops over the years?"

"Yes, but...." he left his statement hanging.

"Bishop Davidson was chosen as a witness for the defense by the same bishops you are trusting to permit and fund the development of a new denomination?"

"Yes."

"Are you telling this jury you have more reason to believe there will be a loving and fair separation offered to pastors like you than Bishop Davidson has for believing there will not?"

Tom, somewhat rattled, simply stated, "I don't know." "Pastor Jenkins, I'm going to ask you to imagine for a moment that Bishop Davidson has valid reasons to believe there will not be a separation. If it ends up that there are no longer enough votes to secure the loving separation you've worked for, will you feel like you have been deceived? Maybe even conned? Maybe even manipulated?"

"Yes. Yes, I would, but we can't predict that for sure!" Tom lightly protested.

"No," I gently agreed. "We can't know for sure either way, can we?"

Tom was finally coming to grips with the reality he had helped to create. I recognized his humbled state and would have liked to give him more time to process what he had just learned concerning Bishop Davidsons' testimony. However, the jury was waiting and I needed to press on.

"Is it true in the history of your organization you have never supported any of the three dynamics that could honestly effect change in the United Methodists institution? You have never encouraged your congregations to withhold payment of apportionments to the institution?"

"No."

"You have not supported facilitating the freedom for conservative congregations to leave the denomination, while maintaining ownership of their church properties and assets?"

"No."

"You have not filed disciplinary charges against any of the church leaders your newsletter chronicles as abusers of the

Discipline?"

"No."

"Pastor Jenkins, didn't you vow at your ordination as an elder to safeguard the doctrine of the church?"

"Every ordained elder has made that vow."

"Yes, they have, but you, and the other members of your coalition, have not pressed charges against the apostate, or opposed the ordination of the apostate, or supported the petitions of those seeking a division of the denomination, or withheld your financial support from annual conference and general conference committees and ministries that support abortion as a means of birth control or other equally antithetical stands, have you?"

"We have supported the rights of others to do so."

"Yes. Well, that is a relatively safe thing for you to do, isn't it? I mean, no one is going to threaten your career over simply supporting the right of other people to fulfill their vows, are they?"

Tom takes time to think of how he might otherwise answer, yet eventually simply responds, "No."

"And meanwhile, the conservative believers that do stay in the church support your coalition. They keep it going. So, you don't want them to leave, do you?"

"We don't want conservative believers to leave because we still have hope for our denomination. We are not closing our eyes to anything that is happening."

"Except," I gently challenge the forlorn man, "for closing your eyes to the possibility the loving separation you've worked for won't be allowed?"

"Yes," he admits, "I hadn't considered that possibility."

"Meanwhile, Pastor Jenkins, isn't it true that hundreds and

thousands of conservative pastors and members are leaving the church?" Without waiting for an answer, I asked, "Do you have any reason to doubt the claims of the 2000 plus lay people, who are among the plaintiffs in this case that, while they were members of UM congregations, their churches were appointed pastors who taught Universalism, or pastors who believe the doctrine of the virgin-birth of Jesus was a myth, or pastors who claim that the doctrine of Jesus' physical resurrection is only an analogy for keeping His memory alive, and the miracles He worked are not to be embraced as literal truths, but only as myths communicating inspirational concepts? Do you have reason to doubt the testimonies of these plaintiffs who claim that their pastors, their district superintendents, and even their bishops have expressed their conclusion that those who oppose their liberal agendas are 'ignorant,' 'sexist,' 'fundamentalist,' 'homophobic,' 'superstitious,' 'hateful,' or even 'unfit parents'? Do you have reason to question their testimonies of being subjected to women endorsing and advertising their lesbian lifestyles at district meetings, or to annual conference worship services in which the guest preacher advocated for support of pro-abortion public policies, or to district superintendents exhorting their congregation to 'not make more of Jesus than you should'? Do you have reason to question these testimonies?"

"No sir. As a matter of fact, our organization has documented many, many such events over the last twenty-five years."

"Right, So, Pastor Jenkins, don't you agree that saying that these pastors and lay people have been driven out of the church is an accurate statement?"

"I can see how some would feel that way."

"Pastor Jenkins," I pressed in, "I am not asking if it is understandable that some might feel that way. I am asking if you believe these faithful believers have been driven away from the denomination?"

Tom had been pushed and pulled by me into considering and admitting how he had been willing to limit his protests of the violations of *The Book of Discipline* to writing about them, but not using the means he had to make it stop. I forced him to acknowledge he was still serving as an unwitting pawn in an ongoing battle. Then, he realized I was asking him to turn his whole testimony into an endorsement of my case against the church. He was obviously unprepared to be seen as a determinative witness for our case. Maybe he realized his answer would put him in the category with those of my clients who lost their careers and their home in the UMC.

On the other hand, if he denied that my clients had been driven out of the church, he knew I would paint him as a willing part of the con, encouraging other believers to take a stand while he hid comfortably in his denomination-approved role. It was time for him to put up or shut up. He would either be known as someone who took a stand for the faith or someone who played within the rules of the organization. He was trapped, and I knew it. He knew it. The jury knew it.

When Tom still didn't answer, I asked again. "Pastor Jenkins, do you believe that my clients have objective reasons to believe that there has been no hope for the reformation of the United Methodist Church?"

"There is hope," Tom said as resolutely as he could manage.

"There is always hope," I agreed, "but is there any objective reason to believe?"

Looking again at his hands, he said, less resolutely, "Not that I can offer at this time."

"Thank you, Pastor Jenkins. Since you, the chairman of the Conserve our Faith Coalition, cannot offer any objective reason for my clients to trust for renewal of the denomination, isn't accurate to say that my clients have been driven out of the UMC?"

Finally looking up, Tom found his courage. "Yes, Mr. Richards, I do believe that your clients were driven out of the denomination."

"Thank you, Pastor Jenkins. Your Honor, I have no further questions."

It was late in the day by this time, and Judge Browne adjourned for the day. Bob remained seated at his table after the jury was excused. As his partner packed their notebooks, Bob sat frowning at the jury box. The only witness I had left for him to call, and of whom he had been so pleased with during his questioning of him, had been fully turned against him. I knew he had no hope of re-directing Tom to serve the defense. All Bob had left was his closing statements. He knew, as I did, it wouldn't be enough. He was going to have to talk to his clients about a settlement offer. He assumed they would rather pay out now than hear the verdict announced against them and then, possibly, file for an appeal.

He could use his closing argument to try to justify a smaller award from the jury than we would be asking for. It wouldn't be a hard case to make. He could point out my clients were not really injured in any physical sense, and that none of them are claiming any long-term emotional distress. He could suggest a judgment against the denomination would be devastating in and of itself, even with minimal financial awards being made to my clients. And, he would be right.

Or … he could talk to his clients and see what they wanted to do.

The card game was over. We held all the aces.

I didn't need to talk with my clients. They had given me total authority in accepting or declining an offer. I already knew what they wanted. They wanted to be heard, and they had been heard. If the council of bishops instructed Bob to make an offer, I would run the number up appropriately before accepting it. If they wanted to let this play out with the jury, I would be happy with that also.

# CHAPTER 46
# UNINTENDED CONSEQUENCES

*"You must give people the freedom not to learn from their own experiences."* — EDWIN H. FRIEDMAN, *A Failure of Nerve*

Bob made a settlement offer. I countered at double what he had offered and sweetened the deal by offering to let him make any and all announcements to the media. Allowing the denomination to present the settlement to the media was not as big a concession as you might think. The only issue the media seemed to be interested in was the charge we made of systemic racism in the church. You may recall the defense never even tried to deny this accusation.

In an ironic twist, the apostates got caught in the same trap they had used against the believers. The apostates insisted the divisive issues in the denomination were the social issues of homosexuality and abortion. They were very successful in diverting attention away from the issue of their apostasy. The media, who really had no interest in Christian theology, had their own agenda. They were eager and willing to represent the divisive issue in the denomination to be the social issue of systemic racism. The council of bishops issued a public letter assuring its readers of their good intentions and efforts to make systemic changes after the denomination resolved the issue of dividing into two denominations. In other words, they would only give the African churches equal representation after they could no longer affect the future of the UMC in the United States.

This letter, inadvertently, verified the systemic racism and drew more media attention, which led to two unintended consequences. First, the churches in Africa held their own convention and decided to disaffiliate from the UMC, naming themselves the African Methodist Church. They issued a letter claiming their independence from the United Methodist Church, and would not be joining the Global Methodist Church, if it were to be formed. In short order, the denomination had lost over half its membership. Since the African church properties and assets were protected from seizure due to their distribution throughout the African countries, they had no fear of the United Methodist Church. And worse was to follow.

When the media reported on the African Methodist Church's response to the letter from the Council of Bishops of the United Methodist Church, comedians began using parts of the letter in their depiction of an ignorant council of bishops eager to change the systemic racism they created and enforced, just as soon as it stopped serving their purposes. The comedians did what the news media did not do by drawing attention to the issue of apostasy in the UMC that the African Methodist Church stated as their reason for disaffiliating. They characterized the African Methodists as those who innocently asked if it was okay to limit membership in a Christian church to those who believed in the Christian faith, while the council of bishops pointed fingers at them and called them homophobes and racists.

The message that the news media ignored was communicated to the American public primarily by the late-night comedians.

# CHAPTER 47

# MY CLOSING ARGUMENT BEFORE THE JURY

Because Bob settled, I never made a closing argument to the jury at court. But they were never the jury I intended to present my case to in writing this book. You are my jury and you have not yet heard the full case. My concern is for you, my readers. You are just like the people of the United Methodist Church, both those who stayed and those who left. You are a part of a culture that doesn't like to take stands and cause waves. You are stuck in your own political parties, just like Bob said. You may be stuck in marriage difficulties. Of course, you are required to make your decisions for or against God. If you decide for Him, then you will find yourself stuck with the reality of all these imperfect churches and imperfect leaders. Maybe your ethical dilemma will come at your job or workplace. When should you speak up? When should you step back? When should you allow things to go on without you?

I hope you don't wait until you are in one of these quandaries to decide what kind of person you want to be. I hope you have practiced establishing your identity in easier situations along the way, maybe even imaginary situations like this story is for you non-Methodist readers.

So, I want to share with you my closing arguments — plural. The closing argument I prepared for the case and my closing argument with Dan.

Of course, you knew ending the case didn't end my need to understand Dan. I want to share as much of it as I can remember. I won't claim total accuracy in recounting my argument with Dan. I have learned no matter how hard we try, we cannot be totally neutral concerning a disagreement in which we are personally involved. But I will try.

First, the closing argument I prepared for the jury:

*"You may remember, in his opening statement the defense counsel explained his defense of this case with two analogies. The first analogy was comparing the United Methodist Church to any other large organization and his second analogy was to a no-fault divorce.*

*"The point of his first analogy was that there will be people who don't get along in any large organization. Wasn't that his point? Well, I believe it is true, as far as it goes, but his analogy does not go far enough.*

*"He said the courts of this state practice 'no-fault' divorce. He explained this means the courts have recognized they do not have the ability to determine who was most to blame for the break-up of the marriage. Well, in this case, I think you will agree we have made it very clear who tried to keep their promises, yes, even their vows, and who has not. Let's put that aside for a moment. Instead, let's consider the defense counselor's comparison of this case to a divorce trial.*

*"Let's imagine a man and a woman have been married for, say, twenty years. They have two teenage children. They own a house that is almost paid for. They own two cars. They have a retirement account. And they simply cannot stand each other any longer, so one of them moves out; it doesn't matter which one. They file for divorce. They go to court and the judge tells the one who moved out, 'Since you are the one who moved out, I award the home, the cars, the savings, and the retirement account to your*

spouse. And, since you are the one who moved out, I am giving your spouse primary custody of the children. You can see them every other weekend if they still want to see you. You must be okay with all this because, after all, you are the one who moved out.'

"Sounds ridiculous, doesn't it? Yet, this is what the defense wants you to say to my clients. And this analogy is really a good one, especially for the pastors I represent because they were asked to enter into a 'covenant' relationship with the denomination. Like the covenant relationship of marriage, they went through a long courtship where the pastors were to reveal everything about themselves their leaders wanted to know. Back when these pastors were ordained, there was a big ceremony before hundreds of people. In this sacred ceremony my clients made vows, one of which was to do everything possible to protect the church from apostasy. My clients tried to keep their vows. To their surprise, they found out they were in a very small group of people who were willing to risk it all to keep their vows. Their efforts were rejected, and these honest pastors were treated like troublemakers. When they separated from the denomination, it truly was like a divorce for them. They were heartbroken.

"But the defense counsel may say, they were the ones who separated. Shouldn't they be content to lose everything? When these honest pastors left the denomination, they left without homes, leaving behind the careers they had spent years preparing for and practicing, and with their reputations damaged. Meanwhile, those who were content to violate their vows were allowed to keep their parsonages, their churches, their multi-billion-dollar foundations, and their reputations. Because, as we know, they were not the ones who separated. So, the denomination breaks its vows, its honest pastors 'divorce' the church, but the church goes on like nothing happened at all.

"I think you will agree with me not only is this not right, not only is this not fair, not only is this not good, but we don't have to accept it. We do not have to accept it!

"The United Methodist Church is not exempt from the expectations that it will be true to what it says are its own doctrines and procedures. It is not exempt from the common decency that prohibits swindling, con-games, the manipulation of trusting people, religious abuse, systemic racism, or, in the legal term of this case, breach of contract. And, the United Methodist Church, no matter how large an organization it is, is not exempt from the judgment of you, the jurors in this case. You have the power, the position, and the responsibility to tell this denomination that what it is doing is wrong, and that there will be consequences for what they have done to the good people I represent."

During the speech, I would have improvised a little – maybe even quite a bit. However, this is mostly what I intended to say. I'd also like to assume that the jury would have been wowed and swayed, but I suppose the witnesses had done most of the work on that point.

# CHAPTER 48
# MY CLOSING ARGUMENT
# WITH DAN

*"Who is worthy to break the seals and open the scroll? But no one in heaven or on earth or under the earth could open the scroll or even look inside it. I wept and wept because no one was found who was worthy to open the scroll or look inside. Then one of the elders said to me, 'Do not weep! See, the Lion of the tribe of Judah, the Root of David, has triumphed! He is able to open the scroll and the seven seals.'"*
— THE REVELATION TO ST. JOHN

We met at IHOP for breakfast the Saturday morning after the trial ended. I think we were both hoping against hope we could somehow reach a basis for continuing our friendship.

"You never answered me," I began. "I have learned so much about you. I've actually studied you: your childhood, your education, your ministry, your marriage, your divorce, and your tenure as a bishop." I pause, weighing my next words carefully. "And I can't understand what you have done. I can't find a reason for how passive you have been toward the apostates in your denomination, or how actively you limited others who promoted actual reforms. It is not like you.

"I want you to know that as important as I think this trial is to my clients and to the whole United Methodist Church, the person I've really hoped to persuade is you. I respect you so much that it caused me to really resent you for being on the other side of this case. Then I realized I never really had a chance of convincing you what you've done is wrong. You already faced the most important person in your life over this issue. You let Sharon leave you over this. I guess you never explained yourself to her, so I shouldn't expect you to explain yourself to me."

"Sonny G.," he said, "I want to tell you, I been passive toward the apostates in the church because I don't want a denominational divide. It would be like a divorce. I don't want the church to conform to the world's perspective that divorce is okay. I was willing to speak my mind to one person at a time. That's why the council of bishops chose me to represent them: they all knew what I believed. I was the one fighting for the hope of healing. I was the one who gave everyone a chance to make this work, to find the good in each other. I wanted us to love each other enough to listen to each other and care for each other. If someone is apostate, love them through it. I never agreed with any heresy, but I didn't condemn the heretic. I loved them. I worked with them. And, when I became a bishop, I did what I've always done: I gave them opportunities to work it out.

"That's what I was doing when I shut down the debates over Kyle's petitions. His petitions were not going to do anything other than exactly what this trial has done. They would have forced people to choose their side and fight against the other side. That kind of debate could only lead to further division.

"Understand, I never shut Kyle down. I wouldn't do that to anyone. What I did was to control the damage so that healing would still have a chance. I allowed enough fire to bring light to see by, but not enough to burn the place down. After all, these are men and women who have been carefully screened and selected to be in ministry. *To be in ministry!* Don't you understand what that means? These people should be the experts in reconciliation and redemption. These were the people whose lives, like mine, were given over to helping people love God and each other." Dan had started out speaking calmly, but he must have noticed the anger in my eyes, because he began to get angry also.

"Then there are people like you, Sonny. People who are more concerned about proving who is right and who is wrong than about caring for each other. People who value justice over mercy, and truth over love. You see, you've given up on having both. You've given up on mercy leading to justice and on love leading to truth. You've forced people to choose between good and good. To help them make their decision, you try to convince people your good is the only good, and the other good is really a conspiracy to work something bad. That's not just wrong, its worse than wrong.

"Sonny, why do you think I've let you know all there is to know about me? Why did I accept your friendship and give you access to everyone I know? I did it so you might look at me and say, 'Maybe there are good reasons for what Dan has done. I might not understand why Dan is passive toward apostates, but I think maybe I can trust him. He is not evil. He isn't the type of person to go along with the crowd. Maybe there is something very valuable he is fighting for. Maybe I shouldn't tear down what Dan is trying to build up.'

"Is it so hard to believe I might know what I'm doing? Is it so hard to give me the benefit of the doubt? And is it possible God has a plan that is more complicated than you understand at the moment? Do you really think I've been following my own path and trusting my own judgments rather than following God?

"One last question: Do you really think God needed the help of the American legal system to accomplish His purposes? Do you think it serves the purposes of God for the church to have to defend itself to a small group of jurors?"

My temporary silence gave him a moment to check his anger. He offered me a reconciling comment: "Well, maybe so. It has happened, and there is no turning back."

I didn't need the reconciling comment, because I still didn't believe that we had gotten to the heart of the matter. As one of my favorite authors has said, 'Conflict resolution cannot begin until the parties have moved beyond their first lines of defense and begun to identify the heart of the matter.' "Can I tell you what I think," I asked Dan, "or do you need some time?"

"No, I'm sorry if I sound bitter," he replied. "Please, go ahead and tell me what you think."

"I think God hates divorce. I believe we break His heart when we can't find it within ourselves to identify and bridge the gaps between us. I believe He made a way. He bridged the greatest gap possible, the gap between sinfulness and holiness. He made a way for us all to be united to Him through His Son, Jesus. You know the theology better than I do.

"On the other hand, as much as God hates divorce, He was the one who created the 'writ of divorce.' God is not a pretender. He does not pretend a divorce hasn't occurred when it has, even for the sake of 'the institution of marriage.' He was the one who gave us the way to face the reality of divorce. Write it down. Put it in black and white."

Dan saw where I was going with my thoughts, and it pricked his anger again. "You still don't get it, Sonny! Up until the moment the 'writ of divorce' is signed, there *is* no divorce. Until that moment, there is still hope for the marriage. There is still the chance for healing. Being hopeful is not the same as pretending. There is still an opportunity for reconciliation and redemption."

Now we were getting to the heart of the issue. I jumped in with both barrels blazing. "That's only true if you were fighting for the marriage like my clients were. You, Bishop Davidson, were not. You pretended there was hope for the denomination while the faithful ministers and laity were wounded over and over until they limped away one by one."

Not giving an inch, Dan countered, "That is your perspective because you don't love the church like I do. You haven't given your life to strengthen this historic movement of God. You haven't t –"

"That's right. You love the institution, but not the people! The institution has been your spiritual home, your profession, your acclaim. The fact is, the institution has loved you. You are a favorite son of the institution. You are the institution's chosen defender. But you do not love the people. Not the over two thousand lay people I represent. Not the one hundred and forty clergy. Not Kyle Fedder. Not even Sharon. Oh, but you love the institution."

Taken aback by my onslaught, Dan visibly deflated. "So, the truth comes out. You do judge me, don't you, Sonny? I'm the 'pretender'– no, worse – I'm the swindler and the con man. Is that what you think?"

Obviously, Dan thought I had overstated my case. I had not. I am the trial lawyer. I know not to assert a position I cannot support. "Yes. You have pretended there was hope beyond hope. You have conned yourself. You have swindled yourself out of your integrity, your real identity, and your marriage. I'm sorry, Dan, but yes, you have become an idol worshipper. You worship the denomination. In my eyes, you've simply become a tool of the apostates."

Dan, speaking slowly and quietly, placed the blame on others. "No. Your clients gave up. They walked away when they could have stayed. No one sent them away. No one abused them in any way. I would never allow that. Kyle could have continued to challenge the executive session. My parents could have stayed together … Sharon didn't have to leave me. They took the easy way out. They stopped trying."

I really believed the heart of the issue had been revealed. Whether he knew it or not, by blaming others, Dan had joined me in the very thing he asserted I've done wrong: he has made a judgment as to who is right and wrong. Instead of pointing out the fact of his judgment, I attacked the credibility of his judgment. He had been so wrong, but he could still make the next right step. He didn't have to continue on this path.

"Really? Come on Dan, get real. You know that is not true. You told me the story yourself about how your mom confronted your dad. Your mom left because your dad did not want a real marriage. She didn't give up. She just acknowledged your dad's choice. Just like my clients acknowledged that the United Methodist Church has chosen not to respect *The Book of Discipline*. Just like Sharon begged you to stand up for the underdogs, to stand up for your own faith … to stand up for your marriage. And you wouldn't do it.

"Dan, it only takes one side to break a covenant. Your dad broke covenant with your mom. The United Methodist Church broke covenant with my clients. You broke covenant with Sharon.

"But I'm not judging you. I've been divorced myself. I've broken covenant. God has forgiven me. He forgives you. I'm no better than you. So, you listen to me. Now, you have to decide what this means to you.

"Here is my advice to you. Go to Sharon. Tell her again about the worst thing you ever did. You didn't speak up when your parents divorced. You just watched it happen. And you did it again as a bishop in the United Methodist Church. You didn't speak up. You didn't take a side. You let the church destroy itself. You even did it as a husband. You didn't fight for your marriage. You let Sharon walk away and then you blamed her for it. The worst thing you ever did became the pattern for the most important things in your life."

In my mind, this was Dan's moment of truth. He had the opportunity to set aside the peacekeeper role he had been playing, to acknowledge his role as the offender in need of forgiveness. In my mind, Dan had always put himself on a pedestal. He was not like others who are sometimes selfish, egotistical, jerks. No, he was the one who keeps the jerks from hurting each other too badly and hopes to help them reconcile. He "ministers" to jerks, but can't see himself as one also. "Sonny, you are a good man, but you are not God. You do not know my dad rejected a 'real marriage,' as you called it. Nor, do you know that I didn't stand up for my marriage. And that's okay because you had no hand in either of those relationships.

"However, what you have done in bringing a Christian denomination into a secular court is not okay. It is sheer arrogance on your part to think you are serving God well by having a denomination judged based on which side had the best attorney and which jurors ended up on the jury. Swap lawyers or change out the jurors and the other side might just as well win the trial. How does that serve godly purposes? No, you go reconcile with your ex-wife, then come explain the covenant of marriage to me."

He was doing it again; everyone can be a jerk but him. I was losing him. Having gone this far, I suspected I must help him find a crack in his own self-justifications or I would lose his friendship forever. So I set aside my anger and addressed him with a sad, pleading tone.

"Dan, I know you are upset with me. What I am saying to you may not seem fair, because, in truth, I am holding you to a higher standard than I have myself. But, believe me, I am doing this because I believe in you. You are, without a doubt, a remarkable man of faith and integrity. Yet, at the same time, you are a flawed man, just like the rest of us. The difference is, you have made your worst flaw known to me. You never tried to hide it. You told me the story yourself about that crisis conversation with Sharon, early in your relationship. You almost lost her when you didn't know what to tell her about why you had never said anything to your parents about their divorce. Then you thought it through and told her that you couldn't risk not being loved by either of them. You remember? Well, your ministry as a bishop has become characterized by that same sin; you've needed the 'parents,' the church authorities, to love you.

"Dan, I'm not trying to hurt you. I want you to get back to the man you were, the man who could take a stand and risk being rejected. That man would not have been passive about apostates in the church."

I had more to say, but Dan was through listening. "You think you know me so well but, Sonny, you have put me in a position I wouldn't have chosen. You have forced me to do the same thing to you that you are doing to me. I will tell you where your fault is. Your sin is that you can't believe that I would have good and godly reasons for my role in the United Methodist Church. Because you cannot understand my reasons, you think my motivations must be bad. So you take the precious pearls of my life story and use them against me. You trample underfoot my lifetime of humility and integrity because you don't understand my motives or can't agree with my decisions.

"You've painted us into a corner we don't need to be in. I can respect the values you have represented throughout this trial. But it seems you are not able to show me the same respect."

Dan had drawn the line in the sand: respect. We had very different ideas of what that word meant. Still, I couldn't argue semantics. I knew my time with Dan was running out, so I throw a lifeline.

"But that is just the point. I do respect you very much. I wanted you to represent yourself in this trial. Instead, you just towed the party line and gave no insight into your motivations."

"True. I didn't reveal my motivations for two reasons. One, I was concerned you would try to dissect them and turn them against me, and two, because I don't believe a court of law is the place for trying to understand each other. Prior to the trial, I gave you all the information about me that anyone could give. Did that make you reconsider your agenda? No. You were determined to create a winner and a loser. So, I lost. "If the United Methodist Church does split it will be because most people, even Christian people, are like you. When things don't look right to them, they want to determine a winner and a loser. Well, the jury probably would have said that you won. But the truth is we have all lost. You wanted a trial because it is your place to shine. It is where you know how to manipulate the setting to your advantage and spin the truth your way.

"The only consolation I can offer myself is that I didn't play the game. I didn't defend myself or attack your clients. I answered every question honestly and let you, and Bob, and the court, and the jury do their things. Now, I can only hope and pray for the good that God promises to bring from every bad thing."

And that was it. He slowly got up, turned and walked away. I imagined if we saw each other again, it would just be coincidental. He would be pleasant toward me, and I would be pleasant toward him. One of us might make a reference to the other, which would remind us of how close we really were at one time. If that happened, I know my heart would feel a stab of pain. I felt that stab over and over while writing this account. It is the pain of unresolved conflict.

I can't admit to being wrong about bringing this case to court like he needs me to, and he can't admit to being wrong in his passiveness toward apostates. We have become the embodiment of the conflict in the denomination.

# CHAPTER 49
# DAVIDSON / DAVID'S SON / SOLOMON

*"As Solomon grew old, his wives turned his heart after other gods, and his heart was not fully devoted to the Lord his God, as the heart of David his father had been."*

*"Although he had forbidden Solomon to follow other gods, Solomon did not keep the Lord's command. So the Lord said to Solomon, 'Since this is your attitude and you have not kept my covenant and my decrees, which I commanded you, I will most certainly tear the kingdom away from you and give it to one of your subordinates.*

*"'Yet I will not tear the whole kingdom from him (your son), but will give him one tribe for the sake of David my servant and for the sake of Jerusalem, which I have chosen.'"*

— I KINGS 11:4, 10 – 11, and 13

I've asked myself how King Solomon could have become the leader God held responsible for dividing the kingdom of Israel. The same Solomon who asked for and was granted the gift of wisdom by God. The same Solomon who completed his father David's vision for the new Tabernacle of the Lord. The same Solomon who wrote two books of the Old Testament that have been preserved for passing on some of his wisdom to all future generations. The same Solomon who led his nation to its greatest splendor and glory. The same Solomon whose leadership was praised by leaders of other nations.

How could he end up failing his one true love, the Shiamite shepherdess to whom he proclaimed his love? Yet even then the ultimate failure of their relationship was guaranteed by Solomon's decision to continue 'browsing among the lilies' (having sex with his other wives and concubines). So, it seems Solomon's wisdom did not safeguard his most desired personal relationship. I guess it should cause me no surprise that the same character flaws sabotaged his kingdom as well.

Of course, the division of a kingdom can't be entirely the blame of any one person. In II Chronicles the story is told a little differently. In II Chronicles the process of Solomon's corruption mirrors the story given in I Kings, but blame for the coming division of the nation is shared with Solomon's son, Rehoboam, and a multitude of political advisors. Both stories tell of Solomon conscripting slave labor, swapping his nation's wealth to provide the Queen of Sheba and other dignitaries huge personal gifts, as they did the same for him, and gaining great wealth (666 talents of gold a year) on the power and threat of his ever-growing military.

In II Chronicles, we are told how the people requested a reprieve from Rehoboam from the heavy taxation Solomon had leveled on them. But Rehoboam replied, *"My father laid on you a heavy yoke; I will make it even heavier. My father scourged you with whips; I will scourge you with scorpions."* After the political divisions and wars of rebellion that resulted, the kingdom was divided into Israel, consisting of just two tribes, and Judah, consisting of ten tribes.

Similarly, Bishop Davidson's actions can't be said to have directly caused division in the United Methodist Church. Many other leaders encouraged and then exacerbated his broken covenant vows to the institution they served. Surely Solomon was surrounded by corrupt advisors and powerful political supporters who persistently insisted upon the gradual, ever more corrupt policies that Solomon adopted. Bishop Davidson was called to lead in the midst of many such promoters and practitioners of corruption.

Am I wrong to see a parallel between King Solomon and Bishop Davidson? Doesn't it seem as if the most wonderful leaders also became the hinge pins for demise of the nation/denomination in which they were so successful? Didn't they both set aside a woman they loved to fulfill responsibilities they considered more important? Didn't they both get drawn into the glory of the institution they served at the cost of their simple obedience to God?

Nevertheless, the Biblical writers did not condemn Solomon. They limited their conclusion to, "*his heart was not fully devoted to the Lord his God.*" Therefore, I will be content to conclude no more than that about Bishop Davidson.

# RESOURCES

Heirs of the Prophets; Chicago: Moody, 1946 – pg. 109

9 781960 810168